THE WRATH OF THE *BANSHEE*

Rose bracketed the *Marauder* with the Shigunga missile launcher and fired again. He also triggered the medium pulse lasers, but at this extreme range, only two of the four scored hits. He knew it was too little, too late. Moving to the side, he saw the *Banshee* emerge from the trees and approach the *Marauder*. Rose knew he was finished, but something screamed at him to keep moving. He checked the scanner and saw that Rianna was still too far away for a shot.

The *Marauder* was bringing up both arms and the *Banshee* was raising its right. Rose kept moving, but knew there was little chance either of the pilots would miss. The Shigunga was still in the midst of reload. By the time his missiles and lasers were ready to fire again, Rose wouldn't be around to press the trigger. As he took one final look out the cockpit, the *Banshee* aimed its arm and fired.

MAIN EVENT

BATTLETECH®

MAIN EVENT

James D. Long

A ROC BOOK

ROC
Published by the Penguin Group
Penguin Books USA Inc., 375 Hudson Street,
New York, New York 10014, U.S.A.
Penguin Books Ltd, 27 Wrights Lane,
London W8 5TZ, England
Penguin Books Australia Ltd, Ringwood,
Victoria, Australia
Penguin Books Canada Ltd, 10 Alcorn Avenue,
Toronto, Ontario, Canada M4V 3B2
Penguin Books (N.Z.) Ltd, 182-190 Wairau Road,
Auckland 10, New Zealand

Penguin Books Ltd, Registered Offices:
Harmondsworth, Middlesex, England

Published by Roc, an imprint of New American Library,
a division of Penguin Books USA Inc.

First Roc Printing, May, 1993
10 9 8 7 6 5 4 3 2 1

Series Editor: Donna Ippolito
Cover: Boris Vallejo
Interior illustrations: Terry Pavlet
Mechanical drawings: FASA Art Staff

REGISTERED TRADEMARK—MARCA REGISTRADA

BATTLETECH, FASA, and the distinctive BATTLETECH and FASA logos
are trademarks of the FASA Corporation, 1026 W. Van Buren, Chicago, Illinois, 60507.

Printed in the United States of America

Prologue

It is the year 3054. Mankind inhabits the stars, but has taken his warlike nature with him. The thousands of human-occupied worlds of the Inner Sphere were once bound together in a glorious, prosperous Star League. With the fall of the League in 2781, a Dark Age descended as each of the five surviving star empires warred for dominion.

For almost three centuries, the five Successor Lords fought among themselves in the endless conflict that became known as the Succession Wars. Millions died and a few worlds changed hands, but for all the fighting and dying, little changed until 3049, when the Inner Sphere met the Clan juggernaut.

With their superior war machines and superhuman infantry, these warrior descendants of the legendary Aleksandr Kerensky's vanished Star League Army came to reclaim the Inner Sphere. For three years, the Clans were unstoppable, until the Com Guards battled and bested them on the world of Tukayyid. Their victory bought the Successor States a fifteen-year truce, paid for by countless lives.

The Truce of Tukayyid has held for two years, but simmering hatred on both sides threatens to tear it asunder. Rival Clans raid each other's holdings, fanning the flames of civil war. Once more, the Inner Sphere trembles on the edge of apocalypse.

This time, no one may survive.

Part 1

1

As the hatchway of the *Bristol* began to open outward, a cool breeze and a host of fresh scents rushed into the cramped interior of the DropShip. Shuffling from one foot to the other, the passenger nearest the door waited impatiently for the opening hatch to meet the rising gangway. The moment the two connected, the man bounded through the hatchway and down the steps. Elsewhere on the ship other hatches began to open as spaceport workers began bringing in the trucks and cranes they would use to unload the huge DropShip.

Jeremiah Rose stopped to draw in a deep breath. The dawn breezes on Northwind had a scent all their own, one he had never forgotten in all the years away from his homeworld. The real thing was far better than any memory, but he had no time to tarry. Moving quickly Rose headed toward the customs building where his gear must first pass inspection before he would be free to enter the streets of Tara, capital of the planet.

Muscling his twin bags with practiced ease, Rose stepped lightly between and around the port workers as they hurried to and fro with their burdens. He trotted across the slightly damp tarmac and shouldered his way through the main entry. Startled custom agents in their regulation Stewart tartans stared at Rose as he pushed the unexpectedly light door open with a crash. Across the room a small man with service bars up his entire left arm turned to stare at Rose, while all around him the junior custom agents tried, and failed, not to show their amusement.

The hawk-faced old man, obviously the senior member of the staff on duty, motioned Rose toward his table with an evil leer. Rose had seen and worked with this petty-minded type before. King of this one small room, he was going to make sure Rose knew it. Rose's clumsy entrance had embarrassed him and now Rose would have to pay. All thoughts of a quick and easy entry into the city vanished as the man moved with deliberate slowness to examine Rose's belongings. For what seemed an eternity, he poked and prodded through Rose's cases, none of which contained anything unusual or even vaguely suspicious.

Rose was born and bred a warrior and his clothes reflected it. The warrior life was his heritage and, until recently, it had been his occupation. Returning to his homeworld, he believed it would be again. Like most soldiers, he traveled light. The three flight suits in the first case were identical to the one he wore. His single set of dress clothes was piled in a heap after the senior agent's search, but the mistreatment did not bother Rose at all. The clothes had been stored during the entire trip from Terra and they would continue to be packed away, in their current disarray, after the agent was finished. Shaving kit, underwear, socks, belts, and boots received the same treatment, winding up in the same tangled pile. Thirty minutes later the man moved to the second case. Around him the room filled with the passengers Rose had earlier outdistanced.

"So much for the first one, son. Now, what's in the second case?" The agent lifted the bag on end and attempted to work the double latches. Despite his best efforts, the case refused to open even though it was apparently unlocked. Rose smiled as the man looked up at him.

"Allow me." Rose set the case on its bottom and pushed open the two latches with his thumbs. Spinning the case around, he stepped back slightly. "It's keyed to open only on my thumbprints." The agent shot Rose an evil look. "Sorry," he added quickly.

Lifting the top of the custom case, the agent could not contain his surprise to see a single laser pistol with three energy clips. Without looking at Rose, the agent lifted the pistol out of the case.

"Fancy weapon you've got yourself, son. It's a little over-balanced, though."

Rose shrugged. The weapon was his remaining pride and joy. Custom-made for his large hands and long arms, it had more range and penetrating power than any laser pistol he had ever seen. It fired more like a rifle with a short grip.

"Why do you need a pistol like this?"

"I didn't know pistols were forbidden on Northwind," Rose said levelly.

"They're not. Not unless you look like trouble or have a criminal record."

"I assure you I am neither." Rose held out his open palms, smiling slightly. The agent seemed unconvinced.

"This is a MechWarrior's weapon, though I don't recognize the brand. You fancy yourself a MechWarrior?"

Yes, Rose was a MechWarrior, but one without a 'Mech, which put him among the ranks of the dispossessed. The agent's remark hit too close to home and he glared back at the small man.

"So you're a 'Mech jock." The man replaced the weapon in the case and closed the lid. "Let's see some papers."

Even in this modern age of computers and microprocessors, most people preferred to have the titles to their lands and valuable property on paper or on plastic. There was something solid about looking at the signatures and knowing the property was yours. In addition to the electronic back-up, many people liked to personally carry the legal titles to their property when relocating.

The customs agent was expecting Rose to show him the title to the 'Mech he assumed was on the DropShip. Rose reached into the inner pocket of his leather jacket and tossed some papers onto the gun case. The agent picked them up and quickly read through them.

"No 'Mech?"

Rose shook his head, unwilling to utter the words aloud.

"Dispossessed." The man's voice rose above the noise of the crowd. Heads turned, all eyes on Rose, who stood frozen. Had he been facing the crowd, he would have seen the mixture of pity, amusement, and scorn that rippled through the crowd. A MechWarrior was a member of the elite fighting force that controlled the balance of power in the Inner Sphere. He enjoyed an elevated position in society, just as the knights of the Middle Ages were elevated above the people they protected. To lose one's BattleMech was the height of shame for a member of this warrior elite.

Behind him Rose heard the crowd murmur and knew that people were pointing. He regarded the customs agent with silent intensity. Though publicly shamed, the insult did not register on his face. The agent smiled and tossed the papers back to him.

"Welcome to Northwind and Tara, son. Enjoy your stay." Keeping his eyes on Rose, the man pushed the two cases down the short ramp and out of his way. "Next."

Rose sidestepped to the end of the ramp and rearranged his belongings into a loose order, then closed the case. Without looking back he walked down the short corridor and into the main terminal of the spaceport. Crowds of people milled near the doors, waiting for loved ones to finish with the customs procedures.

Pushing through the crowd Rose crossed to the far side of the huge room. Having been away for so long, he was not used to the clash of colors that was the cornerstone of Highlander apparel. Tartans of every shade swirled about him, some traditional and easily recognizable, others unfamiliar. As always, however, he also felt the unmistakable undercurrent of Northwind: the joy of living.

Of all the people and places Rose had seen, none could match the vigor of the Highlanders when it came to enjoying life. They seemed to relish everything it had to offer, the good with the bad. Ever since the Highlanders' return to Northwind when Rose was just a small boy, they had discovered new enthusiasm for old work. Twenty-five years had gone by and it was still the same.

Rose paused near the main doors of the terminal and drank in the mood of the spaceport. "Opening the soul," his mentor would have called it. Rose looked around once more at the scene, then went out through the heavy doors.

A long line of cars stood waiting in the circle drive just outside the terminal building. Approaching the first in line, Rose opened the rear door. The driver hopped off the hood and slid into the driver's seat just as Rose was closing the door behind him.

"The Fort, please."

The driver glanced over his shoulder and gave Rose a look of obvious confusion. When the man made no move to put the vehicle in motion, Rose returned the look.

"The Fort," he repeated. "I'm not some stupid tourist or dumb mercenary. Take me to the Fort, *now.*"

Cowed by Rose's forcefulness, the driver faced front again and eased the car into traffic. Rose was grateful to be left alone with his thoughts during the brief trip to the Highlanders' Assembly Hall of Clan Elders, the chief government building on Tara. Set exactly in the center of the city, it was flanked by attendant buildings that supported the work that went on in the central building's hallowed halls. It had been called The Fort ever since the Highlanders had come back to Northwind in 3028. In that year the Highlander Clan elders had reached an agreement with the Federated Commonwealth in which the Northwind Highlanders renounced their allegiance to House Liao in return for being allowed to garrison their homeworld as part of the armed forces of the Federated Commonwealth.

The returning elders had declared that they would defend Northwind from the fortress of these walls against any and all who threatened. From the little Rose could remember, the speech had been a passionate one, but politics had mostly gone over his seven-year-old head.

Rose knew that the Highlander elders were meeting in full session today. The yearly event was a gathering of the elders of Tara and all the chiefs from the outlying provinces. When in session the High Assembly served as the main Highlander governing body.

The Assembly decided matters of planetary importance and considered proposals that would affect all the Highlanders and Northwind. Although powerful, the High Assembly was actually in session for only two to three weeks each year because most governmental matters could be handled and decided by the sub-assemblies that met year-round. Each sub-assembly was responsible for one aspect of Highlander life. The arts, science, medicine, education, and warfare, as well as dozens of other issues, were all directed by an individual governing assembly. The largest, and most prestigious, was the Assembly of Warriors, which controlled all aspects of the Highlanders' military. Composed of exactly one hundred proven Highlander soldiers, the Assembly of Warriors was the first to meet at High Assembly and the last to leave. In all ways the group was the cornerstone of Northwind.

The cab pulled up next to the curb, and Rose stepped out. He slid a fifty C-bill note through the driver's window and started up the stairs without waiting for the change.

Taking the steps two at a time, he only slowed his pace upon reaching the courtyard. The court marked the entryway into The Fort and protocol must be observed. Undue haste was definitely not seemly.

Silently sliding doors parted as Rose neared the entrance. He proceeded through into the foyer, heading straight for the main desk. Flanking the wooden desk were ceremonial guards, silent and steely-eyed. Ignoring them Rose spoke to the small woman behind the desk. Everyone who entered The Fort was required to register with the desk, but traffic was unusually light this early in the morning. Normally Rose would have had a long wait, but it looked as though he'd beaten the rush.

"Rose, Jeremiah. I'm here to speak before the Assembly of Warriors." Rose looked at a point above the woman's head, careful to keep his back straight and his eyes forward. Out the corner of his eye he could see the eyes of one of the guards reacting to his unexpected statement, but like Rose he kept his body perfectly still and his head straight.

"You are expected. The Assembly has already begun. You will wait until summoned," she said sternly.

"I have just arrived on Northwind and could not deposit my belongings." Rose stopped, knowing the simple statement would be enough. Within seconds a boy appeared with a plastic token. Rose handed him the bags, took the token in return, then went to the row of elevators lining the wall. Pressing the third button, he waited until one set of doors opened.

Once in the car he was again forced to wait until the car's automatic sensors decided that he was clear of the door and that no other passengers were entering. Then the doors closed with a soft whoosh and the car began to rise.

Rose glanced at his chronometer, recently adjusted for Northwind's current time, and waited. Seconds later the car stopped smoothly at the third floor, the doors sliding open with the same soft whoosh.

The corridor before him was bare and silent. Twin guards flanked the doors to his left, the only ones on the floor. Behind the massive oak frames he could just hear the sounds of the Assembly. Though the guards did not turn to look at him, Rose knew they could see him perfectly.

Quietly, he stepped off the elevator and went to sit on the single bench across from the Assembly Hall door. What had started six months ago with a request to speak before the Assembly of Warriors was finally coming to fruition. His numerous requests had initially received a poor response, but with persistence he had finally managed to win a place on the agenda. After almost three months aboard ship, he finally arrived by JumpShip at the nadir jump point for Northwind. The trip insystem had been aboard the DropShip *Bristol*.

Since that time Rose had been in daily communication with the office of the Assembly secretary. He had always known protocol was important, but he'd never realized how little he knew about it until the secretary uplinked a two-hundred-page document on the subject. If he was to speak successfully, Rose was expected to know, by heart, the procedures described on those pages and to behave accordingly. He'd studied them long and hard, enough that his confidence was high. Sitting on the solitary bench outside the Assembly of Warriors, he waited with high hopes.

Nine hours later he was still waiting, his confidence a shadow of its former self. The doors had opened several times during the day and the guards had been replaced twice, but Rose's name was not called. Soon the session would end for the day. Forcing himself to remain calm, he looked up slowly as the doors opened once more. Voices spilled into the hallway as a special guard stepped into the hall.

"Jeremiah Rose, the Assembly of Warriors would hear you speak." Rose stood and followed the man into the room. If his speech was successful, this would be the first step in a long road to come. With a slight sinking feeling, Rose noted that his stomach had decided not to accompany him into the room.

2

As Rose followed the man through the door it was almost like walking into another time. Unlike the rest of The Fort, the U-shaped Hall of Warriors was constructed of wood. The door guard stepped to the right to let Rose descend the shallow stone steps to the wooden speaker's platform. The lighting built into the walls and ceiling provided dim, but adequate illumination.

To his left and right, warriors sat on wooden benches behind solid oak tables equipped with computer terminals and sophisticated communication arrays. Many of the gathered soldiers wore traditional kilts and the heavy boots favored by MechWarriors and aerospace pilots. Dress uniforms were considered inappropriate for the Assembly of Warriors, whether for members or for speakers. All manner of knives were, on the other hand, openly displayed by many, and Rose knew that on more than one occasion the weapons had been used to resolve differences of opinion between speaker and audience.

Reaching the foot of the stairs he crossed the sod floor, with each step feeling the press of stares against his back. His every move was under constant scrutiny, the warriors searching for the slightest hint of weakness or indecision. Either one would heavily influence their voting on Rose's proposition.

He climbed the five wooden steps to the speaker's platform and looked at the three people seated there. In the center chair was Colonel Edward Senn. As the commander of the First Kearny Highlanders, the senior regiment of the Northwind Highlanders, Senn presided over the Assembly of Warriors when not on active duty. Rose acknowledged the man's presence with a quick meeting of the eyes, but did not allow his gaze to linger. Confidence, but not pride, was required, as many speakers discovered too late. To his right was Colonel James Cochraine, leader of the Second Kearny. Rose tried to acknowledge the giant, but Cochraine's attention was completely devoted to a communications link built into his chair. Rose doubted the man even knew he was on the platform.

To Senn's left were two chairs, but only the far chair was occupied. The empty seat was normally occupied by the commander of MacCleod's Highlanders, but that unit had recently been redeployed. Although it was unusual for the chair to remain vacant during a High Assembly, MacCleod had refused to stay behind when his unit shipped out. It was typical for the man and the wild bunch he commanded to fly in the face of convention.

Sitting in the final chair was Andrea Stirling, commander of Stirling's Fusiliers. With one leg draped over the arm of her chair and her head resting firmly in her opposite hand, she was the image of boredom. She idly played with a strand of long dark hair and regarded Rose through heavy lashes. No wonder they called her Cat, thought Rose. Of the three Highlanders on the platform she had been a commander the shortest amount of time, but Rose judged her the most deadly. Her green eyes gave away her secret even in the dim light of the room.

At the top of the steps, Rose crossed the platform and stood directly in front of Colonel Senn. Before speaking he waited patiently for Senn to acknowledge him with a nod of the head.

"Greetings, Colonel Senn. Thank you for the opportunity to speak before this assembly." Rose bowed slightly from the waist, careful to keep his eyes firmly on Senn.

Again Senn nodded. "It is our pleasure, Adept Rose, but I am told you no longer go by that title. Perhaps I should call you Jeremiah." Heads turned at the mention of Rose's former ComStar title, but he pressed ahead.

"As you wish, Colonel. My title matters little. Your consideration, however, means a great deal to me." Senn watched Rose calmly as he went through the traditional greeting. Ritual courtesy was expected and Rose was determined to live up to Highlander expectations.

"I bring a token of appreciation to thank you for your hospitality." Carefully, Rose reached into the left leg pocket of his jumpsuit, from which he removed a leather-wrapped bundle. With his left hand he presented it to Senn, who immediately began loosening the thongs that held the leather in place.

"I acquired this during a battle against the Smoke Jaguars. It is a simple item, but crafted with precision as befits a warrior." Senn unfolded the last leather flap and withdrew a boot knife. Patterned after the legendary skaen doo, the grip of the silver weapon was constructed of a dark cherry-colored wood Rose had not been able to identify despite repeated attempts. He suspected that the wood had not been seen in the Inner Sphere previous to the Clan invasion, making the weapon as unique as it was valuable, as beautiful as it was practical.

"Thank you, Jeremiah Rose. I accept your gift in the spirit it was given." Senn removed his own knife from the top of his heavy right boot and replaced it with the Clan version.

"Now, Mister Rose, I believe you wished to address this assembly."

"Indeed I do, Colonel." With a sudden turn, Rose faced the gathering. For the first time he noted the glass-enclosed gallery where sat the spectators of the Assembly. Hidden behind the darkened glass, hundreds watched the proceedings in silence. Rose felt the weight of their attention as he looked down at the assembled warriors.

With the formalities finished, they stared up at him expectantly. Private conversations began to fade away as Rose walked across the platform. He had hoped for a podium, yet such a prop would have been out of place here. The open stage left him no place to hide, which was just the way the Highlanders wanted it.

"I would speak to you of the Clans—the Ghost Bears, the Nova Cats, and the Smoke Jaguars. The Jade Falcons, the Steel Vipers, and the Wolves. Like many of you, I have fought against them and their high technology. I have stood against their OmniMechs and survived. I have seen the Clan invaders crushed on the battlefield, and watched their retreating DropShips light the night sky above our campfires." Murmurs broke out among the warriors as Rose spoke. He was asking them to believe quite a story. The Clans had rarely been beaten, and only twice had they ever retreated as Rose described.

"I speak, of course, of the battle of Tukayyid and ComStar's victory over the combined forces of the Clans." The murmurs grew louder. ComStar was still not held in high regard, despite the success of their military forces on Tukayyid and the resulting treaty with the Clans.

"Today, however, I speak of the future, not the past. Too long the Inner Sphere has allowed the Clans to dictate the ways of the war. We react to their attacks and are forced to play the defender. To that I say, no more. It is time to take the battle to the Clans. It is time to fight them on our own terms." A few warriors nodded, while others leaned forward as though to listen more closely. One warrior thumped on his wooden table, encouraging Rose to continue.

"I was at Tukayyid when the Com Guards defeated the Clans. It was a great victory for the Inner Sphere, but it was paid for at great price. Because of that battle the Clans have agreed not to press their attacks below the line of the planet Tukayyid. Yes, the invasion downward has been halted, but what about the planets to the right and left of the Clan advance? What of those planets that lie above Tukayyid, those worlds not covered by the treaty? Will the ravenous Clans allow the inhabitants of those planets to live in peace? You know they will not!''

More nods, a few more thumps on the wooden desks by other Highlanders. Rose began to pace the platform like a caged beast, his confidence growing, his voice pitched slightly louder. In his heart, however, Rose knew the warriors were not responding only to him. Like most warriors of the Inner Sphere, the Highlanders wanted to stop the Clans, political boundaries be damned. Mercenary units were especially vocal, and the Northwind Highlanders, despite their recent return to Davion space, were among the most outspoken.

"So, what do we do? While the politicians scramble for cover and the Great House leaders try to protect their dwindling empires, the Clans prepare to strike to their right and left into Commonwealth and Combine space.

''I know the Highlanders have a just and legal contract with House Davion. I also know the Highlanders will fight without equal while they fulfill the remainder of the contract. Highlander honor will not allow them to break that contract and do what their hearts cry out for them to do. The Highlanders must abide by the contract and co-ordinate the use of their battalions with the forces of the Federated Commonwealth.'' Rose paused and looked at the empty chair of Colonel MacCleod. The move was not lost on the Assembly.

''It doesn't have to be that way.'' Rose waited for his words to fully sink in. He walked back to the center of the platform in silence as his audience waited.

''My plan, like all good military plans, is a simple one. The Highlanders have contracted to provide four regiments for the defense of the Federated Commonwealth. There is no contract, however, that prevents the Highlanders from forming an independent unit that might further hire itself out to take the fight back to the Clans.'' A few shouts of agreement rang out, mostly from the younger warriors.

''The purpose of my address to you is a simple one. I

ask simply that the Northwind Highlanders allow me to recruit warriors and technicians to be hired out solely to fight the Clans.

"Further, I ask that the Northwind Highlanders allow me to purchase any 'Mechs not necessary to fulfill the Davion contract in order to equip warriors capable of fighting the Clans but who lack the 'Mechs to do so.

"Finally, I ask that the Northwind Highlanders allow me to use their name for this new unit, which I would call the Northwind Black Watch." One warrior jumped to his feet and raised a fist in the air. More thumps and shouts of agreement rose up here and there. Rose turned toward the Northwind commanders and saw that his plea had also touched them. Colonel Stirling was sitting upright in her chair. Senn and Cochraine gazed at him with bright eyes, although their bodies did not show the tension of their junior counterpart. Rose nodded once to Senn and moved to the right side of the platform.

Senn waited for complete silence before speaking. He held out a hand to Rose and gazed around at the assembly.

"Jeremiah Rose has spoken eloquently on a subject near to the hearts of all warriors assembled in this hall. Before we cast judgment on his petition, I call upon any who would speak against him."

Rose had known this was a required part of the procedure, but he did not expect any serious opposition to his speech. Senn was right, the Highlanders had become very vocal about taking the fight back to the Clans in recent months and Rose was offering the chance to do just that. He was surprised when a strong voice called out from the back of the room.

"Colonel Senn, I too would address the Assembly of Warriors." Heads turned to face the old man walking down the center aisle with the aid of a brass-tipped cane. In the dim light Rose could not make out who he was, but warriors near the aisle bowed their heads in silent respect as the man passed. Whoever he was, the man was obviously well-regarded by these warriors, despite his advanced years.

When the newcomer reached the sod floor, Rose could tell by his garb that he was not a warrior. He wore an old but clean tech's uniform without rank or insignia. Looking down on the man, Rose could still not see his face. He was suddenly nervous as the man reached the bottom of the platform stairs, then he stared aghast as Colonel Senn introduced him.

"Master Technician Cornelius Rose will address the Assembly." Jeremiah had tagged another name to the man: Father.

"Thank you, Colonel. The hour is late and I am an old man, so I will make my statement brief." The elder Rose turned back to the suddenly silent gathering and leaned heavily on his cane.

"Fire and brimstone, Highlanders. Fire and brimstone. You're born to both when you take the seat of that grand invention called the BattleMech and stride off in search of glory and honor.

"Honor can be a heavy burden to bear in such a world. Don't think for a moment that I don't know what it's like to face the fire, the shells falling around you and the heat of your 'Mech spiking higher by the second. I understand all too well what that's like.

"Before you stands a man who would take you into the heart of that firestorm. The Clans. We've faced them before and it looks like we'll continue to face them for some time to come. I don't need to tell you that they're tough opponents. My son Daniel died facing the Clans."

Jeremiah's head came quickly around to regard his father. He had not known his younger brother was dead; the news came as a shock. He wanted to know why and how, but trapped here on the platform, he was forced to stand with growing numbness as his father wiped his eyes quickly, then went on.

"Now my long-lost son Jeremiah returns. Yes, he is my eldest son.

"He returns after better than twenty years and asks

you to follow him against the Clans. After twenty years away from his home, he returns and asks us to place our trust in him. To entrust him with our lives and our honor while he goes to fight the Clans."

The old man dropped his head and shook it slowly. The assembly remained quiet, waiting for the man's next words as Jeremiah saw his dreams slipping away. After long moments, the head came back up.

"This once-Highlander returns with visions of glory and dares talk of honor? After leaving like a coward and staying away for twenty years while his father grew old and his own brother died, he talks of leadership? After returning without a BattleMech, he asks for warriors?

"I know the Clans are a serious threat to us all. They must be stopped, once and for all. Taking the fight to the Clans is a fine idea. You have discussed the same idea before in these very halls and know well the merits of such a plan." Standing straight for the first time since entering the room, Cornelius Rose held the assembly with his gaze as he lifted his cane toward his son. The effort cost him considerably, but the cane did not waver as he spoke.

"I say to you simply: Right plan, wrong leader." The cane crashed down onto the platform to punctuate the remark. "To defeat the Clans you must have able leadership from a man you can trust. Jeremiah Rose is not that man. If you must strip away the reserve strength of the Highlanders, then entrust those 'Mechs to a proven leader."

Without waiting for a response, Cornelius Rose left the stage and walked toward the long flight of stairs to the exit. Warriors who moments before had seconded Rose now sat in silence as the old man passed. Senn also remained silent until the doors had closed behind Cornelius Rose, then he began to address the Assembly.

"I call the vote. Jeremiah Rose proposes to use our name for a fighting unit that will oppose the Clans. What say you?" Throughout the hall the warriors used the comm units built into their desks to register their decisions. In moments the anonymous votes were compiled and displayed on the screen built into the arm of Colonel Cochraine's chair. After a pause, he shook his head and announced the result.

"The proposal fails.

"I call the vote. Jeremiah Rose proposes to purchase such 'Mechs that may become available to equip warriors to fight the Clans. What say you?" Another instantaneous tally of the votes. Another shake of the head from Cochraine.

"The proposal fails.

"I call the final vote. Jeremiah Rose proposes to recruit MechWarriors from the Highlanders to fight against the Clans under his leadership. What say you?" Rose fought the urge to hang his head and somehow escape the stares of the crowd. If he was to be defeated, he would do it with his head high.

"The proposal fails.

"Jeremiah Rose, the Assembly of Warriors rejects your proposal and denies you the right to recruit, train, or lead the warriors of the Northwind Highlanders.

"However, as you remain a Highlander by birth if not action, you shall be allowed to remain on Northwind as long as you desire or until such time as you violate the edicts of this Assembly. Further, by virtue of your birth and Highlander tradition, you shall be allowed to recruit such warriors among your family who choose to follow you, provided these warriors are not already under existing contract or in any way obligated to Northwind. Any warriors so recruited shall understand they are not fighting for Northwind, but only for you personally.

"Are these points clear, Jeremiah Rose?"

Stunned by the sudden turn of events and the speedy decisions of the Assembly, Rose could only nod. Senn stood abruptly, followed closely by the other commanders and the warriors of the hall.

"The decision of this assembly is final. Warriors, we stand adjourned until tomorrow."

3

"**H**ey, Rose, wait up."

Rose turned at the sound of the female voice calling him as he walked down Delancy Street away from The Fort. He was surprised at being hailed in the poor light, but he recognized the caller as someone who had known Rose in even dimmer surroundings.

"Good evening, Captain McCloud." Rose kept his hands in his pockets as Rachel McCloud slipped her small hand into the crook of his elbow.

"So, now it's Captain McCloud. Isn't that a bit formal, considering our past few months together? Or have you forgotten it was me and my DropShip that personally brought you home to Northwind?" She looked up at Rose, but he refused to return her gaze as they walked on.

His mind drifted back to the trip from Terra to Northwind. He and Rachel had hit it off almost immediately, becoming almost inseparable for the entire trip. He smiled unconsciously at the memories that suddenly seemed so far away and long ago. After leaving Terra and ComStar, he had foolishly believed anything was possible. Now he was convinced otherwise.

"I take it matters didn't go well at the Assembly."

Rose stopped suddenly and looked down at her. Rachel McCloud was tall for a woman, but Rose easily towered above her. He rarely used his height to an advantage, but now he made an exception.

"You were obviously waiting for me and the Assembly has been over for two hours, so you tell me." He turned to walk away, pulling McCloud's hand off his arm. He had walked three paces when something solid stung his ear. The sharpness of the pain stopped him, but even as he raised his hand to cover his ear, the pain began to recede. He looked back at Rachel, who was conspicuously out of arm's reach.

"What the hell was that for?" His ear still stung, but whatever she'd done hadn't broken the skin. It was the perfect attention-getter.

"Reality check, Adept."

"Don't call me that. You know I don't like it." Rose squared his shoulders and faced McCloud, who had stopped in the middle of the sidewalk.

"Don't behave so stupidly and I won't have to."

"I'm not acting stupid." But even as the words came from his mouth, Rose knew she was right. He was acting stupid, or at least defeated, which was just as bad. He relaxed and held out a hand to her.

"All right, I'm acting stupid. I'll try to stop."

McCloud crossed the brief distance to Rose and slipped her hand in his. There were few things she liked as much as winning a fight, even a brief one.

"What do you already know?" Rose resumed walking in his original direction. Although he had no destination in mind, it felt good to be under the open sky again after traveling so long through space. He doubted that McCloud shared that sentiment, but she was here just the same. Rose felt a tug at his heart, but ignored the feeling, as he had in the past.

"I only know that the Assembly voted down your proposal, mainly because of your father's speech. You're still welcome on Northwind, but your dream of starting a 'Mech unit was dealt a pretty harsh blow."

"I'd say a death blow," Rose sighed. "If not, then the meeting afterward was the killer."

"You had another meeting? I wondered where you went." McCloud snuggled closer to him as they walked, making the footing dangerous. Despite the warm air, she was not used to the cool breeze—or draft, as she insisted on calling it—blowing down from the mountains. She was a born spacer.

"Damn, I forgot my two cases." Rose glanced at his chronometer and slammed his fist into his open hand. "The Fort is closed by now."

"Don't worry. We can get them in the morning. It's not like they're going anywhere." Rose looked back along the route they'd just taken, considering the option of returning.

"You were saying?"

Rose shook his head and continued walking.

"Two boys stopped me on the way out," he told her. "Dear old dad called a family meeting on the spot to hear my proposal and was telling anybody who'd listen not to follow me."

"He sounds thorough."

"Vindictive is more like it. I was still reeling from the Assembly of Warriors when I was escorted to an adjacent room and propped up between my two keepers.

"The room was full of family I hadn't seen since leaving Northwind, but did I get the chance to speak to them or greet them? Hell, no. Dad announced me to the family and then proceeded to tell them what a rat I was. He explained my proposal to them as I listened, then called the vote. It was all over in less than ten minutes." Rose kicked a stray rock into the street and watched it skip to a stop in the middle of the lane.

"Could you have stopped him?"

"Yes, but not really. As a tech, he doesn't really have any clout in the Assembly of Warriors, but as the oldest male in the Rose family he's got a hell of a strong pull. I could have stopped him in front of the Assembly or the family session, but in either case it would have been considered very rude. Not even the prodigal son can go against his father—especially when he's the patriarch—and get away with it. Speaking at all would have been proof of my father's claims.

"Seventeen family members present and all seventeen rejected my offer."

McCloud let Rose walk on in silence. Despite the short time she'd known him, she knew he had not really given up on his dream, despite his current mood. He'd figure something out if he took the time. She began to shiver as the temperature continued to drop.

She looked up at Rose, trying to come to terms with how strongly she felt about him. She'd always prided herself on being independent. Being a DropShip captain was hard work, and McCloud considered herself as good as any in the business. Then along came this MechWarrior who made her question her lonely way of life. Not that it was anything he ever said. His company was enough.

"So what now?" McCloud spoke the words more to keep her lips moving than because she expected an answer. She shivered again, thinking that one day scientists would look back and declare climate control as the invention that separated men from monkeys.

"Now I try to see my sister, Rianna, and take it from there. She wasn't at the Assembly today, so she missed the vote."

"I thought she was a warrior."

"She is, but so far she's unproven. The public records indicate that she's a good 'Mech pilot and an excellent planner, but she's still a year away from her first contract. She could have come to the Assembly as a member of the gallery, but that's about as exciting as watching 'Mechs rust, especially without the frame of reference you get in combat. I doubt anybody thought the meeting would be as explosive as it turned out to be."

The pair continued in silence until McCloud remembered.

"Hey, you said the meeting with your family took only

ten minutes. Where have you been for the last two hours?''

"Talking with Colonel Stirling."

"Cat Stirling?"

"One and the same. How do you know the colonel?" Rose looked over at McCloud, who only shrugged.

"Just one of the people you hear about in my line of work. I believe the term is 'larger than life.' ''

"That sure sounds like her. There were times in the conversation when I swore I could hear her purr." Rose laughed at the thought and McCloud relaxed a little. Rose was already putting the past behind him and concentrating on the future.

"Did you talk about anything important?" McCloud tried to taint the question with a hint of jealousy, but Rose either missed the inference or else chose to ignore it. The idea was silly anyway.

"She more or less agreed with my father."

"Really?"

"Well, not really, but she told me she'd predicted the results of the vote yesterday after learning that my father was going to speak."

"Did you find out anything interesting?"

Rose nodded. "She was the commander of Danny's battalion when he died on—"

"Your brother is dead?"

Rose nodded. He'd forgotten that McCloud didn't know. Though he'd only learned it himself a few hours ago, Rose was surprisingly at ease with the news. He and his brother had never been really close. The death of lancemates had hit him harder. McCloud, however, seemed to take the news as a great shock. He was greatly surprised when she stopped to give him a hug.

"Jeremiah, I'm so sorry." He struggled with what to say, afraid of diminishing her compassion and suddenly ashamed of his own lack of feelings. After a moment's hesitation, he hugged her in return.

"You're shaking." Rose loosened his grip and pulled back enough to see her face.

"It's freezing out here," she said. Rose squeezed her close and she returned the grip with fervor. Looking over the top of her head for suitable refuge, he noted a small restaurant across the street.

He pulled free and pointed across the street. "How about some food, on me?"

"Anyplace warm is fine with me."

Rose gripped her hand and led her across the street and into the restaurant, where they were greeted by the smell of freshly baked bread and by a rotund woman in green tartan. Behind the woman, in the restaurant's even smaller bar, men and woman mingled with loud humor.

"Two for dinner, please."

"Am I blind? Of course two for dinner." The woman slapped Rose good-naturedly on the arm with a pair of menus. "You wait a second in there while I get the table ready." Rose knew there were plenty of tables available, but the bar was where the restaurant made its highest profits and nobody was going to eat without first relaxing. Rose raised an eyebrow toward McCloud. He'd known her for two months, but this was their first social situation outside her DropShip. Did she even like bars?

McCloud looked into the small room and nodded quickly. Rose smiled back at their disappearing hostess and followed McCloud into the noisy room. The single waitress was already leaving the table McCloud had acquired by the time Rose maneuvered his way through the press of occupants.

"Loud bunch." Rose leaned closer as if to whisper, but in the noise he was almost shouting. Still, McCloud barely heard. She nodded in agreement. The pair waited for several minutes, but their drinks still did not arrive. Rose looked over to the bar for the waitress, but she was nowhere in sight.

"What are you lookin' at?" It was one of the Highlanders propped up at the end of the bar. Rose hadn't even noticed the man until he spoke. As he turned away, the man pushed away from the bar and headed toward

Rose's table. "Hey, aren't you the guy from the Assembly this afternoon?"

"Trouble at six o'clock." McCloud stiffened, but did not turn around. Rose watched as two more Highlanders followed their friend over to the table.

"Hey, I was talkin' to you." Rose looked up at the lead Highlander. Red-rimmed eyes stared back with malice. Rose could feel the atmosphere of the room change as people vacated a nearby table.

"I was just looking for the waitress, friend." Rose considered standing, but the challenge of the gesture would be too much to miss. The drunk leaned into the back of Rose's chair, throwing the balance forward. Rose was forced to lean onto the table or rest his head on the man's stomach.

"Friend, of a coward like you? Not on the longest day you ever lived." Rose stiffened at the words, but managed to remain in his seat. His smile was plastered in place for the three drunks, but a knot was growing in his stomach.

"He doesn't like us much, does he, Ian?" Rose looked up at the second bully, who moved behind Rachel's chair. He leered at Rose above McCloud's head, his yellow teeth poking through a tangle of black beard. The third man laughed in false mirth as he ran a hand through his blond hair. Rose felt the knot harden and start to burn.

"Can you imagine," asked the first, "this man leading Highlanders into battle?"

"Then coming home to a woman as beautiful as this?" finished the second. He dropped his hands on McCloud's shoulders for emphasis. Despite the attempt to remain calm, Rose stiffened as he waited for McCloud's reaction. He knew she was ready to react, but she continued to stare straight ahead.

"I'll give you some credit," continued the first. "Coming back to Northwind took some guts. I mean, I didn't think anybody was stupid enough to try to return to the Highlanders after running out on them."

"How about it, Angel? Is this guy really that brave,

or is he just stupid?'' Rose and the three Highlanders all looked toward McCloud, who continued to stare straight ahead. The second bully had begun to rub her shoulders, evidently encouraged by her lack of response. Rose tried to relax and let the tension flow out of his muscles, but the fire that had started in his stomach was spreading quickly. He was shocked when McCloud actually answered the question.

"I can't say much about his courage." She turned her head toward Rose and slowly reached across her body to pat the top of the hand massaging her right shoulder. "And as for brains, hell, this table top has a higher I.Q." She stopped patting the Highlander's hand and threw a look of disgust at Rose. The three standing men began to laugh, mirthlessly at first, but with genuine feeling once they saw the crushed look on Rose's face.

Rachel reached up with her right hand and slightly rotated the laughing Highlander's right hand off her shoulder, twisting the palm out. He looked down at her, but his alcohol-wrapped brain did not register what was going on until McCloud gripped his ring finger with the other hand and swiftly yanked it back.

The bone let go with a pop, but McCloud kept up the pressure, bending the digit all the way back to the top of the man's hand. He tried to yell, but nothing came out. He tried to back away, but McCloud came out of the chair and followed him.

Rose took McCloud's lead, reacting immediately with the pop of the Highlander's broken finger. Leaning forward on his chair, he shot his right foot into the shin of the leader. The mule kick slipped off the bone, however, merely cracking it instead of breaking it cleanly in two. The man came down heavily on the chair, pushing Rose into the table. With a quick spin off his left foot, Rose was free of the chair and facing his attacker.

The man had recovered quickly and was already picking up Rose's discarded chair. The few customers remaining in the immediate area scattered as the man charged Rose, the chair over his head.

With a roar he brought the chair crashing down in a two-handed blow intended to drive Rose through the floor. Rose, however, was no longer in the chair's path.

Stepping inside the chair's arc, he seized the man's left wrist as the chair continued to fall, simultaneously driving his right hand into the man's stomach. Pivoting to the left, Rose continued the motion started by the punch and spun in a half-circle, crouching slightly as he turned. The attacker's momentum carried him forward, but the punch had broken his balance. He slammed into Rose's back, his extended left arm over the top of Rose's shoulder. With a quick upward thrust, Rose catapulted the man through the air, pulling in the left wrist as the man cartwheeled over his head.

The Highlander slammed into the ground, his legs forming a clapboard that smashed his testicles and expelled what little air remained in his lungs. Finishing the move, Rose stepped on the man's ribs just under the armpit and jerked up on the wrist. The shoulder popped out of the socket with a hollow sound and the fingers went limp. Rose dropped the wrist and looked for McCloud.

The first attacker had lost all interest in the fight, but McCloud would not release his hand. Instead of fighting back, he was trying to keep the hand as still as possible to save the finger from further punishment. His friend, however, was not thinking of defense. As Rose looked up, he hit McCloud behind the ear with a bottle. The glass splintered just above the neck as McCloud went down to one knee. The Highlander with the broken hand finally managed to pull free as his friend continued the attack. With his free hand he grabbed the back of McCloud's hair, forcing her head back. Rose looked for something to throw at the attacker, but nothing was in reach. In desperation, he yelled.

It was not the yell of a frightened or angry man. The single note was more like the release of an avenging spirit into the room. For an instant everyone in the bar stood motionless.

Rose used the moment to dive across the table that

separated him from McCloud and her attacker. He landed on his hands and tumbled over his landing spot to rise in a crouch. McCloud's attacker had regained his wits and resumed his strike with the broken bottle. As his hand went down, Rose shot forward. Their hands met centimeters above McCloud's face. The force of Rose's blow diverted the bottle attack, but the glass ripped through McCloud's shirt and drew three thin lines of blood along her shoulder.

The attacker dropped McCloud to the floor and slashed wildly at Rose. The Highlander knew he was outmatched, but was beyond caring. He slashed again each time Rose feinted. Although his moves were crude, the man had a solid defense and was beginning to build an offense. By constant movement and use of the slashing bottle, he held his ground against Rose until McCloud reentered the fight.

The constant movement had forced the Highlander toward the bar and McCloud's coiled legs. With his attention focused on Rose, he never noticed McCloud's kick until his ankle broke. He fell to the ground, face to face with McCloud, a look of amazement on his face. McCloud kicked him several times as she hastily stood, but the man was no longer interested in fighting.

Rose placed his hand lightly on her good shoulder. "Are you all right?"

McCloud looked at him as if he were crazy until she noticed the object of his gaze. Her entire arm was red with blood. She glanced at the man on the floor, her head cocked in question. Rose simply nodded.

With stunning speed, McCloud kicked the man squarely in the stomach. The man groaned and heaved his mostly liquid dinner onto the bar's floor. McCloud was ready to kick him again as Rose placed a restraining hand on her shoulder.

"We'd best be going," he said. McCloud looked up at him in amazement. "Come on, Rachel."

"Listen to the man, lady."

Rose and McCloud turned to the final attacker. He

stood across the room, one hand cradled to his chest, the other holding a needler. The few customers who had not fled into the restaurant seemed to side with the locals. Although none seemed to be armed, they all looked ready to let the remaining Highlander finish the fight as he saw fit.

McCloud was stunned. "You provoke a fight, then threaten to kill us when we beat the snot out of you?"

The gunman did not answer, but his eyes told her the truth.

"So much for that Highlander honor you've been telling me about, Rose." Backing away from the man she'd been kicking, McCloud allowed Rose to lead her out of the restaurant.

The cool air was bracing against their sweat-soaked skin. Rose grabbed McCloud's arm and began to walk her away from the bar as quickly as possible. Although the hour was early, the streets were temporarily deserted. Heading back to The Fort, they glanced about for a cab.

"You know, Rose, I think you saved my life in there."

"The hell you say. I damn near cost you your eye, not to mention your life." He spotted a cab and waved frantically. McCloud was leaning heavily on him as the adrenaline wore away.

"No. You saved my life. Now I owe you." The cab started forward and Rose quit waving. He used both hands to hold McCloud up. "Hey, where did you learn all those fancy moves?" she mumbled.

"I was stationed on Luthien for years, remember? I guess I learned the basics here on Northwind, though, from my mom." McCloud slumped against Rose, barely conscious. As she started to fall, he scooped her up in his arms and waited for the cab.

"What about that shout?" she said groggily. "Where'd you learn that?" Rose looked down at her, surprised to see she was still conscious. The cab pulled up and the driver got out to open the door, concern etched on his face.

"My spirit shout, if you believe such nonsense. My

sensei said that if you were ever in great need, you could release part of your spirit to stun your opponents. That's the first time I've ever tried it in combat, though.''

Blood dripped from Rose's fingers onto the pavement as the driver opened the door and tried to help Rose with Rachel, who by now was definitely unconscious. The door closed behind him and the driver trotted around to the driver's seat.

Rose looked down at McCloud and held her close. ''That's also the first time I've ever heard anything that sounded like that.''

4

Tara, Northwind
25 April 3054

For the next two days Rose stayed at the hospital with Rachel McCloud. The jagged wound on her shoulder had sliced through the skin and muscle, but there was no permanent damage. It had been impossible to stitch the wound, however, so McCloud was forced to keep the arm perfectly still until the injury could begin to heal itself.

Rose hovered around her bed during visiting hours and in the waiting room during the night. Twenty-four hours after being admitted, Rachel had seen enough of Rose. In no uncertain terms, she demanded that he leave her alone for the rest of the day. The duty nurses were equally glad to see him go. They had rarely been criticized as harshly for their care, or what Rose perceived as a lack thereof.

Leaving the hospital, Rose walked without purpose for a few hours, his head and stomach churning over the past days' events. Eventually he stopped for lunch at a small restaurant within the shadow of The Fort, but the meal did little to improve his darkening mood. Picking over the remains of his meal, he finally decided to go home. I'm already in a bad mood, he thought. I might as well make it really bad.

Two hours later Rose was standing in the street in front of his former family home. The cab fare had cost a small fortune, but he hadn't felt like taking the monorail to the Warrior's Quarter.

Rose wondered at the location of his father's home. Cornelius Rose was considered one of the best techs in the Highlanders, but the home the elder Rose now owned had come to him as a legacy from his wife. Although Marie Rose had died when Rose was still a child, he knew she'd been an excellent warrior and leader. He tried to recall her face, but as always, could only envision her standing in front of her *Thunderbolt* in a cooling vest, shorts, and neurohelmet. A MechWarrior and her 'Mech just seemed to go together.

Rose studied the house his mother's skill had purchased even though she had never lived there. Like many others, Marie Rose had died fighting in the ill-fated War of 3039. Yes, she'd been a warrior, but Rose had never reconciled himself to the waste that was her death. Any child mourned the loss of a parent, of course, but his loss went even deeper than that. Rose believed that Prince Hanse Davion of the Federated Commonwealth, and others like him, had killed his mother with their greed and megalomania. Fighting an invader like the Clans was one thing, but going to war over the ownership of a few depleted planets was another matter entirely.

The strong anti-Davion sentiments that Rose could not help but feel had earned him his father's wrath. To Cornelius Rose, Hanse Davion could do no wrong. But Rose did not believe that Davion was a saint because he had allowed the Highlanders to return to the planet Northwind, especially when it was the Davion rulers who had forced them off the planet in the first place. Rose had never forgiven Hanse Davion for his mother's death, yet the Prince's recent death had somehow softened Rose's opinion of the Federated Commonwealth. Besides, he reasoned, the loss of his mother and the split with his father had forced him into ComStar, which had been a good thing, despite the recent turn of events. Although it may not have been a fair trade, he valued his time with the Com Guards.

As always, the house looked strange to Rose. He had lived here for almost eleven years, but it had never really seemed to belong to him or his family. He'd always thought of it as his mother's personal property, just like her *Thunderbolt*. Rose wondered what had happened to Tea Bowl.

As a child, his brother Danny had never been able to pronounce the 'Mech's real name. The *Thunderbolt* had transformed from a T-Bolt to a T-Bol and finally to Tea Bowl. Even when Danny was grown up enough to pronounce the word correctly, Marie had continued to call her beloved 'Mech the Tea Bowl. Now that Danny was gone, his father had probably sold the 'Mech back to the Highlanders.

"Hey, you."

Rose was startled out of his reverie by a shout from the front porch. He had no idea how long he'd been standing in the middle of the street, but his presence had evidently attracted someone's attention.

"Why are you standing in the middle of the road staring at my house?" The woman, or girl, on the front porch seemed genuinely offended. Rose guessed her age at no more than eighteen years as she stood confidently before the open door, hands firmly on her hips. Her tight-fitting clothing revealed an athlete's figure, thin and long-limbed with broad, muscular shoulders. Rose guessed she was a swimmer, but the girl's long dark hair seemed out of keeping with the supposition.

"Sorry." Rose stepped from the street onto the sidewalk in front of the house. "I was looking for the home of Cornelius Rose." It had not occurred to Rose that the family might have moved, but with both his mother and Danny gone, the old man might well have wished to relocate with his daughter to Northwind's Tech Quarter. Then it hit him.

"Rianna?" Rose began walking forward, increasing his pace as he neared the front porch. The girl's annoyance changed to alarm as Rose picked up speed. Instead of running, however, she dropped into a defensive

crouch. Realizing the effect he was having, Rose drew up just short of the porch steps.

"Rianna Rose?"

The girl relaxed and stood up, her face equal parts caution and question.

"Rianna," he said. "It's me, Jeremiah." Rose stood still, his hands at his sides.

Rianna looked him over as if the name did not register, then she realized what he was saying.

"Jeremiah!" Without warning the girl jumped from the porch into Rose's arms. Nearly thrown off balance in his surprise, Rose recovered quickly and braced himself for the impact. Rianna was heavier than he expected, but he wrapped her up in his arms as she hugged him about the neck.

"I knew you'd come home. I just knew it." Rose remained still, hugging the sister he hadn't seen in fifteen years. He tried several times to set her down, but she wouldn't let go of his neck. Eventually he had to settle for half-dragging her to the porch and sitting down on the steps with Rianna in his lap.

"Just like old times, eh, Ria?" His sister nodded.

"I found out yesterday that you'd come back to Northwind, but didn't know how to find you. I had no idea you'd come looking for me." She hugged him again. "Let's go inside where we can talk. The neighbors have already seen enough to last them."

"Is the old man inside?"

Rianna hesitated. "No, he's still back at the repair bay. After missing a day of work, he said he'd have to stay late tonight."

Rianna ushered Rose inside. Standing in the living room he marveled that so few things had changed since his departure. Maybe a few new pictures on the walls, and the colors seemed subtly different, but the mood was still the same.

"I was just fixing some tea. Want some?"

"Sounds good." Rianna disappeared around the corner and into the kitchen. Rose followed at a more leisurely pace, absorbing all the sights and sounds of the house. As he reached the dining area Rianna reappeared with a pitcher and two tall, ice-filled glasses. She set the trio on the hardwood table and pulled out a chair.

"Something to eat?" Rose shook his head and continued to look around the room. Rianna watched him as she poured two glasses, then sat down facing him.

"Does it seem the same?" Rose stared at his sister for a moment, thinking about the question. Her tone made the query seem more important than it should.

"Yes, exactly the same. I know some little things are different, but the feel hasn't changed. Your handiwork?"

Rianna nodded and smiled.

"You've done a wonderful job." Rose reached for his glass and smiled sheepishly at his sister. "You know, I didn't recognize you on the porch."

Rianna laughed lightly. "And I was sure you were some real estate broker, the way you just stood there staring at the house. You really had me going when you started running at me."

"Will you stay the night? Your room is mostly the same. We'd love to have you." Rose regarded his sister from under lowered eyebrows. "All right, *I'd* love to have you," she said. "Papa can deal with it as he sees fit."

Rose considered the offer. He'd expected it, had even planned a response, but now that he was actually seeing his sister, the resolve was slipping away. "I wish I could, but I can't."

Rianna looked crushed. She began to speak, then stopped and stared at her frosty glass with sudden interest.

"How long will you be on Northwind?" she asked the glass.

"Two, maybe three more days." Rose stared at his glass too. He had known the conversation would reach this point, but hadn't expected it to come so soon.

"Then where?"

"Solaris . . . or maybe Outreach," he said, referring to two of the most famous planets in the Inner Sphere.

From far and wide MechWarriors traveled to Solaris, seeking fame and fortune in the 'Mech duels for which the world had become renowned. As for Outreach, it had in recent years become the center for mercenary hiring throughout the Inner Sphere. The planet was also the home of Wolf's Dragoons, a crack mercenary unit in their own right.

"But tell me what you know about the outcome of the Assembly," Rose said.

"Well, I know that the High Assembly decided against you. I'm sure it must have looked like they were swayed mainly by Papa's words, but most likely they turned you down because of the Clans."

Rose held up a hand. "How's that?"

"The High Assembly has decided that the Clans will continue to be a major threat for the next fifteen years, no matter what the Treaty of Tukayyid says."

"Smart guess."

"They've proposed that the Assembly of Warriors restrict the sale and transfer of all 'Mechs outside the Highlanders except in case of emergency." She paused to let the words sink in.

"So, even if Papa hadn't spoken against you, one of the unit commanders would have been forced to echo the High Assembly's decision."

"So I never really had a chance with the Assembly of Warriors, did I?"

Rianna refilled the two glasses and thought for a moment. "Not really. But the family assembly was another matter.

"Since the personal 'Mechs of Highlander warriors are excluded from the High Assembly's decision, anybody not currently under contract could have signed up with you. Unfortunately, Papa axed that idea.

"I don't know how, but he managed to learn that you were coming back before anyone else in the family knew about it. Most of the warriors on Mama's side are currently under contract and the few that aren't weren't told of the meeting. As you saw, there were plenty of available pilots from Papa's side of the family, but he, as patriarch, pretty much controlled their votes. Some of the younger ones might have gone against him if you could have spoken with them one on one, but in an open meeting like that . . ." Rianna let the words trail away. Rose knew that none of the younger pilots would risk earning a reputation as a troublemaker by speaking against the family elder in open assembly. It was too quick a method of killing a career.

"I would have signed up on the spot, but I got stuck with maintenance duty over at the 'Mech bay, and had to spend the entire day with my head in the elbow of a *Phoenix Hawk*. I didn't even know about the meeting— or your arrival—until the entire business was already over."

Rose rapped the table in frustration. Had he not come to the house today, he would have left Northwind convinced that his entire family hated him, instead of just his father.

"It really hurt him when I left, didn't it?" Rose knew the answer by the solemn expression his sister took.

"I don't think you have any idea. Mama had only been gone six months and you were so outspoken against Hanse Davion and the Federated Commonwealth. With the pressure of the war and his increased duties, Papa was on the edge. When you joined ComStar, he just snapped." Rose winced at the thought. He'd never really gotten along with his father, but neither had he wished him any harm.

"The outward anger went away pretty fast, but the rest he's held inside all these years." Rianna let the silence hang. "You can see the results."

"Yes, I can," Rose said softly. "So, where does that leave me, the family, you?" He looked up at his sister, who was biting her lip in concentration.

"Well, you're probably still out of luck when it comes to the family. At least as far as putting together a mercenary unit. There are only two warriors with 'Mechs who would even consider joining you." Rose nodded and gestured for her to continue.

"Angus Lochart is the first. He pilots his father's *Valkyrie*."

"Lonny Lochart's son?"

"Yeah, he's only a half-cousin, if that makes any sense, but he's a member of the family and a good warrior. He's just returned from his first contract along the Periphery and has some experience, although I'm not sure what good it will be against the Clans."

"Experience of any kind is good. What about the second pilot?"

"The second pilot is Rianna Rose." Jeremiah's eyes widened as he looked at his sister with open shock.

"You? I can't . . ."

"Don't even say it."

Rose shut his mouth and studied his sister. The athletic build certainly fit the image, and she had the air of confidence absolutely required of any MechWarrior. But it was hard for him not to view her as the little four-year-old in pigtails, plastered with mud and dirt.

"I'm sorry, it's just that I never dreamed you'd be interested in becoming a MechWarrior."

"Watch out," Rianna chided. "Your chauvinism's showing." Rose could tell she was getting angry, and he wondered if her temper was as bad as their father's. He decided not to risk it.

"Not at all. Some of the best 'Mech jockeys I've ever known were women. I just didn't imagine it would interest *you*, that's all." Rianna was obviously not convinced. She threw her head back and gazed at Rose intently.

"For your information I graduated at the top of my cadet class here on Northwind. Not only am I a certified pilot, but I'm also a certified assistant tech. I've qualified on thirteen different 'Mechs, and my I.Q. is seventeen points higher than yours." Impressed, Rose nodded appreciatively.

"And to top it all off—and nobody knows that I know this—I'm considered a logistical genius." She smiled as

Rose raised his eyebrows. "Something to do with the way I organize my thoughts. It makes supply and distribution a breeze for me." She snapped her fingers and looped an elbow over the back of her chair. "So there."

"All right, you're an ace student, but what about actual combat time? Academy training is great, but have you ever been shot at by a full-strength laser? Have you ever been on the receiving end of an LRM flight? I didn't think so." Rose paused for breath, somewhat surprised by the strength of his emotions. He tried to calm himself before speaking again.

"How long have you been out of the academy?"

"Six months." Rianna looked crestfallen, but tried to hide it.

"And no contract? From what I remember, most of the top pilots had a slot straight out of school."

"I had a couple of offers, but I passed them up."

"Why?"

"My business, not yours." Rianna set her jaw and glared at her older brother.

"It's my business if you want to sign on with me. So what's the story?"

Rianna hesitated before giving in. She leaned forward to match her brother's posture in the chair.

"The only contracts I could get were the standard five-year 'newbie' ones. Mostly dull garrison duty or training-cadre stuff away from the front lines. I wanted to be closer to the front."

"Where the action is. Just like a newbie."

Rianna's eyes flared and she stood up suddenly. Rose had no doubt in that instant that she'd inherited her father's temper.

"No. Not like a newbie. Like a sister who hasn't seen her brother in fifteen years. That's why I wanted to be near the front lines. I wanted to be closer to Terra and the Com Guards, because I knew I'd have a better chance of finding you." Without waiting for a response she stormed into the kitchen. Rose waited a moment, but when she did not return, he got up and followed.

She was standing by the sink, looking out the window into the back yard.

"I know you had to leave, Jeremiah. I know that and I can accept it. I also know that you left behind a four-year-old girl who probably didn't have a very big part in your teenage life, but you were such a big part of mine that I almost couldn't stand to see you go.

"I've remembered and thought about you for the last fifteen years. It wasn't so bad while Danny was still around, but when he left, it got even worse. Now Danny is gone for good and you're back, except now you want to be gone again.

"You made a choice, Danny made a choice, and Papa made a choice. I want to make my choice, right here, right now.

"I don't know you and maybe I won't even like you anymore after I do, but I want the chance to find out for myself." Rianna looked at Jeremiah for the first time since he entered the kitchen. "Do you understand that?"

He slowly crossed the room and stood beside her, also staring out the window.

"Yes, I understand," he said. "If this is your choice, I'll give you the chance. You'll be my first recruit." He placed a hand on her shoulder. "If half of what you say is true, and I'm sure it is, you'll make an excellent executive officer."

Rianna beamed up at him and he slid his whole arm around her shoulders.

"It will be good to see the Tea Bowl again."

Rianna looked up at him in alarm. "The *Thunderbolt* is gone, Jeremiah. Danny lost it when he was killed."

"What?" Rose couldn't believe his ears. "I spoke with Colonel Stirling on the day of the Assembly. She didn't say anything."

"What is there to say? The Clans captured the 'Mech when Danny died. I thought you knew." Rose couldn't conceive of the loss of his mother's 'Mech. Being the oldest, it would have passed to him, but the honor had fallen to his brother when Jeremiah joined the Com Guards.

"What about you?" he said. "You'll need a 'Mech if you want to become part of a mercenary unit."

Rianna smiled, but did not respond. Rose tried to be patient, but lost the struggle. "Well?"

"I've got a *Phoenix Hawk*. As the valedictorian of my class I was awarded a rebuilt model by the Assembly of Warriors. I'm sure they thought I'd be fighting with the Highlanders, but I don't have to, because it's all mine.

"I've only had it for the last few months, but it handles like a dream. It came straight from the Achernar BattleMechs factory on New Avalon." Rianna was practically jumping up and down in place as she spoke. Suddenly Rose saw his mother in her eyes, a warrior through and through.

"Come on, I'll show him to you."

"Him?"

"Of course it's a him. It's only a few minutes from here." Rianna was already pulling Rose by the arm to the door.

"All right, but just for a bit," he told her. "You and I have some other things to discuss before I leave. A lot of things."

5

Jeremiah and his sister spent the next two days together. After inspecting the *Phoenix Hawk,* the love of Rianna's life, Rose had taken his sister to the hospital to meet Rachel McCloud. Though he and Rianna arrived too near the end of visiting hours for a prolonged visit, the two women began almost instantly to chatter together like long-lost friends.

Rachel was outgoing and friendly and Rianna definitely had the gift of gab. Locked in conversation, the two seemed to have completely forgotten Jeremiah until the floor nurse poked her head into the room to say that they had only five more minutes. Rose took advantage of the opportunity to break into the conversation.

"Sorry to interrupt, but if I could have a moment of your time, Captain."

The two women regarded him in silence.

"Rachel, Ria and I have an idea we'd like to discuss with you. I'll keep it brief for now, but tomorrow morning we can go into detail.

"Rianna is going to be the nucleus of the new unit I've been wanting to form. Now that I know I won't be able to gather the strength I need for an effective mercenary unit here on Northwind, I think my best bet is Outreach."

"It makes the most sense," Ria interrupted. Jeremiah and Rachel smiled at each other as she took the floor. "Jeremiah heads for Solaris and the 'Mech games. It could take some time, but he can probably find a 'Mech there for a good price. And if he waits until the end of the season, he might also be able to recruit some independent warriors."

"Sounds like a good plan," Rachel said. "As you say, going to Solaris definitely adds some time to the venture. The planet is all the way over on the Steiner side of Federated Commonwealth space."

"I know, but what choice have I?" Rose began to pace the small room as he went over his plan again. "If I want to be taken seriously as a mercenary commander on Outreach, I've got to have a 'Mech of my own when I get there. Solaris is the obvious solution, despite the delay. Once I've got a 'Mech, I can transport it directly to Outreach and join Rianna to finalize the recruiting process."

"Right," Ria piped in. "I'll head for Outreach ahead of Jeremiah. Assuming Angus agrees to join us, and I think he will, we two can represent the unit."

"Angus?"

"A cousin on our mother's side. He's just back from his first contract and fits under the Assembly of Warrior's edict that only family members can accompany Jeremiah off Northwind."

"Considering the travel time involved, I'm hoping that Ria and, possibly, Angus can leave within the next three to five weeks. They can register the unit with the Mercenary Review and Bonding Commission and conduct preliminary interviews until I arrive."

"Which will be when?"

"Barring a breakdown during transit from Solaris, I'll arrive four to six weeks after they do."

Rachel straightened the covers on her bed with her one good hand. "And where do I come in?"

Rose caught his breath before continuing. This was the only part of the plan about which he was uncertain. "You contract to take Rianna, Angus, and the two 'Mechs to

Outreach.'' Rachel looked at Rianna and then back to Jeremiah before nodding. Rose continued, letting the words tumble out faster and faster as he went along. "We'll pay standard rates for the transport. Once we have a contract, however, Rianna and I would like you to serve as the transportation agent to our destination.''

McCloud was silent.

"Obviously it will mean more to us than to you, but I think it's a good business proposition.''

McCloud looked up at him. "What do you know about business?''

"Just what I read in the papers, but consider it. We'll be in a stronger position to make a contract because we'll have our own transportation. The *Bristol* is a *Union* Class DropShip. It can carry an entire company, plus aerospace support. We can take the profits from the stronger position and pass most of the cash straight to you.''

"You're right, as far as you go,'' Rachel told him, "but there's plenty you haven't considered.

"First, the *Bristol* is just a civilian carrier, a commercial ship. It may have started out as a military vessel, but most of the 'Mech bays have been reconfigured to haul bulk goods. It would take a major overhaul of the cargo compartments to accomplish what you want.

"Besides, I've never had to use any of the *Bristol*'s firepower. It's true she still carries a full range of weapons, but I don't carry enough crew to man those weapons. It's too expensive.

"And finally, what makes you think I want to be a mercenary? I'm a transport captain and I like the work.''

"Rachel, don't get me wrong. I know you're a good captain. I just thought this was a good idea.'' Rose glanced at his sister, who'd been watching the exchange in silence. McCloud dropped her head back against the pillows.

"Rose, it's late. My shoulder hurts like hell and this is my ship you're talking about. I owe you, but I don't want to make a decision right now.''

"I don't need a decision right now, Rachel.'' The door

opened and the floor nurse motioned Rianna and Jeremiah out of the room.

"I just want to know if you'll take Rianna to Outreach."

"Sure, I'll take her. Standard carrier rates for all equipment."

Rose nodded toward the door and Rianna took the hint to leave the two alone. "Rachel," he said, when his sister had slipped out the door, "I know your shoulder is bothering you, but what else is going on?"

From the way McCloud looked at him Rose thought he must have stepped over some invisible line. Then her features softened and she shook her head.

"It's nothing, really. I just get edgy when I have to start looking for another contract. I hate that part of my job. Looking for a cargo and trying to judge how safe it will be to make the run. Ask my crew. They can't stand to be around me during this part of the process."

Rose looked at McCloud quietly, trying to tell if she were speaking the whole truth. He had no idea what McCloud was like while trying to find cargo, having only just managed to squeeze aboard the *Bristol* on the trip from Terra.

"I call the *Bristol* my ship," McCloud went on, "but the bank owns almost half of it and if I can't get a decent cargo while I'm in port, they take a bigger chunk when I'm forced to go short on my payment." She looked at Rose with a harsh stare.

"That's what I mean about business. You've got to be one step ahead of the bankers. Being a good fighter isn't enough if you want to be a mercenary. You've got to be a good accountant too."

Rose knew she was right. He also realized that it wouldn't stop him from trying to create a mercenary company. Still thinking, he crossed to the door, then paused briefly and turned back to speak.

"Thanks, Rachel. We'll stop by tomorrow, and by the way, you owe me nothing."

Rose eased the door shut and followed his sister to the elevators at the end of the corridor.

Captain Rachel McCloud spent long minutes staring at the door before she finally addressed it aloud. "That's just great, Rose. I finally decide to care for someone and then he tells me goodbye." The station nurse heard McCloud speaking over the active intercom, and shook her head sadly.

Unaware of all this, Rose and Rianna waited in silence for the elevator car to arrive, but as the door opened, Rianna laid a hand on Rose's arm.

"She'll get me to Outreach. That should be enough." Rose entered the car first and punched the lobby button.

"It is enough. It's just that having her in on it would have made the entire plan so perfect."

"Are you two . . . involved?"

Rose looked at his sister, then caught a nasty look from the station nurse, whom he had never met. Returning his gaze to Ria, he wondered if it was amusement he'd heard in her voice. He saw not a trace of it on her face.

"Yes. No. Yes, but it's not serious. Hell, I don't know. It's just that I trusted her and this would have worked out so well for the unit."

The elevator door opened and Rose held it for his sister.

"Speaking of the unit, we'll need a name," she said, the excitement back in her voice. "I've got some ideas. How about you?"

Rose shrugged. "I haven't really thought about it. I just figured we'd be the Black Watch or the Northwind something. What have you got in mind?"

"Well, I thought about all the standard ones—Rose's Rangers, Rose's Roughnecks, et cetera, et cetera. Too boring. If we want to attract quality people, we need a catchy name."

"Such as?"

"The Black Thorns."

"The what?" Rose stopped at the hospital doors and

looked at his sister. She was grinning from ear to ear. As he stood there staring, she opened the outer door and walked toward a single cab waiting at the curb.

"It's a great name."

"It's a name, all right. Great, I don't know about."

"Just think about it."

Jeremiah nodded without enthusiasm.

"I've got to get back home," Rianna said. "What's the plan for tomorrow?"

"Tomorrow we talk to Angus. If we can come to terms, we're on our way."

"Great. Where are you staying?"

Rose opened the cab door and Rianna flopped inside. "I had my things moved over to the Hightower," he said. "I haven't actually been there yet, so I don't know my room number." Rose closed the door behind her and reached through the open front window to pay the driver in advance. As he waved away the change, Rianna rolled down her window.

"I'll talk to Angus and arrange a time to meet." She held out her hand and Rose grasped it in both of his.

"This is really happening, isn't it?"

"It really is, and Papa's going to be furious."

"Let him." Ria's voice grew hard. "It's my choice and I want this too bad to bow to his selfish desires." Rose did not respond, and Rianna's features softened. "Besides, I'll have almost a month to say goodbye. That should be enough."

Rianna pulled her hand away and the cab inched forward.

"See you tomorrow."

Jeremiah waved as the cab pulled out of the drive and into traffic. Turning in the other direction, he decided to walk the six blocks to his hotel. He could use the time to think and plan. The Black Thorns had been born and he intended to be a good father.

6

Solaris City, Solaris
2 August 3054

"I've told you more than once, Mister Rose. We'll be on the ground in fifteen minutes. Per your instructions, and generous tip, I've moved all your gear to the front of the bay. Sixty minutes from now you'll be past dirtside customs officials and anywhere in the city you want. Please return to your cabin for landing."

Jeremiah Rose was more than prepared to argue with the steward, mostly for the fun of it, but a burst of static over the intercom interrupted him.

"Passenger Jeremiah Rose to the bridge, please. Jeremiah Rose."

Rose looked up at the intercom as if the page were some kind of ruse. Then he shot the steward a narrowed-eye stare. The steward, eyes heavenward, missed the look, but evidently considered the conversation ended as he began to walk away.

"Hold on, slick. This isn't over just yet. When we hit the ground, I'll be at the Level Two cargo doors. Have my black case ready. I guess I can wait for the rest of the gear. Got that?"

"Yes, Mister Rose, black case, Cargo Hold Two."

Rose wasn't sure he could trust the steward to remember the request or the order. Damn civilians. Why couldn't anything ever be easy—or at least predictable?

His mind wandered aimlessly over the point as his feet moved purposefully toward the bridge, three decks up. He was not exactly a stranger to the ship's bridge, but the request to report there was something of a surprise. Until now most of his visits had been rather impromptu and not especially well-received. He decided to pass the lift and take a service ladder. The ladder wasn't exactly a standard entrance, but the lift was faulty even at the best of times and Rose was slightly suspicious of the captain. The ladder had become a standard service pathway during the last two weeks of the trip, even when the lift was operational. Rose reached out to grasp the sides of the ladder and began the short climb. It took less than a minute to reach the bridge.

"Rose reporting as ordered, Captain," he said, noticing the heat of the bridge. The portly captain jumped at Rose's sharp announcement and looked away from his viewer toward Rose.

"So, you're still on the ship after all. When the crew reported you missing during the final cabin check, I thought you'd finally gotten impatient enough to walk."

"The thought hadn't occurred to me, Captain, but now that you mention it . . ."

The captain rubbed a fleshy jowl and glanced toward the lift doors. "Took the ladder, eh?"

"Well, Captain, I wouldn't put it past you to stop the lift between floors just to twist my tail." Rose smiled at the other man as he realized that was just what the captain had intended.

"Well, now that you're here, I just wanted to take the opportunity to say 'bye.' Not 'goodbye.' Not 'God speed.' Not 'see you later.' Not anything but 'bye.'" The captain took a swift look at the screen as the ship shuddered slightly. Two red lights blinked to life on the master console, but he gave them only a brief glance. Though the ship was in the final stages of landing, Captain Waterson was taking the time to speak to Rose. The captain either had plenty of faith in his computers, his crew, or both, or else he had something to tell Rose that just couldn't wait. Jeremiah wondered if he should be concerned about the two red lights.

"Mister Rose, I must say that in over twenty years of commanding a DropShip, I have never, and I mean never, had the occasion to encounter a man like yourself. To say you are universally hated by my crew would be an understatement of major proportions. I am surprised they haven't mutinied just to get you.

"In short, Mister Rose, please take the earliest opportunity to disembark my ship and never, I mean never, return."

"But Captain . . ."

"No buts, Mister Rose. No smart answers. No witty replies. Just sit in silence and then leave. Since you will not remain in your cabin, I have decided to allow you to remain here on the bridge. If you keep quiet until we hit the ground, my steward, Mister Pulanski, will personally escort you to the customs office, with your gear."

"Why, Captain . . ."

"No words, Mister Rose. Just nod your head. Do we have a deal?"

Rose considered the pleasure of verbally jabbing the captain, but decided that the steward would be a welcome ally in getting off the ship as soon as possible. He smiled and decided to take the offered emergency seat. The captain sighed and rubbed his fleshy neck as he returned to the duties at hand.

With Pulanski's aid, Rose was able to hit the customs office well ahead of the rest of the DropShip's passengers. Pulanski refused to speak with Rose, even when Rose attempted to be polite. Rose didn't really blame the steward for his silence. Just before the final jump to Solaris, the JumpShip had ruptured a fuel cell. Although the danger to the ship and crew had been quickly eliminated, the ship had to remain on-station for more than a month while the damage was being repaired. The delay had meant that Rose would not arrive on Solaris until the final week of the dueling season, practically guaranteeing the failure of his mission.

Caged in the DropShip while repair crews attended to the damaged JumpShip, Rose took out his frustration on the crew and other passengers. Within days he was spending most his time alone. His mood improved slightly when they finally made the jump to the Solaris system, but very few people were willing to spend any time with Rose on the DropShip journey from jump point to planet.

As a result, he spent the entire transit glued to the video, watching the Solaris games. He'd finalized his plan seven hours ago. If there was a 'Mech to be purchased, or stolen, on Solaris, Rose was sure he would find it. At three past seven, exactly sixty-seven minutes after the DropShip set down, Rose left the customs area with his single black case.

Entering the spaceport's main terminal, he let the crowd sweep him along. Despite the hour, the terminal was packed. Following the icons, he pushed through the crowd to the taxi area, intending to give himself the luxury of a private cab to the hotel.

Rose's destination was The Imperial, a hotel located in the "international" sector of Solaris City. Despite its grand name, the hotel was only average except for the fine views offered by its south-facing rooms. That feature alone had made it one of the most popular inns in the capital.

The cab driver didn't try to talk during the trip down through the hills from the spaceport, which Rose appreciated. When they pulled into the hotel's circular drive, he paid the fare and tip in C-bills, earning a nod of thanks from the man. Rose had made his room reservation during the inbound flight, and so checking in did not take long. He also took the time to store his black gun case in a safe deposit box, sealing the lock with his left thumbprint. Then, instead of going up to his room as his exhausted body desired, he headed straight for the main doors.

It took several minutes to flag down a cab that would take him into Black Hills, the Davion sector of Solaris

City, but eventually one showing the Davion flag on the aerial pulled over. Over the years Solaris City had become divided into six major quarters, one for each of the Great Houses that ruled the Inner Sphere, and the sixth being the international quarter that housed most of the public buildings and the relatively powerless local government.

Though most of Solaris City did not live up to the glamour some associated with the bloody 'Mech games, the metropolis was unique in the Inner Sphere. Each of the city's sectors reflected the national and cultural bias of one of the five different star empires, yet citizens from the different states lived side by side in multicultural harmony.

Rose's destination was Seventh Heaven, an infamous bar in the Davion sector. He used the brief respite of the cab ride to massage his neck and rub his eyes. Having been without sleep for more than forty hours, his body was slowing down.

The cab driver was confident and aggressive, making the trip in what seemed to be record time. When Rose paid him, the man seemed disgruntled that payment was in C-bills rather than Davion house script, but accepted the money just the same. By the time Rose got to the front door of the bar the cab was long gone.

Three hours later Rose still hadn't found what he was looking for. Six different bars and nothing to show for it but a throbbing headache and bloodshot eyes. The only satisfaction he felt was in observing how gloomy and squalid was the Black Hills sector, a grim contrast to the almighty Davions' public image as paragons of virtue and defenders of civilization. He thought more people should see the crime, corruption, and violence of these slums lying in the shadow of the magnificent Black Hills.

He'd come to what he promised himself would be his last stop of the night—or the morning. The sign read The Pelican, and it was the haunt of elite MechWarriors and their friends.

Be that as it may, the Pelican was as wild as any bar

Rose had ever visited. Towering trivid screens replayed the 'Mech matches of the day with full stereo sound. The place was brighter than most of its type, but not so light that Rose could see into all the corners. The noise and lights gave him an artificial jolt of energy as he mingled with the crowd. What little vigor he picked up, however, he quickly spent fighting his way to one of the secondary bars. The crowd was the usual mixture of avid game fans, MechWarriors, MechWarrior wannabes, groupies, and people just out for a good time. He saw some patrons trying to have conversations, but most seemed to be concentrating on the trivid. With effort he managed to make a space for himself at the bar and catch the bartender's attention.

"A bottle of Li Lung," he called out, and the young man behind the bar looked like he'd been shot.

"Easy going, ace," the bartender said in a low voice. "You're a little south of the river to ask for a bottle of that snake juice. Of course, if you really want Snake brew—" the bartender leaned across the slick surface and looked both ways—"ask again just a little louder and I'm sure one, or ten, or more patriotic customers will be happy to toss you all the way to Kobe." The young man smiled and straightened up. "Now, how about a nice bottle of Conner's Dark?"

Rose nodded silently and thanked the stars the noise level was loud enough to cover his mistake. He should have known better than to order a Kurita beer in the middle of Davion territory. He blamed it on the lack of sleep, but that was precious little consolation. Rose was still grinding his teeth at his stupidity when the beer arrived. This would definitely have to be the last stop. Any more and his fatigue could get him into real trouble.

"One warm Conner's, just the way you like it. At least, just the way you should like it if you were a real beer drinker."

"Thanks, and thanks. I'm not usually that stupid."

"Shot goes wide and it's a clean miss." The youth smiled at Rose's obvious confusion. "Lord, you must be new. Don't you listen to Ian Owans and Buck Blaylock? They're the number-one announcing team at F-C Broadcasting. It's what Buck always says when a 'Mech pilot misses an easy shot in the games. You know, 'No harm done, but you got lucky.' By the way, they call me Dillon.''

''Rose.'' Jeremiah leaned across the bar and shook Dillon's hand. ''Here's for the beer.'' Again Rose reached across and handed Dillon a twenty C-bill.

''C-bills? You must be new in town.'' Rose shrugged his shoulders and tried to smile. He was beginning to think his plans to get a new 'Mech were not going to work as smoothly as he'd hoped.

''Problem with C-bills?''

''Not really a problem.'' Dillon held the note to the light and examined the other side. ''It's just that, well, you see . . .'' He reached under the bar and stashed the bill in a drawer. He squinted and began counting to himself as he made change. ''It's just that C-bills are so . . .''

''Conspicuous?''

''Yeah, conspicuous. It's a dead giveaway that you're new in town and haven't learned to fit in yet.''

''I see.''

''It's not bad, really. It's just that most merchants in this quarter, and all the others, for that matter, would rather be paid in house script. National pride, and all that. Now, C-bills are the next best thing, but with that little affair up in Tukayyid last year, C-bills just aren't what they were.''

Rose hadn't thought about it, but what the bartender said made perfect sense. Despite the fact that the Com Guards troops had stopped the Clans on Tukayyid, many people of the Inner Sphere still held a grudge against ComStar for its centuries of monopoly on interstellar communications. He'd been warned that nationalist feeling ran high on Solaris, but he hadn't really expected it would run this high.

''So you're suggesting I get some D-bills as soon as possible.''

Dillon handed over the change and smiled. "I can see that a man of your obvious mental abilities doesn't need a humble bartender to tell him which way a 'Mech tumbles."

"Maybe not, but then again maybe there's something you can do to help me."

"Help, in this city?"

"Help is probably the wrong word. Any chance of hiring you to lend me some temporary assistance that will not in any way conflict with your current employment at this establishment?"

"I'm your man," Dillon said.

Rose leaned into the bar, and Dillon did the same. He palmed a fifty C-bill note, slid it toward the barman. "I need a contact with one of the stables. Someone who might be willing to take on a new pilot this late in the season. All I need is a name of someone I can make a pitch to."

Dillon stared at the note and glanced up and down the bar. Most of the patrons were enthralled by the final stages of the latest Blackstar-Tandrek battle. A jarring right-handed punch by the Blackstar *Victor* had knocked the rival *Orion* off its feet just as Dillon opened his mouth to speak.

"You've got a better chance of wedding Isis Marik than hiring on with a stable. There's less than a week left in the season. Next season's tryouts won't start for another few months. Why don't you wait till then?" One look into Rose's eyes and Dillon knew later was not acceptable. "Okay, if you need a name, I can give you one, but my normally sterling conscience forces me to warn you first."

Rose forced himself to be patient, but only with effort. He was convinced that Dillon wanted to help, but the young man just didn't understand how important this was to him. He decided to concentrate on breathing as Dillon searched for the right words. This was worse than combat.

"Brachall. As far as I know, that's his only name. He's

kind of like a broker. Probably the only guy in Black Hills who can put you in touch with a stable, assuming you don't want an independent.'' Dillon's eyebrows went up in a silent question, but Rose didn't even acknowledge it. ''Anyway, he hangs out at Seventh Heaven. Oh, you've been there?'' Rose dropped his head and took a deep breath.

''I was there earlier this evening and was told nobody was around who could help me.''

''Yeah, that makes sense. Those techs are a strange bunch, and if you'll pardon me for saying so, you don't exactly look the part.''

''Okay, so I don't look like a tech. Shoot me.''

''Easy. Easy. Tomorrow, or later today, depending on when you sleep, go to the main bar and ask for Brachall by name. He'll be there, but you've got to ask for him by name. That's the only way he does business.'' Dillon looked down at the C-bill. ''That good enough?''

''Yeah, that's good enough. Thanks.''

''Oh, by the way, if he asks who sent you, don't mention my name.''

''Any reason?'' Rose lifted his hand and left the C-bill on the bar. Dillon scooped up the note in a smooth, practiced motion.

''Yeah. I don't think I want to be any part of what you're about to get yourself into. Nothing personal, you understand?''

''Shot goes wide and it's a clean miss.''

7

"**J**eremiah Rose, to see Mister Warwick."

Rose turned toward the security camera mounted high on the gate. Though there was little light this late in the day, he had no doubt the camera's operator could see him in vivid detail.

He'd met with Brachall the night before, a meeting brief and to the point, exactly the way Rose liked it. The man had turned out to be an entirely unpleasant fellow who charged Rose an astronomical fee to put him in contact with the "only man on Solaris still looking for a 'Mech pilot." Like every weasel Rose had ever known, Brachall could sense when another man was desperate. After a quick exchange of funds, Brachall was on the phone to Desmond Warwick, owner of the aptly named Warwick Stables. Twenty-four hours later Rose was standing in the drive of Warwick's home—or mansion, as it turned out. The estate was huge, with extensive, beautifully manicured grounds to match the imposing three-story villa that dominated the landscape.

The side gate buzzed open and Rose went on foot up to the building. The walk took well over ten minutes, but he was not surprised that no one came to escort him to the house. He felt like a beggar approaching the king's

table, which was doubtless how Warwick intended him
to feel.

With only a single day to learn whatever he could about
his prospective employer, there hadn't been enough time
to do a thorough investigation. The little Rose had been
able to learn was that Desmond Warwick, like many
wealthy members of Solaris society, had arrived on the
game world already possessed of a sizable fortune. Although originally from Quincy in the Federated Commonwealth, he quickly became known as a man without
loyalties, except, perhaps, loyalty to money and power.
He'd started his stable modestly, competing only in the
secondary circuits until his group of warriors had proven
themselves against a variety of opponents. It was only
last year that he'd become a minor player in the Solaris
City circuit, but to date his team had yet to score any
victories against the major stables. Yet, from what Rose
could discover, Warwick sounded like an able manager
employing some good talent and, more important, he
was the owner of 'Mechs. Rose ran the facts over in his
mind one last time as he knocked on the gigantic door.
Midway through the second knock the door pulled open.

"Yes?" Rose was greeted by a towering doorman. Well
over two meters tall, the ancient man's gray hair flowed
with abandon over his elegant uniform. It was one of the
rare times in Rose's life when he was forced to look up,
rather than down, into someone's face. He hated that.
Another point for Warwick.

"Jeremiah Rose. I have an invitation for dinner with
Mister Warwick." The giant stepped aside and motioned
Rose inside. The foyer was like something out of a dream.
A marble floor and staircase were framed by gilt-framed
paintings over teakwood paneling. Arches to either side
of the stairway led into other parts of the house, providing glimpses of even more opulence. Everywhere Rose
looked, the house screamed elegance and money. Having
been forced to walk up the drive, then dwarfed by the
doorman and overawed by the entryway, many another
individual would have been intimidated by Warwick long

before the man ever stepped into the room. Rose, however, had a reaction exactly opposite. The ire that had begun to build during the walk surged within him by the time of the greeting at the door. Now that he was in the house, it turned into a fury. How dare this man, who did not even know Rose, try to intimidate him, try to make him feel insignificant? Rose refused to let it work on him.

Or perhaps it worked only too well. Down on his luck, dispossessed, and frustrated, Rose had had enough. He wanted, or needed, a 'Mech, but not bad enough to put up with a man so obviously self-important. He felt like a caged animal standing in the elegant foyer. Although it had been only moments since he'd entered, Rose felt as if he couldn't stand it another instant. He was just turning toward the door when he heard a sound at the top of the steps.

"Mister Rose, how good of you to join me for dinner." Rose turned to look up at his host, instantly seeing how right he'd been about the man's self-importance. A tiny, little man, Warwick was dressed in a formal silk suit. A garment undoubtedly tailored to his diminutive frame, the suit's gray silk caught, then reflected, the light of the room, making Warwick appear almost to shine. His close-cropped black hair was perfectly in place, and the too-perfect white teeth threatened to dazzle Rose in a too-sincere smile. Warwick stopped on the third step, which made him slightly taller than Rose.

"I trust you had no trouble finding me."

Now it was Rose's turn to smile. "No trouble at all. Brachall was most explicit." Warwick's nose wrinkled as if what Rose said had an unpleasant smell. "In fact, I was pleasantly surprised to be able to find you as quickly and easily as I did." Warwick looked annoyed at the suggestion that it was easy to get to see him, especially in person. Turning away from Rose, he descended the final three steps and began to walk across the foyer.

"If you'll accompany me, we can begin our dinner. I'm sure you'll understand if I'm forced to dispense with some of the normal formalities. With the upcoming match, I suddenly find myself in much demand." Warwick began to lead Rose through the house, with only an occasional glance over his shoulder to make sure the other man was still following. Rose discovered, with some delight, that he could look over Warwick's head and still see perfectly.

"I should think you would find that very gratifying," Rose said, making Warwick stop suddenly and turn toward him.

"I beg your pardon, Mister Rose."

"Having your team in the upcoming match. I understand this is the first time you've placed a team in a Solaris City championship."

"Yes, it is quite an achievement. Considering this is only the second year my stable has been dueling in Solaris City, it *is* very gratifying." Warwick turned back to face front, talking as he continued the trip to the dining room. Rose could barely keep from laughing aloud at the little man. Not only was he vain, but sensitive about it, too.

"I understand this is something unusual for Solaris City. Haven't the games always avoided team championships in the past?" Warwick turned and smiled back at Rose as he entered the dining room, where a waiter was quietly serving soup at two place settings.

So, thought Rose, I got to take the long road to the dining room. Like the other rooms of the house, this one was expensively, if gaudily, furnished with linen cloths, oak furniture, china place settings, and silver utensils. The soup, which seemed to be some kind of chowder, smelled delicious. Despite himself, Rose found his mouth watering. Warwick took the seat at the head of the table and motioned Rose to the place at his right.

"This is something of a new event for the city, I must admit," Warwick said as Rose took the offered chair and unfolded a linen napkin. Then Warwick crossed himself and mumbled into his chest, before resuming the thread of his discourse. "There have always been various kinds of team championships in the matches held outside the city, but the idea has never really caught on in the major circuit.'' Warwick paused to sample the still-steaming chowder. Rose did likewise and discovered it tasted even better than it smelled.

"The chowder is quite good, isn't it?" Rose looked up to see Warwick smiling at him and realized he must have inadvertently allowed his opinion to creep onto his face.

"Quite good."

"As I was saying, the Solaris City games have always featured individual matches, but lance versus lance combat is growing in popularity. I've tried to get the audience to identify with my team, rather than with a single pilot.

"People are growing jaded here in the city, Rose. They want something new. More conflict, more carnage. One-on-one combat is all well and good, and it will never go away, but melees are where the future of the sport is heading."

"Oh, really?"

"Yes. It's a situation where everybody wins. The gamblers have more angles to cover with the different potential confrontations, the spectators have more action packed into the same amount of time, and the stablemasters can register for events by team instead of by pilot."

"And the pilot, does he win?" Rose had stopped eating while Warwick talked. Even with his limited time on Solaris he could well imagine that the crowds had become desensitized to the violence of the duels. It was even starting to happen to him. On a planet where life was held so cheap, it was easy to forget that the 'Mech pilots putting on the show were also made of flesh and blood.

"The pilot? Well, sure the pilot wins. He's part of a team and has his lancemates to back him up. Somebody will be there if he makes a mistake." Warwick smiled triumphantly. It sounded all right, but Rose had broken in enough rookies to know that real teamwork, the kind that solves more problems than it creates, could take months to develop. So far he'd seen nothing on Solaris to indicate that any of the teams ever got that kind of time to practice before a match. Only the best, or luckiest, teams would advance more than a few rounds in any tournament. His opinion of his host, and the power brokers backing this plan, sank to a new low.

"I believe the concept will only increase in popularity over the coming years, which is where you come in," Warwick was saying. Rose snapped back to attention and refocused on his host.

"Where I come in?"

"Yes. You told Brachall that you were a pilot in need of a 'Mech. Well, I need someone who can lead my team to victory. I currently run a stable with five pilots and five 'Mechs. All are suitably skilled, but none have the spark."

"Spark?"

"Spark. That elusive ability to snatch victory from defeat. That extra edge that makes a contender a champion."

"Not that I disagree, but you don't even know me," Rose said, laying down his spoon and leaning back in the chair. "Besides, you've gotten this far without me."

"I know you, Mister Rose. I know you called nearly every 'Mech shop in Solaris looking for a heavy or assault class 'Mech in working condition." Warwick smiled briefly. "I know you didn't find one. I also know there's nobody matching your physical description who has a service record with any of the Great Houses of the Inner Sphere. Of course, that doesn't necessarily tell me that you've never served any of the five House rulers, just that the record is buried deeper than normal. How's that for information?" Warwick's too-sincere smile returned.

"Not bad, but it still doesn't explain why you want me." Rose didn't like the way the conversation was going, or how much Warwick already knew, or what he knew he did not know, about him.

"You obviously want a 'Mech, and you're willing to pay for one. With the Clan invasion, prices are high and quality 'Mechs are, shall we say, scarce. Since you went looking for a 'Mech before a stable, I'd have to say you're more interested in the equipment than money or fame.'' Rose sat in silence. Warwick was good and he must obviously have an efficient network to gather this much information in so short a time.

"In short, you want a 'Mech, and you're willing to fight to get one. Now, the only question that remains is what do I want in return for helping you?" Rose smiled. Warwick didn't appear to need any encouragement to continue talking and it looked as though the next course would not be served until the conversation was finished.

"I need someone who can guarantee me victory in the final match. The fact that I can't turn up any information on you prior to your arrival on Solaris leads me to believe you are either very, very good or else only a Mech-Warrior wannabe. In either case, I can discover the truth in short order. I'm prepared to wager that you fall into the first category.

"What can I offer in return? No need to ask, I can see the question written on your face. In exchange for your services, I'm prepared to offer you the 'Mech you pilot in the final match, the price of the 'Mech to be determined by an independent appraiser after the match.''

"And the 'Mech?"

"I'm not prepared to divulge the actual type until we're further along in our negotiations. However, I can tell you it is an assault class machine, one that was refitted in the Federated Commonwealth.'' Warwick was smug. He had presented Rose with a neat answer to his problem, and the entire offer came gift-wrapped. "What do you say, Mister Rose? You're not likely to receive a better offer.''

"I say no.'' Rose stood, forcing the chair out in the same motion. Warwick's eyes went wide as if the only possible answer to his proposal could be an unqualified yes. Rose wiped the corner of his mouth for emphasis and threw the linen into his chowder. "I haven't been long on Solaris, Warwick, but I know you. I know men like you. I'm not desperate enough to cast my lot with you, even if you seem to have all the answers. Thanks for the hospitality, but I'll see myself out now.''

"Rose, don't be a fool!"

"I may be a fool," Rose shot back, "but you're a chopped-off little runt with delusions of grandeur." Warwick was out of his chair in an instant, overturning it onto the hardwood floor. He slammed one hand on the table and pointed the other at Rose, shouting something incoherent at the same time. He was the picture of righteous fury, except that instead of striking the oak table, Warwick hit the edge of his bowl, flipping chowder across the room and burning his hand with still-hot liquid. His roar of fury quickly turned into a yelp of pain. At the sound, the door behind Warwick flew open and two men rushed into the room.

The doorman, who entered first, went immediately to his master and took the injured hand in a gentle but firm grip. The second man was much smaller, with the body of a wrestler. His small head was perched atop a thick bull neck and broad shoulders. He smoothly stepped over Warwick's chair and prepared to seize Rose.

"No!" Halted in mid-stride, the wrestler tried to look at Warwick and Rose at the same time. Rose, despite the volume of Warwick's command and the obvious authority in his voice, never took his eyes off his opponent. "Scoggins, show Mister Rose to the gate, then return to this room at once.

"Rose, I swear you haven't heard the last of this. You want a 'Mech so bad you can taste it, and I could have given it to you on a platter. But not now. Nobody's going to sell to you, Rose—not after what I tell them—nobody."

Rose started to turn on Warwick, then saw Scoggins reach into his jacket. By the look in the man's eye Rose knew he was outgunned. He was just waiting for Rose to make a move on Warwick, but Rose pulled up short.

"No man mocks me in my own home, Jeremiah Rose. No man!"

"I'll see you later then, Warwick. Just be sure to bring a lot of friends." As Rose walked out of the room under Scoggins' watchful eye, he left Warwick thrusting his hand into a pitcher of water, teeth clenched, eyes ablaze.

8

"**R**ose, I didn't expect to see you back here." Rose smiled at Dillon and wondered how anyone could keep his sanity constantly surrounded by trivids of assault 'Mechs locked in battle. Rose hadn't noticed it the night before, but Dillon seemed oblivious to the racket. He simply observed the patrons of The Pelican intently while constantly smiling at some private joke.

"Evening, Dillon. Does that mean you didn't think I'd find Brachall, or that I'd be so grateful I'd leave you alone?" Dillon's smile grew even wider as he began wiping at the bar. It was obviously a nervous reaction. Not that the bar wouldn't benefit from a little care, but Dillon was studying the plastic just a little too hard. Rose had meant the comment as a simple conversation-starter, but it seemed that Dillon had a lot on his mind.

"Feeling guilty about something?" Dillon looked up and smiled, but still didn't speak. Rose was starting to become annoyed when the bartender moved to the beer rack and pulled out a Conner's Dark.

"I can't really say I feel guilty, but if I'd known where Brachall was going to send you, I'd have simply played dumb. I've been told I'm very convincing."

"You know where I've been?" Rose took a long pull from the brown bottle and tried to savor the taste. Evidently dark beer was an acquired taste. Dillon hadn't asked for money yet, so maybe now was the time to acquire it. Even after a second mouthful Dillon hadn't moved from the spot, or given an indication that he was planning to. Rose looked around the bar and wondered if the comatose barman would be missed, but things were still slow at The Pelican. It looked like some Mech-Warrior groupies had arrived early to mark their territory, but the available crew seemed to be coping with the clients very well. Rose continued to drink.

"Yeah, I know where you've been. Half the Black Hills knows where you've been." Rose raised an eyebrow interrogatively as he set down the empty bottle. Dillon seemed to be caught in some inner struggle. He walked silently back to the beer rack and extracted another Conner's.

"Did you accept?"

"Accept what?" Rose sipped his beer. His stomach rumbled in slight protest. A stomach filled with half a bowl of chowder was definitely not the location for mixing in alcohol. He smiled innocently and reached for a bowl of pork skins.

"His offer. Warwick must have made some kind of offer. I mean you were invited to his house, after all." Rose looked up from the bowl of disappearing pork skins and was genuinely surprised to see that Dillon was upset. Very upset apparently.

"I take it people don't get invited to the Warwick estate just any evening?" Rose looked around for another snack bowl while taking another sip of his beer. His stomach was still rumbling, but not as seriously as before.

"No, they don't. Most people get 'invited' to his mansion on the south edge of town. What do you have that he wants?" Dillon's eyes were locked with Rose's. He obviously expected an answer, which made Rose even less than normally inclined to give him one. Dillon had been a source of information, however. Maybe he shouldn't antagonize the man just for fun.

"Well, I didn't exactly get invited to his home, at least not initially. I was scheduled to meet him at the stables, but as I was walking out the door I got a call from a Mister Butrix."

"Yeah, that's Warwick's doorman slash butler slash bodyguard."

Rose nodded at the information. It was always good to have a name to go with the face. Down the bar he spotted another snack bowl just as his fingers were hitting the last of the pork skins. Two groupies were rummaging through it, spearing the snacks with long fingernails.

"Got any more?" Rose tipped the empty bowl of pork skins toward Dillon, who nodded and reached under the bar for a plastic sack.

"I caught a cab at the hotel," Rose told him, "but the driver wouldn't take me to the gate. I got out about half a block away and walked the rest of the way.

"Warwick's sure got a nice place."

Dillon, who had almost finished refilling the bowl, nodded appreciatively. "It's nice, all right. The previous owners, now they had class. A duke, or maybe it was a baron. Some sort of Steiner nobility. That fellow sure had the blue blood."

"But not Warwick."

"No, Warwick is definitely a commoner made good. No class." Rose liked listening to Dillon more than talking to him. Despite the barman's earlier anger, Dillon seemed more at ease now, chattering almost cheerily, urged on with only occasional comments from Rose.

"Any idea where he got his money?" Dillon nodded, but was called away from the conversation by a pair of fans. Rose used the time to take a better look around the bar, which was filling up fast. The first of the evening's matches was due to start in less than an hour and most of the good tables were taken. Now that he was better attuned to it, he noticed that both the noise level and the air of excitement had begun to build. Rose had finished his second bottle when Dillon returned.

"Ready for another?"

"No. How about some citrus juice?"

"All we got is apple, but it's not bad." Dillon had to fill two other orders before he got back to Rose with the juice. "As I hear the tale, Warwick was some kind of merchant. He happened to be in the right place at the right time with God-only-knows-what during the first few months of the Clan invasion. He made a killing, folded his tent, and came to the game world, just like every other loser, fool, and shark."

"You don't say?"

"Sorry about that. Just a little bitterness spilling out. I am definitely a fool."

"Which makes me . . . ?"

"Either a loser or shark."

Rose considered the analysis and wondered if the barman was really that perceptive. He had indeed come to Solaris as a shark, but things had not gone his way for the last two days.

"So, what about Warwick's offer?" Dillon pressed.

Rose studied the other man for a moment, then decided to tell the truth. "I had to turn it down," he said. Dillon let out a long breath that Rose hadn't realized he'd been holding. "You ever meet a guy who you knew at first glance that you were going to hate?" Dillon almost nodded, but it was his eyes that said yes. "That was Warwick. The fact that I made it through half a bowl of what was surely the best chowder I've ever tasted is testimony to the cook and my patience."

"I'm glad to hear that. You seemed like a good guy when you came in here the other night. I'd have hated to see you working for that man."

"Well, I need the work, but I could never answer to a man like Warwick." Rose looked up from his juice to see Dillon smiling from ear to ear. The grin was infectious, even without the beers.

"Cheer up," the young barman told him. "Who knows what's around the corner? Hey, there's someone you'd like to meet and you don't even know it.

"Jaryl, over here!" Rose had started to half turn around

when he felt someone slam into him, driving his ribs into the bar and the air from his lungs.

"Dillon! How about a pair of shooters?" Rose gasped for breath and tried to look up at Dillon's friend, nearly gasping again when he saw her.

Jaryl was dressed in black and red leather from head to toe. Her red pants, cut low to flatter rounded hips and a firm stomach, were tucked into the tops of her knee-high black boots. She wore a black leather jacket with a red skull on the arm nearest Rose. He tried to get a look at her face, but a tangle of black hair obscured his view.

"Jaryl, you know I can't drink on duty, at least not this early in the evening. Besides, you almost incapacitated the man I wanted you to meet."

Rose was still partially bent over the bar when Jaryl lifted one arm to brush the hair from her face. Perhaps the hair in her eyes obscured the fact that she was too close to Rose to bring her hand up that fast. Her left arm caught him under the chin, slamming his teeth together and catching the tip of his tongue between the incisors. Rose closed his eyes in pain, then started when he opened them again and got a look at the woman who'd just whacked him.

He guessed her age at probably close to thirty, but no more. She was beautiful, her skin smooth and pale with a hint of laugh lines at the corners of her mouth. She was every cadet's dream, except for a black patch covering her right eye.

Rose looked into the other eye, which was green, and saw the challenge, fear, joy, and fire in the woman. The outfit, the devil-may-care attitude were all part of what she had become; a beautiful woman whose beauty had been forever ravaged. Rose smiled as warmly as he was physically able, coughing slightly as his lungs reinflated.

"I can't be altogether sure at this moment, Jaryl, but I believe I will be forever grateful to Dillon for introducing us." He held out his right hand and tried, almost successfully, to suppress a cough. Jaryl eyed the hand warily before taking it in a firm grasp.

"Who've we got here, Dillon? I don't believe I've ever seen him before."

"Mister Rose. You've heard of Mister Rose?" Jaryl nodded slightly and fixed Rose with an icy stare. Though she had stopped shaking his hand, she did not let go. Rose could feel her body tense, but didn't understand why. He returned her stare, but with warmth.

"Mister Rose has decided he doesn't like stablemaster Desmond Warwick and has but recently returned to the company of decent people." Jaryl relaxed slightly and allowed a ghost of her previous smile to return.

"Jeremiah, to my friends," Rose said.

"Jaryl here is the fifth pilot with Carstairs Stables. Her team is scheduled to go against Warwick in the upcoming lance final."

"Dillon, don't be so melodramatic. What he means to say is that I'm almost good enough to be on the team, but unless somebody slips in the shower, I'm in the audience like everybody else."

Her smile returned. "So, if Dillon won't drink, how about you? Ever had a Pelican Shooter?" Dillon grimaced and turned away from the bar as if afraid to see what was coming next.

"Pelican Shooter?"

"Just a harmless little drink," Jaryl said. Rose looked into her one green eye and tried to gauge just how harmless the brew might actually be. "Come on. It's on me. Dillon, set 'em up." Rose was far from convinced, but decided not to argue with Jaryl.

"Two Pelican Shooters on the way." Rose craned his neck to see, but whatever the barman was concocting was obscured from view. Several patrons turned to Rose and Jaryl. Most looked amused, but Rose thought he could see real concern on the faces of others. Jaryl obviously loved every bit of the attention.

"Just what are these things?" he demanded jokingly. Jaryl only smiled in reply.

"Well, if you won't answer that one, perhaps you'll answer another." Her smile indicated that she might, so

Rose continued. "Why buy me a drink? And by the way, how do you know who I am?"

"Well," she said, looking over at Dillon, who was apparently in the final stages of mixing, "I'm buying you a drink because I know who you are and I know who you are because I make it my business to know anybody I might have to kill." Rose's entire body went tense for a moment, but Jaryl was no longer looking at him. Around them, he heard the crowd gasp as Dillon brought two tumblers on a tray held high above his head.

"Two Pelican Shooters," he declared in a loud voice. Around the bar other patrons began to crowd around Rose and Jaryl. Rose was beginning to question the wisdom of accepting "a harmless little drink." As Dillon set the tray on the bar with a flourish, Rose knew he'd been had.

Before them were two tumblers, each half-filled with a brownish liquid Rose only guessed was alcohol. Celery, or onions, or something equally undesirable floated on top. As the crowd gathered closer, Dillon reached onto the tray and grabbed a sardine with each hand. He waved each fish above his head, prompting the crowd to a cheer.

"With every Pelican Shooter comes a story," he said, producing a murmur of general approval from the crowd. "The pelican is a survivor, just like the inhabitants of Solaris. One day, a pelican was gliding over the river, just north of this bar, looking for something to eat."

People gathered around and began to smile. Obviously, a real pelican had never flown anywhere near Solaris, but like any inside joke, it did not need to be funny for the listeners to share in the camaraderie. "Pollution was bad in those days, the debris and sewage so awful that you could almost walk across the river from bank to bank. But the pelican was determined. They even tell that the river caught fire, but the pelican didn't give up.

"Suddenly, through the smoke and flame, the pelican spied a fish, but at the same moment another pelican approached, its sights set on the very same fish."

Dillon dropped one sardine into each drink and placed

the tumblers in front of Rose and Jaryl. "The two mighty birds began a race to the fish." Dillon pulled a small lighter from out of an apron pocket and leaned close to Rose. "No fair blowing on your drink first, Mister Rose. To the winner, a meal, but to the loser . . . ?" Dillon flicked the lighter and passed the flame over each drink, which began to burn with the clear flame of an alcohol fire.

As Dillon backed away Jaryl leaned forward and began fanning the flame with her hand. The crowd meanwhile had begun to chant, setting up a current of air that nearly put out the diminishing flame. Rose jumped forward and began to fan his drink too, but Jaryl's head-start proved the difference. Her flame went out first. As she was raising her glass to drink, Rose had just managed to extinguish the flame in his. As he grabbed for the glass, the crowd roared, urging him on.

Next to him Jaryl was trying to gulp down the brown liquid through tear-stained eyes. His own eyes began to tear at the smell of the drink, which was as bad as Rose had feared it might be. Closing his eyes and holding his breath, he opened his throat as wide as he could. He poured the drink down in a single smooth motion, barely feeling the fish slide over his tongue on the way to his stomach. With a wide smile he overturned the glass and set it back on the tray while Jaryl struggled with the last of the dregs in hers. Rose risked a breath and discovered that the aftertaste was terrible. He glanced at Dillon, who stood smiling behind the bar. Jaryl coughed slightly and slammed the tumbler down on the tray, wiping her mouth with the back of her free hand. The crowd broke into wild applause.

"Damn!" she exclaimed. "Dillon, why didn't you warn me I was going against a professional?" The crowd broke into laughter as Jaryl's face turned red.

"Rose is the winner! Drinks on the house all night!" Dillon reached over and raised Rose's hand above his head. Those near Rose clapped him on the back and shouted their approval.

"And Jaryl . . ."

". . . PAYS FOR A ROUND OF DRINKS!" Dillon grinned as the applause grew louder. Jaryl, still red-faced, rolled her eyes and smiled at the crowd.

"Yeah, yeah, yeah. One round, Dillon. Put it on the tab." Jaryl turned to go, but Rose stopped her.

"Just a second, Jaryl. Mind if we talk for a second?"

"Sure thing, but let's get a table near a trivid. The first match is about to start."

Rose ordered two bottles of Conner's and followed Jaryl to a booth just off the main viewing area. Despite the nearness to game time, the booth was still open. As Rose slid into one side and Jaryl into the other, he noticed that the booth offered an excellent view of the main trivid, near-perfect viewing without the press of the crowd on the main floor. He pushed one of the bottles over to Jaryl as she turned on the speaker built into the booth back.

"Hope you like Conner's." Jaryl nodded and adjusted the volume. Rose couldn't understand the announcer's words, which were in Chinese but might as well have been Greek as far as he was concerned. Jaryl, on the other hand, was obviously picking up on all of it.

"Hey, I'm sorry if I made you mad," he said.

"No, not mad. It's just that I don't lose often and I don't like it when I do. Nothing personal. Really."

"You're good."

"Thanks. It was a trick I learned at the academy. It's not too hard to do with a little practice. Just concentrate on opening your throat and let the liquor slide right down."

"Neat trick."

"But still just a trick."

"As you say."

"Before Dillon brought the drinks, you said something . . ."

"Yes?"

". . . about having to kill me?"

"Yes?"

"Could you, maybe, expand on that point?"

"I guess. I mean, you did buy me this nice, WARM beer." Rose decided not to meet the challenge in her voice or her eyes. She wasn't kidding when she said she didn't like to lose. He let the silence linger as he listened to an announcer he didn't understand go through the warm-ups for a fight he didn't care anything about.

"Sorry, again." Jaryl lapsed into silence and partially turned to the main trivid. A *Stalker* 'Mech was lumbering through the doorway of the 'Mech shed. Rose tried to guess the arena, but couldn't place either the pilot or the location. He'd have recognized one of the five major arenas instantly, for each of those was as distinctive as the sector of Solaris City that spawned it. This must be a match in one of the lesser-class arenas of either the capital or one of the other nearby towns.

The announcer became even more excited as the trivid image switched to a *Banshee,* presumably the *Stalker*'s opponent, but Rose still found it difficult to get enthusiastic about the prospect of men dying for the amusement of others.

"Do you have any idea how nervous you make people?" Jaryl asked suddenly.

"Pardon?"

"Do you have any idea how nervous you make people? People like Warwick or my boss Carstairs?" Rose eased back into his seat and thought about the question.

"I guess not. I'm just one guy. What's to get nervous about?"

"Plenty. You're an unknown. That drives the odds-makers crazy, but, god, what it does to the stablemasters."

"I hadn't thought of it that way."

"You'd better start. Do you know that within half an hour of your first call for a 'Mech, half the stables in Solaris City knew about you? By the end of the first day, most of the stablemen in the city had placed calls checking on your service record, which came up empty."

"Really?"

"Yeah. Any idea why nobody would sell you a 'Mech?"

"Not at all. Most of the people I contacted said they didn't have what I wanted, but that got a little hard to believe after a while." Rose thought back to all the calls he'd made during the inbound flight aboard the Drop-Ship. Out of all the 'Mech dealers on Solaris, not one would sell him even an abused heavy or assault class machine?

"Finals week, that's why. This is the last week of the season. A new guy like you isn't much of a threat for the grand championship—that's handled by a process of elimination. On the other hand, there are plenty of other competitions you could enter if you had a 'Mech. Events like the match between Carstairs and Warwick. Events where the team is entered, not the individual competitors."

"Were there any 'Mechs on the ship that brought you here?"

"I don't know," Rose said. "Most of the cargo bays were off-limits."

"Probably not. If there had been, they'd have been impounded until the end of the week—no new blood until the end of the season. What little manages to get into the city is roadblocked."

"If new blood is so dangerous to the odds, and money, of the gamblers, why am I still walking around? Why was Warwick the only one to approach me?"

"You don't have a service record. Most stables probably passed you off as a 'Mechbunny or ghost." Rose simply stared at her. "That's wannabe or spy to you out-of-towners. Either way, only a desperate manager would touch you, a guy like Warwick."

"And if I'd arrived a month ago?"

"No problem."

Rose slammed the table and rocked both bottles. Only a quick grab by Jaryl saved her beer from spilling all over her and the table.

"Sorry," he said. "What about next week, when most

of the battles have been decided? Can I get a 'Mech then?''

"Probably, but still not for sure. Most of the stables have you pegged either as idle rich or trouble. Either way, a tech is only going to sell to you if he's willing to risk their anger or if the profits are so good he can't pass up the opportunity. Until the major stables figure out who you are and what kind of trouble you're going to be, you're dispossessed.''

"I'm nobody to these guys. Why do they want to make my life so damn rough?''

"Because they can. You can get a 'Mech. You're just going to have to wait a while to do it. In two or three months most of the stable owners will have forgotten about you.''

Rose could only growl and slam the table again. "I leave in ten days.''

"Then you leave without a 'Mech.'' Rose didn't want to believe her, but thinking over the past few days, he realized Jaryl was right. Few, if any, of the locals would talk with him, and those who did seemed on edge. The Pelican was the only place in town where he felt even halfway welcome, and that was mostly because of Dillon. There had to be a way to get a 'Mech, but he couldn't guess what it might be. He concentrated on spinning his empty bottle until he realized he was ignoring his companion. Looking over at Jaryl, he saw that she was engrossed in the trivid on the main floor. Rose followed her eyes and watched as the *Stalker* and the *Banshee* caught sight of one another for the first time in the fight.

The orange and gray *Stalker* let fly with every missile it had. The black *Banshee,* seemingly surprised by the encounter, triggered both its PPCs, but the blast of the missiles and the suddenness of the *Stalker*'s attack made both shots go wide. As the smoke cleared, Rose could see how good a shot was the *Stalker* pilot. He'd targeted all four flights of missiles at the *Banshee*'s torso, blasting away armor and threatening the 'Mech's delicate interior.

The *Banshee* attempted to back around a corner, but

the *Stalker* pressed its advantage. Rose wondered where they were fighting. The announcer was practically screaming in his ear, but the volume didn't help his comprehension. Jaryl was studying the fight intently, yet without the air of bloodlust that had gripped the rest of The Pelican's patrons. The spectacle held everyone in the room in its thrall.

As Rose turned back to the trivid the *Stalker* continued to close with the *Banshee,* which had fired its shoulder-mounted missile rack, but made only scattered hits along the *Stalker's* left leg. In return the *Stalker* delivered a single large laser into the *Banshee's* already-damaged right torso, melting rivulets of plasteel and setting off a series of minor explosions inside.

Rose knew the battle was already decided, but the *Banshee* fought on and the *Stalker* continued to press its advantage. Viewers unconsciously edged closer to the trivid, sensing a kill as the *Banshee* attempted to fight on.

As it staggered back, the *Banshee* fired its pair of front-mounted medium lasers and one of its PPCs. Rose saw the pilot also attempt to line up the Gauss rifle, but the *Stalker* pilot was keeping well to the right of its humanoid enemy, preferring to take the laser and PPC fire as the *Banshee's* heat rose. Again the *Banshee* pilot had aimed low, succeeding in hitting, but not damaging, the powerful legs of the *Stalker,* which were driving toward the nearly stationary *Banshee.* Rose turned away with a slow, sad shake of his head, knowing what would come next.

The *Stalker* continued to fire its medium lasers as it collided with the *Banshee,* driving its armored snout into the battered center torso of its foe. Picked up off its feet and driven backward, the *Banshee* folded around the *Stalker.* As the force of the blow slowed the *Stalker,* the *Banshee* uncurled from around the other 'Mech and flew backward, its remaining PPC firing blindly through the air in a slow, graceful arc. As the *Stalker* fought to regain control, the *Banshee* landed on its hip, then rolled onto its back, whiplashing its head against the ferrocrete floor.

Sparks flew along the back of the fallen 'Mech as the *Stalker* succeeded in maintaining its balance by staggering into the nearby wall. Although the 'Mech punched completely through the wall, it succeeded in remaining upright. With only a slight wobble, the *Stalker* approached its fallen foe.

Rose was still shaking his head when he glanced over to Jaryl, catching, by accident, the face of a man just a few steps away. Shoulders relaxed, feet slightly spread, he was standing near one of The Pelican's several fire doors. Rose stared for a moment before realizing who he was seeing. Jaryl, with the man to her blind side, did not realize that Rose was looking past her and continued to watch the combat.

As Rose met the man's eyes across the roomful of humans mesmerized by the destruction of the *Banshee*, Scoggins drew a gyrojet pistol from his jacket and aimed it at Rose's table. Rose was halfway across the table when the shot hit Jaryl in the side of the head. As flying bits of blood and bone blinded Rose, the murderer crashed through the door and escaped into the night.

9

Six hours after the shooting, The Pelican stood silent and vacant except for Rose, Dillon, and a Lieutenant Viets of the Federated Commonwealth Police Department. As Dillon went over what little he knew of Jaryl's too short life, Rose sat in what was becoming his customary seat, silently sipping a Conner's, his first since the shooting. With ill-concealed contempt Rose watched the policewoman work. She was beautiful, if somewhat short for Rose's taste, but he had long ago learned never to judge a woman by appearance, either for good or bad. In another circumstance he might have been impressed with her soft features and athletic body, but tonight she was just another officer. An officer he did not care to be around. An officer who, for six hours, had done nothing but ask questions, covering the same ground over and over.

As the adrenaline wore off, Rose went numb from the shock. He was no stranger to death in most of its grisly forms, but he had never been this close to the work of an assassin. The juxtaposition was almost too much for him. People had been laughing and having a good time. People weren't killed the way Jaryl was killed. They died on the battlefield, or in some accident, or at home in bed.

The situation started to play on his nerves before his

professionalism and experience took hold and glued him together. Jaryl was a soldier, wasn't she? Not like any he'd ever met, but then most of what he'd been experiencing on Solaris was unlike anything he'd ever encountered. Life in the Com Guards had certainly been more straightforward, if not easier. Dogma and duty his lancemates had called it, the Twin Dees.

Rose had been questioned for only an hour by Lieutenant Viets. She obviously hadn't learned much, or else she didn't like what she'd learned because she'd ordered the bar closed and made everyone go home. Dillon had howled like a wounded animal when she threw everyone out. He continued to mumble about the lost profits while shaking a weary head. When the questioning was done, Rose drifted back to the bar to sort out his thoughts. Most of the police left within the next few hours after wandering in and out in twos and threes to take evidence, trivids, and whatever else police did at the scene of a murder.

Rose observed the proceedings with halfhearted interest. Another lead, another dead end, only this time he could do no better than watch as the woman who'd tried to help him was gunned down. He briefly considered the possibility that he was somehow to blame, but quickly gave up the idea. He doubted that Warwick, or anyone else, would have killed Jaryl just to get back at him for something. Jaryl had obviously been Scoggins' target because of something she had—or hadn't—done, or something Rose couldn't even begin to guess at.

He stared down into the half-empty bottle of Conner's, sloshing the liquid inside. It had long since stopped foaming from the agitation and now simply swirled around in a small whirlpool. This was not the first time Rose had seen death, but cold-blooded murder was different than death on the field of battle.

He glanced again at Viets and Dillon, who were talking quietly behind the bar. Rose guessed that the two knew each other well, at least professionally. Who knew how much further it went? Whatever the situation, Dillon obviously had more patience for her than did Rose, who'd stopped answering even her occasional questions more than ninety minutes ago.

Rose continued to fume into his bottle, silently cursing Solaris, Warwick, Lieutenant Viets, the Clans, and everything else that came to mind. How could a society function when divided into five independent, supposedly equal, governments within shooting distance of one another? How could these governments let a killer walk the streets? How could they ever bring anyone to justice when each sector of the city operated under its own separate police? And how could Viets just sit there when Rose had positively identified the assassin as Scoggins? He'd shouted that very question at her in his best commander's voice.

The lieutenant had been surprisingly polite in the face of his hostility, pointing out that he was, after all, an offworlder, with no ties to the victim or the alleged assailant. "Of course we'll follow up the lead you've given us," Viets said with a polite smile, "but I'm not sure anything will come of it. Mister Scoggins is a Liao national and likely safe and sound somewhere in Cathay right now." Rose finished his beer in one gulp, then stared again at Viets and Dillon, who were conversing in whispers.

Feelings were boiling in him—his frustration at not being able to find a 'Mech anywhere in Solaris, exhaustion from going without sleep for something like forty-eight hours, and then the horror of Jaryl's murder. Even a man as controlled as Rose was cracking under the strain.

"So, Lieutenant Viets," he said bitterly, "I suppose this means you'll just saunter on back to the station house and fill out your report? Just grab a bite to eat, maybe some nice young cop groupie, and head home for the evening. Nothing more about the so-called 'incident' tonight?"

Viets gazed at Rose, her jaw clenched angrily. The knuckles on her near hand went white as she slowly

turned away from Dillon, but Rose continued to taunt her. "You slack-jawed, blue-chested clods are all alike. This bottle has more brains."

"Oh, so the wise MechWarrior wants to show this poor, stupid clod how to conduct a police investigation. Do tell me, wise one, how should I proceed?" Viets scoffed. Rose had expected anger, but not the instant confrontation.

"Wait, I know," she went on sarcastically. "I'll assemble the whole rest of the force and we'll march into Cathay, kick the bejesus out of anything that moves and drag back this Scoggins character you say killed Jaryl Whillins."

"He did kill her!" Rose jabbed an accusing finger at the officer and pounded the bar for effect. The bottle danced to the vibration as it had on the table earlier. Lieutenant Viets didn't even acknowledge that he'd spoken.

"Better yet, we'll just ask the Cathayans to turn him over. That wouldn't be such a problem. 'Yes, that's right. It seems like one of your malcontents shot one of our citizens at a local drinking establishment this evening. Could you just send him over with a note that says you don't mind if we hang him? Thank you very much.' " Rose gripped the edge of the bar and fought against the anger that threatened to overwhelm him. He'd wanted to provoke her, but now she'd turned the tables.

"At least you'd be doing something." Again Viets ignored him. She continued to pace behind the bar, her eyes cast upward as if for heavenly inspiration. Suddenly she clapped her hands and turned to Rose.

"I've got it. We'll just call in those limp-swords over in the international sector. They'd just love the chance to show off all those shiny new rifles they carry around." Rose roared and vaulted the bar, one hand acting as the pivot as his legs came sweeping over the surface. His top leg shot forward and the toes of his boot sought Viets' exposed head. The lieutenant ducked under the blow. With a sharp movement, she struck the inside of the elbow of the arm supporting his weight. Rose's entire body, which a moment ago had been perfectly poised on that one arm, came crashing down. Momentum carried him across the bar's flat surface, allowing him to land mostly on the padded runway. His head, however, bounced off the stainless steel sink just below the bar's surface.

Fighting off the initial dizziness, Rose was attempting to stand when the other side of his head exploded in pain. Stars shot off behind his eyes, but he managed to rise to one knee before something reached under his chin and rocked his head. He felt his teeth chip as his head flew back and forced his body to follow. Flat on his back behind the bar, Rose tried to roll away from the stomp he knew was sure to follow, but the attack never came.

Rose rolled over backward and came up into a crouch, eyes searching for his opponent. He stood slowly as waves of nausea threatened to knock him back to one knee. Just out of the range of his foot stood Lieutenant Viets, her hands easily balancing her tonfa. Rose had seen, and recognized, the martial arts weapon earlier during the interrogation, but he'd mistakenly passed it off as merely ornamental or clumsy. Clearly it was neither. Risking a look away from the weapon, he glanced up at the officer holding it. To his surprise, Viets was smiling.

"You find this amusing, Officer Viets?" Rose began to relax, but only after his opponent shifted her weight firmly onto one foot.

" 'Mechboy, this is my idea of a real good time. Pounding the snot out of you tough guys is a dream come true to us poor, stupid clods."

"Touché." Rose straightened and felt the adrenaline flowing out of his system. His head began to pound from the twin lumps he'd received. He tested the second knot, not surprised to see that his hand came away bloody. He looked over at Viets, who continued to smile as she twirled her tonfa around a seemingly unmoving hand. With a snap of the wrist the weapon was back in its place at her side.

"Dillon, I'm officially off duty. I need something to drink."

"Yes, ma'am. One on the way, and I'll bring some ice for your head, Rose." Rose waved an affirmative without looking at Dillon. A check of his chin revealed that it was bleeding too, but not as severely as the head wound. Rose realized he was lucky to be alive, but that only slightly eased the pain.

"Viets, I've been beaten, stabbed, and twice ejected from an exploding 'Mech, but I've never had a fight go against me that quickly, or that surely." Rose reached for a nearby cloth and dabbed his head. Lieutenant Viets let the silence linger as she crossed to the other side of the bar and took a seat next to the one Rose had only recently occupied.

"Well, Rose, I'm just guessing, but since we're on a planet known for gambling, I'd wager you've never underestimated an opponent so badly, never let an opponent make you so angry, and never fought a ninth *dan* black belt. But, hey, I'm just guessing. You could have been one hell of a lucky guy all your life." Rose walked around the bar and sat next to Viets. He wondered about Dillon, but the bartender seemed to know when it was time to make himself scarce.

"I'm sorry that I insulted you and your police force. Thanks for going easy on me and giving me the chance to learn from my mistake. It isn't a lesson I'll need again."

"Apology accepted, Mister Rose. Now, if Dillon will only get back here with my drink. Ah, speak of the devil." Dillon emerged from the back room with a plastic bag full of ice, which he gave to Rose, and a small porcelain bottle, which he gave to Viets. Reaching into his apron, he produced a matching porcelain cup that he also handed to the policewoman.

"Now that the two of you are on speaking terms, maybe we can get back to business." Dillon was obviously pleased that Rose was no longer shouting and that Viets was "off duty."

"Lieutenant, can you tell me what's going to happen, and how fast? I know, I know. You don't run the department and there are a lot of things that *can* happen, but I've already figured out that you must have a pretty good idea which way this one will go. I really need to know." Rose did his best to make the request humble but not groveling. If he guessed right, and this particular guess wasn't very difficult, Viets was the type of woman who wouldn't respond well to weakness or begging. She might, however, tell him some of what he wanted, or needed, to know if he could convince her it was important.

"I don't know why I'm bothering to tell you any of this. Not only would my butt be in a sling if the captain found out, but you'd just use the information to get yourself killed. That or you'd kill somebody else."

"You think that little of me after such a brief time?"

"You did attack me, remember, 'Mechboy?"

" 'Mechboy? Just what does that mean? You don't know me, what I do or how I make a living." Rose let equal parts of anger and calm slip into his voice. How did she know?

"Oh, 'Mechboy, I know you. I know you and your kind. Strutting around like you own the place. All full of attitude and just itching for a fight with some poor local. I can see it in the walk, the talk, the way you drink your beer. You're a 'Mechboy all right, even without that tin-plated, fusion-powered, death-giving machine you call a BattleMech." Rose was impressed with the passion of Viets' response. He'd met people who didn't like MechWarriors. He'd even met people who hated them, but he'd never met a person who made the word 'Mech sound like something dredged up from the bottom of a cesspool.

"If you hate us so much, why are you on Solaris?"

"None of your damn business, 'Mechboy." Rose saw the fire in her eyes. Adrenaline was pumping through her again. Rose took a quick mental inventory of both his body and his few assets. He knew in an instant he couldn't take her in a fight, either fair or foul, at least not without a 'Mech. He also knew he had to keep her talking if he was going to accomplish his personal mission.

"Then why are you talking to me?" Like someone throwing a switch and plunging a room into darkness, Rose saw the anger flow out of Lieutenant Viets. She held him in a rigid stare, unblinking for long seconds as she examined him. Rose imagined that with a stare so intent she could look into his soul. He held her eyes with what he hoped was equal intensity. When she spoke, Rose was shocked by the power and conviction in her voice.

"I keep hoping, 'Mechboy, that one of you will turn out to be different from all the rest." She broke the stare, glancing away. Rose unconsciously relaxed, exhaling a long breath. When she turned back to him, the intensity was gone. She stared at him, but it was not the same.

"Since you're new to the area, I'll make this as simple as possible." She poured a cupful of clear liquid from the bottle and held it to her nose for a brief instant before downing it in a single swallow. "If I assume you're right about Scoggins, and I'm willing to do that, I need a sworn affidavit from you that says you saw him murder Jaryl Whillins and are willing to testify to it in court." Viets held up her pinky to accentuate the point.

"I go to my boss, a man known far and wide as an impartial dispenser of justice, and tell him that just before a championship fight, a back-up pilot was killed by a man in the employ of the other stable." Up went the ring finger.

"I fill out more forms than you'll see in ten years and pass them on up the ladder, explaining why Scoggins has to be brought back to the Black Hills for trial." Up went the middle finger. Rose shifted his ice bag, sensing where the lieutenant was leading.

"Eventually the whole thing gets handled by the bureaucrats, and Scoggins does, or doesn't, stand trial, depending on who owes what favors to who or how much money is brought to bear on the issue." Viets' index finger uncurled from her thumb. "That's what we call a four-step ladder back at base. Any one of the rungs goes and nobody gets to the top."

"So you're saying it won't be easy to bring Scoggins in for trial?"

"Rose, I'd have to take off both boots to count the steps in that ladder, and you'd like it all to be finished by the start of the fight—I can see it in your eyes." Rose tried, with surprising success, to conjure a mental image of Viets without boots, or anything else for that matter. He forced his mind to shift gears and concentrate on the problem. She deserved more respect than a mental undressing. Even with his resolve, however, it took longer than he anticipated to dispel the image. Viets was just finishing her second cup as Rose began thinking aloud.

"So, again time is against me. If I'm right, Warwick is out to get Carstairs' pilots and change the odds of the fight everyone is trying so damn hard to keep the same.

"Even if Scoggins comes to trial, it won't be until long after the fight, and it won't bring Jaryl back or change Warwick's plans." Rose could see the man sitting like a pack rat atop his pile of gold. "Warwick wants this championship and he had Jaryl killed as part of his plan to win it." To Rose the facts were as plain as the pain in his head. He looked at Viets, who only shrugged and poured another drink.

"Maybe so, maybe no."

"Lieutenant, have you ever met Warwick?" Viets absently shook her head. Rose continued although he was only partially sure Viets was even listening to him anymore. As he spoke she stared into the empty porcelain cup, head cocked slightly as if hearing something very far away.

"He's the type of man you meet once and either hate or love. There's no middle ground, just ask Dillon. I found myself falling on the side of the former emotion, even before he had Scoggins murder Jaryl."

"You don't know that."

"You're right, but I know the way Scoggins looked at

me before he pulled the trigger. It was like we were sharing a secret, something only he and I knew anything about. I know that Warwick stands to gain a lot more than he loses if one of Carstairs' pilots dies. I also know that after spending ten minutes alone with the man, I can't stand the sight of him. It's probably unreasonable, but I'm going to go with my guts on this. Warwick is to blame, even if there's no proof.'' Rose stood and started to walk away.

"Where're you going now, 'Mechboy?'' Viets looked up from her empty cup. "You going to start something nobody wants to see happen? You going to make my life miserable, 'Mechboy?'' Rose could see the challenge in her eyes and hear the frustration in her voice. She deserved better than to have to deal with this, to deal with him. She deserved a chance to do her job without Rose's quest getting in the way, but he'd let events control him too long. It was time for him to seize the initiative and regain control of his life. For all the right reasons he lied to her.

"No, Lieutenant Viets, I'm going back to the hotel for some sleep and a couple of pain pills. I'll not bother you again.''

10

Light spilled into the street as a single metal door was suddenly thrown open, the noises and commotion from within a sharp contrast to the quiet and deserted street. A single man stumbled out, backing out onto the dimly lit sidewalk. Roars and curses followed him out, but the giant seemed not to hear. As he cleared the doorway, a second figure, definitely female, darted into the street, almost dancing within reach of the man. Within seconds she was halfway up the street.

The giant paused and looked after the departing figure, then back through the doorway with a broad grin.

"Good night one and all. I'll return on the morrow, prize in hand." Roars of laughter echoed from the room.

"You'll be lucky to survive the night, let alone the match, O'Shea. Elaine is more than a match for your oafish advances." Roars of laughter followed the insult. O'Shea staggered in feigned shock.

"You wound me, but I've no time for the likes of you." O'Shea spun around, as if to leave, but instead lifted his kilt to the building. Pausing only a moment, he jumped out of the direct line of fire as several bottles and a full mug of ale flew through the doorway into the street. Jeers chased the giant as he hustled away, finally catching up with the woman who had followed him out of the bar.

"I swear, O'Shea, one of these nights you'll be plucking glass out of your bum. You've tried that trick once too often."

O'Shea laughed at the memory of his crude jest, and scratched at his full beard as he considered the possibility.

"Perhaps you're right, my dear. Tonight, however, all my parts are glass-free. Perhaps you'd care to make a personal inspection?"

"Restrain yourself, man. You've got a big match tomorrow." She thumped O'Shea's sternum with the flat of her hand to emphasize the point, but as always, O'Shea was unconcerned.

"Am I not Badicus the Bold? Bonnie Badicus? The match tomorrow will be nothing." He started forward again, but his quarry resumed her walk down the street, temporarily eluding him.

"I'm not so sure about this one. Warwick has something up his sleeve."

"That Steiner lackey? He hasn't got the brains to pour water out of a boot with the directions on the heel."

"If you truly believe that, then you've underestimated your opponent." O'Shea and his companion stopped at the sound of the new voice. O'Shea judged the speaker to be in one of the adjacent doorways, but he couldn't be sure which one. Adrenaline kicked in as he reached instinctively for his trusty Sunbeam. Maybe those last three drinks hadn't been such a good idea after all. He slipped the safety strap off the pistol and scanned the sidewalk.

"Knowledge of your foe is half the battle," came the voice.

"Well, well, Mister Expert, what do you know about it? Warwick is a fool, and if he's sent you after me before the match, he's a damn fool. Many men have tried to take on Badicus but few have lived to tell the tale. You'd better kill me quick or run back to your master and tell him you lost your nerve, because you're starting to annoy me."

Badicus was not really sure what to expect next, but

he had no doubt that he could deal with it. Despite his size and considerable bulk, he was one of the fastest draws on Solaris. Of course, few men who discovered the fact lived to tell about it. Somebody, probably Warwick, had already killed Jaryl, but the obvious danger hadn't stopped Badicus from having his usual pre-fight "relaxer." If anything, the death of his friend had made him drink even more than normal.

Seconds passed and the stranger remained unseen. Badicus was about to convince himself that the entire conversation, such as it was, was merely a figment of his slightly inebriated imagination when Elaine let out a brief gasp of surprise. Simultaneously, his left hand, which had begun to draw the Sunbeam, went numb and a shower of light and pain erupted from the corner of his left eye. Had he been sober, the blow would have felled him in a heartbeat, but the eighty-proof anesthetic seemed to soften the blow. He was only driven to one knee. Stars danced across what remained of his vision as the big man fought to rise and make his hand work. He side-kicked to his left, but smashed through nothing but air.

"I am sorry, Mister O'Shea, but you have something I need." O'Shea managed to stagger up to both feet and look at his assailant. Whatever features would have been revealed were hidden under the high collar of the man's long coat and the gloom of the night. Badicus shook his head like a dog shaking off water, but his whole world seemed to spin.

"Believe me, there is nothing personal in my actions," the voice said. Then, in a blur of motion, both his hands reached out and clapped O'Shea over each ear. In the fraction of the second he remained conscious, O'Shea could not help but notice that the air trapped in his outer ear made a sound just like that of a landing DropShip. The pitch of the engines increased as the attack forced the air past his eardrums and into his middle ear. When the DropShip landed, O'Shea lay unconscious on the street.

Rose stepped clear as the big man hit the sidewalk.

O'Shea's head bounced lightly off the concrete, but Rose was sure the man was not permanently injured. He knelt down beside him and smiled when he felt a strong pulse.

"Very impressive, mystery man." Rose looked over at O'Shea's girlfriend. He'd spotted her when the pair had first left the bar, but she'd retreated into the shadows when he initially spoke out to Badicus. Rose stood and watched as Elaine stepped back into the glow of the streetlight.

"Your boyfriend will be all right. He should wake up in an hour or so, but it might take longer if he's as drunk as he seems." Rose continued to watch as Elaine emerged fully into the light. She moved with her right arm at an odd angle, which Rose at first thought was merely an unusual way of walking. A closer look at her midsection revealed that she held a slim black needle pistol. The way she clutched it against her blue dress in the shadows of the street, Rose had almost missed it. His shoulders slumped slightly.

"In a city with gun control laws, why is it so damn easy to pack a pistol in this place?"

Elaine laughed lightly, but held the gun rock-steady. "Dangerous times like these require extreme measures," she said. "As a warrior, I'm sure you understand that."

"I didn't hurt O'Shea, so you can put down the gun. I just needed him out of action for a couple of hours, that's all." Rose carefully eyed the gun that didn't move a hair.

"Oh, I'm not worried about O'Shea. In fact, you've just made my job a little easier." Rose felt his stomach drop. The adrenaline that had begun to dissipate after O'Shea's fall began creeping back into his blood.

"Your job?"

"Yes. Mister O'Shea was about to have a terrible accident. Of course, I'd have waited until the morning, but you can't have everything you want."

"So you're not Elaine, his girlfriend?" Rose hoped to keep her talking, but he didn't have much of a plan other than that. He hated needlers. Of all the weapons he had ever encountered, only needlers caused such an irrational fear. He knew he would not be any deader than if a laser or an old fashioned slug-thrower killed him, but that didn't seem to matter. He still hated the weapon, even more now that one was pointed at him.

"Oh, I'm Elaine, all right." Stepping carefully, she closed the distance between her and Rose. From her position, she had a full view of the bar, which was to Rose's back. "I'm also known as his girlfriend, but I'm just a girl who needs a paycheck."

"You really seemed to care for O'Shea back at the bar." Rose kept his eyes on Elaine, shifting his view between the pistol and her eyes.

"I'm a natural actress. Could you really like, let alone *love*, a man like that? Just look at him. Go on, take a good look." Rose was not at all inclined to take his eyes off Elaine, but the urgency in her voice forced him to reconsider. Inside he was exploding with energy as his heart sent adrenaline-filled blood racing through his veins, but Rose willed his muscles to remain calm. If, and when, it came time to act, he would move quicker if relaxed. One last look into Elaine's eyes and Rose turned to study Badicus O'Shea. A quick glance told him all he needed to know. Next to his prostrate body was the Sunbeam laser pistol he had tried to pull on Rose. Rose doubted that Elaine knew O'Shea had tried to draw the pistol because she'd been on his right and the pistol on the left.

"Well, could you really love someone like that?" Rose was no longer listening. Elaine's voice had risen in pitch and he could hear the decision in her voice. She had already rationalized the need to kill Rose and was about to pull the trigger.

Rose lunged down and to the side just as Elaine triggered two quick bursts at where Rose had just been standing. The first shot, aimed at his chest, caught him in the right shoulder as he tried to lean out of the way. He could feel his jacket pull slightly as the plastic slivers effortlessly parted the threads of the jacket and the skin underneath. The second shot, corrected as the trigger was being pulled, flew past his ear. As his fingers first touched the Sunbeam, Rose shifted his attention to Elaine. Either she did not know Rose had the laser or she was making very sure of her next shot. Although she had the needler pointed directly at him, she did not pull the trigger. As Rose was bringing the Sunbeam up for a single desperate shot, Elaine was aligning her pistol for the kill.

Rose fired without aiming, praying for the first time since he'd left the Highlanders. His lunge had left him completely off balance, lying on his left side. He heard, then felt, the quiet staccato of the needler as plastic skipped off the sidewalk and raked his left ribs.

He brought his pistol back in line, aimed, and fired before he realized Elaine was already falling backward. The second shot struck her fully in the chest, hastening her backward flight. The needler fell from lifeless hands as her body crumpled into a heap.

Rose tried to stand, stopped short at the pain in his shoulder and chest, then continued the motion. He crossed quickly to Elaine, who stared sightlessly at him. He held a finger to her neck and discovered the entry point of his first shot, just under the chin. From his angle on the ground, the shot must have passed up into the woman's brain, killing her instantly. Two centimeters to the right and Rose would have missed her completely. He drew back bloodless fingers from the already cauterized wound. Behind him he heard a man shout and a woman scream. Without so much as a backward look he fled into the night.

=== 11 ===

"Let me get this straight." The man behind the desk leaned forward to stare intently at his visitor. Like a bear defending his territory, he bunched his shoulders and prepared to engage the individual standing across his desk. "You 'happen' to hear that one of my pilots is out of the match. You 'happen' to hear I need a fourth pilot or else I have to scratch the match. You 'happen' to be checked out on O'Shea's 'Mech. You 'happen' to know Warwick. You 'happen' to be in my office and you 'happen' to want to fight for free. Chromium fire, man! Do I look stupid?" A pair of thundering fists crashed down on the desk as the man stood up. The ancient wooden piece creaked with the pressure, but held together. His eyes blazed with anger and frustration, but he was still in his home territory and would not be cowed into a corner.

"I didn't come to own four 'Mechs by being stupid. I don't know who you are, and at this point I don't really care. What I do want to know is why you're here and why I shouldn't have Esmeralda toss you out on your butt—and don't think she couldn't. She's the only other person ever to take O'Shea in a fight."

The man on the other side of the stablemaster's desk paused for just an instant to allow the nearly berserk owner to fall back into his desk chair. For most people this would have signaled the end of the confrontation, but for this man, it seemed more like a willingness to take a few rounds instead of dishing it out. He reached out and stabbed a cigar, which smelled disturbingly like real tobacco, into the corner of his mouth, his eyes daring his visitor to say something. Behind the stablemaster's chair an overworked and ineffective air purifier hummed quietly. Judging the moment to be right, the visitor leaned forward and placed his hands flat on the other man's desk.

"Mister Carstairs, although you are not interested, my name is Jeremiah Rose." Rose waited a few moments to see if the name would mean anything to the stable owner. Rose had no doubt that Carstairs was intimately familiar with everything that had been going on with his pilots and the role he had played. Carstairs didn't so much as blink at the name. The bear—Rose couldn't help but think of the giant stablemaster as anything else—worked his cigar to the other side of his mouth, but did not speak. Suddenly unsure of his strategy, Rose hesitated slightly before continuing.

"For the last two years I have been fighting the Clans in the Draconis Combine. I was a company commander for more than half that time. Five months ago my company was crushed by combined elements of the Wolf Clan, leaving me the only survivor out of twelve men and women. My 'Mech, like many others, was a one-of-a-kind creation. Now there isn't enough of it left to build a doghouse. I am in Solaris to regain a 'Mech." Rose paused to let Carstairs digest what he'd said. When the stable owner didn't immediately explode again, Rose was certain he'd be allowed to finish his speech. Heartened, he continued on.

"As you are doubtless aware, there are fewer and fewer 'Mechs available, even for seasoned veterans such as myself. My last unit offered me a staff position and placed me on a waiting list for a replacement. I was sixth in line, facing a prospective wait of twenty-four to thirty-six months. That is unacceptable.

"I attempted to purchase a 'Mech from several sources, but even that failed. With the recent Combine and Federat losses, it's a seller's market. I was finally forced to come to Solaris to acquire a 'Mech, as this seems to be the only planet within a year's travel that actually has more 'Mechs than pilots. Now I discover I cannot purchase one even here.

"The JumpShip on which I was traveling developed a fuel leak, delaying my arrival on Solaris for over a month. I came within a week of missing the entire season. Again, that is unacceptable.

"Your lance is scheduled to fight Warwick this evening in the final confrontation of the season. Jaryl, your only back-up, was killed by someone obviously working for Warwick and you are up the creek without a paddle. The damage done to O'Shea's middle ear will be fine in another eighteen hours, but for now he's got a PPC-sized headache, a persistent ringing in his ears, and the balance of a town drunk. The only reason O'Shea isn't dead is that I got to him before Warwick's hired assassin." Rose shifted in his chair as he thought about the med-patches under his shirt and the sting in his ribs.

"Now, Mister Carstairs, you have a choice. You can accept my original offer to purchase a spot on your team and participate in the upcoming conflict or you can have the lovely Miss Esmeralda toss me out." Rose leaned back in his chair and again allowed his words to sink in. He tried to shift in his chair as the owner thought over the matter. His wounds would heal eventually and he doubted the scars would amount to much, but right now it felt as though someone had taped a couple of angry hornets to his side and shoulder. Rose concentrated on his breathing, trying to will the pain away. He hadn't come even close when he noticed Carstairs shift in his chair and prepare to speak. The bear waved away the gray-blue tobacco cloud that had formed around his head and leaned forward.

"All right, Mister Rose, here's the offer. This is a one-time deal, so you can take it or blow.

"First, you buy the *Shadow Hawk* O'Shea's been riding. That way if you get toasted by one of Warwick's gunslingers, it's no skin off my nose. If you manage to make it out alive, the 'Mech, or what's left of it, is yours. Second, you forfeit all rights to salvage and your share of the purse.

"You didn't know about the salvage, did you? It's usually not much of an issue on Solaris, but tonight we got us a real treat. Warwick and I had to agree to make this last fight an actual battle. Winner take all. If we win, we, meaning I, get the titles to the four 'Mechs in Warwick's lance. If I, meaning you, lose? Well, you won't have to worry much about your new 'Mech and I've got to start looking for some new rides for my pilots." Carstairs leaned back in his chair and propped his huge feet on the desk. With a satisfied sigh he blew a series of smoke rings into the stale air.

"Third," Carstairs looked between his feet at Rose, "if you live through the night, you'll tell me about that last encounter with the Wolves. I've heard rumors and I want to hear the real story from someone who was there. I know you didn't fight with any of the regular House units and you're certainly not a merc, at least not yet. Far as I can see, that makes you ComStar or Clan and also one rare bird."

Carstairs grinned as Rose's eyes snapped up. To Rose it had always seemed elementary that others would assume he'd once been a member of the Com Guards, but everyone on Solaris seemed to think he was a spy for one of the Great Houses. Hearing the truth spoken out loud, however, was something of a surprise. Rose had given himself away, but did not answer. The smile on Carstairs' face grew even bigger.

"Now, do we have a deal?"

Jeremiah walked out to meet his new lancemates in the underground locker room. He set down the heavy suitcase and eyed them with the same caution and suspicion he saw mirrored on their faces. Not that he could blame them. They were being asked to trust their lives to a complete stranger at the apparent whim of their boss. Jeremiah was in the same situation, but of his own choice. He could imagine the anger, frustration, and fear these people must be feeling. He examined the two women and one man, all of whom had already donned their gear and cooling vests. The silence was almost a tangible creature, stalking the room with them, until the biggest of the three spoke.

"I'm Esmeralda. This is Jackson and that's Little Mary. This is my lance and these are my people, no matter what that jerk Carstairs says. O'Shea didn't have a problem with that. What about you?" Rose considered his options and, although the arrogance and antagonism in the woman's voice would have normally led to a confrontation, he knew he must ease their fears even if he could not expect their trust.

"Message received and understood, sir." Esmeralda glared at him for a moment, weighing his words for sarcasm, then reluctantly accepted his reply. Although it was obvious she did not trust Rose completely, she launched into her battle plan.

"Here's the scoop, people. The main arena is set for a nearly open confrontation. They've built a couple of one-story buildings in the center, but only a couple and the construction isn't that good."

"How do you know that?" All eyes turned to Rose as he questioned Esmeralda.

"Look, Ace, I make it my business to know what's going on when I step into that arena. If you don't, you die. If I say it's so, then it's just like you heard it from God himself. Got me?

"Do not attempt to stand on the buildings. The roofs won't hold even Mary's *Stinger,* so stay away.

"Rose, word says you're the first target. You seem to have somebody truly upset with you. The odds-makers say you'll be the first to go down."

"I know," he said dryly. "I visited one of the local

bookmakers on my way over.'' Esmeralda gave him a condescending smile.

"We'll try to cover you, but. . ." She let the words trail away to silence. It was obvious she expected little out of Rose in the match, except maybe to absorb a few of the opening shots.

"I understand." He understood all too well. The look on Jackson's face said he'd also bet against Rose.

"Okay, lock and load. Rose, I want to talk to you a minute." Little Mary and Jackson headed off toward the 'Mech bay without a second glance. Rose admired the firm command Esmeralda had over her lance.

"I'll get to the point. I don't know you and you don't know me. That means we've got a problem. Despite what O'Shea says, Warwick's goons are very good. I need to know, right now, just how good you really are. Look me in the eye and answer one question—how good are you?''

Rose leaned forward, his nose almost touching Esmeralda's.

"I'm the best there is."

"Great," she said. "So, now I've got another Kai Allard. Well, I hope that's good enough." Like her teammates before her, Esmeralda walked off toward the 'Mech bay, leaving Rose to follow in her wake.

Following her down the tunnel and then emerging into the cavernous bay, Rose smiled with true joy for the first time in weeks as he looked at his new 'Mech. He trotted across the bare floor and ran his hand across the freshly painted foot of his machine. He stepped over to the attendant scaffolding and rode the gantry elevator up to the cockpit. Opening the rear hatch he carefully set his suitcase inside and ducked through the low opening. Although the cockpit was smaller than he remembered, it felt almost like home.

Like his grandfather and his mother, Rose had learned his piloting skills at the controls of a *Shadow Hawk*. Although he'd graduated to command a larger 'Mech, the *Shadow Hawk* model had always held a special place in his heart. He tried without success to remember the face of his grandfather, dead long before Rose had left his home among the Highlanders. His inability to remember frustrated him, but he shook off the feeling and stepped inside. Home seemed so close and so far away. He wondered how Rianna was doing on Outreach and if she'd been receiving his frequent messages. Specific thoughts of his family began to fade quickly as he began preparing for combat. With an ease born from countless repetitions, he opened the battered case and withdrew the single item. Placing it gently aside, he closed the case and tied it down by the attached restraining straps. He could feel the rush of impending combat as he settled into the command chair and began to strap in.

Unlike most MechWarriors, Rose did not strip down to the bare essentials and don the bulky cooling vest designed to keep a MechWarrior's body temperature cool enough to remain conscious. Instead he wore something resembling a full flight suit, and that was half his edge. What looked like a flight suit was really a Star League-era combat suit. A marvel of engineering, even for the time, it had been handed down from warrior to warrior until it had finally come to Rose, along with the Star League neurohelmet he'd pulled out of the suitcase. The suit and helmet were priceless and Rose treated them that way, storing them in a bank vault the moment after they'd been unloaded from the DropShip his second day on Solaris. As a boy growing up with the Highlanders, he could only dream of such technology, but enlistment in the Com Guards had given him access to gear he'd never even imagined existed. Although the helmet and suit were not technically his, he had managed to keep them when he left Terra. Even with the inferior cooling system of his new 'Mech, which looked to be only fifty or sixty years old, he could run the internal temperature into ranges not even dreamed of in a standard cooling vest.

His helmet was an even greater technical marvel. It provided better transfer of his sense of balance to the giant 'Mech and operated at a much faster speed, allowing Rose to virtually dance when piloting a 'Mech. He pulled the helmet over his head and secured it to his shoulders. Now the dance was about to begin.

=== 12 ===

Solaris City, Solaris
8 August 3054

"Ladies and gentlemen, we are proud to present our feature event, a lance-on-lance battle to the finish between the warriors from Carstairs Stables and the warriors of Warwick Stables.

"Entering from the north and painted in blue and white are the warriors of Carstairs. *Stinger, Hunchback, Shadow Hawk,* and *Warhammer.*"

Jeremiah got his first view of the arena as the giant doors went up and the spotlights hit his 'Mech. Esmeralda had been right about the tiny "town" constructed in the center of the arena. Part of his mind reviewed his weapons while another part considered the tactical advantages of the small cluster of buildings.

"Entering from the south and painted in maroon and gray are the warriors of Warwick. *Javelin, Hatchetman, Centurion,* and *Charger.*"

A *Hatchetman* and a *Charger?* Warning lights began to go off in Jeremiah's head. They matched the warning lights going off on his control panel.

"Per private agreement between the stablemasters of both sides, tonight's duel will be fought without the use of ranged weapons. This contest will be decided up close and personal, the way you like it. Now, let the match begin."

Rose's blood ran cold. All MechWarriors dreaded facing the *Hatchetman*'s axe, preferring to take out the forty-five-ton brute before it could get close enough to use the hatchet. That was not an option tonight. The *Charger*'s weight and speed made it a formidable enemy in close quarters. In a match where each 'Mech used all its available resources, the *Charger*'s small lasers did not provide enough ranged firepower to be a real threat, but in this situation, those two 'Mechs changed the balance of power dramatically.

Jeremiah could hear Esmeralda cursing as the electromagnetic field dropped and he sprinted out of the gate. He tried the trigger of his long-range missile system and was met by the silence of a failed launch. Checking his tactical readout, he confirmed his suspicion that he was carrying a full load of ammunition, which meant the LRM equipment must have been disconnected in the torso. He tried to dump his ammo out the rear ejection port, but nothing happened—just as he'd expected. Those lines must have gone the way of the launch system, leaving him with no way to get rid of the explosive munitions. No doubt the other members of the team were experiencing the same problems and reaching the same conclusions.

Warwick's crew didn't seem to mind at all, so that probably meant they were in on the private agreement. The more Rose thought about the conditions of the fight, the more he worried. Esmeralda's *Warhammer* lacked lower arms, hands, and jump jets, making her little more than a slow-moving target. The rest of the lance had arms and Mary's 'Mech could jump, as could his *Shadow Hawk,* but the lance gave away a lot of tonnage, maneuverability, and raw speed, especially against the *Warhammer.* It took only a few seconds for Jeremiah and Esmeralda to realize that the fight was almost over before it began. The commlink suddenly came alive with her voice.

"Listen up. We've stepped in the guano up to our knees and that's no lie. Pick your targets and give each other some support. I'll take the *Charger,* but the best I can hope for is a draw. It'll be up to you to do the rest.''

Jeremiah felt renewed admiration for his lance commander. She knew her 'Mech was the least-suited for a slugging match and had decided to do her best before she was taken out. It was the same conclusion he had drawn, but she'd come up with it sooner. He tried to keep an eye on Esmeralda's progress as she headed toward the center of the makeshift town, but the *Hatchetman* and the *Javelin* were heading his way. Ignoring the sensor readings and data screens, he concentrated on the front view screens and prepared to make his move.

The *Hatchetman* was definitely the better warrior. As the duo moved closer, the *Hatchetman* pilot used the bulk of the *Javelin* to conceal the movement of his arms, especially the one with the hatchet. When the *Javelin* attacked, however, the *Hatchetman* was there almost immediately. The *Javelin* began to smash down on the *Shadow Hawk*'s head with both arms in an attempt to finish Rose with a single raining of blows to the cockpit. Moving laterally, Rose managed to deflect the first blow with an upraised forearm and then take the second blow on the shoulder. Metal screeched in protest and he could feel the *Shadow Hawk* lurch to the left as the second blow connected. Moving with the blow, Rose brought the *Shadow Hawk* nearly to a crouch. He could almost hear the *Javelin* pilot gloating as he imagined Rose's 'Mech downed with one attack. But if there was a shout, it was one of frustration as the *Shadow Hawk*'s left foot shot out and into the left knee of the *Javelin.*

Armored plates popped loose from the force of the blow and the frame buckled back as the joint was hyperextended. Myomer bundles tore free from the joint, showering the sand with thousands of blue-green sparks. Rose attempted to follow up the attack with a punch, but the flashing axe of the *Hatchetman* forced him to jump back. He was quick, but the axe still caught a portion of the *Shadow Hawk*'s right torso, burrowing into the metal, but failing to breach the thick armor.

A second blow from the axe went wide of the mark, but Rose was again forced away from the damaged *Javelin*. Attempting to circle the *Hatchetman* did no good as the constantly moving axe threatened to strike whenever he got close. Although wounded, the *Javelin* was providing effective protection to the *Hatchetman*'s back and being protected at the same time.

Rose was about to rush the *Hatchetman* when much-needed assistance arrived. Little Mary in her *Stinger* had managed to circle wide around the embattled pair and land near the *Javelin*. The *Stinger* was not normally much of a threat to a *Javelin*, but the pilot had barely regained control of the damaged leg when Little Mary arrived. Kicking was out of the question, however, as a continued shower of sparks marked the 'Mech's every movement. Little Mary charged just as Rose feinted with a kick toward the *Hatchetman*'s leg. The axe flashed down, but failed to strike the *Shadow Hawk*. Overbalanced by the force of the swing, the *Hatchetman*'s misstep let the nimble *Stinger* through.

Little Mary hit the wounded 'Mech at a dead run as the *Javelin* attempted to limp out of the way. Her *Stinger* crashed into the right side of the *Javelin*, whose damaged leg snapped at the knee as the pilot attempted to stay upright. The two 'Mechs went down as the smaller 'Mech lost balance and crashed on top of the one-legged *Javelin*.

Both 'Mechs lay still for a moment, then Rose moved in on the *Hatchetman* as it started toward the prone pair of 'Mechs. As the *Shadow Hawk*'s foot shot forward, however, the *Hatchetman*'s deadly axe swung in a back-handed arc toward the *Shadow Hawk*'s head. The blows struck simultaneously, but the results were dramatically different. As the kick buckled plates of steel and ceramic in the *Hatchetman*'s leg, the axe took off the top of the *Shadow Hawk*'s head. All the head armor, as well as all the communications arrays and sensor equipment, were neatly sheared away. The force of the blow sent the

Shadow Hawk staggering backward. Rose managed to stay upright for two clumsy steps before his 'Mech fell flat on its back. As the force of the impact tore through him, he felt the wound over his ribs reopen. The cockpit immediately filled with smoke and sparks as the communications system shorted out. Rose fought for the internal fire extinguisher, but repeated attempts proved useless. He was reaching for the manual fire extinguisher when he noticed the primary screen.

The *Hatchetman* was poised above him, the axe already falling. Rose managed to move just enough to take the blow on the *Shadow Hawk*'s heavily armored chest. He could feel the impact of the axe, but the smoke was so thick it was becoming impossible to see the front viewscreen. Throwing caution to the wind, he ignored the pummeling hatchet and groped for the fire extinguisher. The heavy axe fell twice more before the flames were put out and the smoke had cleared enough to see. Rose immediately wondered why he'd bothered.

His front armor had been breached, lighting up the status display like Luthien on New Year's Eve. He glanced at the main view screen and noticed that the *Hatchetman*'s axe dripped fluid where it had sunk into the insides of the *Shadow Hawk*. The axe was about to fall for the fourth time when Little Mary saved him.

Ramming the *Hatchetman* from behind she pushed the 'Mech over the prone *Shadow Hawk* and sent it sprawling face-down onto the arena floor. Rose managed to regain his feet and thanked his god that the axe had not severely damaged either the *Hawk*'s gyro or the engine.

Mary continued to press her advantage, but when she got close enough to make a second attack on the *Hatchetman,* it was already standing. She moved in for a strike, but the longer reach of the axe struck first, severing the *Stinger*'s left arm with a single fluid move, then biting into the torso. Although the *Stinger*'s kick damaged the wounded leg of the *Hatchetman,* it did not seem to have any effect on the 'Mech's movement. Little Mary went

down hard as the *Hatchetman* pulled the axe free of the torso.

Rose began to move as the *Hatchetman* neatly cut off the *Stinger*'s left leg. Blood was flowing freely down his side, but Rose blotted out the pain and concentrated on the *Hatchetman*. The *Stinger* struggled to rise, but could only flop ineffectively as the *Hatchetman* prepared to deliver the coup de gráce.

Rose, however, struck first. As the axe began its back swing, he punched into the *Hatchetman*'s damaged back. His fist drove through the delicate circuits, finally stopping when the 'Mech's gyro ground itself into a thousand pieces against the armor-plated fist. Instantly the *Hatchetman*'s joints locked up. Over-balanced by the extension of the axe, the 'Mech teetered for a moment, then tipped onto its side.

Rose scanned the remains of the battlefield, prepared to continue the fight. Esmeralda and her *Warhammer* stood on the far edge of the arena among the remains of the *Charger* she had fought. Her *Warhammer*'s remaining arm had impaled the *Charger*'s chest, evidently destroying its gyro, but the *Charger*'s repeated attacks had destroyed the *Warhammer*'s right leg. She made no effort to disentangle herself, because removing her 'Mech's PPC from the *Charger*'s chest would no doubt have sent her crippled 'Mech to the ground.

The *Hunchback* and the *Centurion* were slightly harder to find. The two had fallen into a smaller building and become entangled. The *Hunchback* had landed on top, effectively pinning the *Centurion* in the building. Until the *Hunchback* moved, the *Centurion* was trapped. He surrendered when he saw that the *Shadow Hawk* was still in the fight.

Seconds later the ring announcer began broadcasting over the arena's loudspeakers, but Rose's attention was elsewhere. He had managed to acquire a 'Mech and none of his lancemates had died in the process. He reached across his body and pulled open his flight suit to stop the flow of blood. While pressing firmly on the pad that cov-

ered the wound, he planned his future. Now he could
return to the front lines and strike back at the invaders
who had taken so much from him—a pay-back that was
going to cost the Clans dearly.

═══ 13 ═══

Solaris City, Solaris
9 August 3054

Rose walked into Carstairs' office and collapsed into the overstuffed chair facing the stablemaster's desk. In the hours since the match his wounds had become increasingly painful and now even the walk here had left him short of breath. He rubbed his side and stared at the stablemaster.

"You don't stand much on ceremony, do you, Rose?" Carstairs said. "Most people knock before they barge into a man's office."

The man seemed nervous, probably frightened about Rose's reaction to the way the two stablemasters had secretly manipulated the conditions of the 'Mech battle. But what did Rose care about any of that? He'd come to Solaris for only one reason, and at last he was going to get what he'd come for—a BattleMech.

Rose shrugged. "I thought I had a standing invitation. You did say you wanted to hear the rest of the story."

Carstairs relaxed visibly when he saw that Rose hadn't come to make a scene. "So I did, so I did," he said, perhaps a trifle too heartily. "I tell you, Rose, I always feel good after a victory, but tonight. . .tonight I feel better than I have in years. What a match!"

The stablemaster got up from his desk and walked

around behind Rose, who then heard ice dropping into glasses and the sound of splashing liquid.

"I bet Warwick is still crying his beady little eyes out over this one." Carstairs gloated, returning to view and offering Rose an unrequested tumbler. Rose took it without comment and set it on the arm of his chair.

"Swing that chair around, Rose. I want to sit over here." Rose muscled the chair toward where Carstairs had taken up residence on a matching couch.

"Have you seen the replays?" Rose smiled, but did not respond. He had not seen any of the actual tapes, but he'd heard several commentators reviewing the match. By all accounts Carstairs was a genius and his team incredible.

"I've had so many calls in the last hour I've had to disconnect the service."

"So, you're set." Rose raised the glass and took a small sip. Like every hard liquor he had ever tasted, this one burned all the way down, but instead of sitting like a lead weight in the bottom of his stomach, it seemed to seep away and leave a warm glow. Surprised, he regarded his glass.

"Good stuff, eh? I've got a connection over in the Montenegro quarter who can get me a bottle every now and then. I try to save it for important occasions, and tonight I cracked the seal when the gates went up." Rose took another drink and savored the same warming effect. He knew it was only his imagination, but the pain in his side seemed more remote.

"So, Mister Rose, what now?"

"I leave Solaris tomorrow night aboard the *Gentle Wind*, and God willing, I'll never be back." Carstairs laughed and drank deeply.

"I don't blame you, Rose. This place is not for the weak of heart."

"Weak of heart? The people here are nothing but a pack of animals. The killing, the violence, the destruction. It's all they live for."

"Right you are, Rose, but it still served your purpose,

as it does theirs. It's a necessary thing, Solaris, and I'd not live anywhere else.'' Rose shrugged and drank again. He would never understand this planet, but Carstairs was right. It had served the purpose.

"So, Rose, you were going to tell me a story."

"Yes, per our agreement." Rose thought for a moment about his deal with Carstairs. In his rush to acquire a 'Mech, the telling of a simple story seemed like a fool's bargain on Carstairs' part. It had been easy to say yes at that moment, but now that the time had come to tell the tale, Rose realized he had given in too easily to the stablemaster's wishes. It had been more than two years since he last fought as a member of the Com Guards. Since that day he'd never talked about the fighting on Tukayyid.

Rose had by now come to accept the guilt and frustration he felt whenever he remembered the events of the fateful battle on that world, yet the pain was fresh, undiminished by time. Looking over at Carstairs, Rose decided that if it was time to tell the story, it was not for the reasons the stablemaster thought. Confession was said to be good for the soul; now he would find out if that were true. Rose would tell Carstairs the whole story and see if that helped diminish the pain. He smiled and lifted his glass toward the couch.

"I do like a man who pays his debts." Rose drained his glass and held it up in silent request for another. Carstairs heaved himself from the couch and returned with two more full glasses. Rose took a sip and then settled back into the chair.

"I am, as you suspect, a former member of the Com Guards. For most of my adult life I have served as a member of that fighting corps, stationed on one planet or another in the Draconis Combine. I desired little more than to pilot my 'Mech, but that was not to be.

"After several years as a 'Mech pilot, I was sent to Terra to learn the art of command at the Sandhurst Royal Military College. Three years later I was reassigned to the Ninety-first Division, Visions of Words, stationed on Luthien as an officer adept. In Inner Sphere terms that would be equivalent to the rank of captain. I was on Luthien when the Clans first invaded the Inner Sphere.

"Despite what you may have heard, ComStar was as ignorant as everyone else about who and what the Clans were. We watched with growing frustration as the Clans drove further and further into Steiner and Kurita space. We drilled and we waited.

"Eventually the drive came to a halt, and we believed the Clans had ended the invasion, but still we trained and practiced. When the attacks began again the soldiers of my command felt almost a sense of relief. A sense of purpose. Finally the grim news arrived that the Clan armies intended to attack Luthien. Here, finally, was the test of our trials and efforts. We would help the Draconis Combine defend its capital world.

"When the invaders arrived, however, the Com Guard forces were ordered to return to our base. Although we were allowed to protect the ComStar compound, we were not to engage the Clans. I sat for more than fourteen hours in my cockpit listening to the Kuritans fighting and dying. I listened to the arrival of the Kell Hounds and Dragoons. I sat and looked out over a seemingly peaceful city as thousands died just a few kilometers away.

"At the time I was furious. I even attempted to resign my commission, but Precentor Commander Brockton would not accept it. He finally placed me under house discipline to keep me from leaving. Three days later I was on a ship heading for a planet called Tukayyid.

"It all seems so ironic now. I was like a caged animal on that voyage. I wanted combat with the Clans so bad I was ready to fight my commanders to get it. Six months later I had seen enough battle to last most men a lifetime."

Rose held up his empty glass and waited silently as Carstairs refilled the drinks once more. He had tried unsuccessfully for months to forget the killing and battles on Tukayyid. He had refused to talk with anyone about the fighting and the killing; now he was practically telling his life story to a complete stranger.

Rose sighed deeply and rubbed his slightly numb face. Was the liquor making him talkative? It seemed like a good excuse, but Rose knew he had carried the grief around long enough. Unexpectedly, one of his few happy memories of his father leapt into mind.

The two had been walking back from the 'Mech bay late one night. Rose was barely ten, but already he loved to explore and play around the repair bay. On this night his father had discovered him among the servo motors along a bay wall, nearly inconsolable over some childhood disappointment. His father had simply taken him by the hand and begun to walk home. They went all the way in complete silence until they came finally to the front door of the house. At that point Cornelius Rose turned to his son and said, "When something is too bad to bear, tell someone that it hurts. When you do that, it passes your pain to them. All that will remain is the memory of the pain." Without another word, his father had opened the door and gone inside.

Maybe Carstairs was the perfect person to tell. A stranger whom Rose would never see again. Let him live with the deaths; he didn't seem to have any problems with the idea of human misery. A tap on the shoulder jolted Rose back to the present moment. Carstairs stood above him with an outstretched glass. Taking the offered drink, Rose made his decision and resumed his story.

"From the time the Clans landed, we were in almost constant combat. We were initially stationed in the Dinju Mountains, such beautiful country that it was hard to imagine fighting in it. Every view was like a holopicture.

"The battle began on May first. The Smoke Jaguars were the first to land, and other elements of our troops engaged them almost immediately upon their landing. Besides six 'Mechs, my command included tanks and infantry support, but once we arrived on Tukayyid the non-'Mech elements were reassigned as part of Precentor Martial Focht's plans. The overall redeployment made good strategic sense, but, tactically, it left us undermanned. We were used to fighting with combined arms and that hurt us at first.

"Six hours into the fighting, five of the Jaguars broke through the initial battle line, a trio of those damn fast *Ryoken* backed by a pair of *Vultures*. We outnumbered them six to five and we had position on them, but they seemed to hold us in absolute contempt.

"Two of the *Ryoken* charged my *Shootist*, firing at extreme range. The pilots were excellent marksmen, but their large lasers didn't inflict enough damage to even breach my armor before we unloaded on them. Jenkins, in a *Thug*, and Hopper, piloting a *Crab*, added their PPCs and large lasers to my lasers. By the time the first *Ryoken* reached me, its armor was paper-thin, but still unbreached. I slammed a full clip of depleted uranium shells smack into its center torso as Jenkins and Hopper concentrated on the trailing *Ryoken*. Sparks began to fly and thick smoke began boiling out of the opening I'd created. Explosions rocked the machine as it continued its charge toward me. I was just about to fire again when the entire 'Mech disintegrated before my eyes. It was almost as though we'd severed the cords that held it together.

"I charged through the wreckage to add my firepower to that of Jenkins and Hopper. Emerging from the smoke of the *Ryoken*, I discovered Hopper had taken much of the *Ryoken*'s fire. Gouges crisscrossed his 'Mech where the Clan lasers had melted away his armor. I fired as I ran, taking the other *Ryoken* in the leg, but failing to divert its attention. Jenkins breached the armor near the right shoulder and set off a plume of blue-white smoke that usually marks the death of a heat sink, but the Clan 'Mech continued to fire exclusively at Hopper. We gutted that 'Mech and still it clawed its way toward Hopper's *Crab*. As Jenkins clubbed it to death with his 'Mech's stocky arms, the *Ryoken* fired a final time, severing the *Crab*'s left arm.

"In most fights, that would have been the end of it. Outnumbered three to six, any sane person would have turned and fled. Not these guys. The two *Vultures* had been engaging the rest of my unit with LRMs, using the remaining *Ryoken* as a spotter. Despite repeated attempts, nobody had hit the quick 'Mech, and the missile launchers were well-concealed behind a low hillock.

"I ordered Hopper to stay back while Jenkins and I flanked the two *Vultures*. As we rounded the hill, I ordered the rest of the lance to charge the *Vultures*.

"If the tactic surprised the two, they certainly didn't act like it. They each made a half-turn and put their backs together. Jenkins and I exchanged blows with one *Vulture* as Morressy, Batteil, and Tiegard took on the other and the remaining *Ryoken*. Missiles arced toward us and we returned fire. As the range decreased, the *Ryoken* added its own lasers, mostly directed at the *Thug*. It wasn't a fight, it was an endurance test. The two Clan pilots just sat in one spot and traded shots with us as we attempted to finish them.

"My heat was climbing fast and Jenkins was only able to fire his SRMs when Tiegard killed a *Vulture* pilot with a Gauss rifle shot to the head. Sometime during the fight Batteil destroyed the other *Ryoken* by setting off an ammunition explosion, but I didn't see that 'Mech fall.

"I offered the remaining two warriors a chance to surrender, but they didn't respond. Maybe they never heard me. Tiegard killed the other *Vulture* with a shot to the back. It all seemed so stupid. We had them beat and they forced us to prove it, dying in the process.

"We were still licking our wounds when we got word that another group was on the way. We limped back to our original positions and tried to support Hopper as much as possible during the next fight, and the next, and the next. Those Clanners were like some unstoppable wave crashing into the shore. By the end of that first day we had killed fifteen Clan 'Mechs, but none as heavy as the first two *Vultures*.

"Night came on, and the supply trucks brought ammunition, but we stayed in the field. Batteil and I made what repairs we could, but except for simple armor repair, most of the damage was beyond our meager ability to fix. Hopper's *Crab* looked like a one-armed target and Morressy's *Exterminator* limped badly from a severed foot actuator. I could barely believe my 'Mech had not been touched in the fighting. Tiegard said I was marked to survive the campaign, but I laughed off her comment. The next morning she gave me a letter she asked me to open only if she did not survive.

"What do you do in a situation like that? This woman had already decided she was not going to make it and most of the unit shared her feeling. From that moment on it was as though I commanded a unit of dead men who believed that I was the only one destined to live. They had given up on themselves and were channeling all their strength into ensuring *my* survival. How do you deal with that? They don't teach you how to live with a person who already knows he's dead, not even at Sandhurst.

"The next day we remained in our position and waited. Fifteen hours later we were still hiding, waiting for the Jaguars to stumble into our position. Our power down to a trickle, communications gear set to receive only, each warrior waited alone with his or her thoughts. We listened to the progress of the battle and wondered if, and when, we would receive the call, but fate is fickle. As the sun slipped behind the mountains we received word to maintain positions. The Jaguars were on the run and it looked as though they were about to abandon their position in the mountains. If the line began to collapse, we were to add pressure and make sure they didn't try to regroup. It was just past seven when we got the order to move out.

"We were directed across the valley and toward the retreating Jaguars. Soon we passed the remains of many beaten and broken 'Mechs, Com Guards and Clan alike. We had just entered the valley floor when we saw one of their huge DropShips take off at the far end. External speakers began to pick up the sound of distant conflict. As we approached, we could see other elements of the Com Guards engaging the Jaguar rear guard. My unit broke into a run and threw its weight against the Jaguar line. Almost immediately I lost sight of everyone but Tiegard.

"Despite the press of 'Mechs around me, I fought like a man alone, screaming at my enemies and firing at any Jaguar 'Mech that moved. I fought first with the autocannon, but soon exhausted the munitions. I fought like a man possessed and all the while Tiegard was next to me, matching my fury with icy calm.

"Dozens of times the Jaguar line threatened to break, and just as often one of their warriors would stop the tide. DropShips rose into the sky above us, lifting the Jaguars out of our reach. Frustrated, we threw ourselves at the remaining defenders, but they would not be broken.

"Eventually even my battle lust abated. There was Tiegard at my side, her 'Mech gouged by laser fire and missile impacts. We began to look around for the rest of the unit, eventually discovering three of the other members standing around the remains of Morressy's blackened *Exterminator*. A Clan strike had bored into the heart of the 'Mech, destroyed the engine shielding and the man above it. We stood there dumbstruck until the recall sounded and the salvage crews arrived.

"Morressy had been right. He did not survive the battle. I was numb from the shock of losing my first unit member in combat. The greatest shock, however, was delivered by Hopper. As we moved out of the mountains he remarked about my 'Mech's condition. Despite having participated in the thickest part of the fighting, it had only taken damage from two Clan attacks. Switching to Hopper's video feed, I saw that a nearly perfect 'X' had been stitched across my 'Mech's chest by the fire from twin lasers.''

14

Solaris City, Solaris
9 August 3054

Carstairs gulped for air and stood up from the couch.

"You're joking."

"I'm not."

"I've been in this business nearly all my life and I've never heard anything like that. You're joking, of course. I need another drink."

"No more for me."

Carstairs disappeared behind Rose, reappearing quickly with his glass refilled. As he returned to the couch and sat, Rose abruptly stood.

"You're not leaving me, are you?" Carstairs said. "You said I'd hear the whole story."

"No, I'm not leaving," Rose told him. "Just need to stand up."

Carstairs swung his feet around on the couch and settled back into the arm. With his drink on his chest, he motioned Rose to continue.

"Before I do, where is Esmeralda tonight?"

"What? I guess she must be over at O'Shea's place. He's bound to be depressed after missing the fight. Why do you ask?"

"No reason. Just curious."

"You were saying?"

"I was saying we pulled out of the mountains and redeployed to meet the rest of the Smoke Jaguars in the Racice Delta. For the next three and a half days I fought marsh, swamp, farmland, and river bottoms. Through it all, my 'Mech took only light damage, most of which the tech crews assigned to the unit were able to repair overnight.

"Despite some hard fighting, most of the Jaguars seemed to think the campaign was finished. They took us on at every opportunity, but not with the same intensity they'd showed in the mountains. Seven days after landing, the Smoke Jaguars left Tukayyid.

"By that time, the Nova Cats and the Diamond Sharks were gone, too, but the Wolf Clan had arrived to take their place. What remained of my unit was now transferred into action against the Wolves. There were other Clan units still on the planet, but only the Wolves and Ghost Bears were making any headway against our forces. By the time we were redeployed, the Jade Falcons were gone and we'd backed the Steel Vipers into a corner.

"Command always kept the exact figures on our losses a secret, but we knew we were getting at least as good as we were giving. Everywhere you looked, field-rigged 'Mechs were trying to hold the line. With the chances still good that we'd lose the planet to the remaining Clans, the Com Guard warriors fought like it was the Inner Sphere's last stand.

"The night of May fourteenth my unit was deployed along a ridge line that paralleled the Porozistu Mountains. The Wolves were pulling back all along the line, and we were there to make sure they didn't try to return to the city of Brzo. Storm clouds had been gathering in the mountains all day, and as night fell they moved down into the lowlands.

"Just past midnight we started picking up sensor readings. Batteil got them first in his *Black Knight*. By the time the rest of us got fixes, Batteil already had them tagged. We were in over our heads, facing twice our number. Given the enemy's technological edge, I did what any sane commander would do. . . ."

As Rose continued to tell his tale, the memories replayed themselves like battle tapes against his mind's eye. The heat, the fires, the smoke, the radio chatter, he saw and heard and felt it all. . . .

"Central, this is Station Three-Seven Bravo," Rose said. "I've got multiple inbound 'Mechs. Strength is at two Stars. We cannot hold. Request permission to withdraw to coordinates Zulu Seven-Seven."

"Hold the line, Bravo. We will advise." On Rose's control panel the tactical channel blinked to life. He made the switch.

"ETA is two minutes, Adept. If we plan to leave, now's the time."

"Hold on, Tiegard, Central is on the line."

"Three-Seven Bravo, hold your position. Reinforcements are on the way."

"Central, what is the ETA on reinforcements?" Rose's stomach lurched as he thought about another engagement. Didn't these Clanners know when to quit?

"Bravo, ETA twenty minutes. Can you hold the line?"

"That's a negative, Central. We cannot hold." Suddenly a new voice was on the line.

"Bravo, this is Precentor Luarca. You were put there to hold the line, and by the Word of Blake, you'll hold the line or die trying."

"Precentor, neither your threats nor the Word of Blake is going to matter in thirty seconds. Either we pull out now or those reinforcements will be giving us last rites."

"Then the Peace of Blake be with you, Adept. Do your duty." Abruptly the channel went dead. Rose gazed through the viewscreen and watched as the first of the Clan 'Mechs came through the trees and spotted his position. Without taking his eyes off the lead machine, Rose keyed the unit comm channel.

"All right, people, we stand and fight. Reinforcements are on the way, but we've got to hold them until we get some back-up."

"Then this is the end." Rose could hear the finality in Tiegard's voice. "Here we make our last stand."

"Damp the heat, Acolyte. Just hold them until reinforcements arrive." On Rose's tactical readout the emerging red dots were tagged and identified. Most of the Clan 'Mechs looked to be lights and mediums, but the last three out of the woods were yet to be confirmed. Rose watched as a *Fenris* continued its cautious approach. Running on minimal power, it was unlikely the enemy 'Mech even knew Rose was on the other side of the hill until his *Shootist* opened fire.

Rose started the combat with a long, steady burst from his large laser. In the darkness he would not see the shot until the first of the autocannon shells sparked against the ferro-fibrous armor of the *Fenris*. Shots danced up the *Fenris'* leg, stopping at the hip. Sparks flew from the ravaged knee, but the pilot managed to keep the 'Mech upright. Both arms swung toward Rose, but twin beams of azure electrons shot into the damaged leg from Jenkins' *Thug*. The *Fenris'* knee buckled even as it let loose all four lasers at Rose. Three lasers missed, but the final shot tore straight through the *Shootist*'s head.

Rose's control panel exploded as damaged circuits overloaded and failed. Metal and ceramics ricocheted off his helmet and tore into his flight suit. Smoke filled the cockpit and triggered the automatic fire extinguisher. Halon gas robbed all oxygen from the cockpit except in the emergency line that fed directly into the neurohelmet.

The *Shootist* staggered a half step, but did not fall. As Rose's vision cleared he saw the remains of the Clan force emerge from the woods at a run. Flanking well to the right, away from Rose, were two of the nimble *Dashers*. The *Fenris* lay dead at his feet, a victim of Jenkins' accurate shooting.

"Two *Dashers*, breaking right. Batteil, they're heading your way." Rose waited for acknowledgment, but none came. As the *Dashers* disappeared over the ridge, Rose rechecked his radio. He appeared to be sending, but nobody from his unit was responding. The Clan 'Mechs moved closer as he figured it out. One of the OmniMechs must be mounting an ECM pod, its powerful electronic jamming systems effectively blocking communications among the Com Guard 'Mechs. Rose scanned the Clan ranks for the likely carrier, punching up candidates on the computer at the same time. The computer came up with nothing, leaving Rose on his own.

"It's got to be the *Black Hawk*," Rose said aloud to no one in particular. "Good armor and good protection. It's got to be the *Black Hawk*."

The Clan 'Mechs swarmed up the hill. Normally Rose would have defended the hill, allowing the sharp rise to shield most of his 'Mech while the attackers charged into his guns. This time the situation was too dangerous to be allowed to continue because the ECM was making it impossible to communicate with his unit.

Rose fired as he ran, but only the ER laser had the range for a successful hit against the *Black Hawk*, which had just thrust its boxy left hand in his direction and fired its Gauss rifle. Nickel ferrous slugs ripped at the *Shootist*'s left arm, setting off a train of sparks from the 'Mech's elbow to shoulder. A flight of missiles passed over Rose's head as the Clan pilot misjudged the distance.

"That's all for you, ace!" Rose leaned forward in his seat, screaming at the *Black Hawk*. Despite the advances in Clan technology, Rose knew from previous experience that the *Black Hawk* could mount only a single heavy Gauss rifle. He closed the distance, half-running, half-sliding down the ridge. He fired again with his large laser, burning a gash across the *Black Hawk*'s torso. The laser's acquisition light clicked green, but Rose held off thumbing the trigger.

The *Black Hawk* stabbed his left arm at Rose and again tore into the *Shootist*'s damaged left arm. Red lights leapt to life on the control panel as his arm-mounted heat sink collapsed. Rose knew that his 'Mech's heat was beginning to rise, but didn't bother to look at the gauges. One of the *Shootist*'s main advantages was its ability to run cool.

As the 'Mech reached the bottom of the hill, Rose thumbed the autocannon. Twenty explosive shells slammed into the center of the *Black Hawk,* completely halting its forward progress. Rose pressed his advantage with another shot from the laser. The Clan pilot, staggered by the first two shots, tried to step to the right. Rose watched with a grim smile as the *Black Hawk* tried to plant its left leg on the rocks, only to have the leg slide out from underneath the 'Mech. A flight of SRMs rocketed skyward as the 'Mech crashed onto its back. As Rose rushed over to the 'Mech, a *Thor* and a *Fenris* turned his way. He fired his ER laser at the *Thor* without aiming, his concentration focused on the struggling *Black Hawk*. Laser fire answered his challenge, slicing into his 'Mech's right foot.

As Rose reached the *Black Hawk* it had just managed to regain its balance, but not its feet. The deadly Gauss rifle swung toward Rose, but he managed to move inside the pilot's aim. His right arm knocked away the Gauss rifle, sending the shells arcing over the ridge into the woods behind as his hand jammed into the *Black Hawk*'s head. Ferro-fibrous armor buckled, but did not give as the *Shootist*'s fist stopped just short of the cockpit. The *Black Hawk* struggled to get up, but Rose blocked the attempt with his left hand, which he kept pressed against the *Black Hawk*'s head. The *Fenris* and the *Thor* closed on Rose, but could not fire for fear of hitting the struggling Clan 'Mech.

Rose looked down the *Shootist*'s left arm, and with a moment's pity for the pilot trapped underneath his armored fist, fired the arm-mounted pulse laser. Red light flared briefly, then the *Black Hawk*'s struggles ceased. Sounds of battle flooded the cockpit as Rose stepped away from the dead 'Mech.

"Down, Adept!" The *Shootist* crouched behind the *Black Hawk* as Rose ducked without thought. Laser fire from the *Thor* and PPC fire from the *Fenris* flew all around him, but didn't connect. Rose crouched lower and returned the fire, concentrating on the *Fenris*.

"Jenkins, report!" The *Fenris* split to the left, arcing around Rose as the *Thor* kept him pinned down with laser fire.

"Moderate damage all-round, Adept. We've got the crown of the ridge, but that impromptu charge of yours means you're cut off. We could abandon the crest. . . ."

"Negative, Jenkins. If I keep these two busy, that leaves the last six for you. Can you handle that until help arrives?" Rose watched the screens as the *Fenris* ran along the fringe of his short-range scanner. In another minute Rose would be cut off and surrounded.

"We can if they don't try to rush us. I don't think they know there're only four of us up here because we're bunched so close together. What about you?"

"I'm slower than both of these guys and I've got less firepower. Other than that things are just about even. Rose out." He killed the comm, but left the line open. He needed to concentrate, but the *Thor* was leaving him little time for that. The *Fenris* had almost completed its looping run and would break from the trees any moment now. Unable to think of anything brilliant in the time available, Rose charged the *Thor*.

Weaving slightly as he ran, Rose closed the distance as quickly as possible. Within seconds he was within range of the large laser, so he triggered a long burst and was rewarded with a hit on the *Thor*'s right arm. The other 'Mech's large laser stopped its motion and slumped forward as his fire destroyed its housing. Rose knew he was luckier than he deserved to be, but smiled at the thought that he might live through the combat. He triggered the large laser and medium pulse lasers. Armor boiled along the *Thor*'s torso, but the 'Mech remained firmly on its feet.

Rose closed to within sixty meters of the *Thor* before the Clan 'Mech slowly brought up its left arm. In his heart Rose knew he was dead. The other warrior was so slow and deliberate with his aim that it was obvious he had something up his metal sleeve and that Rose had just run full speed into it. Veins already filled with adrenaline received another jolt as Rose's heart leaped to his throat. Gritting his teeth against the pain to come, Rose risked all and did what he hoped was the last thing the *Thor* expected.

As the *Thor*'s left arm autocannon fired, the *Shootist* dove to the ground. Explosive shells screamed over Rose's head as his 'Mech slid face-first into the rocks and dirt. The *Shootist* jumped and bounced toward the *Thor*, pushing dirt forward and digging a furrow in the ground. His armor bent and popped free as the sliding movement ground away metal and over-stressed the seams. Over his head, Rose could hear the high-pitched whine of the autocannon as the *Thor* released an impossibly long burst. Never had he heard so many shells discharged in such a short time.

Rose rolled over onto his left side and fired his large laser. At such short range the *Thor* filled his targeting screen. Not waiting to see where he hit, Rose continued the movement and brought the *Shootist* to a standing position.

The *Thor*'s shoulder-mounted missile tube opened fire for the first time as Rose fired his large laser. Autocannon shells passed missiles in flight as the two pilots tried to bring their other weapons to bear. Explosions ripped the right torso of the *Thor* as the large laser breached armor and chewed through the insides. Rose meanwhile noted more damage to the *Shootist*'s already-abused torso. Without thinking, he charged the *Thor*, keeping well away from the left arm and the weapon it carried.

As another volley of missiles tore away what armor remained on his 'Mech's torso, Rose slammed into the *Thor*, rocking forward against the restraining straps as the two 'Mechs collided. His left shoulder actuator failed as it was crushed between the two 'Mechs. He concentrated on keeping the *Shootist*'s legs moving as the *Thor* punched into his left side with its single fist. The *Shootist* shook from the impact, but Rose continued to push

against the *Thor*. A second punch tore through the barrel
of his autocannon, but Rose finally succeeded in over-
balancing the OmniMech. As the *Thor* fell it pulled out
what little remained of the laser, sending sparks into the
night and lighting their duel for all the remaining warriors to see.

From behind, the *Fenris* fired its PPC into the center
of the *Shootist*'s back. The armor disappeared under the
shot's power, but none of the energy managed to reach
the 'Mech's insides. Pushed by the force of the blast,
Rose stumbled up the ridge. Half-crawling, half-running,
he scrambled for the crest where the rest of his unit remained in position.

Reaching it, Rose was stunned by the carnage around
him. Jenkins' *Thug* had been torn apart by missile fire
and PPC blasts, and lay face down closest to Rose. Smoke
and steam poured from holes in its back, partially obscuring the fire that raged within the center torso. Rose
could feel the heat from fifty meters away.

Hopper's *Crab* remained standing next to the headless
form of Batteil's *Black Knight*. Scarred and eventually
destroyed by laser fire, the 'Mech held one of the *Dashers* in its remaining claw.

Rose crossed the hilltop and headed down the far side
of the ridge toward the sound of weapon fire. Tiegard
was evidently still alive, but her 'Mech was not trans-
mitting an IFF signal. As he ran through rocks and the
debris of fallen 'Mechs, he knew his unit had given a
good accounting of itself. For the first time since cresting
the ridge he glanced down at his control panel to get a
fix on the *Fenris* trailing him, then remembered he'd
keyed off the comm unit. He slapped down on the receive
switch and cursed himself. His unit had died without him.

"Tiegard, hang on. I'm coming!" Rose fought against
the shame that welled inside him and concentrated on
reaching Tiegard. Rounding a single large boulder, he
discovered her *Highlander* surrounded by three Clan
'Mechs. Her back to an outcropping, she prepared her
last stand. The *Highlander*'s right arm had been de-

stroyed below the shoulder. What little remained trailed sparks and fluid as the 'Mech moved. In her left arm she held the broken remains of an OmniMech's arm. Battered beyond recognition, it could have come from any of the Omnis Rose had seen destroyed on the ridge.

"I'm here, Tiegard! Hold on!" Rose continued forward as the nearest OmniMech turned to face him. The undamaged *Mad Cat* squared off against the battered *Shootist*, daring Rose to approach.

"Forget it, Adept. I'm already dead. The engine shielding is all but gone. The radiation's already killed me, my body just doesn't know it yet."

"Then we'll die together."

"No! You've got to live. You've got to live for the others, and for me." The 'Mech nearest the *Highlander*, a *Man O'War*, started forward as a *Thor* kept Rose covered. Tiegard brought the club arm over her head and waited.

"We all knew you'd be the one to live. Now do it. Don't throw your life away for ours. We're already dead." Another light on the tactical comm unit went green. The reinforcements were near, but still too far away for Rose and Tiegard. The *Mad Cat* took a cautious step forward. Rose bit back tears.

"I can't do it."

"You can, Adept sir, and you will. For us." The *Man O'War* stepped within range, but the club did not fall. Tiegard stepped away from the rocks, renewing the shower of sparks. In the light Rose could see dark fluid spilling out of a destroyed leg actuator.

"You have to live for me, for Jenkins, for Morressy, for all of us who will never leave this world alive." The *Man O'War* lunged forward and rammed a fist into the *Highlander*'s torso. The 'Mech's skeleton collapsed around the fist, trapping it inside as the engine shields failed completely. In a burst of flame that sent a column of flame ninety meters into the air, the *Highlander* and the *Man O'War* disappeared.

The concussion passed over Rose, staggering him, but

he refused to let his 'Mech fall. The *Mad Cat* stumbled forward, fighting to bring his guns into line. Across the flame-engulfed clearing, Rose could see the flattened *Thor* also on fire. It thrashed in the dirt, trying unsuccessfully to douse the flames that covered it. Rose fired on the *Mad* Cat while, behind him, the *Thor* and the *Fenris* appeared along the same trail he had taken.

Rose looked past the *Mad Cat* to the pyre that marked the passing of Tiegard and the rest of his unit. Illuminated by the blaze, he could see the approaching Com Guard reinforcements, but they were still too far away. As the *Thor* and the *Mad Cat* fired, Rose slapped the ejection button.

The *Shootist* collapsed in on itself as explosive slugs tore through the torso from the rear and PPC beams engulfed the front. The cockpit soared above the destruction of its old body, and landed at the base of the ridge well away from the Clan OmniMechs and the advancing Com Guard troops.

When the rescue team found him, Rose was already out of the cockpit and ready to go, his pistol in one hand and a stack of letters in the other.

═══ 15 ═══

Solaris City, Solaris
9 August 3054

Rose stopped pacing and turned away from Carstairs.

"So much for my story." He took a deep breath and let it out slowly, surprised at how deeply it had affected him to relive the events of that night. Having regained some of his composure, he turned back to Carstairs.

"Now that my debt to you is discharged, I'll be leaving. Fate willing, I'll never see you again, Mister Carstairs." Rose turned to the door as Carstairs swung his feet off the couch.

"You seem to be in an awful big hurry to get away, Rose." Rose looked back at the stablemaster, but kept moving toward the door.

"Suppose I were to tell you that I could get you a better 'Mech?" Rose stopped with his hand on the knob.

"Thought that might get your attention," Carstairs said, crossing the room to the bar to begin pouring yet another drink. Rose had long ago lost count of the number poured, but the bottle was nearly dry.

"Why would you do that?" Rose kept his hand on the door pull, torn between leaving and the improbable lure of acquiring another 'Mech. Carstairs chuckled.

"Despite what you think, Rose, I'm a businessman. You strike me as a person who would willingly pay my asking price for a certain 'Mech I recently acquired."

Carstairs slipped a hand into his waistband and rocked on his heels. He grinned and gazed at Rose with bloodshot eyes.

"Too good to be true. Bye, Carstairs." Rose threw open the door.

"It's the *Charger,*" the stablemaster said as Rose waved and walked through the closing door. "It's already been retrofitted." At that Rose shot his hand back into the closing gap between door and frame. He slowly pushed the door open again and looked at Carstairs.

"What's the catch?" Rose came back into the room and let the door close behind him. He knew that he was probably playing the fool. If the *Charger* really were available, it was bound to be a wreck.

"No catch. You pay me the price, it's yours. I could use the cash to buy 'Mechs and pilots better suited to my style." Carstairs crossed back to the couch and collapsed with a sigh. He swung his feet up and pointed his drink at Rose. "You don't believe I'm serious."

"You are very perceptive." Rose remained near the door, suddenly unwilling to approach Carstairs. He felt like the fabled fly at the edge of the spider's web.

"Six, in C-bills." Rose offered, slumping slightly as the tension drained from his shoulders. The man was drunk and he could not help but laugh.

"Three and your helmet," Carstairs said, and Rose stopped laughing.

"Not a prayer."

Carstairs waved his hand, flinging liquor across the room. "Then I was right. That suitcase had your neurohelmet, and a good one."

Rose turned to leave. His Star League neurohelmet was priceless and Carstairs knew it.

"Four and the flight suit." Rose stopped again.

"Three-five in D-bills and the suit."

"Three-eight in C-bills."

"Three-seven in D-bills."

"Three-eight in C-bills, my final offer."

"We finish the deal right now," Rose said.

"Done."

"I've got a call to make." Rose crossed the room with long strides and punched into Carstairs' comm unit. "Yeah, it's me, Sandler," he said. Carstairs shot Rose a quick look, but Rose had already turned away. Although the stablemaster strained to hear, Rose's muffled voice didn't carry to the couch. In less than a minute Rose hit the disconnect.

"A messenger is on the way. You'll have to let him in."

"Not a problem." Carstairs eased out of the couch and crossed to his desk, brushing Rose away as he settled into the chair.

"What about the title for commercial transport?" Rose leaned over Carstairs' shoulder as he unlocked the center drawer.

"It arrived from the arena ten minutes before you did." Carstairs pulled a tamper-proof folder from the drawer and keyed the thumbprint lock. He looked up at Rose, shielding the contents with his body. "Where's the suit?"

"I'll get it, you finish the transfer." Rose rounded the desk and headed for the door. "And don't forget my messenger. He'll probably be here before I get back." Carstairs waved him away without looking up.

Twenty minutes later Rose was back at Carstairs Stables, a duffel bag over one shoulder. As he arrived, a Voltex Cruiser pulled up next to him and the window rolled down. From his office, Carstairs could see a slim hand reach out to hand Rose a plastic envelope, which quickly disappeared inside the MechWarrior's jacket. As the unseen driver released the envelope, the car slipped into gear and disappeared into the night.

When Rose returned to the office, he had the envelope in one hand and the duffel bag in the other.

"A certified draft for three point eight million in C-bills. And one slightly used flight suit." Rose dropped the envelope on Carstair's desk and pulled out the flight suit, which he tossed onto the couch. "One title, please."

Carstairs leaned back from the desk and pushed a two-page document toward Rose.

"Your name and your thumb on the left. Mine are already on the right." Rose threw the still-bulky duffel over his shoulder and scrawled his name illegibly with the proffered pen. Tossing the pen back onto the desk, he pressed his left thumb firmly against the indicated box on the page. The paper warmed slightly, but nothing registered. If necessary, the print could be checked under ultraviolet light.

Carstairs separated the pages with deliberate slowness as Rose tried to wait patiently. He examined the second copy and handed it to Rose, who also studied it briefly.

"You don't read your contracts?"

"Only if I think it's necessary." Rose folded the title and tucked it inside his jacket. "You wouldn't cross me, you're a businessman."

"But what if I did?" Carstairs grinned as he slipped the paper into a desk drawer. "What would you do? I could have an assassin waiting just outside this door."

"In that case, Lieutenant Viets would arrive to find you trying to dispose of my body."

"Lieutenant Viets?"

"Of the Federated Commonwealth's police department in the Black Hills. She's a friend of mine."

"You're bluffing."

"And you're just speculating. You're a businessman, remember?"

Outside, an abused Hermes Rover pulled up to the curb. "I believe my ride is here," Rose said, turning toward the window as a small woman got out of the car and leaned against the open door.

"What about your new 'Mech? How are you going to get it to the spaceport?"

"I've already called the arena and informed them of the new owner. They'll be more than happy to have the 'Mech transported to the spaceport for a fee. It made room in the 'Mech bay."

"All right, Rose, you win. Just humor me. Where'd you get the money?"

"Where does anybody on this God-forsaken planet get money? I bet on the games." Rose opened the office door and paused. "I bet every C-bill I had on Jeremiah Rose to survive the match."

An hour later Rose waved goodbye to Lieutenant Viets and looked up at the ugly apartment building Badicus O'Shea called home. He was lucky Viets had recognized him as he was trying to flag down a cab and agreed to be his temporary chauffeur. Mama always said it was better to be lucky than good, he thought, and Mama was probably right. He climbed the three flights that led to O'Shea's apartment and knocked on the reinforced door. Halfway through the third knock, the door flew open, revealing the expressive face of Badicus O'Shea.

"Who's this banging on the door at all hours of the night?" O'Shea demanded. His full beard hid countless lines and wrinkles, but Rose knew they were all lines of laughter, not worry.

"My name is . . ."

"Jeremiah Rose." Esmeralda peeked around Badicus and looked Rose up and down with cold disdain.

"So you're the one?" Without waiting for an answer, Badicus grabbed Rose by the front of the jacket and pulled him inside the small apartment. With a flick of his wrist he sent Rose sailing into the couch at the far end of the room. Rose started to stand, but O'Shea did not press what Rose had initially interpreted as an attack. Instead the big man pushed the door shut, and jumped onto the other end of the couch. Rose's end rippled in reaction to the weight on the opposite side, but the creaking frame seemed immune to O'Shea's casual abuse.

"It looked like you knew your business out there today," O'Shea said, glancing back and forth between Rose and Esmeralda, who was standing behind O'Shea. Rose shrugged and raised his hands slightly.

"Of course, that axe almost got you. Too bad I wasn't

there. The blow would have missed me clean.'' Esmeralda snorted and flopped onto the only other piece of furniture in the room, a threadbare reclining chair.

''That axe would have taken your head off at the shoulders, O'Shea, and I'd be making funeral arrangements right now. I've never seen anyone react that quickly to an attack.'' Uncomfortable silence filled the room as O'Shea and Esmeralda stared at Rose.

''I wanted to return this to you.'' Rose reached into his duffel bag and pulled out a cloth-wrapped package. He reached over and handed it to O'Shea.

''I'm sorry about what I was forced to do to you, Badicus O'Shea. I let my desire override my better sense and I apologize.''

O'Shea unwrapped the package and discovered his laser pistol. ''I thought I'd lost her,'' he said, handling the Sunbeam almost lovingly, examining it minutely as if for the first time.

''It was so beautifully cared for that I knew how much it meant to you. Again, I'm sorry.'' O'Shea looked up from his pistol and back at Rose.

''Well, this doesn't exactly make up for what you did to me, Rose, but I'm glad to have her back. Essy can tell you, I'm not much good at holding a grudge.''

''That's a damn lie. He remembers everything.''

''From what I understand, you saved my life.''

''I warned you about that tramp, O'Shea, but oh no.'' Esmeralda rolled her eyes and shook her head. O'Shea did his best to look chastised, but with little success. Again the room was silent for a long moment before Esmeralda spoke.

''Tell us, Mister Rose, why are you here tonight?'' Rose saw the challenge in her eyes, just as earlier in the day. This time he was ready.

''Two reasons. First, I wanted to apologize to O'Shea and return his property. Second, I wanted to offer you a contract.'' Esmeralda's eyes flared, but she said nothing. Badicus shot a look at her, then turned to Rose.

''What do you mean, a contract?''

"In just over sixteen hours I'll be leaving this dustball, hopefully never to return. I'm heading to the Dragoons' world of Outreach to put together a mercenary unit to fight the Clans. I'm going to need a lance commander, and I wanted to offer the job to Esmeralda." O'Shea regarded Rose with an open mouth. Esmeralda remained perfectly still.

"What about my 'Mech?"

"You have your own 'Mech?" Rose was shocked. He hadn't considered the possibility.

"Whose 'Mech do you think I took into the fight this afternoon, one of Carstairs' walking tin cans? Not likely." Rose paused a moment as he ran the figures through his head.

"I'll pay for the transport of your 'Mech to Outreach. Once there transport will be part of the contract. Technically, you'll be an officer, with full rights and privileges."

"One of how many?"

"Myself, my exec, you, and one other lance commander."

"You haven't got the unit put together yet, have you?" Rose considered the easy lie, but rejected it. Esmeralda was too wary.

"Not yet. My exec is on Outreach right now getting the recruiting process started, but I haven't talked with her since arriving on Solaris."

"You must be one rich man, Jeremiah Rose. How can you afford all this?"

"In truth, I can't. If you sign on, it'll have to be for a percentage of the contract. I was down to almost nothing before the fight, but with some action on the side, I've got enough for the passage and a little left for expenses when we get there. The truth is that we'll need to sign a contract fast."

"You say I'll be an officer?"

Rose smiled, but only on the inside. So, she did have a soft spot.

"I have to know before I leave the room, yes or no," Rose said. "As it is, we'll barely have time to book pas-

sage and load the *Warhammer.*'' Silence descended yet
again as Rose and O'Shea stared at Esmeralda. Head buried in her chest, she sat thinking for long moments,
oblivious of the two men's stares.

"I'll go," she said at last, turning to look at Rose.
"I'm a fool to follow you, but I'll go."

"I'm going too." Rose looked over at Badicus in confusion.

"I'm sorry, Badicus, but. . ."

"You owe me, Rose. Essy can vouch for my abilities
and I've got cash. I'm willing to pay for a spot in the
unit if I'm in Essy's lance." Rose was still in shock.
What little he knew about O'Shea suggested that he was
good, but to take a complete unknown was risky, or stupid, or both. He looked over at Esmeralda, who nodded,
but did not speak.

Now it was Rose's turn to let the silence hang as he
considered his options. He'd always put trust in his subordinate officers in the past. Now was no time to change
his ways.

"You've got a 'Mech, too?" O'Shea's head slumped
forward.

"No."

"Good, I can't afford the transport costs." The big
man's head shot back up. Rose looked into the bright,
eager eyes and smiled. "You can pilot the *Shadow Hawk*
you've been using for the last few months." Rose clapped
his hands and stood to go. "And I guess I'll have to learn
how to pilot a rebuilt *Charger.*"

16

Harlech, Outreach
24 September 3054

Rose, Esmeralda, and Badicus finally arrived on Out-reach after spending what seemed to Rose like an eternity trapped aboard the *Gentle Wind*. Though a civilian trans-port, the DropShip boasted all the inconveniences and discomforts for which military ships were famous. Over-crowding, abysmal ventilation, poor lighting—and those were just the good qualities Rose could recall.

His companions seemed to survive the trip better, but that was because they spent most of their time in the repair bays working on their 'Mechs. Rose had tried to help out at first, but Esmeralda's skill at fine-tuning was well beyond his journeyman's ability.

They'd also tried to fix up the *Charger*, but Esmeralda had been too good at demolishing the assault 'Mech in the final duel. They'd only be able to reattach the severed right leg when they could get hold of some heavy equip-ment simply not available on the DropShip. When they landed on Outreach, it was embarrassing to see the 'Mech being off-loaded in pieces, but Rose wasn't really wor-ried. Once they got the right equipment it wouldn't be more than a few days before the 'Mech was again ready for action.

While Esmeralda and Badicus went off to oversee the off-loading of the other 'Mechs and to secure spots in the repair bay for Rose's *Charger*, Rose spotted Rianna and Angus approaching the gate with two men in tow. Rose and Rianna had communicated several times during the *Gentle Wind*'s inbound flight from the jump point, but she'd never mentioned a word about them.

The two men were obviously civilians. Everything from their style of dress to the way they moved through the crowd spoke of a lifetime sitting behind desks, safely protected by a hopefully distant military. If these were potential employers, Rose wondered if he might be entering the wrong business. Steeling himself, he put on a polite face and stepped forward.

"Jeremiah, it's good to see you again," Rianna greeted him, obviously wearing her business face too. Instead of embracing warmly, the two shook hands. Then Rose turned to Angus.

"Good afternoon, Captain," Angus said, extending his hand. Coming from him three words strung together seemed like a speech, but the young man immediately stepped to the back of the group. The MechWarrior always seemed to shy away from attention, generally hanging back whenever Rose was around. Rianna could only shrug and say that his attitude seemed to go one hundred and eighty degrees in the other direction when he was inside his 'Mech. Strapped into the *Valkyrie*, Angus was invariably at the forefront of any contest, blending speed and stealth in his tactics. If the young warrior continued to show promise, Rose hoped to assign him to the pursuit lance, maybe as the leader.

"Jeremiah, may I present Mister Wilkins and Mister Hoffbrowse? They have been most insistent about wishing to speak with you about a matter that could be mutually beneficial." Rianna gave her brother a lopsided grin that neither civilian could see. Evidently they would not be put off or else had asked to see Rose personally. In either case, Rianna obviously did not think much of the spaceport meeting.

"Sirs, I am Jeremiah Rose. Perhaps we could go someplace private to talk?" Without waiting for a reply from either of the speechless men, he began walking toward an adjacent waiting room. With one arm around Rianna's shoulders, he pulled her a few quick paces ahead of the civilians.

"What's all this?" he demanded in a whisper.

"They've been on Outreach for almost seven months and can't find a unit to hire. They're offering a one-year garrison and training contract, which no commander in his right mind will touch."

Rianna was right. Though new to the mercenary business, Rose knew that a one-year contract of that type would probably end up costing more than it paid. By the time the unit transferred to the garrison planet, served the time, then returned to Outreach, they would be severely low on funds, especially if the contract contained no incentive clauses.

"Then why are we talking to them?"

"They think the Clans might invade their planet, for one thing. And for another, the contract they offer contains some interesting terms. I thought you'd like to at least hear them out and decide for yourself."

When they reached the waiting room Rose indicated a pair of chairs for the two men. Like most civilians, they took them without thought. Rose noted that Angus had followed at a slight distance and was now standing behind the civilians. The slender young man was hardly intimidating even if the other two men had realized he was there. Yet he was in good position in the unlikely event of trouble.

"Captain Rose, if I may, I will be brief." That sounded like an excellent idea to Rose, who smiled his acquiescence.

"Mister Wilkins and I are here as duly appointed representatives of the planet Borghese." Hoffbrowse paused for a look of recognition, which Rose provided. The small planet was in the Steiner portion of the Federated Commonwealth and very close to Clan Jade Falcon's line of advance.

"For reasons that are unknown and unfathomable to

us, the Federated Commonwealth military command has decided not to garrison our planet. Because of our proximity to the Clan front, we have decided to take matters into our own hands by hiring a mercenary unit to protect our world.''

As Hoffbrowse continued speaking, Rose studied him carefully. The man still acted like a civilian, but there was something more to him than he let on.

"Mister Wilkins and I have attempted to hire a mercenary unit, approximately company size, to beef up our planetary defense force until we can persuade the Federated Commonwealth of the error of their ways. Which we anticipate will take no more than a year.

"We would like to hire your unit to undertake this contract. Standard rates. You supply your own transport to and from Borghese.''

Rose had been warned that the two were desperate, but hadn't expected such a short sales pitch. He let the silence hang for an uncomfortably long time. Mister Wilkins looked as though he was ready to explode by the time Rose finally responded.

"Gentlemen, I appreciate your gracious offer, but I must delay my decision until I can discuss it with my staff. I'm sure you understand. In the meantime, I assume that you can provide more details about Borghese to my executive officer?''

Hoffbrowse nodded and Wilkins produced a data disk from the pocket of his jacket. Rianna accepted the disk wordlessly and slipped it into her thigh pocket.

"The disk contains our Outreach address, where you can reach us at any time. Please let us know as soon as possible; we are most anxious to secure the safety of our planet.''

Rose shook hands with the two men, then remained standing there as the pair made their way out through the crowded terminal. When they'd finally disappeared from view, he turned to Rianna, gesturing her toward the main exit doors.

"Now, what's the story on those two?'' he asked.

"Well, they've approached every respectable unit on Outreach, but nobody will bite. I did a little digging on my own and learned that Borghese has very little to recommend itself to either mercenaries or the Clans. The population is small and the planet is self-sufficient, but that's about it. Their preliminary offer was pretty laughable, but even with a good round of negotiations, any unit stuck there would just barely make a profit.

"I'd have let them walk without bothering you but they're also offering unrestricted use of their facilities for repair and refit. In the event of any real combat, we'd also get all the salvage."

"How did they happen to choose us?" Rose asked as they followed Angus' lead to a small car parked across the street. Without being told, Angus slipped behind the wheel while Jeremiah and Rianna climbed into the back.

"Well, we're pretty much the bottom of the first barrel. They went first to everybody with a decent reputation, but got turned down cold. Next they hit on the new units and got a similar reception. We fall into the 'new unit looking for its first contract' class. If we say no, I imagine they'll start talking to the units with questionable reps."

"They're not too anxious to call the wolves into the fold, are they?"

"No, but they seem determined to hire a unit and they're bound to get to that point soon."

Rose looked out the window at the city scrolling by, trying to put his finger on what bothered him about Hoffbrowse. Angus was evidently heading for the repair bays to meet with Esmeralda and Badicus.

"What's our situation, besides the men from Borghese?" Rose asked, bringing his thoughts back to the present.

"We've been officially recognized by the Mercenary Review and Bonding Commission, but like most other new units, we have a C rating. That's not real good, but it can go up quickly if we do well with our first few contracts.

"Angus and I weren't allowed to start recruiting until we received recognition. That slowed things up quite a bit, but since then we've held preliminary interviews with several independents. We eliminated a few whose transcripts were questionable and a couple of others because they didn't have their own 'Mechs. We also rejected two who we thought were just plain crazy." She stopped and looked at Angus through the rearview mirror. He caught her glance, but did not speak. Rose decided to break the silence.

"Which leaves us with what?"

"Six possibles, only two of which I would say are strong contenders."

Rose shook his head and pinched the bridge of his nose as he thought about the numbers. "When do I meet them?"

Rianna brightened at that question. "Later tonight. I've set up interviews every hour starting in"—she glanced at her watch—"two hours.

"On the up side, I've gotten us a spot on the Dragoons' training field for day after tomorrow. It will give us a chance to get better acquainted. Do you think everything will be ready by then?"

Rose thought about it. "Probably. The *Charger* I got from that thief Carstairs was a pile of junk, but Esmeralda and Badicus have been working on it since we left Solaris. I knew it was a risky deal, but I took it anyway. The 'Mech's not as bad off as I'd feared, but it's not as good as I'd hoped either.

"Esmeralda's *Hammer* and the *Shadow Hawk* should be ready to go by now. I'd say two days would be just about right to finish the *Charger* and conduct a full set of tests on the other two 'Mechs."

"Good, we're scheduled to take on a unit called The Gargoyles and they've—"

"We're what? You mean we're taking on another unit on our first exercise? Whose idea was that?" Rose knew the answer when his sister glared at him.

"Mine, Captain. We had to do it to get the use of the

field. Without use of the field, we can't even try out our weapons, which makes the practice rather pointless. And by the way, you'd better strap on that laser you've had tucked away in the box. Everybody on this planet goes around wearing a sidearm.''

Rose had always heard that Harlech, the capital of Outreach, was a rough place. From what Rianna was saying, it sounded like the rumors were true. The place was nicknamed Wolf City, which suddenly struck him as an ominous name for a town.

The trio finished the ride in silence. When they reached the repair bay, Rose made a quick round of introductions, then left Angus with Esmeralda and Badicus to finish the task of unloading their 'Mechs and their gear. Esmeralda provided the kind of capable, and loud, leadership that Angus seemed accustomed to. Rose knew the three of them would have to work well into the night to get everything ready, but it couldn't be helped. Although they were not yet in the field, he had the same sense of anticipation, and the other members of the team seemed to share it.

Rianna drove him back to the hotel and served as an assistant during the six hours of interviews Rose conducted that evening. They made offers to only three candidates. The two tagged by Rianna as strong prospects said they'd like to think over their decision but eventually decided not to join the unit.

The third candidate's file contained only a question mark. Rianna smiled when Rose asked what that meant. It meant the man was borderline insane, she said, despite an excellent service record with the Third Lyran Regulars.

Rose was initially put off by the man's wild personality and refusal to answer to any other name but Hawg. The more they talked, however, he saw that Hawg was also honest, capable, and very unusual. Besides, his *Zeus* would be a welcome addition to the unit.

When the repair team arrived early the next morning, Rose briefed them on their newest member before sending them to get some rest. He continued wading through the files and records of the candidates until the sun rose the next day, when the recruiting interviews started all over again.

17

Harlech, Outreach
25 September 3054

By dusk of his second day on Outreach, Rose had still not seen much of Harlech except for the Hiring Hall and his hotel room. The groundwork Rianna and Angus had done in the previous weeks had just about played itself out. By mid-afternoon Rose realized that none of the remaining candidates who interested him were interested in return. His unit was simply too new to attract experienced pilots.

He was just leaving the hall for a belated lunch when a small, dark-haired man approached, obviously wanting to talk.

"Excuse me, but would you happen to be Captain Rose?"

Rose gave the man a polite smile. He'd seen him enter the Hiring Hall several hours earlier, but had assumed he'd left after examining the postings.

"Yes, I am. Can I help you?"

Rose was surprised by the man's reaction. Taking Rose by the arm, he beckoned him closer with a crooked finger.

"I'm a MechWarrior in need of a unit. I thought we could discuss the matter." The man looked over his shoulder. "This is not a good place. Perhaps lunch is in order? I know a quiet spot near the spaceport."

Rose's better judgment counseled against it, but he was intrigued. He gave a slight nod of the head, and the two were off.

Rose's lunch companion had his own car and insisted on driving, which was fine with Rose. The unit's rented car had already gone back with Rianna to the repair bay where she would help out with the final work on the *Charger*.

The man drove in silence, giving Rose the opportunity to look him over. He was barely over a meter and a half tall. Rianna—not to mention Hawg—would have towered over him. Despite the heavy traffic, the man seemed perfectly at ease driving through the crowded city. He glanced at Rose several times during the trip, but never spoke, which was also fine with Rose. By the time the car pulled into the parking lot of a small Mandarin Chinese restaurant, Rose would have known the man was a MechWarrior even if he hadn't been told. His movements at the controls of the car were precise and efficient, the way only a warrior could be.

Still following the man's lead, Rose passed into the restaurant, where they took a rear booth. Rose didn't like to sit with his back to the door, but he had no choice because his host slid silently into the seat facing it. He mentally shrugged and sat down opposite. Just when Rose was beginning to believe he must have imagined his companion's ability to speak, the waitress appeared and accepted his order. Lacking a menu and any knowledge of the Mandarin tongue, Rose gestured that he would have the same. At last, the man addressed him.

"You are a patient man, Captain. A most desirable trait in a leader."

Rose nodded at the compliment, but decided that if he was going to play the listening part, he would do it to the hilt.

"My name is Ajax. It is a colorful name given to me by wishful parents. I think they thought it would inspire me to become a great warrior like the ancient Terran hero. I fear I have fallen short of their lofty dream.

"As I have recently become unemployed, but not dispossessed, I came to Outreach seeking to serve a commander of both honor and ability."

"And you believe I am such a man?"

"I do, but I can see you do not understand." Ajax paused as the waitress returned to serve two bowls filled with large, flat noodles and steaming, aromatic broth. Ajax picked up his spoon as he continued.

"I've been going to the Hiring Hall for more than three weeks, and on several occasions Angus and I have talked about you and the kind of unit you plan to form. From what he's told me, I believe I would fit in well with your plans. I also believe you are a leader I could willingly follow." He paused to let Rose absorb the words.

"You must consider yourself an excellent judge of character," Rose said, to which the man nodded with a slight smile. "Be that as it may, I should probably warn you that what little Angus knows of me he has learned from my sister, the unit executive officer, and she barely knows me at all."

"Yet they both trust you."

Rose reflected briefly, then finally allowed that it was true. "You're right, but I'm still not sure why they believe as strongly as they do."

"Force of personality? Charisma? Perhaps divine favor. I cannot say, Captain. I can only say that I have seen its effects.

"You are listed as a potential company. You started with three members and have doubled in size within two days." Ajax held up a restraining hand. "I know you would dismiss this as planning on the part of your sister, your executive officer, but still it happened. You have also been approached by the Borghese delegation."

Rose choked on his soup and reached for his napkin before further embarrassing himself.

"Please, Captain, no need for alarm. I was with Angus when the Borghesians arrived to meet him yesterday for the trip to the spaceport. The civilians announced themselves before I could excuse myself."

Rose tried to catch his breath. He had assumed that the two men were probably careless in the way most civilians were, but the casual manner in which they were conducting business was almost criminal. Whatever little thought Rose had entertained about making Borghese his first employer disappeared like the steam of his soup.

Ajax waited a respectable time for Rose to compose himself, then continued. "I would like to offer my services to your company." He reached into his shoulder pocket and withdrew a memory disk. "Here is a copy of my personnel file. It is current, as of three months ago. If you have the time and are interested, I can go over the highlights now."

"Please continue." Rose set down his spoon and relaxed slightly. He wanted to concentrate on the man's story and be able to remember it when he made his decision later today.

"I was raised to fight with the Warrior House Hiritsu of the Capellan Confederation. For my entire life it was all I ever wished for. It was all I ever wanted to be.

"I was with House Hiritsu for ten years, all of them troubled. From the beginning there was no talk of honor or glory, as I had expected. There was only hate for the Federated Commonwealth and Hanse Davion. We fought engagements of all types, almost exclusively against Davion. As I fought, I watched my lancemates throw themselves at their F-C opponents with complete disregard for their lives. So many died, and in many cases, I suspect they wanted to die locked in combat.

"At twenty-eight, I was the old man of my lance. Despite new recruits, we were constantly under-strength. Eventually I could hate no more. For the sake of my spirit, I had to break from Hiritsu. Outreach was close and I managed to make it here after only minor difficulties."

Rose looked across the table at the other man and wondered what he'd been forced to do to escape his Warrior House. Rose had never seen any of the famous Capellan Warrior Houses in action, but he knew of their tradition as able MechWarriors and fierce fighters. Fanatical devotion to the celestial office of the Capellan Chancellor was expected from all members of the Warrior Houses, both on and off the battlefield. To leave Capellan space at all must have taken tremendous courage and sacrifice.

Rose regarded the man with a carefully neutral expression. Inside he had already made his decision, however. If the warrior's records could be certified, Rose would be glad to have Ajax as a member of the Black Thorns.

"We are drilling tomorrow for the first time as a unit. If accepted, can you practice with us?"

"I regret, sir, that I cannot."

Rose was surprised by the response. He had understood that Ajax had his own 'Mech, and assumed that it was here on Outreach. His eyebrows went up in silent question.

"It is my 'Mech, sir," the man said. "When I left House Hiritsu, I took it with me, although it was undoubtedly the rightful property of the House. I am no thief, sir, and was therefore obligated to inform my commanding officer of my actions."

"I see."

"Before I left No Return."

"Are you telling me that you told your commanding officer you were going to take your 'Mech and leave the planet before you actually did so?"

Ajax nodded his head solemnly.

"It's a wonder you're still alive," Rose commented dryly.

"It is no wonder, sir. My commander refused to act on the information for one day." Ajax's eyes lost their focus, as if he were seeing something very far away. "She was, like me, an old-timer. I had already jumped by the time House Master York knew.

"Now, however, I feel that I must put more distance between myself and House Hiritsu. That is why I have been somewhat secretive about my movements. It is also why I cannot disclose my 'Mech. I am sorry."

"What are you piloting, Ajax, that makes it so worthy of House Hiritsu's trouble?"

"My 'Mech is an advanced *Raven*," the warrior said, making Rose give out a low whistle. "It mounts the latest in advanced weaponry in addition to a Beagle active probe and Guardian ECM suite."

Rose rubbed his chin and considered the place such a 'Mech would have in his company.

"I'll tell you what we can do. I'll have Rianna run a standard check on your service jacket. If everything checks out, meet me back at the hotel tonight around eight and I'll introduce you to the rest of the unit. Come with us tomorrow and watch us in action. I can allow you to pass on the first exercise.

"In the meantime, however, I've got to get to the repair bay to check on my own 'Mech. Can I trouble you for a ride?"

Ajax nodded and Rose grabbed the check, just slightly faster than the smaller man. He paid in silence, then the two walked out to the car. Ajax was as silent as during the first trip, which made Rose wonder if driving reminded Ajax of piloting a 'Mech, possibly bringing out the same personality he showed in battle. Rose was still wondering when Ajax abruptly pulled up at the repair bay.

"Until tonight, Captain." Rose extended his hand across the car seat and shook Ajax's outstretched hand.

Rose watched for a moment as Ajax drove out of sight, then he crossed to the cavernous buildings of the main repair bay. Despite being dropped off right outside the main gate, it still took almost half an hour to walk to the area where his *Charger* was housed.

Crossing the bay toward his 'Mech, he could see that things were not progressing as he'd hoped. The giant machine was still supported by a large winch that rode the massive rails above the length of the service bay. Drawing closer, he could see that the final preparations for refitting the 'Mech's leg were under way, but Esmeralda was locked in a heated debate with a Dragoon technician.

Rianna was shoulder to shoulder with the big woman, but she was not speaking. By the way his sister's arms were crossed and her jaw firmly set, Rose knew that she was on the verge of exploding all over the middle-aged technician.

The three men of the unit were well back of the confrontation, apparently willing to let Ria and Esmeralda handle matters. Resting on the good foot of the *Charger* were three Dragoon technicians. Rose picked up his pace and hoped he'd be in time to prevent anything unpleasant.

"Rianna!"

Ria's head shot up, but Esmeralda didn't bother to look Rose's way. While the larger woman continued her arguing with the Dragoon technician, Rianna stepped around her and met Rose just out of earshot.

"That damn Dragoon tried to tell us how to reattach the leg," she said. "That got me fired up and then Esmeralda jumped into the middle of it." Rose wondered about the rest, but they were now too close to the Dragoon for him to ask any more questions. Esmeralda had the good sense to stop talking when Rose came up alongside her. After nodding to his unit, he turned to the Dragoon.

"From what I hear—all the way across the bay, I might add—there's a problem." Rose smiled politely, but his eyes said he was anything but friendly.

"Sir, my crew was preparing to reattach the leg when these two women demanded we stop. Now I find myself locked in a debate about the correct procedure for reattaching the severed leg." Rose admired the man's cool. Despite the verbal abuse he'd taken from Esmeralda, he hadn't lost his calm. Rose looked inquiringly at Esmeralda, who took a moment to compose herself before speaking.

"Captain, this crew was about to reattach the leg without running a stress test on the hip mount."

"Which is unnecessary," continued the technician,

"because the damage is localized to the main support shaft below the mount."

"And I'm telling you," finished Esmeralda, her voice once again rising, "that it is necessary. I should know, I was the one that severed the damn leg in the first place!"

The technician involuntarily stepped back under the force of Esmeralda's words. Rose knew he was about to order the stress test when another group of men approached.

"Some kind of trouble, Technician Bailee?"

Rose looked beyond the Dragoon tech at the approaching Dragoon captain and his attendants. Although new to Outreach, Rose recognized the distinctive markings on the man's jacket as those of the Dragoon Gamma Regiment. Esmeralda looked into the man's eyes, flashing a silent challenge.

"Just a disagreement over a minor technical issue, sir. Nothing to worry about."

Rose watched as the two Dragoons stared at one another. Although Bailee had fought head to head with Esmeralda, he was not about to let the Dragoon officer win the fight if he could not. Rose hoped the too-dapper young officer would leave, but seeing the look in Esmeralda's eyes, he knew the hope was doomed.

"Perhaps I can help." The captain stepped next to Bailee, but he was staring at Rianna, his eyes suddenly alight. It didn't take a mind reader to figure out what he was thinking.

"After all," he continued, "such beauty deserves the best Wolf's Dragoons has to offer." With oily charm he extended his hand to Rianna, but Esmeralda cut him off.

"Then why don't you be a good boy and go find him. We could use a hand from the best." Rose heard a howl behind him and did not have to turn to know that Hawg was falling over with laughter. Bailee gulped and succeeded in keeping his face neutral, but Rose saw the clenched fist that revealed how dearly the effort was costing him. Even the members of the captain's group were smiling.

"Oh, such a sharp, pointed wit."

"Oh, such a sharp, pointed head," Esmeralda said, and Rose quickly stepped between them. The two were glaring at one another, the captain with obvious hate, Esmeralda with obvious amusement.

"Captain, I don't think this is necessary. We had just reached an understanding."

"You're right about that. The Dragoons understand as well. You malcontents bring your battered jalopies here to be repaired by the best technicians in the Inner Sphere and to learn from the best warriors available." He indicated Rose's 'Mech with distaste. "Then you have the audacity to insult us." The captain shifted his attention from Rose to Esmeralda. "You're cannon fodder. Something for the Clans to destroy before they have to fight the real warriors of the Inner Sphere."

It was Ria who answered. "Oh, will that be before or after the Dragoons betray us the way they turned traitor to their own Clan kind?"

Rose heard the words, but could not believe Ria had actually spoken them. Nothing would offend a member of the Dragoons faster then questioning the unit's loyalty. Rose heard the six men at the foot of his *Charger* moving about, ready to attack or defend themselves as necessary. The captain opposite him looked like he was ready to take a swing at somebody when Bailee placed a hand on his shoulder.

"Please, sir. Not here."

The young captain shrugged off the hand and glared at Rose. "Where else is there? They wouldn't dare face us on the field."

"Dream on."

Rose interrupted the unknown speaker. "Captain, we are scheduled for the practice field tomorrow against a unit known as The Gargoyles. Perhaps you would be willing to take their place?"

The captain seemed not to hear Rose, then his eyes lit up.

"You can't be serious. You really want to fight us? We'll kill you."

"Possibly, but on the practice field we'd live to apologize." Rose stood very still, trying to keep his face as calm and neutral as possible. After several tense seconds, the captain relaxed.

"You're on. One of my lances is down for refit. I guess we'll have to do with only two."

"But . . ."

"That will be acceptable," blurted Rose, firmly stopping his sister's comment. "Until tomorrow."

The captain didn't bother to acknowledge him, but turned and stormed away, his men in close support. Bailee eased his cap back and blew out a long breath. Shaking his head, he walked over to his assembled technicians and began conducting the stress analysis on the hip mounting. Rose's unit assembled around him, Esmeralda with a big grin on her face.

"What in the hell are you smiling at?" he grumbled.

"We're going to pound that creep to smithereens, and I was just imagining the pleasure of it." She ground her thumb into the palm of her hand for emphasis.

"Wait a moment," Rose said. "We're going to fight the best the Inner Sphere has to offer with a unit that has never fought together. We're definitely outnumbered and we're probably outgunned. And, in case you forgot, this is their home field." He stopped and looked around at his team. The smiles had faded with the grim realization of what they'd gotten themselves into.

"Now that may be the reality of the situation," Rose went on, "but we're not beat yet." Cautious smiles replaced earlier grins as his people listened. "I guess we can start building the legend tomorrow. Rianna, I might have a new recruit. Take his files and have them checked. If they're legit, we're up to seven, but don't get your hopes up for tomorrow. Even if he joins the unit, he's unavailable for the practice.

"Esmeralda, I know you've got a map of the field." A predatory grin confirmed his faith in her ability. "Work with Badicus on a plan of attack. There's no sense in standing back and letting them come at us.

"Angus, you and Hawg stay here and make sure all our 'Mechs are ready to go." Rose checked his chronometer. "We'll meet back at the hotel at seven sharp to finalize our tactics."

Rianna cleared her throat. "What about you?"

"You're going to drop me off at the spaceport. As important as this exercise is tomorrow, I've got to talk to Captain McCloud about the *Bristol*. If she wants to become part of the unit, we're in good shape. If not, we'll just have to see. We need to start looking for contracts, not just recruits.

"If there's time, I'm also going to try to find out about that dandy we just insulted. Maybe I can learn what we're up against."

Rose looked once more around the group. Now that they had a plan, their confidence was back, hopefully tempered with a little realism.

"Well, don't just stand there, people. We've got a fight to win."

=== 18 ===

"This is Thorn One. Everybody on-line?"

Rose was still warming up the *Charger*, but decided to break the silence sooner than usual to give the rest of the team time to communicate. Five voices responded in the affirmative.

Running through the system in sequence, Rose was increasingly happy with his 'Mech. Though he'd not had the chance to pilot it before today, he counted on his years of experience to carry him through. Early that morning the lance had traveled as a unit along a carefully marked course from the repair bay and the spaceport storage facilities. It was the first time in more than a year that Rose had watched the sun rise from the cockpit of his 'Mech and the feeling left him somewhat nostalgic.

He had allowed Rianna to take the lead, mostly because she knew the way, but also to get a better view of the unit as they traveled. All the 'Mechs moved with grace, but Angus was by far the smoothest. Walking just to the right of Rianna, his *Valkyrie* traveled with a silky ease it took most pilots a lifetime to achieve.

Once they reached the practice field each 'Mech was swarmed by a host of Dragoon techs. The crews attached sensors, readouts, and inhibitors that would let the 'Mechs duke it out in combat without killing each other.

Although the system was expensive to operate and not nearly as good as the real thing, it was the best one Rose had ever seen outside that used by ComStar. As each 'Mech moved away from the preparation area the pilots put their machines through a series of tests to calibrate the new instruments for the Dragoons monitoring the match. Rose used the time to learn more about his 'Mech.

Despite what most civilians think, each 'Mech is unique. Except for the gross differences between individual designs, each 'Mech tended to take on a personality of its own. Indeed, part of the difficulty in becoming familiar with a new 'Mech, no matter what the design, was learning the subtle changes that were part of the system.

Like all *Chargers*, Rose's was extremely fast, especially considering the eighty-ton weight. It was also capable of jumping one hundred and fifty meters, a phenomenal distance for an assault 'Mech. Before launching those eighty tons into the air, however, Rose wanted to get to know the 'Mech a lot better. Originally built on Luthien, this particular *Charger*'s cockpit was completely annotated in Japanese. Converting that to English had been Rose's first order of business once the 'Mech left Solaris.

The *Charger*'s weapon systems were adequate, but not outstanding. The torso mounted a Shigunga long-range missile system that could fire twenty missiles in under two seconds. The missiles were guided by an Artemis IV fire-control system slaved to a targeting computer. The entire system promised excellent first-strike capability, especially in the hands of an experienced gunner like Rose.

Four medium pulse lasers scattered over the 'Mech's torso and arms backed up the LRMs. The pulse lasers could dish out a lot of punishment, but their limited range made it difficult to use them effectively. Although the *Charger* was well-armored, it was not built to slug it out with other heavy or assault 'Mechs. Its strong point was speed, not stamina.

Rose's reverie was interrupted by a squawk of static. Somewhere in the Dragoon command bunker technicians had overridden his frequency to give preliminary instructions. According to the rules of the field, it would not happen again.

"Black Thorns, this is Wolf Alpha One. You are scheduled for departure in three minutes. Our sensors show all systems green and weapons locked down. This engagement is scheduled for three hours. You have until that time to meet your objective.

"Per individual agreement, the objective of this mission is simple survival. I remind all participants that the only rule of engagement is the prohibition of physical contact between 'Mechs of opposing sides. Other than that, you have free reign to use the field as you see fit.

"Wolf Alpha One signing off. Good luck, Black Thorns."

And we're going to need it, Rose thought.

Esmeralda had learned that the most prominent terrain feature in the training area was a small town of twelve buildings located a little more than twenty-five kilometers from their starting position. That in itself was not bad news, but Rose had learned from Captain McCloud that his opponents were nicknamed the Asphalt Warriors. Unfortunately, that was all he was able to find out about the unit in the short time available.

As he and his team sat down to plan strategy early the previous evening, the odds had seemed to grow longer. By the time he told everyone to hit their racks around midnight, Rose had privately concluded that victory would be out of the question. With luck they could manage a draw.

Making last-minute adjustments to his flight suit and neurohelmet, he thought what a fool Carstairs had been to think he was getting something so dear to Rose. If Rose hadn't possessed the back-up suit, he'd never have traded away the first, no matter what the 'Mech. The suit's advanced technology was too valuable to a man in combat. Satisfied that all was ready, he opened a radio link.

"This is Thorn One. Prepare to move out.

"Ajax, are you on-line?"

"I'm here, Captain."

"Is McCloud with you?"

"I'm here, Rose." Ajax and McCloud would watch the fight from the command bunker. Sensors scattered throughout the practice field were augmented by satellites to provide a full view of the action. Although McCloud had not officially signed on, she and Ajax would be able to observe the whole engagement from a perfect vantage point. Their analyses and critiques would be valuable in debriefing the unit later on.

In an actual battle Rose would have wanted his unit in constant communication with the command center, wherever that might be. On most Com Guard missions, that would have been a forward command post or else the regimental commander. If he could persuade McCloud to join the unit, he would hope to use the Drop-Ship as a command post.

"Black Thorns, move out on my command. Execute Zero One, as we planned. Maintain radio silence until you have contact with the enemy."

Rose moved to the front of the pack and looked back at the assembled 'Mechs. Each pilot was alone in a cockpit, wrestling with his or her own emotions as the countdown continued. It was a hard feeling to explain to civilians, but his preflight state of mind was always one of extreme calm. As though he was in the center of a hurricane. Planning done, there was nothing left to do but execute and adapt. The brief time passed quietly when Ajax came on the line.

"Green signal, Captain. You are free to move." Without responding, Rose stepped forward. Rianna and Angus quickly took the lead and moved ahead of the remaining 'Mechs. When they were three hundred meters ahead of Rose, they slowed their pace and kept the same distance from the rest of the pack.

Per the plan, Rose was in the center of the remaining 'Mechs, with Hawg and Esmeralda on either side. Badicus brought up the rear, occasionally sweeping the rear quarter of the moving formation in the unlikely event that an enemy was behind them. Kilometers disappeared under the giant metal feet of the Black Thorn 'Mechs.

After ten minutes the two lead 'Mechs broke sharply to the left and began a new course designed to bypass the small town. The remaining four 'Mechs followed in their wake, but Esmeralda and Badicus changed places. Hawg was now the closest to the village and the *Shadow Hawk* covered the far flank. Thirty minutes later the unit had completely by-passed the town. Moving steadily, they approached the Dragoon staging area from the far side. While the main body stopped and Angus moved to protect the front, Rianna brought her *Phoenix Hawk* forward.

"I have six sets of tracks, moving quickly," she said. "The deep impressions look like heavies or assaults. It also looks like any of the smaller tracks got erased by the trailers. You were right, Captain. They ran straight for the town at flank speed."

"So far, so good. Let's stick to the plan and follow them in."

Rianna moved quickly to the *Valkyrie*'s side and the two 'Mechs led the unit toward the town along the Dragoons' path. This time, however, the two lighter 'Mechs kept well under the guns of the heavier 'Mechs that followed them. It took sixty minutes of slow maneuvering before the town registered on their long-range scanners. The tracks still led straight into it.

Rianna and Angus stopped and waited for the others to catch up. As Rose covered the distance, he motioned Esmeralda forward with a wave of the *Charger*'s huge hand. Despite her *Warhammer*'s lighter weight, the 'Mech packed the heaviest armament, and Rose wanted to get it into the fight as quickly as possible.

Esmeralda took the point, with the remaining Thorns

following her at a slightly staggered distance. At eight hundred meters, she broke radio silence.

"Bingo! Two targets behind Building Six." Without waiting for a reply, she broke into a run toward the distant buildings. The rest of the unit followed her at their best speeds. As they reached the three-hundred meter mark, Rose's scanner had locked on to six of the Dragoon 'Mechs. Arranged in a classic ambush position among the buildings of the town, they were—fortunately for the Thorns—also facing the wrong way.

Rose continued to close the distance and realized that the Dragoons had not even bothered to watch their backs. Screened by the buildings and with their opponents' attention in the wrong direction, the Thorns had closed to within two hundred meters before the first of the Dragoons began to move.

Rianna hit her jump jets, riding the twin columns of flame to the top of the nearest building. From the roof she had a perfect vantage point to fire at a *Crusader,* one of the two nearest Dragoon 'Mechs. The *Valkyrie* joined her on the roof as she fired both Sunbeam lasers. At pointblank range the twin lasers should have scored easy hits, but the second shot flew wide. As the target moved out of cover, Rose could see the Dragoon *Crusader* return fire, its left torso gouged with simulated laser damage. Two flights of LRMs flew to the roof as Angus also targeted the 'Mech. The LRMs exploded around Rianna's *Phoenix Hawk,* sending chunks of armor into the street below. Her 'Mech staggered, but Rianna quickly brought it under control, jumping off the roof just as the second Dragoon filled the air with charged electrons. Angus followed Rianna deeper into the town.

Rose quickly lost track of the two lighter 'Mechs and concentrated on the Dragoon *Crusader.* Still running, he triggered the Artemis and watched with satisfaction as the computer showed his missiles blasting away armor previously weakened by Rianna's laser. Esmeralda added two solid PPC hits, and the *Crusader* staggered backward. The infrared readings on the Dragoon 'Mech shot into the red as the master computers of the practice field dictated an engine hit. The Dragoon lost his balance, the *Crusader* tumbling backward, out of sight.

Esmeralda tried to press the advantage, but the second Dragoon, a shiny new *Zeus*, lumbered into view to provide cover for his fallen comrade. Joining the fray, Hawg fired his autocannon and LRMs into his Dragoon counterpart. Badicus meanwhile had jumped to the roof recently vacated by Rianna and Angus, and was firing into the side of the *Zeus*. Esmeralda had just reached the nearest building when the Dragoon reinforcements arrived.

Leading the counterthrust was an egg-shaped *Imp*, backed by an *Annihilator* and a Dragoon trademark *Archer*. Rose's heartbeat filled the cockpit as the two 100-ton 'Mechs tried to fire past the *Zeus*.

"Hawg, round the building from the side." Rose hoped Hawg was listening as he looked for cover and fired another salvo of missiles at the *Zeus*. Esmeralda did a good job of keeping the *Zeus* between her and the assault 'Mechs, but that only made them target Rose instead.

The *Annihilator* raised both arms and fired all four autocannons. The cluster munitions scattered like a shotgun upon leaving the barrel, spraying Rose with a hail of simulated shot. The *Charger*'s entire right side was shredded as the shots tore into its arm, torso, and leg. The inhibitors kicked into life and the right leg went stiff for just an instant, simulating the stopping power of the deadly volley. Rose was slammed to the left of his seat as the *Charger* stumbled around. He had almost brought the 'Mech under control when the *Imp* fired both PPCs.

Both shots hit the *Charger*'s left arm, coring through armor and scarring the skeleton below. Rose did not notice until later that the shots had destroyed the arm's medium laser. The second attack was too much and Rose lost his battle with gravity. The *Charger* took one more step, then crashed to the ground. He was sure his fight was over, but Esmeralda moved to cover him. Standing less than thirty meters away from the *Annihilator,* she traded a brief volley with the larger 'Mech as Rose regained his feet.

Though he'd managed to stand up, the *Imp* continued to fire on him as he did. Badicus was attempting to draw the assault 'Mech's fire, but the pilot ignored him. In order to keep the Dragoon 'Mechs confined to the narrow streets of the town and to restrict their fire, Rose and Esmeralda were forced to stand their ground before the *Zeus* and the two assault 'Mechs. The *Archer* fired at Badicus on the roof as the *Shadow Hawk* fired down on the damaged *Zeus.* The armor on Rose's *Charger* was practically gone when the tide of the battle shifted.

A rebel yell filled the commlink as Hawg charged down the side street and caught the Dragoons from the right, gutting the badly damaged *Zeus* with missiles and lasers. Simultaneously, Rianna and Angus landed on the opposite side of the street and began firing at the damaged *Crusader.* The *Crusader* exploded as the two lighter 'Mechs finished off the engine's shielding with a hail of pointblank laser fire. The force of the simulated blast was channeled down the street, engulfing the two attacking 'Mechs and the nearby *Imp.*

Both Thorn 'Mechs flashed from green to red, then disappeared from Rose's screen, victims of the explosion. Although they were blocked from sight by the buildings, Rose knew that the two 'Mechs had been immobilized by the practice field's myomer inhibitors. On his primary screen the *Imp* was briefly highlighted in red before returning to its normal color, minus its right arm. Rose fired his remaining weapons at the damaged 'Mech and was rewarded with computer-generated explosions in the right torso.

Ajax came in over the open channel. "Thorn One, the two missing Dragoons are approaching at high speed. Thorn Three, watch your back."

Rose risked a look at his side scanner and watched briefly as two swiftly moving 'Mechs came up behind Hawg. As the *Zeus* turned to face the new threat, the undamaged Dragoon *Archer* gave up firing at Badicus and targeted the *Zeus'* back.

"Esmeralda, get the *Archer*!" Rose staggered forward and switched his sights to the *Annihilator*. The *Warhammer* lumbered past the pivoting assault 'Mech, limping badly. Rose fired his remaining weapons at the *Annihilator*, stopping its movement. Again the arms came up to return fire, flaying the last of the *Charger*'s armor off in a shower of sparks.

Rose risked a look at the scanner to check on Hawg, but the *Zeus* was already down. Caught in the crossfire between the *Archer* and two MASC-equipped *Wolverines,* the *Zeus* had been torn apart in a single lethal volley. Badicus jumped off the roof and headed deeper into town, the twin *Wolverines* in hot pursuit. Rose did not give much for his chances, but was forced to put it out of his mind as the *Annihilator* lined up for another shot. Knowing he could not sustain another attack, he concentrated on releasing one more volley before he was tagged dead.

As Rose fired what he was sure would be his last hasty shot, Esmeralda abandoned the *Archer* and fired into the back of the *Annihilator*. As the *Annihilator*'s back exploded, Esmeralda's *Warhammer* was rocked sideways by the *Archer*'s lasers. Although the *Annihilator* was heavily armored, it was not able to withstand the full assault of the *Warhammer*. Nearly all the engine shielding was ripped away and the gyro severely damaged.

Rose and Esmeralda both knew that in a real battle she would never have been able to get close enough to inflict such damage, but since neither side was allowed to strike physical blows, she'd gotten away with it. It was a good example of breaking the spirit of the engagement by sticking to the rules. The *Annihilator* staggered forward, but quickly righted itself and turned on Esmeralda. Rose knew the *Warhammer* would be destroyed by the two Dragoon 'Mechs, but he was not prepared for what happened next.

With amazing speed, the *Annihilator* brought its left

arm around and clubbed Esmeralda in the chest. Although the inhibitors of the assault 'Mech softened the blow somewhat, the front of the *Warhammer* buckled inward. Rose screamed a curse and tried to close on the *Annihilator*, but Esmeralda was closer.

Swinging from the waist, she drove the *Warhammer*'s right PPC into the *Annihilator*'s head, lancing the cockpit amid a shower of sparks and smoke. Rose continued to run, despite the fact that he knew it was already too late to prevent retaliation. The *Charger* took two more steps before the Dragoon technicians activated the myomer inhibitors on all the remaining 'Mechs.

All the standing 'Mechs froze in place, except for the *Annihilator*. With a screech of grinding metal, it knocked away the PPC that had impaled its head. Gaining speed as it went, the 'Mech fell straight backward into an adjacent building. Unable to move, Rose watched as the building collapsed on top of the massive 'Mech, completely burying the head and shoulders in stone and mortar.

═══ 19 ═══

Rose lounged with his back against the cool marble wall and watched the rest of his unit deal with having to wait. A casual glance at his chronometer showed that they'd been "detained" in this austere room somewhere in Wolf Hall for more than two hours. Patience was beginning to wear thin on some, but the Thorns managed to avoid taking it out on each other.

He knew that they were not at fault for initiating the physical combat that had put one Dragoon in the hospital, but as time wore on he began to wonder. His unit was sitting on the Dragoon homeworld, practicing on Dragoon fields, their 'Mechs sitting in Dragoon repair bays, fighting a match with Dragoon referees. Technically, he had nothing to fear, but if the Dragoons said it was the Black Thorns' fault, who in the Inner Sphere could argue differently? It wouldn't tarnish the reputation of Wolf's Dragoons if they were bested one time by an unknown mercenary force, but it could mean all the difference to the Black Thorns. The results of the match would be posted in the Hiring Hall for all prospective employers to see. News of such a win would undoubtedly help the Thorns get the kind of contract he was seeking.

Ten minutes after the *Annihilator* had collapsed into the building, a Dragoon medevac unit had dropped in on the scene, followed closely by a security company. Several 'Mechs moved to cover the immobile Thorns, as a *Shadow Hawk* and a *Grasshopper* used their giant metal hands to free the *Annihilator* from the fallen walls.

Rose was surprised to learn that the pilot was still alive, even conscious, as a medical VTOL took him away. The security force, led by the *Grasshopper*, escorted Rose and his company back to the staging area, where their 'Mechs were powered down. Rose had wanted to communicate with the rest of his unit, but the Dragoons had imposed a broad-based jam on the Black Thorn 'Mechs, forcing each pilot to work in silence.

Once out of his 'Mech and on the ground again, Rose had motioned the team to remain quiet as Dragoon foot soldiers with laser carbines quickly surrounded them. Though most of the 'Mechs in his company had gone into battle armed, even for a practice battle like this one, they were no match for the armored Dragoons. Herded like livestock, the Thorns had been packed into the back of an armored van and driven directly to Wolf Hall. Once the van doors closed behind the last Thorn, the unit members had turned to him with a thunder of questions and outrage. Rose shut them off by slashing his finger across his throat.

He'd expected an immediate court case, formal charges or something that would allow him to defend himself, but the guards had merely deposited the Thorns here without so much as a word. Twenty minutes later McCloud and Ajax were added, and the door had closed for the final time.

At that point Rose would have accepted questions, but the other Black Thorns had descended into a gloomy silence. By unspoken agreement, they'd decided to wait out their confinement in silence, at least as long as they were being held in the Dragoons' main administrative building. Ajax had judged the mood instantly and taken a seat on a long bench opposite Rose. He had not moved since. Rachel McCloud was another story.

Rose could see the fury in her eyes as she entered the

room. Although he suspected that she was mostly angry at the Dragoons for throwing her in with the mercenaries, her single hot look at Rose said she blamed him too. She threw herself into the wooden chair nearest the door and stared a challenge at anyone who might dare to approach. The Thorns left her alone.

Rose had initially thought to keep McCloud company, but one icy look from her told him what a very poor idea that was. He didn't understand their relationship any more than before, or even if they still had one. She'd been polite to him prior to the day's events, but that was about all. He knew she was once again concerned about acquiring a cargo, but if she was going to end up sharing the blame for the attack on the Dragoons, the chances of a profitable run dropped to about zero. Rose decided that a talk with her would have to wait until they were out of their current situation.

Looking around the room, he began to take the measure of his men. Hawg had collapsed on the floor, falling asleep with his head propped on his cooling vest. Even asleep, the man's physique was impressive. Rianna had initially paced the room, but eventually she threw herself onto a bench and tried to relax. As always, Angus seemed to come to rest next to her. Esmeralda and Badicus shared the bench with Ajax, but Rose couldn't judge their mood, even after two hours. The only thing he could tell was that this kind of treatment was probably not new to them.

Rose shifted his weight and felt the leather of his holster rub his bare thigh. The laser was still in its holster, as was his boot knife. Dragoon confidence or Dragoon arrogance? he wondered. As he pondered the question, the heavy latch on the single door slid open. Seven heads came up in unison. Hawg stretched slowly and pulled himself to a sitting position, his cooling vest now resting in his lap. The man's right hand was out of sight of the door, but Rose could see it resting on his holster. While his left hand wiped sleep from his eyes, the right unfastened the holster.

As the door swung open a Dragoon security trooper

slipped into the room and stood at the side of the door. Because the guard was so lightly armed, Rose assumed he was there for show only. The second man into the room was the main event. Although small, the dark-featured Dragoon exuded a presence that more than made up for his lack of height. His eyes moved from one Thorn to another, pausing slightly as he looked at Hawg. Rose stood and turned to face him.

Walking forward, the Dragoon extended his hand. Rose considered snubbing the gesture, but reconsidered giving offense. Grace under pressure always seemed to annoy people who did not have it and earned the respect of those who did. As the two shook hands, Rose realized this man fell into the latter category. Releasing his grip, Rose scanned the other's uniform. An officer and an infantryman. In his current situation that could only mean he was . . .

"Major Brubaker, I was beginning to think the Dragoons had forgotten about us."

Brubaker cocked his head and looked up at Rose. "Hardly, Captain Rose." Rose nodded and smiled, the picture of politeness, if not ignorance. "As you may have guessed, we have been detaining you because of your unit's action on the practice field."

No apology. That was typical for a Dragoon. It was even more typical for an infantryman when addressing a MechWarrior. Rose wondered if curiosity might not be as important as he originally thought.

"I understand. I take it that we are free to go?" Rose's eyebrows popped up and he smiled as sweetly as he could.

Major Brubaker chewed his lower lip for a moment. Rose waited politely and gave the major time to speak.

"Upon further review of the holovids, we have ruled that Captain Hawkens broke the rules of engagement by striking the *Warhammer*." Rose heard a sharp intake of breath behind him and assumed that it was Esmeralda breathing again. Brubaker kept his eyes firmly on Rose, choosing to ignore the distraction. "Captain Hawkens will survive and possibly learn from the experience, although I wonder about his chances for further advancement.

"If it matters, the field supervisors have disqualified both teams." Rose was not surprised. They would look after their fellow Dragoons first, even those who broke the rules. "As the head of Contract Command, however, I have overridden their report and entered your unit as the victor in the engagement." Rose nodded his appreciation, not trusting his voice to contain his surprise. To his even greater surprise, Brubaker went on.

"Despite what you might believe about Wolf's Dragoons, we do not tolerate the kind of behavior displayed by Captain Hawkens this afternoon. He struck the *Warhammer* first, obviously aiming for the cockpit. Had his aim been better, he would be in the prison ward of the hospital charged with murder. Your retaliation does not change the fact that Captain Hawkens struck first and violated the rules. At that moment his team forfeited the contest." Rose was impressed. The Dragoons were proving that they lived by the same standards they imposed on the other mercenaries who came to Outreach.

Brubaker had not looked away from Rose once as he spoke, but his voice carried through the entire room. Brubaker knew, as did Rose, that the contest could have gone the other way just as easily and it might have been Esmeralda in the hospital, or dead. Brubaker turned sideways half a step and looked at Angus and Rianna.

"Destroying the *Crusader* with a single salvo was very impressive."

Rianna blushed and smiled slightly. "Thank you."

"I'm afraid you misunderstand. I didn't say you did something good, just flashy. Throwing yourself on an opponent's sword is rarely a sound decision."

Rose could see his sister's blush turn a deeper red. Brubaker turned back to Jeremiah. "Captain Rose, Colonel Parella is going to be very upset when he discovers what you did to one of his lances." With a nod of his head, the major left the room.

They were free to go, and so Rose followed behind, but was the third one out of the room behind McCloud. By the time a security van dropped them off at the staging area, light was beginning to fade. Rose gathered his unit together around one of the *Charger*'s enormous feet.

"Now that we're alone, we can relax. We've got a couple of hours of maintenance work to finish before we start the debriefing. Don't get your hopes up. This isn't the way we'll do it in the field, but I want to be absolutely sure we're alone. Get the 'Mechs back to the bay, then clean up and meet me in my room in three hours for dinner. Consider that an order."

Rose turned to Captain McCloud. "I know I can't order you, Captain, but I'd appreciate it if you'd join us." McCloud didn't bother with a response. For the first time in his life Rose was truly glad that looks could not kill.

Three hours later, Rose was still thinking the same thing as McCloud burst into his hotel room. The rest of the unit was scattered around the room finishing off the remains of their dinner, which had been provided by Ajax. Rose closed the door and returned to his chair.

The Black Thorns had been discussing the rapid deterioration of their current situation when the front desk announced McCloud in the lobby. Rose imagined that it was one of the benefits of command, but he had a hard time getting used to the big suite that comprised his "room." The suite consisted of a meeting room, small office, bathroom, bedroom, and kitchen. The entire unit could have stayed here, and on more than one occasion, a member had bunked on the couch after a late-night meeting. Rose had finally agreed to take the large, and expensive, lodging when Rianna pointed out that it would also serve as the Black Thorns' office. Guests staying in suites could only be bothered by visitors once they'd been cleared by the front desk. It looked like the room would not be a problem for much longer.

"Good evening, Captain," Rose said amiably, "I take it this is not a social call."

McCloud glared, and Rose dug the last piece of shrimp

out of the bottom of a paper carton. He wondered how he'd ever become close to the woman and what had happened to make her change toward him so quickly. "We were just discussing our options when you arrived. It shouldn't take long, and since I understand you are grappling with the same problems, perhaps it's good you're here. Esmeralda."

Rose grasped a half-finished bottle of dark beer and sat back to listen. Esmeralda ran her hand through her hair, forcing it temporarily out of her face. "Well, as the saying goes, we won the fight, but we lost the war. Although none of the civilians has wind of it yet, we're damn near the top of the Dragoons' shit list. The officers are barely civil and the enlisted treat us with open contempt. They might consider Hawkens to be a pain in the butt, but they sure know how to stick together. I guess their own recent troubles have taught them a lot about togetherness.

"We've been challenged by how many? Eight different Dragoon units?"

"Nine," said Badicus, "if you count the armored platoons."

"Twelve." All heads turned to Rianna, who shrugged. "There were three challenges waiting at my room this afternoon."

"In short, you've offended the Dragoons and they want to make me pay for it." Rose looked at Rachel and realized it was the first time he'd heard her speak all day. She still had a beautiful voice.

"I take it," he began cautiously, "that this treatment hasn't been confined to us?"

"The *Bristol* and her entire crew have been painted with the same broad brush." McCloud threw up her hands. "It isn't that they're doing anything you can put your finger on. Yes, some of the techs are rude, but plenty of techs are like that. Parts that were previously available can no longer be found, but that happens too. Service crews are unavailable . . . inspections take longer to complete, forms take longer to process. . . ."

". . . costs are slightly higher than estimated, etcetera, etcetera, etcetera. All right," finished Rose, "we can see that we've worn out our welcome in Harlech. We've got to turn the situation around while we still have the chance—if we wait much longer, we'll be completely out of options. Now what do we do about it?

"Rianna, what about contracts?"

"Slim and none. The only offer we've had is from the Borghese delegation. I talk with them on a daily basis, but I've managed to put them off for now. For some unknown reason, they seem to like us and have stopped looking for another unit until we make a decision. If we want it, the contract is ours."

"Anything else, even remote?"

Rianna furrowed her brow and rubbed her eyes. "Nothing. We've got an outside shot at a couple of longer-term garrison jobs, but the odds are not in our favor. There are too many beat-up units returning from the front lines and willing to accept a cushy garrison billet for us to compete with."

"Anything we can subcontract from another unit?" asked Hawg. Rose looked at the man in wonder. He hadn't thought of it himself and was surprised that the big man did.

"Nothing on the table. Some of the bigger units are offering slots to qualified units, but most of them aren't true subcontracts. Twelve months from now we'd be locked into a long-term contract with little chance of getting out." For a moment, no one spoke.

"Disband?" It was Angus who said it, but nobody looked up. Although the man had posed the single word as a question, Rose feared it was the death cry of his new unit. He decided to remain silent. Despite his contracts with the people in this room, he could not lead if they were unwilling to follow. It was better to get it out in the open now. Hawg again surprised Rose by being the first to respond.

"I said I was in and I meant it. Besides, things are just getting interesting." Standing slowly, he came to attention and threw Rose a salute. Without waiting for a response, he sat back down, grabbing one of the many paper cartons of food on the way.

"I'm not leaving unless somebody kicks me out," said Esmeralda after a brief silence. She too stood up and saluted Rose. As she was sitting down, Badicus stood up. "I've come this far and see no reason to stop now."

Ajax stood next and gave a formal Liao salute. "Though I am unbloodied as a member of the unit, it is my hope to serve as admirably as the rest." He bowed slightly from the waist and sat down.

Rianna stood up and Angus followed, each performing a classic Highlander salute. "We're family. You don't even need to ask."

Rose regained control of his breathing and tried to keep his face and manner calm. Vowing silently to be worthy of such loyalty, he stood slowly and saluted each one in turn. Finally, he looked at Rachel McCloud.

"Captain, I know that you're worried about your ship and her crew. I understand that concern, but I cannot undo what has been done, however unfair the outcome has been for you. I can promise to make the situation as bearable as possible. We need the use of a quality DropShip manned by a skilled crew. You know us, and you know me. I'll do everything in my power to make sure your ship and your crew are provided for."

While McCloud studied Rose for a moment, the rest of the Thorns watched her making up her mind. Long minutes later she rolled her head against the back of the chair and looked at Rose with shining eyes.

"God will take me for being a fool, but I accept. Every hour I spend on this planet now just brings me closer to lifting off with no cargo at all, so you're my best business. However, I must guarantee my crew's safety. You will provide the crew's protection when we reach the Clan border."

Rose smiled and his team smiled with him.

"It looks like Borghese is the only place that will have

us—and as it happens, it's the very place I want to go,''
he said heartily.

"Beats hanging around here," McCloud said, finally
returning his smile.

"Ria, get the Borghesians on the line. Tell them the
Black Thorns are on the way."

Part 2

Houston, Borghese
13 December 3054

The trip to Borghese was every bit as uneventful as Rose had feared it would be. Life on a DropShip was always boring for the soldiers being transported. The spacers in charge had all the work, and the mercenaries were expected to keep out of the way. Several times during the trip from Outreach to the jump point, an angry Captain McCloud had called Rose to the bridge, telling him to keep his people out of the way. Ground-pounders were particularly useless in the confines of the DropShip.

Eventually the spacers and the mercenaries worked out a kind of truce that gave Rose and his people more freedom aboard the ship and the spacers less to worry about. Once they'd made the first jump from Outreach the trip settled into a steady routine. Every six to eight days the *Iron Hand,* the JumpShip carrying the *Bristol,* had to stop to recharge its jump drive via its gigantic solar sails. In those periods Rose and his mercenaries would work on their 'Mechs in the cargo bay where they were stored. Space would usually have been a problem, but because the *Bristol* had been forced to leave Outreach earlier than scheduled much of her cargo hold was empty.

When the engines were fully recharged, the JumpShip captain passed the word to the DropShips it was carrying that it was time to jump to the next star. Gear would be secured and the occupants of the *Bristol*, spacer and mercenary alike, would strap themselves in for the instantaneous jump through hyperspace that would take them some thirty light years further toward their destination. Having made the jump, the spacers would go back to whatever they'd been doing and the mercenaries would return to the cargo bays.

Just as plenty of space was available in the cargo holds, it was also available in the guest cabins. Each member of the Black Thorns actually got his or her own cabin for the trip, an unheard-of luxury aboard civilian and military DropShips. The mercenaries were as giddy as cadets at this unexpected luxury.

Because there were no regular hours for day and night aboard ship, Rose allowed the mercenaries to work when and as they pleased. They held their weekly status meetings in the galley, usually just prior to a jump. At these meetings everyone was updated on the current status of the ongoing maintenance.

Rose had never met a MechWarrior who didn't work on his own 'Mech, at least to some degree. Even House troops, whose 'Mechs were owned by the House ruler who employed them, worked to make their 'Mechs as reliable and comfortable as possible. Independent units and pilots who actually owned their own machines were even more renowned for their tinkering. For pilots like Hawg, whose 'Mech had been in the family for three generations, the amount of tinkering bordered on the insane.

Because the Black Thorns were a small unit, they could not afford the luxury of hiring a full-time technician. Rose hoped eventually to field a large unit with a complete staff of support specialists, but at the moment every warrior had to oversee the care of his own 'Mech. If the task was bigger than usual or beyond the pilot's expertise, Rose assigned other members of the team to assist. Fortunately, he'd been lucky enough to hire several warriors with excellent technical experience.

Rianna undoubtedly had the most formal training, but

much of it did not apply to the kind of repairs necessary to keep a sixty-year-old 'Mech running after countless battles. Hawg, on the other hand, was a fount of information on how to by-pass damaged circuits and repair battle-damaged components. Working together, with the assistance of Esmeralda, the three kept the other four mercenaries busy for their full work cycle.

Rose insisted on working on his own 'Mech, as much to lead by example as to make sure he would know everything there was to know about the *Charger* before having to ride it into a real battle. His example seemed to have the desired effect, for when the *Iron Hand* made the final jump to Borghese, all seven 'Mechs were in excellent condition. They'd been freshly painted and re-numbered according to the system devised by Rianna, and Rose had to admit the demi-company looked very sharp. Sharp enough, he hoped, to impress the local leaders of Borghese. When the mercenaries were not working on their 'Mechs, they were studying what they laughingly referred to as their play books.

Rose had devised a series of commands based on his years with the Com Guards that would allow the unit to deploy and maneuver with a minimum of confusion and conversation. Although he had originally designed the system for a full company, it had not taken long to trim down the manual for use by the smaller unit. Rose had divided the unit into three demi-lances. The pursuit lance consisted of Angus' *Valkyrie* and Ajax's *Raven*. Rianna and Rose formed the command lance, while Esmeralda's *Warhammer*, O'Shea's *Shadow Hawk*, and Hawg's *Zeus* made up the unit's battle lance.

The team held review sessions on a regular basis, during which Rose drilled individual members of the unit on which maneuvers would be called for during a particular action. After one or two times of being embarrassed before their comrades, the unit members began to carry the manuals with them and to quiz themselves. By the end of the trip the Black Thorns were challenging Rose with situations and commands.

Although Rose spent a considerable amount of time with his 'Mech, he also spent many of his off-duty hours with either the delegation from Borghese or Rachel McCloud. Leo Wilkins proved to be good company, despite being a civilian, but Rose considered Hoffbrowse terminally boring. The two men were well-informed about various situations on Borghese and considered it their patriotic duty to make sure Rose knew as much about the planet as they did. Despite Hoffbrowse's best efforts, Rose focused only on the major topics and ignored much of the detail.

"I don't have to know every fact about the planet," Rose told the man on several occasions. "I just have to know who does." Rose did nevertheless end up finding out much more about Borghese than he'd initially intended.

He learned that salt-water oceans covered more than 80 percent of Borghese. The world had one major continent, but it was smaller than Australia where the Com Guards used to practice on Terra. With so little usable land available, the planet's initial settlers had looked to the sea to provide them with sustenance, but the sea turned them away with sudden electrical storms and crashing waves. Eventually the settlers had given up, the population leveling off at its current level. Borghese's ten million inhabitants were mainly involved in the world's only industry, mermaid harvesting.

The creatures were not actually mermaids, but the early settlers' name for the fish had stuck and become official. Because of the storms, the fishing industry was limited to the waters nearest the land, but mermaid fish were considered a delicacy on many worlds and brought a good price. Only the wealthiest could afford to buy it, though, and so the market was limited. Any fisherman who could survive ten or more years supplying the food merchants could retire quite well-off.

The major city on Borghese was Houston. Located on the southern coast, the sprawling metro area was home to more than 60 percent of the planet's population. The remaining cities were mostly small towns or, more often, simply a collection of families who happened to build near one another. The land was able to support several hybrid Terran crops, mostly strains of beans, corn, and wheat, which allowed limited livestock production.

After studying the information supplied by Hoffbrowse, Rose deduced that Borghese was still dominated by pioneers who refused to believe that there was something better than what they had. The planet was completely self-sufficient, but that was about all that could be said for it. Then again, Rose reconsidered, maybe that was saying quite a bit in the current era.

When he would finally satisfy himself that he'd worked enough for one day, Rose usually wandered into the spacers' quarters to look for McCloud. Though he would never forget the support she'd given him during their stay on Northwind, something had changed when they reconnected on Outreach. Rachel seemed like a different person. Despite their previous intimacy, she'd insisted on keeping her distance. He was sure that pulling her, and her DropShip, into the Dragoon fiasco had strained their personal relationship, possibly to the point of no return.

The long trip to Borghese, however, seemed to have smoothed away any anger she'd been harboring toward Rose, and by the end of the trip she was her old self again. At least the old self he'd first met when she'd transported him from Terra to Outreach.

As the *Bristol* cleared the JumpShip and began the nine-day trip insystem to Borghese, Rose began to scan incoming information about the planet. When the nine days were up, he believed he had a good grasp of the planet's political climate, but he didn't like what he'd learned. If the public newscasts were correct, the mercenaries were not being welcomed with open arms. Rose approached Wilkins several times on the final leg of the trip, but the civilian steadfastly refused to give him any more information about the situation.

"Now that we're back in Borghese space, I'll have to ask you to wait for an official answer from the Ruling

Council," he said. Until the *Bristol* had jumped into the Borghese system, Wilkins had been bending over backward to provide Rose everything he needed. Two hours after McCloud made the required announcement to the Borghese port officials, Wilkins was suddenly struck mute. Rose didn't even need to check with McCloud to know that the man had received a message from his bosses and been told to keep quiet. Even while the *Bristol* was descending toward the Houston spaceport, he knew something was definitely wrong.

As the *Bristol* touched the ground, Rose could see pickets outside the landing area. Most of the signs were crude banners demanding that Rose and his "mercenary killers" go home. Although the spaceport crowd was not very large, Rose knew from the broadcasts he'd monitored that others shared their viewpoint. His team hadn't even cleared the DropShip yet, and he was being called upon to make his first command decision. One that would undoubtedly set the tone for the rest of the mission.

It was customary for any 'Mech force to debark their DropShip in parade fashion, at least if they were landing at a secure spaceport. Often the arrival of a new unit would be marked with music and ceremonies that officially transferred the protection of an area from one unit to another, or from the civilians to the new unit. Even as the *Bristol* was still high over the spaceport, Rose had noted the conspicuous lack of typical review stands. He reached for the adjacent handset and dialed Wilkins' room.

"Yes?" Wilkins sounded like he was in a hurry.

Rose didn't bother to identify himself. "You said the contract we signed will be accepted by the Ruling Council, right?"

"Yes. The agreement we signed is technically binding, per the agreement with the Mercenary Bonding and Review Board, but the Ruling Council has final say in all matters that concern the safety of the planet. They will have to ratify the agreement before you are officially accepted."

Rose had asked the question at least three times before, but Wilkins had always given a half answer. Now the line was, "wait for the Ruling Council."

"That's fine. Just tell me where the Ruling Council meets."

"The Assembly Pavilion. It lies at the opposite end of Assembly Avenue. If you'd been watching as the ship landed, you'd have seen the column-lined streets. Quite impressive actually."

"Thanks." Rose hit the disconnect. He *had* seen the column-lined street and the gigantic white building at its end. The avenue led directly from the spaceport to the seat of government. God help Borghese if a surprise invasion ever hit them. They'd have a 'Mech parked on the floor of the assembly before the councilors even knew the enemy had arrived. Rose dialed Esmeralda's room.

"Saddle up the troops, Essy," he said when Esmeralda answered. "We're riding into town."

"You sure about this? Looks like we have friendly opposition."

"I want all pilots in their 'Mechs in three minutes." Rose paused before disconnecting. "Make it a drill." He grinned and grabbed his holster as he disconnected Esmeralda.

Rose hit the doorway and sprinted down the hall, buckling his holster as he went. The spacers were all on decks well above him so he threw caution to the winds and increased his pace. As the commanding officer, Rose's quarters were one deck higher than the rest of the unit, but the same distance from the 'Mech bays. At the end of the hall he slapped the door controls and ducked under the rapidly rising door. Back-slapping the down button without looking, he emerged into the 'Mech bay. Ignoring the stairs directly ahead of him, Rose grabbed the twin railings and flung his feet over the metal rails. Pushing off with his hands, he used the rails as a crude slide, and flew down to the deck below. As he hit the deck floor, the far door opened and Ajax led the rest of the unit into the room. His eyes went wide for a moment as he realized Rose had beaten him into the room.

Rose flashed a grin and ran across the room to his 'Mech. He climbed the chain ladder to the torso handgrips, then hit the ladder's rewind button. As the ladder began disappearing into the *Charger*'s lower torso, Rose continued the climb. Reaching the 'Mech's shoulder, he stopped to take a brief look around the bay. The others were also in the process of climbing up the length of their 'Mechs. Ajax would likely be the first one up, a testimony to his foot speed and the *Raven*'s shorter stature.

Rose slipped around the *Charger* and entered through the back of its head. He closed and sealed the hatch, then dropped into the command chair. Reaching to the rack above the main viewscreen, he pulled out his neurohelmet. Using both hands, he settled the helmet on his shoulders and began the ignition sequence. Electrical power flooded the 'Mech and lights filled the cockpit.

"Authorization confirmation, please." Rose loved the voice of his new 'Mech, but he would never admit it. Speech synthesizers were still not widely used, despite the added benefit they provided. Most pilots had enough to worry about coordinating the movement, firing, communications, and heat levels by sight and feel to worry about listening, and reacting, to another presence. Rose had always used one in the Com Guards, figuring he could look one place and listen another. The *Shootist*'s voice had been firm and unemotional. The *Charger* almost purred. Though the system had been disabled when Rose purchased the 'Mech, he'd just managed to re-engage it prior to the jump to Borghese, and to program the verbal warnings, which were based on a variety of hostile or threatening actions. This was the first time he'd heard the voice except during testing.

"A rose by any other name," began Rose.

"Is still a rose," finished the computer as Rose smiled. "Be wary of the rose . . ."

". . . and fear the thorns."

"Confirmation complete. Welcome aboard, Captain."

Rose hit the command channel. "Thorns, identify."

"Pursuit Two, on-line." Rose was not surprised that Ajax was the first to report in.

"Pursuit One, on-line." That Angus reported second did surprise him. The kid wasn't even winded.

"Battle One, on-line." Esmeralda was flexing the *Warhammer*'s arms, swinging the huge PPCs across the bay.

"Command Two, on-line. Requesting immediate debarkation clearance from the DropShip." Rose didn't bother to respond. As the executive officer, Rianna took care of the details like opening the doors, while Jeremiah checked the troops.

"Battle Three, on-line." That left only Badicus. Rose waited expectantly as the bay doors began to open.

"Battle Two, on-line, almost. Primary visual panel is not responding."

Rose shook his head and looked over at the immobile *Shadow Hawk*. The visual unit had failed immediately after the battle on Solaris. Rose had replaced it twice on the way to Outreach, and then Hawg had rebuilt it completely when it failed during testing on the way to Borghese.

"Switch to secondary. Confirm visual."

"Secondary confirmed. Just don't go running off. I'll have a devil of a time finding you." Badicus wasn't far from the truth. At only 60 percent of the size of the main viewscreen, the smaller screen would make it easy to miss some things. It was good to have it in a battle, but nobody wanted to have to depend on it, especially during close maneuvering.

"Doors are open. We're clear to debark."

Rose noticed that his sister's voice revealed not even a trace of excitement. She sounded very professional. Rose hoped it would last.

"Column formation, Thorns, two abreast. Pursuit, you have the honors. Command Two will follow as a single. Battle One, you have the rear with Battle Two. Try to keep him out of trouble.

"Pursuit, we're heading down the main road. Don't stop until you're standing in front of the biggest white building you've ever seen."

The *Raven* and the *Valkyrie* headed down the ramp. Though their weights were different, they made a good pair. For the entry into the city Rose wanted his column to look good as well as provide a sound military defense. Rianna moved out alone and Hawg fell in along his right side. Esmeralda and Badicus moved behind him.

As the *Charger* moved down the ramp, sunlight hit the new paint for the first time. Rianna, with Ajax's help, had settled on red and black as the unit's primary colors. Given the unit's name, Rose thought the choice appropriate as well as impressive. Each 'Mech was painted in the same colors, but each pattern was unique. When combined with the grays and silvers of the ports, the effect was memorable.

Rose followed his sister across the landing field and through the main gates. Conveyor trucks and cargo carriers moved aside as the procession moved past the terminals and toward Assembly Avenue. Ten minutes later the Black Thorns were causing a major traffic jam as cars veered to the curb to let the 'Mechs pass. The citizens of Houston had probably all seen BattleMechs before, but Rose allowed himself a moment of pride as the civilians stopped their daily routine and stood gaping. Rose stepped around and occasionally over cars as they continued on their way. At their slow pace it took thirty minutes to reach the Assembly Pavilion.

"Crescent formation. Standard defense of the building." Rose stepped forward and the Thorns took position around him. While Rose faced the building, the rest of the unit faced the other way. Rose flipped on the external speakers.

"This is Captain Jeremiah Rose of the Black Thorns mercenary unit. We have a binding contract, as certified by the Mercenary Review and Bonding Commission of Outreach, and we request immediate ratification."

Nothing happened for a few minutes, so Rose settled

back into the chair after turning up the external speakers. After fifteen minutes a barrel-chested man appeared at the top of the stairs. Seeing that the man was dressed in formal coat and vest, Rose guessed him to be one of the Council members, perhaps the chairman. Zooming his cameras in on the man's face, it was easy to see he had an air of command and that he held himself with perfect bearing. With the *Charger* at the bottom of the stone stairs and the man at the top, Rose was only slightly taller than him. When the man began to speak, he did not shout, despite the *Charger*'s size and distance. He simply looked directly at the *Charger*'s head and began talking.

"I am Council Chairman Zenos Cooke. We've been expecting you, Captain Rose. If you will be so kind as to come with me, we can begin. The Council has been in an emergency session for the past two hours." The Chairman turned to go, then stopped.

"You will, of course, have to leave your 'Mech outside." Without waiting for a reply, Zenos Cooke disappeared into the building.

=21=

With little else left to do, Rose shut down the *Charger* and followed Chairman Cooke inside. The rest of the Black Thorns remained on guard outside, linked to Rose by his personal communicator. He doubted it would be needed, but having the small device made him feel better.

The Assembly Pavilion was every bit as impressive within as it was without. The walls, floor, and ceiling were joined together with infinite care to create smooth, flowing hallways. Once inside Rose noticed a handful of guards, but these seemed to be mostly for show. They stood at attention as Rose entered, but he had either been cleared for entry or they did not challenge strangers. He shook his head as he followed the main corridor to a set of huge double doors. These people needed training even worse than he'd imagined.

At the end of the hall Rose was finally stopped by a pair of armed guards. Just as he came to a halt, however, the first guard pulled open the massive door and the second snapped to attention. Rose mumbled his thanks and went inside.

Standing at the door, Rose saw that he was at the far end of the High Council chamber, a room dominated by a semicircular table surrounded by nine chairs. The table and chairs sat on a raised platform that stood under the dome of the main room. From where Rose stood, the members gathered around the table seemed aloof from the rest of the room, but that was probably how they were supposed to appear. Several assistants scurried around the table carrying stacks of papers and memory disks to the Councilors they supported. As Rose entered the room, Zenos Cooke settled into the center chair and began reading his monitor.

Feeling slightly like Daniel in the lion's den, Rose began to move down the short aisle to the platform. The ceiling was much lower in this section of the room, making it easier to imagine the aisle as an access tunnel to the platform. On either side empty chairs faced the platform. He noticed several trivid cameras behind the mass of chairs, but they were also quiet. Evidently emergency sessions of the Council did not get broadcast to the general populace. Rose stepped past the last row of chairs and into the brightness shed by the lights of the dome. It was like stepping into another world.

Eight sets of eyes settled on Rose as he appeared under the lights. Zenos had already been watching him, picking up his movement down the aisle while the rest of the Council members went about their business. Rose climbed the flight of six steps and walked to the center of the semicircle. Conversations stopped as the men and women of the Council examined Rose. He'd spent only a short time in the cockpit of the *Charger,* but he knew he looked scruffy compared to the leaders of the Borghese government. A flight suit was rarely considered correct attire when addressing a government, especially when its members were all formally attired.

"Captain Rose, I have the privilege and honor to welcome you to Borghese." Chairman Zenos smiled and Rose was convinced the salutation was sincere, until he remembered he was dealing with a politician.

"Thank you, Mister Chairman." Rose returned the smile, but it wasn't nearly as warm.

"Captain Rose, am I to understand that you have

brought 'Mechs to the Assembly Pavilion?'' Zenos rolled his eyes and sighed. Rose turned toward the new speaker.

His first thought was *vulture*, but he was thinking of the bird and not the 'Mech of that name. The new speaker was a small man with a huge nose and wide eyes. His voice was raspy, but it carried a certain authority that Rose had always associated with nobility. The man looked to be more than eighty years old, his face a web of lines and wrinkles. Although Rose knew the names of all the Council members, he did not know their faces, or their opinions.

"That is correct." Rose kept any hint of a challenge out of his voice. Just give them the facts, he decided.

"Why?" Rose considered addressing the man, but decided to make his remarks to the entire Council. As such, he looked at Chairman Cooke when speaking.

"Several months ago agents of your government contacted me with an offer of a garrison and training contract. My mercenary unit subsequently accepted the offer and signed the proper documents on the planet Outreach." Rose paused for breath, but continued quickly when the Vulture looked about to speak.

"Per that contract, I have begun the deployment of my force. 'Mechs are of little use sitting in the belly of a DropShip. Despite the lack of official greeting at the spaceport, I decided to press on to the seat of government and introduce myself. Having done so, I need to know where my unit will be quartered." Rose tried to make his speech sound slightly indignant, but if he was successful, it didn't show on the Council members' faces. When he looked back at Cooke, the man was smiling.

"Your quarters, and the need for them, have yet to be established," the Vulture said.

Cooke rolled his eyes again. "Mister Crenshaw, you are out of line," he said. Crenshaw backed down, but Rose could tell the confrontation was far from over.

"I take it there is some question about my contract?" Rose made it sound like a query, but he knew it was a statement of fact. A somber nodding of heads confirmed his words. "Perhaps someone could explain?"

"We can explain all right." All eyes turned toward Crenshaw, who was now standing. "Cooke's boys went to Outreach without the approval of the Council. They signed a contract without authorization and that makes it illegal and non-binding. You came a hell of a long distance out of your way, son, and all for nothing."

A heavy crack resounded through the dome. Rose jerked his head toward Cooke, expecting to see some kind of gavel. Instead he discovered the Chairman pounding on the wooden table-top with his knuckles. The volume alone brought people to attention. Rose suppressed a desire to rub his own hands. Hitting anything that hard with your bare hands had to hurt.

"Mister Crenshaw, considering the gravity of the situation before us, I acted within my rights as the leader of this Council. As required, I fully informed two members of the Council of my decision and filed the necessary papers with the Council Secretary.

"Madame Hillerman, were all papers duly recorded and accurately entered?" Cooke never took his eyes off Crenshaw.

"They were, Mister Chairman."

"Then you, Mister Crenshaw, have *nothing* to complain about." Except that you were flanked and busted, Rose added mentally.

Crenshaw appeared about to reply, but stopped. He nodded at Cooke and glared then sat down without another word.

"Mister Chairman, I agree that you had every right to authorize the dispatching of a delegation to Outreach, but now that the contract has been tendered, we must vote on ratification."

The new challenger to Cooke spoke calmly. Rose looked at the young woman, who was apparently the junior member of the Council. Rose guessed her age in the mid-thirties, fully ten to thirty years behind the rest of the Council members. She looked at Rose, but he could tell nothing about her opinion of the discussion going on around her.

"That's right, Cooke. If the majority votes this down, we send this boy home and take care of things ourselves."

Rose was really starting to hate being called boy. He started to say something, but the young woman interrupted.

"We've been over this for the last two, almost three hours. We know the Clans are a problem, but they do not threaten us."

"Yet," interrupted Cooke.

"The front lines are heavily fortified," she continued, giving no indication that she'd heard Cooke's rebuttal. "Even though the Federated Commonwealth has decided not to garrison Borghese as we had hoped they would, what good is a partial company if the Clans decide to attack?"

Rose watched the two argue. Cooke was getting angry, and emotion charged his every word. Thus far, his challenger had managed to keep her calm, but Rose could tell that was slipping away. The remainder of the Council seemed ready to let the two of them argue it out.

"They can make one hell of a difference. Without them the Federats will have to retake the planet. With some kind of organized defense, the defense Rose and his men will establish, we can provide some safe landing zones. Without them, the Clans would overrun the planet, and that's if there's an invasion. What about a serious raid? The militia can't hope to compete with those Omni-Mechs."

"All of that only matters if the Clans attack, which they won't, because we're below the line defined by the Treaty of Tukayyid."

"We're above the line and open to attack."

"You're *on* the line and you don't want the Clans to decide if you're fair game." All heads looked past Rose as someone walked down the aisle Rose had just traversed. Rose turned partially, watching the newcomer, but keeping the Chairman in his peripheral vision. The disembodied voice continued as the speaker slowly entered the light.

"If you're invaded, you don't have a chance. All due respect to the man standing before you. If you get raided, well, that's a different story." Rose watched as a pair of boots stepped into the light. "If the Clans decide to raid Borghese, this man and his troops could make all the difference." Light crept up the man's trouser legs. F-C regulation boots and britches, thought Rose.

"So," continued the voice, "I ask you again. Do you really want to take the chance? I don't know this man, or his price, but I know you'll need him if the Clans mount a serious raid." The man stepped fully into the light. "And believe me, the Clans are always serious."

Rose turned all the way around to stare at the speaker. More than two meters tall, he was broad-shouldered and slim-hipped. Although dressed in Federated Commonwealth MechWarrior fatigues, he carried himself like a man with general's stars. His thick brown hair and full beard were neatly trimmed, but gave him a wild air that only increased his appeal. Like Rose, he wore a laser pistol, but his was strapped to the right thigh.

"Salander Morgain, I did not know you were in the city." Rose did not like the respect he heard in Cooke's voice, or the way Morgain suddenly calmed the Council.

"Mister Chairman, I apologize for the dramatic entrance. I was unavoidably delayed." Rose hoped his men had something to do with it.

"Hauptmann . . ."

"Please, Mister Chairman, I am just a civilian now." Rose's mind went into high gear. A recently retired MechWarrior who was still in the prime of life. He didn't look disabled, but what other explanation could there be for early retirement of one who seemed to command so much respect?

"Mister Morgain, if you insist. We asked you to come before the Council to give testimony on the Clans. We

are all aware of your record against the Steel Vipers and Jade Falcons.''

Morgain ascended the steps and stood beside Rose. He nodded politely and turned to face the Council. Rose followed suit.

''We've been debating the wisdom of ratifying the contract of the man you see before you, Captain Jeremiah Rose, commander of the mercenary Black Thorns.'' Morgain extended his hand and flashed a warm smile. Rose returned the firm handshake, but could not bring himself to return the smile. ''We had hoped to hear your testimony before the arrival of Captain Rose, but now that you are both here . . .'' Cooke spread his hands and shrugged.

''Mister Chairman, were the Captain not here, I would say the same thing. We must fight the Clans with everything at our disposal.

''I know that I've been away from Borghese for a long time, and I feared people would forget me and the work my father and I started here. You can imagine my surprise, and joy, when I returned and discovered it was not so.

''When Father was on the Council he always stressed self-reliance and preparedness. Mister Crenshaw, you sat on the Council that ratified many of his ideas. Borghese must be prepared to defend itself against those who would steal the precious resources that are vital to us all.''

Rose saw several nods of approval. Who was this guy? And who was his father, other than an ex-Council member?

''So you would fight them?'' It was the young woman who spoke, but she appeared to already know the answer.

''Miss de Vilbis, although I am no longer in the military, I would fight them with my bare hands if that was all I had.'' Salander paused, and Rose thought he caught a wisp of a smile. ''Of course,'' he continued, ''I'd start the fight in the *Marauder*.'' The Council members laughed and Rose knew they'd made their decision.

''I returned to Borghese to find rest and recuperation

from what I suffered at the hands of the Clan invaders, but I would not, I could not, stand by and let them destroy the fairest planet in the Inner Sphere.''

Rose stared at the Council members, but watched Morgain out of the corner of his eye. The speech was slick and very well received. Rose hoped the man was just a gifted speaker. There was something about him that he didn't like, but just what it was eluded him. Jealousy? Rose had always believed he was above such an emotion.

"Mister Chairman, I call the vote. Do we ratify the contract previously accepted by Captain Rose, as presented by Mister Wilkins?'' Rose watched Miss de Vilbis. She had obviously been swayed by Morgain's impassioned speech.

"The vote has been called. All those in favor of the motion to accept the contract with Captain Rose indicate by saying aye.'' Murmured ayes filled the room. "All those opposed, same sign.'' Silence. "Motion carries.'' Chairman Cooke smiled and the rest of the Council members seemed to relax.

"Welcome to Borghese, Mister Rose. Let me show you to your quarters.''

≡≡ 22 ≡≡

Houston, Borghese
14 December 3054

Rose spent the next day moving his team and what little gear they possessed into their new quarters. New, as in previously unoccupied. The brick buildings that made up the little compound were sturdy but unattractive. In addition to the barracks, which housed twelve in a single common room and two officers in separate bedrooms, there was a mess hall, supply building, command post, and—the crowning achievement—six 'Mech repair/storage bays. Chairman Cooke indicated that the remaining six bays would be constructed soon, but Rose didn't mind. The compound was perfect.

Enclosed by a wire fence, the mercenary quarters were somewhat insulated from the civilians who picketed their base on a regular basis, but not so cut off they felt isolated. They also had a small staff of locals to handle the mundane chores of cooking, cleaning, and general maintenance, plus a handful of militia soldiers to man the gate and command post. Rose knew better than to trust the guards without some proof of their political loyalties, but their services did make getting in and out of the compound much easier. Although making the mercenaries feel welcome was not part of the contract, Rose realized that somebody was trying to do it even if other factions were opposed.

After creating a duty roster and settling in, Rose requested a meeting with Chairman Cooke. To his surprise, the Chairman offered to pick him up later that same day so the two could talk. In his previous dealings with planetary officials, Rose had rarely found them civil, let alone polite and eager to help. When the Chairman's official car pulled through the main gate, Rose left Rianna in charge and went out to greet it. Again he was surprised when Chairman Cooke stepped out of the luxury car.

"Mister Chairman, what a surprise. I didn't think you'd be coming here personally."

Cooke flashed a big grin and stretched, bringing his hand down to grasp Rose's in the same motion. "Oh, I like to get away from the office every now and then. Nice day, isn't it."

Rose could readily agree that it was a beautiful day. It was the middle of spring in Houston and the weather was mild. A slight breeze blew in from the ocean, tanging the air with salt. Rose knew that spring was only a brief season on Borghese. Soon the heat and humidity of summer would sap the inhabitants of their strength as the mercury rose and the barometer fell.

"Do you like the facilities?" Cooke asked, gesturing in a sweeping motion that took in the whole compound.

"Very much. Was this your idea?" Cooke nodded and studied the repair bay where Esmeralda and O'Shea were working on the *Shadow Hawk*'s primary display unit. "And the auxiliary personnel?"

"Hand-picked by my chief of staff. They're loyal, but don't count on them to stop a concerted attack, no matter what the source. I thought they might prove helpful, without getting in the way."

Rose nodded. "Thanks. So far they've done a good job." Rose and Cooke continued to stare at the repair bay as the conversation stopped. Abruptly Cooke slapped his thigh.

"Have you had lunch yet?"

Thinking about it a moment, Rose suddenly realized he hadn't eaten since last night. Being the commanding officer of a unit, even a small one like the Black Thorns, was time-consuming work. He shook his head.

"Good. Let's head downtown. It will give us some time to talk." Cooke opened the back door of his limo and climbed inside. Rose followed and the vehicle eased out of the compound and headed downtown. As the driver maneuvered the car between the surrounding high-rise buildings, Cooke asked, "Getting situated?"

Rose nodded. "Things are coming along very nicely. The compound is in a perfect location. It's close to the Assembly Pavilion and the spaceport, but not in a direct line between the two. I'd have chosen a similar location if it had been up to me."

Cooke chuckled. "I'll take that as a compliment. I hope you're almost ready to begin active duty."

Rose paused before speaking. There was a certain urgency in Cooke's voice and he wanted to be sure he knew the reason before answering.

"Is something going on that requires our immediate attention?"

Cooke smiled and looked out the window. "Nothing out of the ordinary. Some of the Council members want you to start producing from day one. They're stoking the media fires, and anything you can do to offset that would be a big help to your own situation."

"As well as your own?" finished Rose.

Cooke's smile split wide open. "You sure you're not in politics?" Rose shook his head. "Well, you've got it right. Crenshaw and his cronies are after my job and this is just another way to make me look bad. Bad, that is, if you don't produce some type of miracle."

"Like a Clan attack?"

"Like something to justify your fee." Cooke shifted in the seat and stared directly at Rose. "A minor raid would be all right, but no property damage."

Rose half-believed the man was serious, but decided he didn't want to know so he let the matter drop. More information was definitely in order. "Perhaps you should start at the beginning."

Cooke rubbed his face with two large hands and exhaled sharply. "All right, I'll take it from the top.

"As you can probably tell, Borghese isn't a big place in terms of land and population. It's a Terran-sized planet, but there's just too much water for the place to be of much use to anyone. We've had our share of Steiner, then F-C, garrisons, but most units seemed to look at Borghese as soft duty. It's understandable. We don't offer much in the way of a military target, and we don't produce enough to tempt the Combine to raid us for economic reasons either.

"All in all, that's made life very peaceful for those lucky enough to be born here. We grew up and lived our lives without the worry about war. Some of the younger lads joined the military, but they were always shipped away for duty. We have a militia, but it's barely worthy of the name, no offense intended. It's just that they specialize in assisting with civil emergencies, not military attacks. Things were going well until the Clans came along."

Cooke looked out the window, talking to his reflection as the car continued to drive through the manmade canyon of Houston's downtown area. Rose was content to hear the whole story, no matter how long Cooke took to tell it.

"For a while the Federats used Borghese as a marshaling point to collect troops to be sent further up to stop the Clan invasion. Things were pretty exciting for about a year, then the front got too close and they shifted the staging area further to the rear." Rose watched as Cooke smiled, lost in memories of recent years. It was not hard to guess that his power had either been established or cemented during that time.

"We were preparing for an invasion when the Com Guards stopped the Clans on Tukayyid. Until that point it looked like Borghese was going to be a prime candidate for a major battle, but now that the Clan advance has halted, that probably won't be happening."

Relief was written all over the man's face.

"At first everyone was overjoyed, which lasted until we realized that the Federats wouldn't be sticking around to defend us. From what I can tell, there are just too many military targets along the Clan border for them to worry about a minor world like Borghese.

"You've probably seen better maps than what I've got access to, but the basic picture amounts to this: if the Clans get past the Federat front lines, there's nothing to stop them from having their way with Borghese."

Again Cooke was correct. Rasalgethi was well-defended by the Sixth Lyran Guards and the Blue Star Irregulars. They'd likely chew on the Clans for a good while, even if they couldn't hold the planet. Tomans was safe, too. They had two regiments of the Kell Hounds and Barber's Marauders. With the Hounds' experience and the Marauders' hundred-ton 'Mechs, the Clans weren't likely to strike. Crimond and Pandora were the only other planets within a jump of Borghese on the front lines with the Clans.

Pandora was practically a fortress. The planet was normally protected by the local military college's training battalion, but the Fourth Davion Guards and the Tenth Federated Commonwealth Regimental Combat Teams had recently taken up station there. An invasion was more likely to be launched from Pandora than launched to it.

That only left Crimond. Of the four planets on the Clan border, it had the weakest defense. Currently defended by only two regiments, the heavily industrialized world had been a tempting target for an attack by the Steel Vipers last February. Only timely reinforcements from Wolf's Dragoons had ended the attack. If Crimond were ever attacked in strength and fell, Borghese would be in serious danger.

Because of the Inner Sphere's current state of technology, JumpShips always traveled from one populated area to another. If a jump drive failed while the ship was in an uninhabited star system, the crew was as good as dead. No Inner Sphere spacer was willing to take that risk. Making a strong defense at the border made perfect sense if a force was battling one of the other Houses of the Inner Sphere, but Rose suddenly realized that the Clans probably didn't care how they jumped as long as the final destination was correct. Borghese was only two jumps away from Steel Viper- and Jade Falcon-occupied worlds. If the Clan invaders were willing to recharge their JumpShips at uninhabited systems, they could be on Borghese less than thirty days after leaving their home base. Rose swallowed against a suddenly dry throat.

"My concern is that the Clans, probably the Jade Falcons, if what little I know about them is correct, will jump past the Federat front lines and hit Borghese and other planets like it." As Cooke talked, Rose's respect for him continued to grow. He shared Rose's unspoken concern, even if the Federated Commonwealth did not. "Using Borghese as a base, they could begin to expand laterally. Technically, they'd be honoring the Treaty of Tukayyid, but they'd make fair game of other planets lying to the right and left along the treaty line.

"That's why I sent Wilkins to hire a mercenary force, even a small one. If the Clans ever learn how weak are our defenses, Borghese would surely move up on their list of possible targets."

Rose knew that if he were the Clan ilKhan, he'd be thinking exactly the same thing. "Which is where I come in."

"Precisely. If the Clans send a unit to investigate Borghese, you'd have to stop them."

Rose sat up and opened his mouth to speak, but Cooke held up his hand. "Before you say anything, let me tell you one more thing. I know the Clans have never 'investigated' anything before. They always arrive in force and pound any target into submission. If that happens, I don't expect you and your men to throw your lives away."

That was certainly comforting. Rose didn't plan to do any such thing, but it was good to know that the man paying the bills felt the same way.

"This is a new situation for the Clans, however. I believe they may have to adapt their tactics to reflect the new conditions, and that situation includes potential raiding.''

Rose considered the possibility of new Clan tactics. They had proved their ability to adapt on Tukayyid, but for the first time they'd been stopped cold. Rose didn't count the two losses the Clans had suffered at the hands of the Kuritans and the Federated Commonwealth on Wolcott and Twycross in 3050. Although the Dracos had fought off the invaders, they'd used trickery to do so. Rose was all in favor of the tactic when necessary, but he still believed that the Com Guards had proven themselves the only military force able to stand up to the Clans in an all-out military confrontation.

The Treaty of Tukayyid might forbid the Clans to continue their advance past the line of that world but it didn't stop them from raiding and even making small-scale invasions of Kurita and FedCom planets above the truce line. And the attacks had been occurring with greater and greater frequency. What Cooke proposed didn't sound so unreasonable, and Rose nodded his agreement. A few things still bothered him, however.

"Even if it is just a raid, we couldn't hope to put up much of a fight without the help of the militia."

"I understand that," Cooke said. "We need training, and we need it in a hurry.

"When the Federats were here we didn't have to worry about defense, because they were going to take care of it for us. Before that, there really wasn't any reason for concern. Now we have a reason and nobody to protect us but ourselves." Rose remembered how difficult it was to grow up. Now the entire population of this planet was going to have to do the same thing.

"So the first order of business is training," he said. "I've got the crew to take care of that. We'll need the cooperation of the militia leaders and support from their administrative division."

"I can have that arranged," Cooke said. Rose was glad to hear that the Chairman was agreeable to suggestions and requests. It would make the situation easier to handle.

"Once the training is underway," he went on, "some of the resentment against us may disappear. That would be nice, but I won't count on it. By the way, how bad is the resistance against us?"

Cooke gritted his teeth and Rose knew the answer wouldn't be good. "There was some heated discussion about bringing you to the planet, even after we ratified the contract. As far as the population is concerned, you're a good thing. The majority supports you, but they're the silent majority. The vocal ones are parked outside the gate of your compound. They make a lot of noise, but they don't represent the way most people feel.

"The Council, on the other hand, is a different story. There are two factions in it right now. For the sake of simplicity, let's call one of them mine and the other one Crenshaw's. My four-member group thinks we should fight the Clans tooth and nail. It will be costly, but it has to be done. Crenshaw and company think we should surrender peacefully and let the Clans occupy Borghese without a fight. Although it would be better for the planet, it will hurt the Federated Commonwealth."

"It's a nine-member Council. Which side gets to make the decisions?"

"Both of us, and neither of us."

Rose cocked an eyebrow and Cooke laughed. "Miss Jessica Ann de Vilbis holds the reins. She firmly refuses to be placed in either camp, and has been the swing vote in the last six Clan-Inner Sphere decisions, voting each way three times. Right now Miss de Vilbis is trying to reconcile duty to Borghese with duty to the Commonwealth." He shook his head and clenched his teeth. "She's a damn strong woman and too young to have such a major voice in the Council."

Rose considered what he knew. The population was behind him, even if they weren't vocal about it. The Council could go either way on the decision to support him. Hopefully, that was the bad news. What about something positive?

"What do we have to work with?"

Cooke considered the question. "Mostly motorized infantry, with a few outdated tanks and APCs. The cream of the crop—which still isn't saying much—is the Green Team."

Rose suppressed a laugh, almost. "Catchy name."

Cooke shared his sentiment and shrugged. "It wasn't my idea. The Greenies have two squadrons of VTOLs and a fixed-wing fighter flight attached to them. Most of the defense budget for the last three years has gone toward purchasing their new Rippers."

Rose didn't think much of using VTOLs in combat, but few MechWarriors did. Helicopters were just too easy to shoot down in a firefight, despite advances in their armor protection. A single light 'Mech would have probably been of more use, but he'd have to use what was available.

"So we'll start with them. I don't suppose there are any retired MechWarriors on the planet, other than Morgain." Rose still didn't like the man, despite having had three days to overcome what he considered an irrational dislike.

"Just Salander Morgain and his men."

"And his men?" More good news. An independent 'Mech unit was on the planet and Rose was just finding out about it.

"Yes. When Morgain returned from active duty, several of his old lancemates came with him. They've been staying on the Morgain estate for the past three months."

"How many?" Rose tried to remain calm.

"Five, counting Morgain. I met them when they returned, but since then they've stayed at the estate exclusively." Rose was somewhat relieved. At least they wouldn't be in the way.

"Any chance they'd participate in planning the defense, if that becomes necessary?" he wondered aloud.

"I'm sure they would, but I doubt that Morgain would

fight except in the face of a Clan attack.'' That sounded good to Rose.

''Morgain and his men returned to Borghese while Wilkins and Hoffbrowse were still on Outreach. The Council immediately approached them about the position you were hired for, but he turned it down.''

''Any reason?''

Cooke shrugged, a gesture that was becoming all too common. ''He hinted at some kind of lasting damage he'd suffered at the hands of the Clans, but he wasn't specific. I didn't press the point.''

''But he's still a major force in the politics of the Council,'' countered Rose, his voice slightly strained. Salander Morgain's presence bothered him.

''A legacy of his father, I'm afraid.'' If Cooke took offense at Rose's comment, he didn't show it. ''Renaldo Morgain was quite a man and the people still remember him, even though he's been dead for almost fifteen years. Salander is a firm part of that memory. He's the only surviving member of Renaldo's family, and made quite an impression on the media at his father's graveside service.''

''I take it that his father was a cut above your standard Council member.''

''You could say that. He was a junior member during the Fourth Succession War and the Chairman during the War of 3039. Somehow Renaldo came to national prominence during the first conflict and then became Chairman during the second.''

''He sounds like quite a man.'' Rose was sincere. Although he didn't like the younger Morgain's too-smooth style, he respected anyone who'd been able to help pull the people of Borghese through the madness of two wars.

''He was,'' said Cooke, his voice suddenly distant. ''I'm not sure his son quite measures up, but then few people could.''

Rose nodded and tried to lighten the suddenly darkened mood. Glancing out the window he saw that the limo had just passed the same landmark for the third time. Evidently Cooke thought the luxury car was the safest place to talk. "I don't suppose it would do any harm trying to enlist Morgain's help, but I think it's probably a waste of time."

"Leave no stone unturned, that's my motto. At least that's one of my mottoes," Rose said.

"Suit yourself."

Rose planned to do just that, despite what anyone else said or did. "There is something you can help me with, however."

"Just ask," Cooke said. "I'll see what I can do."

"I need the temporary attachment of a VTOL with crew to the unit. I want to get a better picture of the continent, and I'll need more mobility than my 'Mechs can provide. I'll need the men and equipment for about three months." Rose would probably need it for longer, but thought it would be easier to get a temporary extension later than to try to get the entire time up front.

"I think that can be arranged."

Rose hid his smile. The VTOL would prove invaluable during the first few months of duty.

"Good," he said, then looked at Cooke in mock seriousness. "Now, are we ever going to eat, or do we just keep riding around the block until this thing runs out of fuel?"

23

Houston, Borghese
12 June 3055

The next six months were busy ones for the Black Thorns. As executive officer, Rianna coordinated the training with the Green Team. Although every one of them was older than she, Rianna worked well with the leadership, which pleasantly surprised Rose. Esmeralda, Badicus, and Ajax performed most of the actual training.

Esmeralda reported that the Greenies had already been trained in the basics of anti-'Mech tactics, but that most of those tactics were hopelessly out-of-date. Sending infantry against a 'Mech was never a good idea. If the Green Team was to have any chance of surviving, let alone succeed in crippling a target, they would require extensive retraining.

Esmeralda, Badicus, and Ajax made a good team, and soon the Militia Training Center was ablaze with the sounds of mock combat. As Rose and the other mercenaries could attest, Esmeralda was a demanding officer. The Greenies, however, seemed to delight in the harsh demands and difficult exercises to which she subjected them. Ajax and Badicus piloted 'Mechs, served as advisors, and generally assisted the forceful woman as the Green Team was brought up-to-date.

Angus spent most of his time assisting Rianna at the base. When not needed at the compound, he too worked with Esmeralda. Rose was initially hard-pressed to find specific duties for the young man, but eventually that turned out for the best. Though quiet, Angus had tremendous leadership potential. He was not afraid to make an important decision when none of the other members of the Black Thorns were available. This ability to make quick, accurate decisions contributed as much to the smooth operation of the unit as did Rianna's ability to coordinate the logistics of training and unit supply.

Rose spent most of the first two months away from the compound. Accompanied by Hawg, he put almost eighty thousand kilometers on the loaner VTOL in the first sixty days he had it. Rose would have preferred to have Ajax or Angus with him on the scouting expeditions, but their experience made them better-suited to the training and support efforts going on back in Houston. Hawg, though knowledgeable about repair and 'Mech operations, seemed to lack the talent to transmit the knowledge to others.

Rose had feared he'd be spending all his time with a backwoods AgroMech jockey, but Hawg turned out to be surprisingly well-informed on a wide variety of subjects. When Rose's schedule allowed him to return to Houston, he rarely spent time at the compound, however. Most nights he spent with Rachel McCloud, determined to keep the relationship alive.

As the commanding officer of the most potent fighting force on Borghese, Rose enjoyed celebrity status. Soon Rianna was coordinating his social calendar in addition to keeping tabs on his scouting flights. Rose tried to make at least one event per week, Rachel McCloud at his side, to explain the purpose of his unit to the assembled guests. Though he was persuasive, Rose reckoned that he owed much of the unit's growing acceptance to Rachel. She may not have started out with much enthusiasm for the mission to Borghese, but she'd warmed to the idea as time passed. She was also much better at dealing with the social elite. Rose didn't know many details of her background, but was beginning to suspect that the kind of parties and social events they attended were nothing new to her.

By the end of the second full month on Borghese, Rose was pleased to find matters proceeding far better than he'd ever imagined. The protesters were still parked outside the main gate, and would likely remain there for the duration of the Black Thorns' contract. A small tent village had sprung up along the side of the road, but Rose let it remain because the protesters were, for the most part, quiet and well-behaved.

Salander Morgain was an increasingly common sight at the compound, soon striking up a friendship with Rianna. Although Rose did not know it, the two had been seeing one another socially for several weeks. The rest of the Thorns knew about it, but no one mentioned it to Rose because the situation seemed harmless. Besides, most of the mercenaries thought their commander was overly protective of his sister. Esmeralda didn't think much of Morgain, but she preferred to keep an eye on Rianna instead of dragging Rose into the situation.

When summer reached its hottest on Borghese, so did Jeremiah Rose. In the course of three days he learned that Rianna had been seeing Salander Morgain, that the VTOL was going to be reassigned, and that Hawg had caught viral pneumonia. It was only a matter of time before the first event came out into the open. Rianna had been behaving like a schoolgirl, which fit her age but not her status. Rose was furious, but directed most of his anger at the unit for not letting him know what was going on. His attention was quickly diverted, however, when a Borghese militia major arrived at the compound with written orders for the return of the VTOL.

Rianna stalled while Rose tried in vain to get in touch with Chairman Cooke. When neither action proved successful, Rianna confirmed the orders with the militia command center and impatiently waved the man away. The VTOL left thirty minutes later. Rose was still trying to procure some kind of airborne transportation to complete the last of the reconnaissance work when Angus called him aside.

"Hawg is sick, sir. I think we'd better get him to the hospital."

Riding in the ambulance with the stricken man, Rose berated himself for having let the illness progress so far. Hawg had caught a summer cold during one of their frequent flights, but refused to give it any attention. The condition seemed to worsen during subsequent trips, but Hawg refused to succumb to the illness. He was simply too robust to let the virus slow him down. That morning, however, Angus had discovered him with a raging fever. Hawg spent the next ten days in the hospital.

With his assistant in the hospital and the VTOL firmly back in militia hands, Rose returned to the Council with a formal request for an assistant and a replacement vehicle. He was not overly surprised when the Council turned him down, Miss de Vilbis again casting the swing vote. He was surprised, however, when a Ferret light scout VTOL landed in the compound yard the next morning. Rose, Rianna, and Angus, the only three Thorns remaining in the compound, gathered around as the pilot emerged. Approaching the assembled mercenaries, he pulled off his helmet, out tumbling the longest blond hair Rose had ever seen. Stuffing flight gloves into his helmet, the man extended his hand to Rose.

"Captain Rose, my name is Antioch Bell. I've been sent to help with your scouting." Rose took the offered hand and returned the warm smile.

"The Council changed its mind?"

The pilot gave Rose a lopsided smile. "Not exactly. I work for Salander Morgain."

"Salander sent you?" Rianna said, and Antioch seemed to notice her for the first time.

"Yes, ma'am. You must be Rianna." He extended his hand. "Salander has spoken a lot about you."

Feeling Rose glaring at her, Rianna's wide smile gradually disappeared. "Pleased to meet you, Mister Bell.

Now, if you'll excuse me," she said, then turned on her heel and went back to the command building. Rose watched her stomp away. Angus meanwhile was quietly introducing himself to Bell.

"Sisters." Rose shook his head and Bell grinned.

"I've got two myself. I'll never understand women, even when they're my own flesh and blood."

Rose considered the statement and Bell's presence in the camp. "Mister Bell, I appreciate the gesture you and Mister Morgain have made, but I'm afraid I'll have to decline. I can't, in good conscience, accept civilian transport."

"Well, Captain Rose, if it will help ease your mind, the Ferret over there has been collecting dust for the past five years. And that's the way it'll stay if you refuse the offer. By the way, I'm not exactly a civilian. I served seven years with the Twenty-sixth Lyran Guard."

"Oh, really?"

"I work for Morgain now. I signed a contract when we left the Guards." From the look on the man's face, Rose knew he viewed the signing as a natural thing to do.

"And the other warriors up at the estate?"

"Same deal, more or less, but I shouldn't be telling tales. You want me to head back home, or shall we do some recon?"

Rose looked the man over. He was roughly the same age as Rose, but he seemed much more at ease with what was going on around him. Everything from his posture to his expressive face told of a life lived in the open. Rose doubted that the man was trying to hide anything, and briefly wondered whether his original evaluation of Salander Morgain might have been wrong. He looked over at the VTOL.

"Can you really fly that thing?"

Bell's face lit up. "Sure. I'm not combat-rated, but all the combat gear was stripped when the militia sold it to Morgain. If we keep it on the straight and level, we're in good shape."

Rose considered the statement. Not exactly a ringing endorsement of ability, but the risk was probably worth the time that would be saved. He glanced over at Angus, who only shrugged.

"I'll get my maps," he said. Fifteen minutes later they were in the air over Houston.

The final stages of the reconnaissance took Rose and Bell three weeks. The Ferret was only a two-man vehicle, so travel was cramped. Like Hawg, Bell was talkative, but on a slightly narrower range of subjects. Their three weeks of scouting was most productive, however, and Rose figured that one more long day of flights to the north of the city would finalize this stage of his plans. He and Bell were on their way back to the compound when Antioch interrupted his paperwork.

"Incoming call for you," the pilot said, and Rose reached for the headset. Normally he didn't wear the communications set while the VTOL was airborne. Though he and Bell sat in separate compartments, the intercom system didn't require the use of the "head clamps," as Bell preferred to call them. Slipping the set over his head, Rose gave a thumbs-up to Bell, who switched the channel.

"Captain Rose, this is Chairman Cooke." Rose stiffened. The use of formal titles was rarely the harbinger of good news. "I understand you're en route to the compound?"

Rose nodded out of habit. "That is correct."

"Please divert to the Assembly Pavilion helipad immediately."

"Something wrong, Chairman?"

"We can discuss it on the ground, Captain. Cooke out." The line went dead and Rose was left staring out into the darkening sky. He slid the headset off and spoke into the intercom.

"I guess you heard that." Bell flashed another thumbs-up. "We're on the way?" Another affirmative. Rose settled back into the seat.

"Doesn't sound like war, so there must be trouble," Rose said, thinking out loud. "Can you raise the compound? I think I want Rianna and Esmeralda there to meet us."

When the Ferret touched ground, Rianna, Esmeralda, and Chairman Cooke were all waiting on the pad. Rose jumped out of the craft even before the blades had stopped turning, and dashed the short distance to the assembled figures. He nodded a greeting to the two women, then turned to Cooke.

"We've got trouble," the Chairman began. "Petr Ivaars, my strongest supporter on the Council, was arrested this afternoon on charges of environmental pollution and profiteering. He resigned in the face of the charges." The huddled group entered the back doors of the Assembly Pavilion and Cooke no longer had to shout to be heard. As the doors closed behind him, the Chairman adjusted his collar and continued.

"We called an emergency session of the Council, and on the way to the meeting—" Cooke paused and Rose braced himself for the worst—"Amanda Hillerman was killed in an automobile accident."

The group continued on in silence as Rose worked through what Cooke had told him. Suddenly it hit him. Two of the four members of Cooke's coalition were gone. Rose had no idea how politics worked on Borghese, but he doubted Ivaars would be back, even if cleared of the charges.

"You're out," said Rose solemnly.

"Not yet. I've got five more months left on the appointment, but there isn't much chance of another term. Meantime the first thing the Council will have to do is recruit two new members." The small group came to a set of closed double doors, which Cooke threw open in a show of strength and frustration. As echoes of the banging doors filled the corridor, he continued.

"Once the seats are filled, they'll move to change official policy. They won't fight the Clans if they arrive."

"What about the people? You said the populace was against the Clans."

Cooke shook his head. "Crenshaw will conduct a media blitz. Soften the edge of the Clans and exaggerate the weaknesses of the Federated Commonwealth. By the time it's over the people will welcome the Clan advance and wonder how the Inner Sphere ever got along without them." He barked a short laugh. "Most of them won't even realize that they were manipulated."

"It's already started," Rianna said. Startled, Rose and Cooke stopped in their tracks and turned to look at her. "I've been monitoring the local news reports. The Clans are being portrayed as unstoppable. Most of the footage is of destroyed F-C 'Mechs and the remains of the towns where the fighting's been heaviest. Things were kind of gloomy, but it didn't seem so bad, until tonight."

Rianna didn't have to be told to continue. She kept speaking as Cooke's face turned redder. "The footage they were showing tonight . . . I thought there was something familiar about it. When you mentioned the media, I remembered. Tonight's footage was from the battle of Twycross. I remember it from the academy. It wasn't available to the public when we viewed it."

"Meaning it's recently been declassified or else somebody has powerful connections," Cooke said. "Did they mention it was old footage?"

"No."

"That's it," said Rose. "If it was above the board, they'd have announced it was old film."

Cooke rubbed the stubble on his chin. "Captain Rose, you're about to become very unpopular. I can stall, but eventually Crenshaw's faction is going to win. That means no resistance if the Clans decide to take Borghese."

"What about a raid?" Esmeralda asked.

"A lance could take over the whole planet, if they looked threatening enough," Cooke said.

"You're joking."

"Biota and Volders fell without the firing of a single shot," Rose reminded her.

"But both planets were threatened. To a population who believes the Clans are about to destroy them, a couple of 'Mechs can seem very threatening."

Esmeralda snorted, and Cooke turned on her.

"Don't doubt it, lady. You're a warrior. Killing and destruction may come easy to you, but this is a planet of fishermen and farmers. They don't fight, and if they're threatened, they'll surrender to the first Clanner they see."

Esmeralda was taken aback by the intensity of the diplomat's gaze, but she recovered quickly. Seeing that Cooke was about to get an earful, Rose quickly stepped between the two.

"Point taken, Mister Chairman," he said, staring hard at Esmeralda until she was back in control of herself. "What about a counterattack?"

Cooke looked at Rose as though the mercenary had lost his mind.

"Crenshaw will try to persuade the people to accept the Clans," Rose said. "You've got to convince them not to. You've still got Morgain. If his reputation is as good as you say, he could slow the tide of support, at least for a while."

Cooke nodded, his eyes lighting up for a moment. "We'll have to wait and see that it happens."

"In the meantime, we're heading back to the compound. Rianna, consider the base on yellow alert." Rose turned to Esmeralda.

"Make sure the 'Mechs are ready to go at a moment's notice. Until we see how bad things are against us, we play it by ear and prepare for the worst."

Cooke checked his watch, then gestured in exasperation. "Now I'm thirty minutes late for the meeting I called." He started down the hall, but stopped after only a few steps. "Perhaps you'd better let your DropShip crew in on the news. They're still considered part of your force."

"The Chairman's right," Rose said, turning to Esmeralda and Rianna. "You two head back to the compound. I'll see if Antioch can take me directly to the spaceport."

24

As it turned out, McCloud was better prepared than Rose for the news of the change in Borghese politics. The *Bristol*'s holds were already being filled for a trip to Cameron. In two days Rachel McCloud and the *Bristol* would leave Borghese. Rose doubted either would ever return.

There were no tearful good-byes, just the harsh reality of the demands of McCloud's job and Rose's contract. Rachel made her living hauling commercial goods from one planet to another. Although Rose had a contract, she did not. The maintenance on the *Bristol* was too high for her to remain sitting on one planet, even if she liked the company. Rose offered her a position as permanent transport of the Black Thorns, but she rejected the offer. The unit didn't make enough to provide for the extended maintenance of their 'Mechs. How could they hope to cover the expenses of a DropShip?

Rose left the ship after securing Rachel's promise to return to the compound tomorrow evening for a farewell dinner. It seemed the least he could do. Stepping off the ramp, he noticed Antioch leaning against a cargo lifter despite Rose's earlier insistence that he head for home. Rose crossed the deserted tarmac. With a sigh, he leaned a shoulder wearily against the same lifter.

"Tough night." Antioch made the statement sound like

a question. Rose didn't respond and Bell let the silence drag. Eventually Rose grew restless and heaved himself away from the lifter.

"You know what I don't understand?" Rose asked rhetorically. "Me. I don't understand myself.

"I meet someone I really care about and things are going pretty well." Rose turned and looked up the ramp into the empty bay of the DropShip. "I have to leave, but we're on good terms. I send a couple of messages via ComStar and a few months later we're reunited. It's not the same, but I figure it's because of the separation." Rose crashed back into his resting spot against the lifter and continued to look up the ramp.

"Things start to get better on the trip here and I actually believe the relationship can last." Rose fell into silence.

"So what don't you understand?" Bell asked.

"When we're aboard ship, things are great. We talk and laugh and everything is fine. But the minute I hit the ground, I have to remind myself that she's even around. I mean, I think about her more than I should, but I rarely have the time to talk with her or tell her what I feel."

"Maybe there's nothing there," Bell said softly.

Rose looked hard at him, trying to pierce the dim light in search of mockery. Even in the darkness, however, he could see Bell was serious.

"Yeah, maybe you're right. But why do I feel so bad that she's leaving?"

"I've only known you for a few weeks, but I like you," Bell said tentatively. "If it's not out of line, I'd like to offer a bit of advice." Rose wasn't sure he wanted to hear what his companion wanted to say, but he was confused enough to realize that another viewpoint might give him some badly needed perspective.

"If you don't want her to leave, tell her. At least give her the chance to say no."

"I offered her a position in the unit."

Bell shook his head. "That's not the same thing. That

was an offer to the DropShip and its captain. Not to the woman. There's a difference.''

Rose knew there was a difference, but he couldn't bring himself to admit it aloud. The same thing had happened with Tiegard, with whom he'd also shared something special, but with Rachel it was different. She wasn't a 'Mech jock and she wasn't a warrior. Rachel looked at life in a completely different way, which was what Rose found so enchanting. Unfortunately, just as with Tiegard, Rose could not bring himself to admit how he felt.

"Let's go," he mumbled, seeing a strobe light come on at the top of the ramp. As the two men walked toward the Ferret, the ramp retracted into the belly of the DropShip. Rose couldn't see it, but he heard the echo of the ship's heavy door as it was secured for the night. There was an ominous finality to the echo that haunted him all the way to the compound.

Across Houston, at Crenshaw's second home, the mood was much lighter. Crenshaw was entertaining a single guest in his study and he was doing his best to make the man feel at home. Following a Council meeting that had been cut short by Cooke, Crenshaw mentally cursed him to Hell, then decided to retire to his home in town rather than endure the ride back to his country estate. When his guest had appeared just as the Council was adjourning, Crenshaw was able to invite him to his home without the other members of the Council noticing.

He smiled and offered his guest another snifter of brandy. This stuff comes all the way from Andro, he thought with a huff of annoyance, yet the man drinks it down like ale. Crenshaw had suspected it from the first moment this fellow had walked into the Council meeting almost three months ago—Salander Morgain was a mere shadow of his famous father.

"Do you like it?" Crenshaw managed to hide his disgust. After his many years as a politician, few could read his moods.

Salander Morgain nodded. The brandy had an intense

warming effect he had never experienced with any other alcohol. He'd have to find out where to get some for himself. Crenshaw smiled and moved to a chair matching the one Morgain occupied. His movements were not those of an old man, despite his physical appearance.

As the councilman seated himself, Morgain could not help but remember the first time he'd seen Crenshaw. Even as a young boy, he'd sensed something sinister about the man. It lay just under the surface, waiting for the right moment to spring to life. His father had managed to keep Crenshaw's ambitions in check, as had the string of other chairmen who'd run the assembly. Only Cooke seemed unaware of what Morgain knew was the man's true nature. Now the beast was free, and he could see it in Crenshaw's eyes as the man prepared to speak.

"Salander, I will not mince words. We sit on the eve of an historic day. A day that will be remembered in the history of Borghese as the day we set our feet on the right path."

Salander was amazed. Crenshaw actually believed whatever tripe he was about to express.

"You know that I oppose Zenos Cooke in the Council?"

Morgain nodded and sipped his brandy. The fact was common knowledge.

"You also know that I would not oppose a Clan landing, if one were to occur."

Morgain hesitated, then nodded. He'd always known as much, but the gleam in Crenshaw's dark eyes was unnerving. "I hear your name mentioned as the leader of a pro-Clan faction, which I believe the media has named the Preservationists. "

Crenshaw snorted. "Populist hogwash. The name matters little, as does my involvement with the faction. I do, however, support their aims. This foolish war with the Clans must not come to Borghese. I am dedicated to preventing that by any means necessary."

Morgain nodded again. Crenshaw leaned forward,

placing his elbows on his knees. "Do you understand what I am saying?"

Morgain continued nodding, then caught himself. The reaction had been reflex until he looked into Crenshaw's eyes. The old man was not joking around. The younger man swallowed the last of his brandy and set the glass on the table between them. He leaned forward, his position mirroring Crenshaw's.

"I understand. I've fought against the Clans, and I know what they're capable of doing. I would also do anything to keep the war from spilling into Borghese."

Crenshaw relaxed. Morgain was now on his side. He smiled and reached out to pat the younger man's knee. "Just like your father. You love your homeland." What a lie, thought Crenshaw. Power and money are all the boy cares about.

Crenshaw leaned back in the chair and motioned Morgain to pour himself another brandy. While he did so, Crenshaw continued speaking.

"I believe we can prevent a war, despite what that fool Cooke has already done. Can I count on you to help?" Crenshaw already knew the answer, but if he could get Morgain to verbalize his position it would seem more like his own idea.

"Of course. Tell me how I can help." Crenshaw hid his smile as Morgain crossed back to his chair, his glass filled to the rim.

"The Council controls the militia. If someone threatens war, the Council can keep the reins on any hothead who wants to start shooting. Since I control the Council—or will after tomorrow's appointments—I can keep the militia from starting something. But. . . ."

"But the mercenaries," interrupted Salander.

Crenshaw bit his lip. He hated to be interrupted. He smiled through clenched teeth and continued. "But the mercenaries are beyond my control. I've tried to talk with Rose on several occasions, but he refuses to see me except during the Council sessions. If the Clans arrive before the end of his contract, he'll definitely try to fight them." Crenshaw let his words sink in.

"The Clans would be forced to fight back and who knows where it would end," blurted Morgain. Crenshaw nodded solemnly.

"We have to stop him." Crenshaw continued nodding as Morgain set the half-full glass back on the table. He looked at Crenshaw and started to speak, then stopped, his mouth hanging open.

"That's what you need me for, isn't it? I'm the only one who can stop Rose."

Crenshaw considered his options. Morgain's statement was not exactly true, but it was close enough. He looked at the young MechWarrior and decided to be a little more circumspect than he'd originally planned.

"I don't want you to stop Rose. I'm hoping it won't come to that. What we, the Preservationists, need is someone with a military background to support our cause.

"You've been very outspoken in your views about what to do when the Clans come. Although I haven't always agreed with you, I respected your conviction. But consider the cost of resistance. Destruction like you saw while fighting with the Federated Commonwealth army. Do you really want that for your home? Could you live with that, knowing that the damage and death could have been avoided?"

Crenshaw leaned forward and impaled Morgain with his stare. Long moments passed, then the younger man shook his head.

"Of course you couldn't. I understand, son, how much home means to you.

"All you need do is support the no-resistance policy that I'll be proposing to the Council in the next week. If you were the first private citizen to announce his approval of the plan, the masses would follow. You'd be a hero."

Morgain cupped his face in his hands. Seeing that the MechWarrior had swallowed the hook, Crenshaw decided that now it was time to pull.

"Just like your father." Morgain's head snapped up. Crenshaw knew he was looking for any trace of deception, but it was too easy to fool the drunken young man. His face was a neutral mask, but his eyes told Crenshaw everything.

"What about the mercenaries' gear?" Morgain tried to sound disinterested, but failed completely. "Somebody will have to be responsible for it."

"I can think of nobody more qualified than yourself. The machines matter little to me or to the other members of my group. Consider them yours." Crenshaw could practically see the C-bills flashing in Salander's eyes. He reeled in his catch as he stood up and extended his bony right hand.

"Glad to have you on board, Hauptmann Morgain. We can use you."

Morgain looked up at the hand and slowly stood to shake it.

"Now, if you don't mind. It's getting late for an old man like me. Why don't I have my chauffeur drive you back to your estate? You can sleep on the way?"

Crenshaw summoned the butler, who woke the chauffeur, who brought the limousine around to the front of the house. Crenshaw said good night and stood watching until the car was out of sight. Then he returned to the study, where another man had taken Morgain's chair.

"You hear?" he asked, flopping back into his chair.

"I heard."

Crenshaw regarded the man, who wore a look of extreme boredom. The man steepled his fingers and placed his index fingers to his chin in concentration.

"We should move tonight."

Crenshaw shook his head. "It's too soon. If anything goes wrong on your end, it could affect the Council's voting tomorrow. Wait until tomorrow night. By then, I'll be in control of the Council and you can be on your way."

The man tapped his fingers against his chin. Crenshaw

could see that he didn't like the idea, but that eventually he'd accept it.

"Young Morgain behaved just as you predicted."

Crenshaw laughed with true delight for the first time that evening. "Thank you, but it really wasn't hard to predict. When you discovered the truth of his war record, all I had to do was put that together with what I already knew about him. Greed and insecurity, what a pitiful combination."

"We had best make sure nobody else finds out about Morgain's past. If the rest of Borghese ever learned that he was cashiered for involvement in the black market, his credibility would drop to zero."

"Believe me," said Crenshaw, rubbing his eyes, "nobody knows that better than I. Fortunately, the only people who know the truth are you, me, and the Records Department on Tharkad. None of whom are likely to volunteer the information.

"We're safe on this one. Besides, Morgain's credibility only has to last another few months. After that, who cares what happens to him?"

The man opposite Crenshaw frowned, then nodded. The two sat in silence for a moment, then Crenshaw stood. "I'm going to bed," he announced through a yawn.

When his guest didn't move, Crenshaw began heading for the doorway.

"And Hoffbrowse, lock the door on your way out."

$=$ 25 $=$

As Zenos Cooke predicted, the new members of the Council were chosen by Crenshaw and his supporters. Although the final replacements could only be elected by popular vote, the Council could make temporary appointments. Only a simple majority was needed for approval because the time actually served by the Council members was so short.

The first candidate seemed to be planted firmly in the middle of the road. Though Calvin Washington was better known for his lavish parties than for his political views, Cooke decided that the man was as good a candidate as he was going to get. In his acceptance speech, Washington promised to work hard, listen to the people he represented, and weigh each decision carefully. He was appointed by a five-to-zero margin.

The second man practically arrived at the meeting in the same car as Crenshaw. During the initial speeches, he declared himself a member of the Preservationists. Despite vehement objections from Cooke, the Council elected Ermando Rashimaln by a vote of three to two. When Washington's hand went up in affirmation even before Crenshaw's, Cooke knew he'd been duped. De Vilbis abstained from voting, which was allowed, but very unusual. Voters expected their representatives to vote on issues, not sit and watch them go by.

The Council adjourned in the late afternoon to give the new members a chance to bring themselves up to date on the current facts. Cooke had no illusions that both junior members were fully aware of the facts, but couldn't do much about it. Though he was still the chairman, the Council decided most issues by a simple majority. Cooke enjoyed a favored status and could sometimes bend the Council decisions to his will. With Crenshaw on the watch, even that would be hard to do now.

As the members filed out of the domed meeting room, Cooke gave Crenshaw his best I'd-like-to-see-you-dead look, but the old man just smiled. He tried the same stare on Washington, but with similar results. Cooke figured Washington was just stupid and unaware. Crenshaw was obviously neither.

Rose got the news as he was preparing for McCloud's good-bye dinner. The rest of the mercenaries knew he was taking it hard that Rachel was leaving, but nobody, even his sister, knew what to say. Eventually they decided to leave him alone, trusting he would work through it on his own, or ask for help if he needed it.

Rachel McCloud arrived promptly at seven. For unknown reasons, Antioch Bell had insisted on driving her to the compound. The ever-present protesters had been much more active of late, but Bell managed to get through them with a minimum of hassle. Rose knew that the dinner would be superb. Their local cook was excellent. His mind was elsewhere now as he stared at McCloud, listening to the conversation without joining in. The apple dumplings were just being served when the comm unit rang.

Rianna stood to answer it, but Rose was faster. Crossing the small room, he picked up the handset and listened. He started to announce himself, but the caller interrupted. Rose's face drained of color as he listened.

Ajax was the first to move, heading for the door even

before Rose had put the handset back in place. Rose followed quickly, giving orders as he went.

"Stand to, Thorns, we've got a problem at the spaceport." The rest of the team crowded toward the door as Ajax raced for his 'Mech. Because they were operating on yellow alert, everyone was wearing combat gear or else had their equipment within easy reach. Rachel remained seated, her face calm.

"What's going on, Jeremiah?"

The rest of the mercenaries were filing out the door, some running directly to the 'Mech bays, others to the barracks. The last to exit, Hawg pulled the door shut behind him with one hand as the other cradled a dumpling. Rose took a deep breath and exhaled loudly.

"Terrorists are attacking the spaceport. It looks like the object of the raid is the *Bristol*. Your crew is trying to hold them off, but it doesn't look good."

Rose expected anger and frustration, but he barely managed to duck as McCloud threw a heavy glass at him from across the room.

"You son of a bitch. You're supposed to protect them." Without waiting for a reply, she charged around the table. Rose dropped into a crouch and prepared to meet the charge, but it never came. As McCloud neared the front door, it suddenly swung open. Running full throttle, McCloud didn't have a chance to avoid it. She hit the door at full speed, getting the air knocked out of her lungs and smashing her head into the reinforced wood.

Hawg, his shoulder still braced against the door, looked at Rose and tried to smile. "It seemed like the only thing to do at the time." The big man peered around the edge of the door as Rose stepped over to the fallen McCloud, who was gasping for breath, her left eye beginning to swell shut. The wounds looked and sounded bad, but she'd be up in a few minutes.

"Sir, now would be the time to get out of here. Unless you think she'll run into the door again when she gets up."

Rose looked up at Hawg and then back to McCloud.

Torn by indecision, he pointed to the cook. "Get a couple of guards in here. Make sure she doesn't leave until we get back."

McCloud was struggling to rise, her remaining good eye focused on Rose's throat. "Sit on her if you have to," Rose said, "but don't let her leave."

With that, he was out the door, Hawg close on his heels. By the time Rose reached the cockpit of the *Charger*, Ajax's *Raven* was already moving toward the main gate. Angus soon followed and the rest of the company closed behind the recon 'Mechs. Running through the gates in his 'Mech, Rose could see that the protesters had gathered in strength at the compound tonight, screaming at the 'Mechs as they went by. Rocks pinged off the *Charger*'s armor, and for a moment Rose feared one of the protesters would be crushed under the feet of one of the 'Mechs in the vain attempt to stop them. Fortunately, he was wrong. The group stayed well away from the road and soon the Black Thorns were past them and moving toward the spaceport.

Ajax and Angus led the way, with the rest of the Thorns close behind. Soon Ajax had outdistanced the rest, and Rose decided not to call him back. It was unlikely that the Capellan would meet any resistance until he got to the spaceport and his timely arrival might be fortuitous.

By the time the rest of the Thorns arrived, Ajax had swept the *Bristol* with his powerful short-range scanners. The Beagle active probe mounted in the *Raven*'s nose gave a grim, but accurate picture.

The terrorists had evidently gained access to the ship by posing as maintenance workers. Rose could see their damaged cargo-lifter parked under the closed door of Bay Number Three. Two bodies lay near the lifter, but in the darkness it was impossible to identify them as friend or foe.

Rose's *Charger* pulled up next to the *Raven*, which was sheltered from the DropShip's guns by an intervening supply building.

"What's the situation, Ajax?" Rose tried to peer over

the supply building, but could see only the top half of the *Bristol*.

"They were just sealing the bays as I got here. Looks like the crew managed to hold them off for a while, but not long enough. I capped the two by the lifter, but the rest got inside."

As Rose listened, the top gun of the DropShip swung their way. The gun lowered, but stopped well above the top of the *Charger*'s head. Because the *Bristol* was basically a sphere, the placement of its guns had posed a design problem. The designers had finally decided to devote most of the protection to the top half of the sphere, as that was the side most often engaged in combat. On the ground, these top-mounted weapons gave the *Union* Class DropShip good defense against aerial attacks. For defense against ground forces, the ship depended on the 'Mechs it normally carried to keep enemies away. Right now the Thorns were positioned under the *Bristol*'s major weapons, and would have to face only the lower set of lasers if they decided to rush the DropShip.

Rose considered his two options. Either he could order his unit to rush the ship, damaging it enough to prevent takeoff or they could sit and watch it get away. In either case the *Bristol* would be lost to McCloud. On one hand she'd never be able to afford the repair costs for such damage; on the other, the hijackers were unlikely to return the ship when finished with it. It didn't take long to decide.

"This is Commander One. Rush the DropShip. Concentrate fire on the closest support stanchion. If we break one of the legs, they might decide not to attempt liftoff."

Even as Rose spoke, a sudden red glow appeared under the *Bristol*. Smoke billowed out from beneath the massive craft as a dull roar deafened the mercenaries.

"Ajax, I thought you said they'd just closed the hatches!" If that was true, Rose should have had ten to fifteen minutes to attack the ship before the hijackers could possibly start up the engines and attempt liftoff. In that amount of time he could have broken all four

DropShip legs. Instead, the ship was now in the final stages of liftoff.

"Go, go, go." Trusting the rest of his lance to follow, Rose rounded the edge of the maintenance building and ran toward the *Bristol*. Triggering his first salvo of long-range missiles, he could see the ship's massive legs extend as the engines began to bear the weight of thirty-five hundred tons. Smoke rolled over the *Charger*, obscuring the 'Mech's bottom half. Rose fired again at the *Bristol*'s nearest leg. Around him the Black Thorns targeted the same leg with PPCs and large lasers. Rose fought closer as the thrust of the *Bristol* increased. Around him the howl of the massive engines reached a deafening pitch.

The ship leaned slightly to the right, and one of the *Bristol*'s legs lifted off the ground. As Rose fired again at the near leg, the *Bristol* finally answered. Three red beams shot from the weapons bay, striking the *Charger* squarely in the chest. Armor dissolved and flowed in three separate rivulets as the intense heat of the lasers melted the ferro-fibrous plates covering the 'Mech's engine. Thrown slightly off balance by the attack, Rose tried to take a step back to steady himself.

Instantly he knew he was going to fall. Although the blasts would normally not have been enough to knock him over, the typhoon around him pushed his balance over the edge. Thick smoke rose around the view ports as the *Charger* disappeared within the smoke. The 'Mech fell hard on its right elbow, snapping off armored plates and slamming Rose onto his right side. By the time he regained his feet, the *Bristol* was airborne. He tried to rush forward to fire at the exposed engines, but the heat was too great.

As the *Charger*'s heat scale climbed into the red, he slapped the engine-shutdown override, watching in frustration as the *Bristol* rose in the air. Esmeralda fired a pair of PPCs as the ship continued upward, but Rose knew the fight was already lost. He didn't even bother sending another flight of LRMs after the retreating craft.

"Black Thorns, this is Command One. Group on me."
Rose moved out of the rapidly diminishing smoke and
led his unit back to their base. He was still trying to
decide what he was going to tell McCloud when he saw
that the main gate had been breached.

The main gate hung on shattered hinges. Near the
guard house Rose could see the still forms of the two
guards. Through the windows of the barracks and the
mess hall rapidly spreading flames were visible. At first
Rose thought that the heavier fortified command post was
undamaged, but when he triggered the *Charger*'s chest-
mounted spot light, he saw that the doors and shuttered
windows had been scored by machine gun fire. Zooming
in on the post's front door, however, Rose saw that the
building remained secure. He saw no signs of heavy vehicles or 'Mechs, but they could easily be hiding behind
the command post or in the repair bay. As he charged
through what was left of the main gate, he noticed that the
protest encampment to the side of the road seemed abandoned.

"This is Command One," he said. "Seek and destroy
any vehicles, but look out for peds. Battle lance, take the
'Mech bays. Pursuit lance, check the perimeter. Rianna,
you stick with me."

Rose led his sister to the command center, scanning
for individual heat sources. It would be nearly impossible
to hide a vehicle on this side of the camp, but an infantryman with a missile, especially an inferno, could cause
considerable damage. After several seconds of tense
searching, Rose was about to declare the base abandoned
when he caught the azure flash of a PPC.

Spinning toward the flash, Rose saw a civilian four-
wheel drive vehicle streak out of the 'Mech bay. Esmeralda's shot had flushed the vehicle from its hiding place
and now it was accelerating toward the main gate. The
driver sent the vehicle sliding in a four-wheel drift around
the edge of the flaming barracks. From the open-top cargo
compartment two missiles leapt toward the *Warhammer*,
trailing gray smoke. Esmeralda fired another PPC, but

the wildly sliding vehicle eluded the shot as both its missiles struck the *Warhammer*'s head.

Rose tried to line a shot, but the vehicle disappeared under the cover of the command post. By the time it had cleared the corner of the building, it was pointed straight toward the main gate. Rose fired hurried shots with both arm-mounted lasers, but they struck to either side of the rapidly moving vehicle. He was about to give chase when Ajax arrived.

The *Raven* bounded around the mess hall in pursuit of the fleeing vehicle. Rose also started the *Charger* toward the main gate, but the *Raven* got there first, its bird-like legs driving the 'Mech's small body with increasing speed. As the vehicle slowed to take the first corner in the road, Ajax fired his Harpoon Six missiles. Someone yelled a warning over the open channel, but Rose couldn't identify the anguished voice. True to their name, five of the six missiles harpooned the side of the vehicle as it slid into the turn. Powered by forward momentum and lateral explosions, the vehicle completed the turn and slid off the road. Although the low buildings between the wreck and the *Charger* obscured Rose's view, the resulting explosion left no doubt about Ajax's marksmanship.

Ajax moved forward to confirm the kill and look for survivors, then reported that all four men had died in the wreck. As Ajax finished his report to Rose, Esmeralda declared the 'Mech bay clear. Angus and Ria quickly followed with identical reports, although they had discovered several of the compound guards dead at their posts, along with a handful of attackers. That left only the command post. Rose turned toward it, and activated his external speakers.

"This is Captain Rose of the Black Thorns. Open the doors of the command post and come out with your hands up. The building is completely surrounded." Rose waited and listened to the sounds of flames licking wildly at the burning mess hall. Several seconds later the door swung open.

Out stepped Rachel McCloud with a Zeus heavy rifle.

The eight-kilogram sniping rifle looked like a cannon in her small arms, but she rested the bulk easily on one hip. Rose could not help but smile at the sight. McCloud was the image of confidence and martial prowess until she suddenly collapsed in the doorway. Zooming in on her, he could see that her hair was thickly matted with blood.

"This is Command One. We've got to get out of here while there's still time. I don't know who attacked the camp, but I bet they'll be back. Without the support of the Council, we've got to assume we're on our own.

"Battle One and Three, watch the perimeter. Battle Two, salvage anything you can in the 'Mech bay. Rig it for external transport if possible. Munitions and armor have first priority.

"Recon Two, patrol outside the gate. Keep the Beagle wide open and let me know if anything comes close. If it looks even vaguely hostile, shoot.

"Command Two, Pursuit One, dismount and clear out the command post. We move out in thirty minutes, people, so hop to it." Watching the flames completely engulf the barracks, Rose suddenly felt sick. Although the building's exterior was of metal and stone, the interior burned readily.

"I'm sorry about your personal gear," he said to his people. It was a hollow statement and Rose knew it, but what else was there to say? Everything the Black Thorns owned had been in the barracks and now it was completely destroyed.

Watching the flames, Rose realized that he had made a terrible mistake. He should have known how impossible it would be to divert the attack on the DropShip, and kept part of his command back at the base. Now the base was destroyed and his warriors left only with the clothes on their backs and the 'Mechs beneath their feet. Considering the recent trail of events he told himself that their current predicament was entirely his fault.

Anger boiled inside him and threatened to erupt when Rose looked back at Rachel McCloud's unconscious form. He gritted his teeth and forced the anger into a new form. Fury turned to resolve, Rose vowing silently never to let such a debacle happen again. He would put the protection of his command above all other concerns, even the contract. He shook himself back into the real world feeling as though the vow were etched on his heart and mind.

"Twenty-nine minutes left, Thorns, and then we're on our own. Make the cleanup quick." Rose locked the *Charger* in place and climbed down the 'Mech, the cockpit's emergency medkit hanging from his shoulder. First he would see to Rachel, then evacuate the city, then figure out how the Thorns might survive the mess they were in.

Once the unit had some breathing room they'd decide how to avenge themselves on the terrorists who'd stolen the *Bristol* and destroyed the compound. Rose could hardly wait for that moment to come.

═══ 26 ═══

The camera swung closer as the speaker glanced down at his few notes. Salander Morgain had always believed that if you could look the camera in the eye and speak with confidence, everything would work out fine. In truth, he knew things didn't always work out as planned, but so far he'd been lucky. He looked once more at the notes Crenshaw's staff had put together for him and slipped them under the podium.

To his right he could see Crenshaw cover his face in annoyance, but Morgain only smiled and looked up at the camera. His timing was perfect. The active light on the top of the camera winked to red and the lens caught the entire movement. It gave him a look of deep concern that the audience could immediately identify, even if most didn't understand the meaning of it.

"Fellow residents of Borghese, my name is Salander Morgain." He had decided to start with a humble introduction; crowds really liked that. "Tonight I would like to take a moment from your busy lives to address a topic of deep concern to us all: the Clans." Morgain kept his voice very neutral. He did not want his auditors to draw any conclusions, yet.

"Ever since the first day of their arrival in the Inner Sphere, these strangers from beyond have been a con-

stant source of dread and foreboding.'' Morgain allowed
his voice to rise in volume and pitch. ''Their weapons,
their technology, and their fighting tactics swept entire
planets clean of defending forces with an almost con-
temptuous ease.'' His voice softened, dropping almost to
a whisper. ''I know because I was on several of those
planets and watched my lancemates die as we fought a
losing battle.'' He shook his head, eyes down. When he
looked back up at the camera, he had a new light in his
eyes.

''When I returned to Borghese, I was hoping to leave
the violence of the military life behind. I hoped to live
in peace on the planet of my birthplace. But now I know
that is not to be.

''From where we stand at this moment, the Clan
JumpShips are only two weeks away. Two weeks.'' Again
he shook his head. ''In spite of this, the Federated Commonwealth chooses not to defend our world. Their regimental combat teams are deployed all around us, but for
Borghese—'' Morgain paused and held out his hands—
''there is nothing.

''So what do we do?'' Morgain looked directly at the
camera. ''In the military, they taught us that there are
only three things to do when you face an enemy.

''You can run.'' Morgain flashed a smile for the first
time in his speech. ''Unfortunately, for Borghese, that is
not possible.

''You can fight.'' The smile disappeared in a heartbeat. ''Again, I am afraid that is not possible. If we had
even the slightest chance of success, I would lead the
battle personally, but I believe the effort would be futile.
The Clans are too powerful. Abandoned by the Federats,
we cannot hope to stand against them.

''That leaves only the third option: surrender.'' Morgain gripped the podium and slowed the pace of his
speech. ''It is not a word to be spoken lightly. In all my
military career, I have never surrendered, and until recently, I never dreamed that I would even contemplate it.
My mind was changed, however, by a counselor wiser

than me who asked a simple question. 'You would fight, but at what cost?' What could I say?

"Could I say that I would fight until the planet I loved was destroyed by the ruthless invaders? That I would fight while thousands died in a conflict they had no chance of winning? Could I fight again and witness the horrors I saw at Kobe and Thun visited on my home?" Morgain paused, evidently exhausted by the intensity of his emotions.

"I could not. I cannot fight against the Clans, should they come to Borghese, and I wholeheartedly urge you to share my belief in nonresistance.

"I have—"

Rose hit the stop button on the replay unit and glanced at Zenos Cooke. The two men were sitting in Cooke's upland retreat, though Rose knew the location would not be safe for much longer. While Rose was conferring with the Council chairman, the rest of the Black Thorns were keeping watch around the villa. The two men had been viewing the official recording of the afternoon's Council meeting, which included a broadcast of Salander Morgain's address. Despite Cooke's protests, the Council had voted to let Morgain speak to the people in an effort to calm their fears about the Clans. Cooke had been forced to endure the carefully orchestrated spectacle and now watched it again in the same mood of despair.

"I take it that he goes on for a while longer in a similar vein?" asked Rose. Cooke nodded grimly. It had been two days since the attack on the Black Thorns' compound and neither man had slept much. Rose looked like he was handling the strain. Cooke did not.

"With Morgain in their corner, the Preservationists should be able to swing public opinion to their side. They won't fight the Clans now, no matter what I say or do."

"What about us?" Rose tried to keep the question neutral, but concern and a touch of fear crept into his voice.

"You want to hear it from him?" Cooke indicated the

frozen image of Salander Morgain on the screen. Rose shook his head.

"The condensed version goes like this," Cooke said. "You are a menace to the planet and the people. Nobody knows why you destroyed your compound or killed the protesters, but you did. If you cannot be persuaded to turn yourselves in to the proper authorities, Morgain and company are going to come after you, probably backed by the militia."

Rose wanted to laugh, but the situation was too serious. He was afraid the official story would read something like Cooke had outlined.

"A roving patrol chanced upon the compound as you left, but there were no survivors among the protesters you killed. They tracked you to the northwest, but were too lightly armed to engage. They lost your trail when you crossed the Garrison River north of Houston."

That had been Angus' idea. The Thorns had waded into the wide, but shallow, river and walked almost twenty kilometers upstream in the dead of the night.

When they finally left the river they were well away from civilization. They'd been on the move ever since, dodging towns and people for the last two days. Despite the risk of Crenshaw and his cronies thinking to look for them at Cooke's villa, Angus and Ajax had slowly led the group there at Rose's insistence. Rose was glad he did. Without support from Cooke, the Thorns were isolated from the rest of the world.

"What about the *Bristol*?" Rose knew he wouldn't like the answer, but he needed to know.

Cooke sighed. "The *Bristol* lifted without clearance from the spaceport under the command of Captain McCloud. Since she was not cleared for debarkation and had not paid for either her cargo or her port charges, she has been declared a pirate."

"Was she reported to the Federated Commonwealth?"

"I don't know. I assume so, but that is really a matter for the port master. Something like that would probably never come to the attention of the Council."

"Then we've got something to work with." Cooke looked at Rose as though he were crazy.

"McCloud was at our base when the *Bristol* blasted off. She's spent most of the last forty-eight hours unconscious in the back of Hawg's *Zeus*. She was wounded in the attack on the compound. We couldn't very well leave her, and Hawg's cockpit had the most space.

"The theft of the *Bristol* must have something to do with Crenshaw and the Preservationists. Assuming that's true, they can't very well report the DropShip as a pirate, or else every F-C ship in the area would be gunning for it. That ship is on a mission and it has to be able to travel. Any idea where it went?"

Cooke shook his head. "It made a non-standard arc in the general direction of the Borghese nadir jump point, then suddenly took off at a ninety-degree angle to its previous course and disappeared."

"Pirate jump point."

Cooke nodded. "The JumpShip was probably already waiting." Pirate points, as they were called, were sometimes used as alternate entry points into a system but only by the most skilled or the most desperate JumpShip captains. They significantly decreased a DropShip's travel time to and from a JumpShip, but use of these points was dangerous in the extreme. Not only were they difficult to calculate, but the slightest miscalculation in the jump through hyperspace could literally tear the JumpShip and DropShip apart during the instantaneous transfer across light years of space.

"But if you can force their hand, we might be able to slow down their plan, whatever it is. Force them to report the theft and see what happens. My guess is that they won't let that happen."

Cooke rubbed the stubble of his chin, reminding Rose that he too needed a shave. He shook off the urge to scratch his own neck as Cooke considered the plan.

"I think I can apply some pressure," Cooke said

thoughtfully. "I've still got some pull as chairman and I might as well use it before it totally slips away. Crenshaw has been gobbling up everything he can get his hands on." Rose's communicator beeped four times, cutting Cooke off.

Rose stood abruptly. "Company's on the way. I've got about twenty minutes to get away from here so I'll say good night."

Cooke stood and extended a hand. "This could be our last meeting, Rose. I'll keep doing what I can, but my support base is eroding fast. They can't replace me as the Chairman, but they can supplant me as a political force. That means Crenshaw will be calling the shots.

"Good luck with Morgain and his gang. He's got a reputation to protect, so I don't imagine he'll pull any punches." Rose nodded and took the man's offered hand.

"Count on me to be careful."

"Where will you go?"

Rose smiled and shrugged. "I don't know yet. I've managed to download the recon maps Hawg and I made over the last few months, so we'll try to figure out something from there." Rose didn't sound optimistic, but both men knew the Black Thorns' best chances lay in reaching the sparsely populated wilderness of the continent's northwest.

"Good luck, Captain. I know it doesn't help now, but I'm sorry I got you into this mess."

Rose nodded and headed for the door. He had similar sentiments toward the other members of his command. As he reached the door, he decided that only one of them should have to shoulder that responsibility.

"Don't worry about us, Mister Chairman. We'll pull out of this. Your contract was honorably offered and honorably accepted. You're not to blame for what's happened." He didn't have to mention who was; they both knew well enough who was responsible for their current grief.

Without waiting for a reply, Rose left the room. His

only hope was that Cooke would somehow manage to provide them some measure of help while Rose led the Thorns into hiding. Without that, he wasn't sure what chances they had for survival.

27

The Cedars, Borghese
14 July 3055

Rose led the rest of the Thorns into what passed for wilderness on Borghese, the flatlands gradually giving way to the winding rivers and the cedar forests that gave the area its name. Rose mentally thanked the original settlers for having transplanted the Terran trees that had thrived on the rich Borghese soil, growing virtually unchecked for centuries.

The first two weeks were relatively uneventful. They moved only at night and camped during the day under the cover of the cedars. Food was plentiful because they'd managed to salvage several weeks' rations from the emergency stores of the base repair bay. Rose had no idea why the items had been stored there, but he was glad for the mistake.

McCloud traveled in the 'Mechs of different warriors, but never with Rose. She had not taken the news of the *Bristol's* hijacking very well, drawing the same conclusion as Rose; there'd been a traitor among her crew. By week's end she and Rose were on speaking terms again, but not quite friendly. Rose thought it natural that she should blame him for the loss of her ship. He'd promised, after all, to protect it.

Rianna monitored the civilian airwaves as the mercenaries camped by day and when they moved through The

Cedars at night. She confirmed that the Thorns were being hunted by the militia and Morgain's lance, but that their pursuers were still more than a hundred kilometers away from the mercenaries' current position. The political infighting in the Council was headline news, with matters going from bad to worse for Cooke. The *Bristol* and her crew were quickly forgotten as the hunt for the Black Thorns went on, leaving Rose to guess what Cooke was up to.

Angus and Ajax listened to the military bands, but they were silent. Despite several fly-overs by Ripper VTOLs, Rose was confident that most of the search vehicles had by-passed them, and it seemed reasonable to assume that they could continue in hiding until they heard how effective any efforts by Cooke had been. The next morning, however, their position was spotted.

Just before dawn, the unit was crossing one of the meandering rivers so common in the area. Coming out in the open increased their chances of discovery, but the unit couldn't afford to be penned in by the water. They were often forced out from the cover of the trees to make crossings. None of the rivers were particularly deep, and so one crossing point was as good as another. This day, Angus and Ajax were on one side of the river and the rest of the unit on the other. Sending three beeps across the comm line, Ajax signaled that the Beagle active probe found nothing in the area.

Badicus' *Shadow Hawk* waded in first, followed closely by Esmeralda in her *Warhammer*. Just as Hawg's *Zeus* stepped off the bank, however, a hovercraft came shooting up the river. The high-pitched whine of the fans announced the craft only an instant before it broke around a bend. Running down the center of the river, it headed straight toward Badicus.

Standing hip-deep in the current, the *Shadow Hawk* turned to face the craft. One giant hand came up, and Rose was sure Badicus was about to fire. The hover pilot was not going to make the shot easy, however. As he jammed the controls hard to the left, the craft came sliding backward toward the *Shadow Hawk*. The pitch of the fans changed abruptly and the craft settled suddenly in the water, killing all momentum. As the back end of the craft bit into the water, the front end reared up, threatening to tip the craft on its back. Then, after a moment's pause, it crashed back into the river amid a giant spray of water. As the craft settled, the driver reengaged the fans and took the hovercraft once more down the river.

Rose doubted Badicus was a good enough shot to hit the craft on its inbound course. The sudden stop had caught Rose by surprise as it must have Badicus as well. When the hovercraft turned, Rose expected the warrior to shoot, but the *Shadow Hawk* simply stood watching it go. Although Rose and the rest of the unit could see the hovercraft, Badicus was the only one in the river and thus the only pilot with any chance of hitting the small vehicle. Instead of firing, Badicus had let the craft escape. Rose sat in shock.

The sight of Ajax trying to run the vehicle down snapped Rose out of his stupor. But even the *Raven* couldn't catch the speedy hovercraft. No one had spoken during the entire incident and Rose realized they were still obeying radio silence. He keyed the commlink.

"All right, Thorns, what was that?"

"Ground Hawk, Mark Two."

"You sure about that, Badicus?" Rose was furious at the man for having let the hover get away, and he let his voice reveal it.

"Yes, sir. The Mark Two is an unarmed recon craft. It's constructed of polymers and heavily shielded, that's why Ajax couldn't detect it."

Rose ground his teeth. The pilot was undoubtedly relaying their current position to the entire militia. It was time to get out of the area. "Pursuit Lance, get us out of here. I don't care where, but we've got to put as much distance as possible between us and this spot in the next two hours.

"Battle Two, meet me on Comm Three." Rose switched to channel three and secured the line. He now had a private link to O'Shea. He wasn't really concerned about the other Thorns listening in, but he wanted to chew Badicus out in complete privacy. When Badicus reported in, his anger turned cold.

"You've got one chance to tell me why you put the entire unit in danger, O'Shea. One chance to justify the trust I put in you, so you'd better make it good."

Rose listened to several seconds of silence as the unit's 'Mechs continued to move, Angus and Ajax leading the group on a direct course through the trees. The unit was racking up the distance, but the trail would be easy to follow.

"The craft was unarmed, sir," Badicus began tentatively. "I couldn't fire on an unarmed vehicle."

Rose exploded over the commlink. "Damn it man, you've just put the entire planetary militia, not to mention five BattleMechs, hot on our butts and you don't want to fire on the unarmed hover that's telling everybody where we are?"

"That's right, sir. I won't fire at an unarmed craft and I'm not sure I would have been able to fire even if the craft had been a Mark One."

"And why the hell not?"

"Sir, I've spent the last few months of my life with the same men who are now trying to hunt us down. Esmeralda and Ajax are in the same situation. How can you live with a group of people one day and expect to treat them like the enemy the next?"

Rose strangled a furious reply. He knew the craft should have been stopped, yet he'd been considering the same ethical dilemma at the back of his mind. He was sworn to protect the people of Borghese and now might be called upon to shoot some of them. That it would be in self-defense wouldn't make much difference. With that his anger seemed to melt.

"You're probably right," he said. "As a unit and as individuals we're sworn to protect these people. I don't like the idea any more than you do, but our first duty must be to one another. You put the whole unit at risk when you let the hover get away. It wasn't fair that you were the one who had to make the decision, but that's what happened and now the rest of us are going to suffer. Think about that next time you decide not to pull the trigger. Dismissed.''

Rose killed the connection and walked on in silence, trusting the pursuit lance to lead the way. He was still considering what to do an hour later when the unit suddenly changed course. Angus was cutting back on their original path, sacrificing some distance for a trail that would be harder to follow. Reaching a decision, Rose opened the commline.

''Thorns, this is Command One. An interesting problem now confronts us. In a few hours we're going to come into contact with the militia. People we've promised to protect are going to try to bring us back to Houston. Given that they burned our compound and stole the *Bristol,* I think you can imagine the type of treatment we'll receive when we get back.'' Rose paused to let the words sink in.

''We can only run for so long. Sooner or later we're going to have to engage the militia and Salander Morgain's 'Mechs. That means fighting, and killing. We can't let that happen, so here is what we are going to do.

''Pursuit, keep us away from them for as long as possible. The longer we can stay away, the longer we have for Cooke to try to help us some way back in Houston. That means nearly constant movement, little sleep, and no room for error. We stick together and make them hunt us down. When they finally manage to corner us, we surrender and take our chances in Houston.'' Rose paused, then decided there was nothing more he could add. ''Questions?''

The comm unit remained clear as the unit moved through the trees.

The next eight days were little more than a blur for Rose and his command. Led alternately by Angus and Ajax, they moved in and around every natural obstacle they could find. The recon work Rose and Hawg had done earlier provided the unit with information the militia either did not have or were unable to take advantage of.

The unit was almost cornered several times by the militia Rippers and Salander's 'Mechs. On three separate occasions, the Thorns were subjected to long-range missile fire from the infantry, but none of the shots came even close to hitting them. The lasers of the Rippers were more dangerous, but 'Mechs traveling among the thickly packed cedars gave the airborne pilots few good shots. The laser attacks finally ended on the sixth day when a near-miss set fire to a copse of trees, the flames spreading to engulf the whole area.

The hunters didn't like it, but they were forced to divert some of their force to keep the blaze from spreading further. The forest fire didn't create as much of a problem as Rose had hoped. True to Cooke's earlier claim, the militia was especially skilled at handling civilian emergencies. While detaching a smaller force to deal with the fire, the main body moved on, driving the Thorns before them. The Ripper VTOLs were still being used for spotting, but their sniping was over.

As the sun came up on day nine, Rose knew his unit was near the end of the line. Lack of sleep and the near-constant tension had sapped the mercenaries' strength and much of their will. Only McCloud seemed to have any energy. Unable to pilot a 'Mech, she'd taken to riding with a different pilot each day. Rose noticed that the various 'Mech pilots were always in a remarkably better mood at the end of a day with McCloud. After she insisted on riding with him, he understood why.

Traveling under radio silence, each pilot was left with his or her own thoughts for the entire day, all the fears, hopes, and futile wishes eating away at the pilot's confidence. Having McCloud for company took the warrior's mind off negative thoughts and gave him or her something positive to concentrate on. Rose had no idea how she'd treated the other pilots, but with him it was almost like old times. They laughed and remembered the months aboard ship when they'd spent entire days together. By the end of the day Rose felt better than he had since the loss of the *Bristol,* and McCloud also seemed to be in good spirits. As she climbed out of the cockpit during one of their infrequent rest stops, she had actually forgiven Rose for the loss of the *Bristol.*

Eventually fatigue took its toll on the unit. Forty-eight hours after his last conversation with McCloud, Rose sat looking over the sleeping forms of his unit. At first the pilots had slept on the ground, but now they were forced to sleep in their 'Mechs in case the militia or Morgain's men arrived sooner than expected. Sitting in his *Charger,* Rose reflected on the noose that was tightening around the unit.

The militia commanders seemed to have figured out that the Black Thorns were unwilling to fight them, and had repositioned their men to the front and sides of the unit. While the militia kept the mercenaries in place, Morgain was closing the noose with his lance. To travel more than ten kilometers in any direction meant they would have to fight through one of the pursuing units.

Rose kept his eyes on the long-range scanner and watched the five heat sources his computer had long ago tagged as 'Mechs come cautiously closer. Opening the commlink he woke the rest of the unit as another channel on his comm blinked green. He was beyond hope that the call might be from Cooke, the only member outside the lance who had the frequency, but in spite of that, he opened the channel.

"Rose here."

"Good morning, Captain Rose." Rose didn't need an identification, instantly recognizing the voice as Salander Morgain's. He had no time to wonder how Morgain had obtained the frequency, but he knew things had just taken a turn for the worse.

"Mister Morgain, or is it Hauptmann now?"

Rose thought he heard light laughter on the line before Morgain answered. "Hauptmann it is, just like in my army days." Rose reached out to the comm unit and patched the feed from Morgain through the open channel. Now all the Black Thorns could hear his words, though only Rose could respond.

"Captain Rose, it is my duty to order you to surrender yourself and your unit immediately. As the rightful representative of the leadership of Borghese, I am authorized to accept your surrender and assure you that you will be treated fairly upon your return to Houston."

"What about the charges against us?"

Morgain seemed taken back by the question and did not respond immediately. "You will be tried in a court of law, as would any other citizen of the planet. Given the serious nature of the charges, I imagine you will appear before the Ruling Council.

"What about the charges against Captain McCloud?"

Morgain was ready for that question and answered immediately. "All charges against Captain McCloud have been dropped."

"What?"

"Upon the subsequent return of the *Bristol*—"

"The *Bristol* is back on Borghese?"

The comm unit was silent. For a moment Rose thought he'd misunderstood Morgain. Then the incoming light on channel three went green. That had to be McCloud trying to open a channel to Rose. He decided to ignore the light for a moment, waiting for Morgain to continue.

"Well, technically, Captain Rose, the answer is no. But the *Bristol* is insystem and should arrive back on Borghese tomorrow."

"So Chairman Cooke convinced you they weren't pirates after all?"

"On the contrary, Captain Rose, the late Chairman Cooke had nothing to do with it. The *Bristol* arrived of its own free will, piloted by the first officer."

"Cooke is dead?"

"Unfortunately, yes." Rose could tell Morgain was smiling as he spoke. "He died last night in his office at the Assembly Pavilion. An apparent suicide. I imagine the media will receive word of the event any moment now.''

Rose wanted to reach through the commline and strangle the man. Morgain was too self-assured. He obviously thought he had all the answers.

''You're a liar, Morgain. Chairman Cooke would never take his own life.''

Morgain scoffed. ''How little you know about it, Rose. His note stated quite clearly why he ended his miserable existence. He was afraid of the new order that is coming to Borghese. He could not live with the change.''

Rose was instantly sure he knew the answer, but he asked the question anyway.

''What change?''

''The change brought about by the *Bristol*. She's leading a Clan DropShip to the planet. The Jade Falcon commanders will formally accept the surrender of Borghese and claim the planet as their newest conquest.''

Rose heard the words, but refused to believe them. Cooke's worst nightmare had taken place and the people of Borghese were the ones to blame. It wasn't good enough to just wait for the Clans, they had actually invited them to take their planet.

''You're with them, aren't you, Morgain?''

Again Rose didn't need to hear the response to know the answer. Morgain had too much information for a mere Hauptmann, especially one so far out in the field. Cooke had been killed to clear away any political opposition to the Clans. If Rose surrendered, there would be no further resistance to the Falcons. Borghese would be forced to surrender without a chance to defend itself. As the thought hit him, Rose also realized something else. The militia couldn't know about the death of Cooke or the arrival of the Clans. They were being kept out of the way and in the dark. By the time they returned to Houston, the capital would be firmly in Jade Falcon hands.

''Morgain, you and your Preservationists back in Houston can go straight to hell. You're as bad as the Clans you support, maybe worse, because you were born here, and now you're going to turn Borghese over to the invaders.''

If Morgain bothered with a reply, it was quickly cut off as Rose killed the connection. The line to the Thorns, however, was still open.

''You heard the man, Black Thorns. Morgain is with the Clans. At this point it's probably safe to assume the militia doesn't know what's going on, but they will soon.'' On the scanner Morgain's lance closed on Rose. ''Once the militia realizes they've been played for fools, they'll probably come over to our side.'' Even so, Rose realized that Morgain wasn't likely to give the militia the chance to figure out the truth. If the Black Thorns were wiped out, Morgain's lance could force the militia to accept the Clan invasion without resistance. As if to confirm his thoughts, the militia began to close in on either side of the Thorns.

''Morgain is going to try to squeeze us on all four sides. By the time the militia figures out we're the good guys, they'll already have helped eliminate us.

''Prepare to engage enemy 'Mechs. Keep away from the militia and do not, repeat do not, engage. Battle Lance, you'll form the center with me. Command Two and Pursuit Lance, stay to the rear. Attempt to engage the flanks as they open up.''

Rose suddenly remembered McCloud. She'd been riding with Ajax for most of the day. Ajax had quietly suggested they leave her behind for the militia to rescue, but McCloud had steadfastly refused. Now that the fight was about to be joined, she was in the lightest 'Mech.

''Pursuit Two, do you still have your passenger?''

''Affirmative.''

''Keep the passenger safe, Pursuit Two. All other considerations are secondary. Do you understand?''

''Affirmative, Command One. I understand.'' Good, thought Rose to himself, because I'm not sure I do.

As Rose spoke, Morgain's 'Mechs closed the distance. Although outnumbered, they obviously thought they had the advantage. And with the militia, Morgain was probably right. Now it was time for the Black Thorns to earn their pay and prove to themselves, and to the people of Borghese, that they could fight.

While the Thorns were maneuvering into position, Morgain's 'Mechs were picking up speed. As they came within four kilometers of the Thorns, Rose ordered his unit forward. Moving at cruising speed, they prepared to carry the fight to Morgain.

$$=== 28 ===$$

Esmeralda and Hawg anchored the center of the Black
Thorn advance, with Rose and O'Shea on either side.
Watching the distance close on his scanner, Rose
searched through the cedars for the first glimpse of Morgain's 'Mechs. The dense tree growth would make the
fighting close and personal. Rose flexed both arms of
the *Charger*. Physical attacks and mass could well carry
the fight.

As the range closed to under a kilometer, Rose caught
a glimpse of metal reflected from the rising sun. It had
to be a BattleMech, but the trees hid its outline. The next
instant the 'Mech had vanished. As Morgain's force drew
closer, his 'Mechs shuffled positions. What had initially
been a cluster altered to become a vee, with the point
directed squarely at Esmeralda and Hawg. Rose had no
doubt that the heaviest 'Mech in Morgain's force would
be the point of the vee. Ahead, the ground began to rise
slightly. Rose could tell from the scanner that Morgain
was at the base of the rise on the other side.

"Battle Lance, charge!" The four 'Mechs charged up
the hill, trying to gain the high ground and the advantage
that went with it. Easily the fastest in his *Charger,* Rose
reached the crest just ahead of the rest of his lance. He
dropped his targeting cross hairs onto the first metal shape

he saw, which happened to be the second 'Mech in line on his side. The Artemis IV confirmed a lock and Rose triggered a flight of missiles. Only after the missiles had fired did he carefully examine his opponents.

A shining *Stalker* held the point of Morgain's vee. It was this 'Mech's reflective paint that Rose had seen briefly as the two sides closed ground. The 'Mech didn't even turn in Rose's direction, but kept its attention focused on the rise where Esmeralda would soon appear.

Rose's initial target was a *BattleMaster*. The *Charger*'s computer tagged it as a newer model, but it was impossible to confirm the identification because the 'Mech was wreathed in the smoke and flame of long-range missiles striking its head and shoulders. The pilot brought up his PPC, but the shots went wide of the *Charger* as the impacting missiles spoiled the pilot's aim.

The final 'Mech in the vee on Rose's side was a *Banshee*. Rose didn't need the computer to tell him it was a 5S model; the multiple weapon ports were proof enough. Something about the 'Mech's movement was familiar, but Rose couldn't place it right now and he had no time to figure it out. The *BattleMaster* recovered and triggered a salvo at the *Charger* as Rose's missiles recycled.

The azure PPC beam caught the *Charger* squarely in the chest, blasting armor into ionized flakes. Then came the aligned ruby light of a laser firing from the *BattleMaster*'s left torso, gouging into the *Charger*'s right arm and leg an instant later. Rose fought to control his 'Mech, quickly regaining his balance and triggering another flight of missiles.

Guided by the Artemis fire-control system and Rose's gentle hand, the flight again struck the *BattleMaster* around the head and shoulders. Rose knew the pilot was taking a beating from the multiple missile hits. Despite the 'Mech's thick armor, the pilot was bound to feel the effects of explosions going off just meters away from his seat. Rose topped the hill and closed the range on the *BattleMaster* and the *Banshee* just as Esmeralda and Hawg popped over the hill. On the far side of the battle line Rose saw the brief flash of a PPC and knew Badicus had engaged the remaining 'Mech of Morgain's lance.

At virtually the same instant both sides fighting in the center of the line triggered everything they had at each other. The *Stalker* and the *Awesome* to its right each targeted a separate 'Mech. Esmeralda and Hawg, however, ganged up on the *Stalker*. At close range, the hits were almost guaranteed.

The *Awesome* fired every one of its weapons and hit with every shot. Its pilot gambled that Hawg could not survive the salvo as its heat went from cool to critical in three seconds. Hawg took two of the PPC hits to the chest and the other to his right arm. The supporting laser and missile fire further damaged the *Zeus'* right arm and blew away armor plates from the left knee. Under that barrage Hawg had no chance of controlling his 'Mech, which spun partially around before crashing onto its left side. The undamaged *Awesome* moved toward the fallen *Zeus*.

Hawg's attack on the *Stalker*, combined with Esmeralda's shots, had stopped the lumbering 'Mech in its tracks. Lasers and missiles streaked toward the armless machine, followed closely by PPC fire. Lasers burned and armor exploded away in a cloud of fragments as the combined firepower of the two Thorn 'Mechs breached the *Stalker*'s right-torso armor, ravaging its powerful legs. Like Hawg, the *Stalker* pilot could not control the 'Mech during the vicious assault. Unlike Hawg's 'Mech, the *Stalker* fell head-first into the slope, plowing up rocks and dirt.

Esmeralda also staggered under the *Stalker*'s attack, but through fate or uncanny skill, she managed to keep the *Warhammer* upright despite the barrage of missiles exploding across her 'Mech's chest and lower torso. As the *Zeus* struggled to rise she moved to defend Hawg, leaving the flailing *Stalker* to stand if it could.

Rose considered shifting targets, but abandoned the idea as the *Banshee* moved to support the *BattleMaster*. Rose centered the cross hairs on the chest of the

BattleMaster for a third time as the missile-reload light flickered green. He was about to engage both missiles and the medium pulse lasers slaved to the same control when the *BattleMaster* started to topple forward. As Rose watched in amazement, the eighty-five ton 'Mech fell flat on its face. Unlike the other two 'Mechs that had gone down, however, the *BattleMaster* made no attempt to stop its fall. Rebounding off the trunk of an ancient cedar, the 'Mech crashed to the ground and then lay still.

Rose allowed himself a moment of amazement. Despite scoring only two hits, neither of which had breached the assault 'Mech's armor, he'd taken out the *BattleMaster*. The pilot had undoubtedly been pummeled into unconsciousness by the concussion of the missile explosions. He doubted the pilot would wake before the fight was over, but decided to make sure.

"Pursuit, swing right. One *BattleMaster* down, but a *Banshee* has moved to support. Make sure that 'Mech doesn't get back up. Two, protect yourself and your civilian at all costs. That's an order.''

Rose swung to the left and moved toward the center of the battle line on Morgain's side of the ridge. He kept one eye on the *Banshee*, which had yet to fire as it moved through the trees, and the other eye on the *Stalker*, which was still trying to stand. As he broke through the trees, the *Stalker* had managed to make it to one knee.

Rose had always considered the *Stalker* a poorly designed 'Mech. Although the 'Mech mounted considerable firepower, it was slow and clumsy. Compounding the problem were two "wings" that served as arms. Though the 'Mech was regarded as a good firing platform, the lack of arms severely hampered its ability in certain situations. And this was one of them.

Without arms, it was extremely difficult to get the 'Mech back upright once it fell to the ground. If this *Stalker* hadn't fallen on a slope, Rose doubted that it would have ever gotten up again without some kind of assistance. The pilot had almost succeeded, but Rose thwarted the attempt by charging across the intervening ground.

Rose fired all four of his pulse lasers as he closed, every one of them hitting the *Stalker*'s right side as the pilot tried to get the 'Mech's other leg underneath it. He managed to keep the 'Mech upright as Rose's lasers cut away vital armor, but he couldn't keep his footing when the *Charger* slammed into his side.

Beginning to run, Rose charged the *Stalker*. Normally he'd have tried a shoulder slam, but with the *Stalker* partially bent over and on slightly lower ground, Rose had decided to try another tactic. As he closed the distance, he adjusted the *Charger*'s stride so that his left foot was planted next to the side of the *Stalker*. Continuing the motion, he brought the right foot forward and threw his weight backward. Like a football player blasting the ball past a defending goalie, Rose powered the right foot forward.

If the *Stalker*'s shape had been more human, Rose could have hit it in the ribs, but the *Stalker* had only the right wing. The *Charger*'s giant foot caved in the other 'Mech's previously damaged armor and crushed the short-range missile launcher underneath. Then came a bright flash that made Rose fear he'd caused an explosion in his eagerness, but there was no chain reaction from the missiles stored in the torso. As the *Stalker* rolled away from the blow, the *Charger*'s foot caught on the ruptured endoskeleton and pulled Rose off balance. The *Stalker* fell again, this time taking the *Charger* with it.

Rose tried to roll with the fall, but the trapped foot made that impossible. The *Charger* fell across the *Stalker*, further damaging the 'Mech underneath. Though Rose was able to use the *Charger*'s outstretched hands to absorb some of the impact, he still hit the ground hard. Armor buckled and seams popped free as Rose immediately attempted to rise. With the *Charger* being face-down, its lightly armored back was exposed and vulnerable to Morgain's 'Mechs. Rose searched the scanner for the

Banshee, his mind filled with images of when his 'Mech had been knocked over on Solaris.

The *Banshee,* however, wasn't close enough to take a shot through the densely packed cedars. To Rose's surprise, the 'Mech had paralleled his course, but had made no attempt to get closer. Rose continued to stare at the scanner as he tried to rise because all he could see through the main viewer was dirt and crushed cedar needles.

Esmeralda had moved closer to Hawg and was slugging it out with the *Awesome* while Hawg was still struggling to stand on the slope. The thermal readings on the two standing 'Mechs were well in the danger level, but the *Awesome* seemed to be running hotter. It had obviously been firing all three of its PPCs as soon as they came back on-line. Chances were good that the waste heat generated by the weapons' fire would eventually shut down the 'Mech; in the meantime those same weapons would take a heavy toll on the mercenaries. Rose finally found Badicus still engaged with the fifth enemy 'Mech well to the left of the main line. Rianna was moving to support him, but it would be several seconds before she was clear of the trees.

The pursuit lance had moved to cover the fallen *BattleMaster* and were wisely staying in position. Neither of the lighter 'Mechs could stand the punishment being dished out by the heavy and assault 'Mechs of Morgain's force and they knew it. If they kept the *BattleMaster* out of the fight, Rose would consider it a better than even exchange and a good use of the lance. It also kept McCloud out of harm's way, no matter what happened to him.

"Battle Two, this is Command One. What is your status?"

O'Shea opened the link and a burst of static filled Rose's cockpit. "I've got him right where I want him, Command One." An explosion filled the line and Rose heard O'Shea's involuntary cry of alarm. In the background the *Shadow Hawk*'s heat warning bell went off.

"Cancel that last transmission, Command One. That last shot nicked the engine shielding."

"How bad?" Rose struggled harder to free his 'Mech's entangled leg. He could feel the *Stalker* resisting, however, and the leg remained trapped.

"I can shut it down now, or I can blow up in three minutes."

"Shut the damn thing down, O'Shea. That's an order." Rose heard the heat warning bell go off again.

"Command One, automated shutdown sequence has been initiated, but I don't think I'm going to be able to stick around for the finish. This guy's coming back for the kill. Sorry about the 'Mech, Rose, but I'm ejecting."

"Battle Two, what is your opponent?"

Rose heard the restraining pins explode and a split second later the cockpit rose into the sky above the battlefield. "Marauder Twooo . . ." and then the connection went dead.

Rose began thrashing in a vain effort to free the *Charger*'s trapped leg. He was about to call for Angus to help when the leg began to come free. With his other leg he kicked at the *Stalker* while repeatedly trying to pull the trapped leg out of the *Stalker*'s torso, but it would not come away. On the scanner the *Marauder II* moved closer to the embattled *Warhammer* and *Awesome*. Its hundred-ton weight would easily swing the battle against the Thorns unless Rose could free himself. Finally Rose could wait no longer.

Throwing caution to the wind, he pushed off with his outstretched left arm. Though he could not hope to stand, the sloping ground gave him enough leverage to roll over onto his back. He was reasonably sure the maneuver would succeed, but he feared that if the foot were wedged too tightly in the *Stalker*'s torso, the sudden movement would snap it off.

As the *Charger* flopped over onto its back, Rose heard the grind of metal as armor tore free and the skeleton underneath bent, then popped free. The foot was still trapped in the *Stalker*, but Rose could tell that the "toes" were pointed up. Kicking with his left leg, Rose sighted down the trapped right leg and fired the arm-mounted pulse laser. Armor boiled away, and with a heave the foot came free.

Rose rolled over to his right side and struggled to stand on the uneven ground. In doing so, he noticed the damage to the *Stalker,* whose torso had been reduced to bits of crushed steel by his charge and subsequent thrashing. The pilot had shut down the engine at some point in the struggle and emerged from the cockpit as the *Charger* stood up.

Rose started to climb up the hill and immediately saw how severely the trapped leg had been damaged. Both the foot and knee actuators had been destroyed, reducing the *Charger*'s progress to a stiff-legged shuffle. Despite the shorter distance he had to travel, Rose reached the embattled *Warhammer* and *Awesome* immediately after the *Marauder II.*

As Rose was arriving, the *Zeus* was just regaining its feet. Unlike Rose, Hawg had been able to fire some of his weapons even though down, and he had evidently decided to do so. The *Awesome* was little more than charred steel, the pilot having apparently decided to punch out when he could no longer ignore the heat build-up. The driverless 'Mech still showed up as a beacon on the infrared sensor, but it was no longer a threat.

Rose shouted a warning as the *Marauder* fired at Hawg's *Zeus.* Although Hawg was in the process of turning, he didn't quite make it all the way round. The LB-X autocannon sent two shells into the *Zeus'* back. The second shell followed the first and tore into the gyro heart of the 'Mech. The rapidly spinning gyro ground itself to death on the shards of the cannon shell.

Standing on the uneven slope, the *Zeus* suddenly pitched forward. Hawg tried to bring the legs under the falling body, but there wasn't a pilot in the Inner Sphere who could have accomplished the feat. As the 'Mech began to stumble-fall down the hill, Hawg struggled to keep up with the fall. Bouncing off trees as it went, the *Zeus* ran down the hill completely out of control. When it hit the bottom of the slope the change in angle ended Hawg's attempts at control. The 'Mech fell to the ground, disappearing behind the cover of the cedars.

Rose turned to the *Marauder,* which showed signs of recent damage, but none of it serious. He called up the schematics for hundred-ton 'Mechs and looked for a weakness as he triggered a flight of missiles.

"Command Two, try to get behind it, and make it fast. We won't be able to hold it for long."

Rose moved away from Esmeralda's *Warhammer,* forcing the *Marauder* to choose between the two targets. For a moment the huge arms hovered between the two Thorn 'Mechs, then they zeroed in on the heavily damaged *Warhammer.* Esmeralda fired her PPCs as the *Marauder* did the same. The *Warhammer's* fire struck undamaged armor, but the thick plating resisted both shots. The *Marauder's* shots were luckier, punching through the damaged right leg of the *Warhammer,* its armor already destroyed by the *Awesome's* repeated attacks, leaving only the 'Mech's skeleton to absorb the damage. The internal structure simply disappeared under the azure beam. The *Warhammer* hopped once, then crashed to the ground. Rose knew that Esmeralda, whose 'Mech had guns instead of arms, would never get the *Warhammer* to stand without assistance. That left Rose and Rianna against the *Marauder* and the *Banshee.*

As if sensing Rose's thoughts, the *Marauder* pilot triggered its powerful jump jets. Guided by the thrust of the jets and the fins protruding from its back, the massive 'Mech touched down almost a hundred meters away from its previous position. Now Rianna would have to travel even further to get behind it. Rose thumbed the Artemis as the *Marauder* grounded and limped to a new position, his missiles exploding along the 'Mech's elongated legs.

The LB-10 tracked the slow-moving *Charger* and sent two shells streaking across the clearing. The first streaked across the clearing, one shell blowing away the remaining armor on the *Charger's* right leg, scarring the skeleton underneath. The rest hit the hill behind Rose, showering the 'Mech with dirt and rocks. Shifting position, Rose tried to protect the damaged leg. Another hit like the last one and he'd suffer the same fate as Esmeralda.

Rose bracketed the *Marauder* with the Shigunga and fired again. He also triggered the medium pulse lasers, but at this extreme range, only two of the four scored hits. He knew it was too little, too late. Moving to the side, he saw the *Banshee* emerge from the trees and approach the *Marauder*. Rose knew he was finished, but something screamed at him to keep moving. He checked the scanner and saw that Rianna was still too far away for a shot.

The *Marauder* was bringing up both arms and the *Banshee* raising its right. Rose kept moving, but knew there was little chance either of the pilots would miss. The Shigunga was still in the midst of reload. By the time his missiles and lasers were ready to fire again, Rose wouldn't be around to press the trigger. As he took one final look out the cockpit, the *Banshee* shifted its arm and fired.

Rose stopped in his tracks as the *Banshee* placed the muzzle of its right arm missile launcher lightly against the cockpit of the *Marauder II* and fired. Fired at point-blank range, all six missiles ripped through the cockpit armor and shredded the inside. The controls, the command chair, and the pilot simply ceased to exist. The *Marauder*'s limbs locked firmly in place as the feedback circuit to the cockpit was severed.

Rose continued to stare as the *Banshee* lowered its arm and began to power down. Rose's scanner confirmed that the *Banshee* pilot had disengaged the engine and taken all weapons systems off-line. He sent a warning to Rianna not to fire as she entered the clearing, and remained watching in amazement as the *Banshee* completely shut down.

Rianna's *Phoenix Hawk* walked into the battle area with both large lasers up. She too stood facing the *Banshee* and waited for the pilot to emerge. It took almost five minutes, but eventually he opened the hatch at the back of the *Banshee*'s head and climbed around to the right shoulder. Rose didn't need to zoom in on the pilot to see that the man emerging from the *Banshee* had long blond hair.

=== 29 ===

The militia was still closing in on the Thorns, but their progress had slowed to a crawl. Despite the battered condition of Rose's 'Mech, there was no chance he would abandon it to talk face to face with Antioch Bell. The *Charger* limped over to the still form of the *Banshee* and the man sitting on the shoulder.

"Pursuit Lance, this is Command One. What's going on with the *BattleMaster*?"

"Command, this is Pursuit One. Ajax has exited his 'Mech and is administering first aid to the *BattleMaster* pilot. I can see them both from here."

"Is he crazy? The militia is still closing. Get him back into the cockpit, and scan the incoming units. Get back to me when you're finished." Rose closed the channel and fumed while he stared at the primary screen. A trained professional like Ajax would never have left his 'Mech unless something unusual was going on. Rose concentrated on breathing deeply, trying to calm his adrenaline-heightened nerves. When his heartbeat had slowed to an acceptable level, he engaged the 'Mech's external speakers.

"I'm not sure why you did it, Antioch, but thank you for saving my command, and my life." Rose zoomed in on the seated pilot. Bell gave a halfhearted salute and pulled his knees tightly to his chest.

"I take it that the *Marauder* was piloted by Morgain." Bell nodded and Rose continued. "The militia is closing in. We've got to either leave or fight. Since I won't fight them, we'll leave. Will you make sure that Esmeralda, Hawg, and O'Shea are treated fairly by the militia?"

Bell lifted his chin off his knees and spoke, but the *Charger*'s external microphone did not pick up the words. Rose increased the gain. "What's that?"

Through the static Rose could just make out Bell's words. "The militia won't engage."

Rose was shocked. "Why not?" He adjusted the microphone and Bell's voice became clearer.

"I fed them the last transmission you had with Morgain. They know what's happening in Houston and they know about the arrival of the Clans." Bell paused, his chest heaving massively as he fought to control his emotions. Rose had killed men before, but he had never fired on anyone he knew. He could barely imagine what it must be like to kill a friend.

"Why, Antioch? I know that I owe you, but I want to know why."

With one last sigh, Bell unwrapped his legs and looked up at the *Charger*. With Rose's camera on zoom and the microphone on high, Bell seemed almost to be standing right next to Rose. On the other end, however, Rose knew his voice was coming across on an amplified mechanical speaker. Bell could see where Rose was sitting, but could not look him in the eye. Rose wanted to help his friend, but until he knew more, he could not risk leaving the *Charger*.

The words came tumbling out. "I knew Morgain was up to something. I've always been able to tell when he's in over his head." Bell spoke without expressing emotion, but Rose could see the pain on his face.

"A war hero? What a pile of drek. Morgain was offered an honorable way out of the Twenty-sixth when Colonel Farnsgate discovered that he was selling stores to the black market. If the old man could have proved it, I'd be in prison right now.

"Twelve men and women in the company, and only two of us were not directly involved. Not that it really mattered, because we both knew about it and we both went along."

Rose could see the anger and frustration building in Bell as he spoke. He was standing now and had begun to pace. Rose listened, keeping his eyes on the scanner. He wanted to know why Bell had fired the missiles, not the story of his life.

"First I throw away my career for Salander Morgain and then I follow him to Borghese." Rose was impressed. He'd never heard the name pronounced with such contempt. "I signed on to form a mercenary unit, not to sit back and watch the war go by.

"You probably didn't know that he kept us virtual prisoners on the estate. Morgain held our 'Mechs to ensure our cooperation and support. The day I met you was the first time I'd been off the estate in months. I'd have carried you on my back for those recons if it would have gotten me off that property. I hated the place and the cronies Morgain surrounded himself with. I guess I even hated myself for being fooled by him." Bell sighed and ran his hand distractedly through his long hair. When he spoke again, his voice was softer. Rose could hear sorrow fill the void created as the anger drained away.

Bell looked at the immobile *Marauder*. "I hated him, but I didn't want him dead.

"Then I found out he was involved in a scheme with Crenshaw. I knew it was bad, but I figured it must be something like a repeat of the black market. This time I decided to get to the truth before things got out of control. Which is when I found out about the Preservationists. Crenshaw is the head of the group and Morgain is, or was, the muscle.

"The Preservationists captured the *Bristol* and traveled to Clan-occupied space. They actually invited the Falcons to come to Borghese. Crenshaw saw it as an opportunity to make sure the planet not only survived an invasion, but to turn a profit as well. I guess he figured that if the Clans were invited, they'd treat us better, especially the planetary rulers.

"You and Cooke were the only problem. Crenshaw got rid of Cooke, and Morgain was supposed to get rid of you. I learned of the plot the night you were attacked. Morgain was furious that the soldiers didn't hit you before you got to the 'Mechs." Bell paused and rubbed his chin.

"They were supposed to attack your base before the DropShip. If the troops had been better trained, we wouldn't be having this conversation. In any event, I've spent the last few weeks trying to decide what to do.

"I could have left, but Morgain would never have let me take my 'Mech. My only other choice was to go along with them. I was going to do it, too." Bell paused and Rose realized how close he'd come to receiving that final shot instead of Morgain. Bell began to shake his head. He turned to climb down the *Banshee* and Rose increased the volume of the microphone.

"Like always, Morgain got cocky. I was the second-in-command, so I knew all the frequencies we were using. It was supposed to be a private conversation between you two, but I decided to listen in. When I realized the importance, I fed the link to the militia commanders." Bell lowered himself to the *Banshee*'s ladder and began to climb down. "The militia knows they've been played for fools. Once they're sure this is over between you and Morgain, they'll come in." As Bell started down, soon only his head was visible. "Oh, by the way, I surrender. I'll wait for you on the ground."

Rose sat in his 'Mech as Bell climbed down the *Banshee*, then calmly waited on the 'Mech's foot to be taken prisoner. Rianna contacted the militia leaders. Being on the opposite side of the *Banshee*, she couldn't see Bell, but her microphones were slightly better, so she'd heard the entire conversation. While Rose considered what to do, Rianna arranged a truce with the Green Team.

The first order of business was to inform the Thorns of what was going on. Opening the unit-wide channel, Rose gave his team a summary of their current situation. He had keyed the commlink to one-way communication because he didn't want to answer a lot of questions, but by the time he was done, every one of the pilots was signaling requests for a private line. Rose told them as much as possible, postponing further questions until they could assemble in one location.

When Colonel Bahlyard, the Green Team commander, arrived thirty minutes later, Rose was sitting on the foot of the *Banshee* alongside Bell. He still hadn't figured out what to do about the unit's current situation, but he hoped to get help from the sandy-haired infantryman. His first requests to the colonel were for help in retrieving the rest of the Black Thorns. Rianna, Ajax, and Angus were clustered around the *Banshee* and *Charger*.

Hawg had crawled out of the remains of the *Zeus* under his own power and taken a seat on the *Banshee*'s other foot. Although he looked fine physically, the death of his *Zeus* was hitting him hard. Rose had seen the look before on the faces of other MechWarriors, something between amazement and horror. At least he wasn't crying, but that would probably come later.

It would take some doing to retrieve the final two members of the team. Esmeralda would have to be cut free from her 'Mech, but only because a severed support spar had jammed the cockpit hatch shut. A 'Mech could pry the spar away, but the militia probably had the tools to do the job better and with less collateral damage to the supporting structure.

Badicus' ejection seat was still emitting a strong signal, but he'd landed in a dense copse of trees. A 'Mech could probably retrieve him, but only after battering aside the trees that hemmed him in. Rianna had requested a VTOL retrieval, which Colonel Bahlyard immediately authorized. The flight crew had found O'Shea strapped to his chair and sitting in a tree twenty meters above the ground. They were still working on the rescue.

Rianna crawled down from her *Phoenix Hawk* with the unit's portable communications system slung over one shoulder. She sat it on the ground at her feet, slipped the headset over her ear, and adjusted the microphone. She could keep track of the two militia teams assisting the mercenaries and still listen to what was going on. Rose waited until Ajax and Angus joined them at the *Banshee*'s feet before beginning.

"I guess we all know each other," he said. "I'm sure you all remember Commander Bahlyard, who also happens to be in charge of the force that's been making life so hard for us for the last few weeks." Rose noticed the colonel's face was slightly flushed and hoped it was the red of embarrassment instead of being his natural color. In Rose's experience no commander could accept looking like a fool, and the higher the chain of command, the worse they took it.

"Gentlemen, and lady," Rose said with a nod to his sister, "this is strictly an information meeting. We've got precious little of that right now but I need a better picture of what's going on." Rose looked around the group. The Black Thorns were practically dead on their feet from fatigue and the usual post-battle slump. "We'll make this quick," he promised, then waited until he was sure he had everyone's attention.

"We're about as far as we can be from Houston and not be under water. We know that the Clans are coming and that they'll probably be received as honored guests at the capital. Antioch, is there anything else?"

Antioch Bell rubbed his eyes and looked around at the mercenaries. "From what little I know about it, the Preservationists weren't too worried about your command. I guess they had a lot of faith in Colonel Bahlyard's men and our 'Mechs." He shrugged and smiled slightly. "Go figure."

"That confirms my last orders." All heads turned to Bahlyard. "They came directly from the Council. I'm supposed to report when you either surrender or have been eliminated. They didn't seem to think an engagement would go any other way.

"I haven't heard anything about the arrival of the Clans, but it makes sense, given my latest orders. Despite three hangars full of new Rippers, we were only authorized to take one group. I was ordered to leave the rest in the hangar. I was also told to keep half the Green Team back at the capital, in case you tried a flank attack. What a crock. As far as I know, that's the first time the Council has ever dictated to a field commander what hardware he can use."

Rose picked up the scenario as Bahlyard suddenly stopped talking. "So, your best equipment is back at the base with half the troops. Very effective. Not only are we too far away to protest the landing, but the planet's own force is divided into two easily digested pieces. To top it off, the leader is sent away with the troops while the bulk of the equipment remains safely in the hangar." Rose calculated the remaining men and equipment near the capital and came to an instant and demoralizing conclusion.

"I think we can pretty well rule out any form of assistance. By the time we get back, the capital will be firmly in the hands of the Jade Falcons."

Ajax cleared his throat. Rose was mildly surprised to see that he actually wanted to address the meeting.

"Perhaps we should consider something," the Capellan said. "The Clans have been invited to Borghese by the current government. I do not suggest that their actions can be excused or justified, but the Clans are not invading."

"Ajax is right," Rianna said from the other side of the loose circle. "The Federated Commonwealth will never allow it, but the leaders of Borghese are preparing to hand the planet over to the Clans. The invaders only came to collect the passkey to the world."

"So, they're not invaders, technically," Rose put in, "but does that make any difference?"

Ajax nodded. "From what we've learned about the

Clans, they do everything according to a ritual bidding process. The honor of performing any deed is bid for by the contestants until the final force is determined.

"If this were an invasion, they would bid for how many men, or OmniMechs, it would take to wrest control away from the Federated Commonwealth. If intelligence is correct, the Clans will not bid on how many OmniMechs it takes to invade, but how many it will take to accept a surrender."

Rose stared in amazement. Of course Ajax was right. He'd been at Tukayyid where the Clans had died rather than break their rules of ritual engagement. Ajax continued with a spreading smile.

"They will, if intelligence is correct, send a force capable of accepting a surrender behind enemy lines. It must be strong enough to fight its way back to Clan territory if it turns out to be a trap, but it must also be weak enough to make the taking of the planet glorious."

"Which means we have a chance," interrupted Rianna.

Ajax tilted his head and nodded slightly.

"If intelligence is correct," mimicked Rose with a smile. "You don't trust the gang in military intelligence, do you? No need to answer, I doubt any of us do, but your point is well-taken. We just may have a chance."

Bahlyard, temporarily forgotten, interrupted. "Any Clan force that lands on Borghese will have to be persuaded that it isn't a trap. Once they're convinced, the Clan that claims Borghese will have to move quickly to reinforce their foothold before the Federated Commonwealth can react. We have to get word to General Dmowski at Kelenfold. She has the authority to shift troops to our defense."

"Any chance the word has already gone out?" asked Rianna.

"Not much," Bahlyard said. "The Preservationists must know enough to restrict interplanetary messages. Breaking into the ComStar compound or protecting it from the Clans and the Council are about the only ways to make sure a message gets sent."

Several people started talking at once. Rose held up his hands for quiet and looked around the assembly. He noticed Hawg had gone to sleep. "That's enough for now. We're worn out, physically as well as mentally. A couple hours' sleep and a hot meal will do us more good than rushing into a plan of action.

"Colonel Bahlyard, no matter what we decide, we must keep the outcome of this engagement a secret." The stocky Bahlyard grinned like a wolf.

"I'm sure I can arrange for a report on the destruction of your unit and on the mauling of Morgain's command. It would be close enough to the truth. If I paint the picture pretty enough, they might agree to a couple of extra days in the field for rest and repairs before recalling us to Houston."

"That would be perfect. We'll be officially out of the way, and with luck, Crenshaw won't even consider the possibility that we're still alive." Rose checked his chronometer. "Can you meet us back here in eight hours?" Without looking at his watch, Bahlyard agreed.

"Black Thorns," Rose said, "meet back here in six hours with a full report on your 'Mechs' readiness and any ideas about raiding a hyperpulse generator station in the heart of a friendly city that's defended by Omni-Mechs."

Rose turned to Ajax. "I take it the *BattleMaster* pilot has been turned over to the militia medics?" Rose received the customary nod. Evidently Ajax had spoken his fill earlier.

"All right, people, you're dismissed. We have an objective and a reason to hope." The gathering broke up as the pilots drifted away. In moments only Ajax and Hawg still remained at the feet of the *Banshee*. As silence descended on the clearing, Ajax joined Hawg in deep, but troubled, sleep.

The Cedars, Borghese
14 July 3055

Rose looked around at the members of his unit. Badicus and Esmeralda were back, and the Black Thorns had once more gathered at the feet of the *Banshee*. McCloud and Antioch joined them, but Colonel Bahlyard was still with the militia. Rose looked over his unit again, but the situation wasn't any better than a few moments before.

Despite strong life signs and initial reports, Badicus was not fit for combat. When he'd ejected, one of the release clamps that anchored the cockpit to the 'Mech's head had not released properly. The *Shadow Hawk*, like most other 'Mechs, relied on a controlled explosion to propel the command chair clear of the 'Mech. Once the chair reached a preprogrammed altitude, the flight adjusters kicked in and controlled the descent. Under normal conditions it was all pretty simple and predictable. Even if the pilot lost consciousness after engaging the system, he stood an excellent chance of surviving the ejection.

When the clamp failed to open completely, however, the explosion ripped through the back-right quarter of the cockpit. The command chair had shielded Badicus from most of the blast and flying metal fragments, but his right side was covered with cuts. The faulty clamp had torn free, sending the chair flying skyward. But with the altitude adjuster nearest the blast completely destroyed, the ride down was anything but controlled. Badicus was lucky to have landed so high up in a cedar tree. If he'd fallen all the way to the ground, it would have killed him. As it was, the landing had broken his left hand and dislocated his right elbow. Covered with bandages, braces, and a cast, he was attending the meeting under heavy medication.

Esmeralda had fared much better, but the *Warhammer*'s fall had triggered a brief cockpit fire. After vainly attempting to escape the cockpit, she'd managed to put out the fire with the two emergency extinguishers. Her legs above the heavy combat boots had been badly burned during the process. She still wore her combat shorts, her burned thighs covered with a thick balm of burn gel. She had refused pain killers and faced Rose with a determined, if tense, expression. He winced every time she moved.

"Pursuit, what is your status?"

Angus drew a circle in the dirt with his toe. Knowing that the rest of the unit had suffered tremendous casualties, he was slow to report. "Both 'Mechs are fully functional, sir. Both pilots are combat-ready." Rose thought that the young man stressed the word combat too much, but he let it pass.

"Very good. Battle, give me the bad news."

Esmeralda shifted, apparently searching for a more comfortable position. Perhaps she found it because much of the pain Rose had heard in her voice earlier was gone. "Battle Three is dead. As you already know, the gyro was destroyed. But we've just found out that the remaining seven million pieces were scattered all over the engine compartment, ruining the engine shielding. Hawg did a good job of shutting down the reactor before the shielding went and the engine blew. It'll take a new gyro and the better part of a new engine to get it running again."

Rose looked at Hawg, but he remained very calm as Esmeralda described the destruction of his family heirloom. He wanted to say something, but now was not the time. Instead he just nodded as Esmeralda continued.

"Battle Two can be repaired, but not without a full electronics bay. Any ejection is hard on the system, but when the clamp failed, it destroyed most of the communications and tracking system. Houston is the only place on the planet where we can get that kind of gear."

"Can we get it mobile?"

Esmeralda considered the option. "If we took a VTOL and replaced the command chair, we could probably patch something together, but we'd have to pilot with visuals only, and shooting would be impossible.

"My 'Mech is down, too," she said. "The leg could be repaired, but again, we'd need a full repair bay to do it. The break came right about here." She drew a finger through the green gel on her leg, indicating that the break had occurred across the middle of the thigh. She left the gash in the gel as she continued talking. "We could reattach the leg and weld it back on with the vehicle repair gear the militia is carrying, but it wouldn't hold if stressed. It can walk, but that's about it. Even running would probably snap the leg in half.

"Hawg and I are combat-ready, but O'Shea is out because he can't use either arm. He could pilot the damaged *Shadow Hawk* if we got it going again, but it could only move at a walk and both arms would be useless."

Esmeralda finished and began smoothing out the crease in the burn gel with a careful finger. Normally Rose would have looked to Rianna to provide the report on the command lance, but he took the duty instead.

"Command Two is fully functional. Command One can be repaired, but with the tools we have available, it will take a couple of hours. The leg will be the worst problem, but I think we can get it back into operation. Rianna and I are both combat-ready."

Rose paused. The entire unit already knew they'd been mauled by Morgain and his 'Mechs, but hearing the results was a hard mental blow. Many 'Mech pilots went their entire careers without ever facing the kind of toe-to-toe fire fight they'd just been in. Of the ten engaging 'Mechs, seven had been either killed or knocked out. Rose didn't mentally count the pursuit lance since it had been kept out of the battle. Seventy percent casualties were unheard of in modern war. Hell, thought Rose in anger, seventy percent had always been unheard of, no matter what the century.

He rubbed the stubble on his chin and picked himself up off the foot of the *Banshee*. Despite having gone more than forty hours without sleep, he felt surprisingly alert. His unit didn't seem to share his energy, however. He'd ordered all six pilots to sleep at least four hours prior to the meeting and most of them looked as though that had only primed them for more. They didn't look like a team that had just been mauled, but they weren't especially confident about what the future held. Now was the time to rally the troops.

"All right, that means we're down to six pilots and four 'Mechs." He paused and walked into the midst of the group. "I can live with that." All eight heads came up at the same time. "You've all had a little sleep and some hot food and for the last hour you've been inspecting your 'Mechs for damage."

Rose paused and looked each Black Thorn in the eye. "Well, the light duty just ended."

With a sudden whirl he faced Esmeralda and pointed an accusing finger. "Esmeralda, forget about repairing the *Warhammer* for the time being. What do you know about *Marauders*?" Esmeralda stood there with her mouth open. Finally she began to stammer an answer, but Rose cut her off.

"It was a rhetorical question. It doesn't matter what you know, or don't know for that matter, because you're our new *Marauder* pilot. The head of that beast was savaged by Mister Bell when he saved my butt from Morgain. I think it can be repaired, though. When the meeting's over, find out.

"Hawg, I know that I can't replace your 'Mech, but I'm willing to try. About five hundred meters from where we stand is a fully functional *BattleMaster*. You just became the new pilot.''

If Rose had turned blue and floated into the air, Hawg could not have been more surprised. Rose returned Hawg's sudden smile and soon the two men were beaming at one another. "Until the *Charger* is fully repaired, the *BattleMaster* is our best repair vehicle. The *BattleMaster* is the only 'Mech with two hands. We're going to need it for salvaging parts from the downed 'Mechs.''

Hawg snapped Rose a formal, parade-ground salute. Rose knew the *Zeus* would be missed, but for the moment Hawg would be too busy to mourn the ancient machine. That left only two items to finish.

"Black Thorns, I have the privilege of announcing that a new recruit has offered his services to the unit and has been accepted for immediate duty.

"Welcome aboard, Antioch Bell.''

Now it was Bell's turn to be amazed. "I didn't volunteer for anything. Besides, even if I did, my side was taking shots at you this morning, or don't you remember?''

Rose remembered, but he knew he had little to fear from the former member of Morgain's band, and the rest of the Thorns probably felt the same way. After all, Bell had always been a friend to the unit and he hadn't fired on any of them during the fighting. "I'm sorry about that, Mister Bell. Perhaps I should explain myself better.

"Black Thorns, a MechWarrior of considerable experience has announced his presence with uncharacteristic resolve. He saved the Black Thorns from destruction and probably saved my life in the process. Do we want that type of ability in our unit?''

"Yes!'' The unanimous chorus was deafening.

"There you go, Mister Bell. A fine example of military protocol in action. You've been accepted by the Black Thorns, whether you want it or not. Consider yourself drafted.''

Rose gave the unit a few moments to shake hands with

the stunned *Banshee* pilot. Like Hawg, Rose wanted to give his friend some kind of direction, even if only temporary. As the mercenaries sat down again, Rose continued the meeting.

"With that out of the way, we have only one more thing to discuss. The Clans. While you were sleeping, Colonel Bahlyard transmitted his report to the Council. I'm sorry, but the Black Thorns were destroyed. I, of course, died fighting. The rest of you were captured." Rose stood in the middle of the unit, striking his best heroic pose. A chorus of boos made him break his pose as the mercenaries groaned at the sarcasm.

Rose checked his watch and continued, relaxing as he went. "The *Bristol* is leading a single Clan DropShip toward Borghese. Both ships will hit the spaceport tarmac in six hours." Rose could see McCloud light up at the mention of her ship. "Colonel Bahlyard has been summoned back to the capital, where he is ordered to turn over his prisoners. He's also been ordered not to interfere with the Clan 'Mechs he's going to find in Houston."

"How many?"

Rose turned to Esmeralda. "Unknown at this point. I'm guessing one or two Trinaries, but we shouldn't count on it until we get more information. I've thought a lot about it, however, and I agree with Ajax.

"The Clans will use some kind of bidding to determine the force they send here. Two Trinaries, or thirty 'Mechs, is about the most I think they'd send. Hopefully, they'll only send one Trinary, say, fifteen 'Mechs. We should know more when Colonel Bahlyard gets more information from his men in Houston.

"Until that time, here's the plan. We have to get word to the Federated Commonwealth before the Clans can reinforce their position. That means a raid on the hyperpulse generator. For the time being, that's as far as we need to go in the mission.

"Getting ready is going to be difficult, to say the least. If we had to leave right now, we'd have only four 'Mechs in fighting shape and one wounded to make our run. To have any chance of success, we have to make that seven 'Mechs in fighting shape as soon as possible.

"For the time being we're going to trust the militia for security." Rose held out a stalling hand. "I know your objections, but we don't have much choice. If the militia wanted us, they'd have already made their move. The Council has nothing they can throw at us that the militia can't stop, and these trees should provide cover from the Clans if they try something."

"Captain, I don't believe the Clans even know we're here." Rose turned to Ajax and wondered why the mercenaries always waited until his back was to them to make a point. "Since the Council believes us to be destroyed, they have nothing to gain by telling the Clans we were ever here. The militia can easily be explained as being on maneuvers. The Clans aren't likely to be much interested in them, especially since we're so far from the capital."

Heads nodded in agreement and Rose's was one of them. "Even without interference, time is critical," he said. "We have to be ready to move out as quickly as possible if we're going to be successful. If things get speeded up for any reason and we want to move out, we've got to be able to do so with as large a force as possible.

"Angus, you and Ajax are going to be in charge of the surface repair. Bahlyard has already confirmed that the militia has some maintenance personnel who can help us repair our armor. Start with the worst damage and work your way down. Questions? If you need more to do, I'll have it.

"Badicus, you get ordnance."

O'Shea shook his head sadly. "I knew I'd be punished for letting your *Shadow Hawk* get beat up. I never knew you were so cruel, and me a cripple." Around him the mercenaries scoffed. Going through a downed 'Mech to retrieve live ammunition was dangerous work, even under good conditions. Because of the danger to the crews,

Liao ordnance crews were often composed entirely of criminals. In many cases O'Shea would have been right to consider the duty a punishment.

Rose smiled at the mock sadness in O'Shea's eyes. "Knock it off, bumblebutt. You're overseeing the militia ordnance crews. Most of them have never seen the inside of a 'Mech ammo bay, let alone worked in one. We should be able to produce some possible reloads for the working 'Mechs, but don't let them get killed in the process. Distribute any ammunition you find among the 'Mechs that can use it."

O'Shea smiled and wiped his brow with the back of his cast in exaggerated relief.

"Rianna, you and Hawg are going to assist with the repair of all internal damage. Bahlyard doesn't have anyone who can provide expertise, but he's agreed to give us a couple of assistants. Start with the *Charger* and the *Marauder*. Esmeralda, stick with the *Marauder*. If time permits, and I don't think it will, work on the *Shadow Hawk*.

"Bell, you and I need to talk, then you can help the others. I need to know everything you know about the Preservationists. Give me another fifteen minutes, then we'll get together. I'll want you to cover the same ground for Colonel Bahlyard."

Rose looked around the circle. The mood had definitely lightened. Although the Black Thorns were still tired, they seemed to be in much better shape than at the start of the meeting.

"Questions?"

"Just one, Captain." Rose happened to be looking at Angus when he spoke. "We're relying a lot on Colonel Bahlyard. Is that wise?"

"Probably not, but we've got our backs to the wall. We're the only force on the planet that can stop the Clans and Bahlyard knows it. This is his home planet, remember?

"Most of the people of Borghese don't want the Clans and Bahlyard is a part of that majority. Unfortunately, the people in power, who represent only a very small minority, seem to have a misguided vision of life under the Clans and they're determined to drag the rest of Borghese into that vision, even if the population has to go kicking and screaming.''

Rose paused again. ''Anything else? No? Then get off your butts and on your feet, out of the shade and into the heat. We're wasting daylight.'' As the mercenaries scrambled to their various duties, Rose remained standing in the middle of the empty circle. He was looking at McCloud, who remained seated. Ajax had the presence of mind to wander away from the area.

For the first time in a long time, Rose and McCloud were alone. There was so much Rose wanted to say, but lack of time forced him to stick to the basics. When this was all over, he promised himself, then he'd tell her how he felt.

''Captain McCloud, have you ever flown a 'Mechbuster?''

=== 31 ===

Despite nearly constant work, it took four days for the repair crews to finish work on the damaged 'Mechs. It was the *BattleMaster* that had monopolized their efforts and cost them the most time.

All BattleMechs are keyed to their pilot's brain waves and unique starting sequence. They can be reprogrammed, and subsequently unlocked, but only with the proper tools and time. Rose had not given the problem much thought because the current *BattleMaster* pilot was still alive. Unfortunately that man viewed the 'Mech as his personal property and was not about to give it up. Rose was counting on the extra firepower and refused to leave without it.

The cockpit of the 'Mech was actually a converted command module, which allowed both a pilot and a commander to ride in relative comfort. Although the commander's compartment had long ago been stripped of useful equipment, the chair and restraint system were still installed. Since Badicus had refused to accompany the militia when they left on the third morning after the battle, the heavily armed and armored 'Mech would prove particularly useful. Per their agreement, McCloud was traveling with the militia.

For several days Hawg and Rianna tried to bypass the

'Mech's security system while the rest of the mercenaries
worked on the other 'Mechs, but their best efforts were
defeated. Rose had tried to reason with the pilot, but he
remained defiant. Finally the other repair work was done,
and Rose could wait no longer. He was about to approach
the pilot himself when Ajax stopped him and offered to
retrieve the information.

Rose was initially skeptical, but Ajax was confident he
could succeed. As Ajax and the pilot disappeared into
the back of a Ripper VTOL, the mercenary smiled briefly
as he pulled the door shut. Fifteen minutes later Ajax
emerged with a very pale pilot and the security sequence.
Rose considered asking Ajax how he'd gotten it, then
decided he didn't really want to know. Once Hawg was
into the *BattleMaster*'s main computer, he began the re-
programming process.

When they finally began their trek back to Houston,
Angus and Ajax were in the lead as usual. Rose and
Rianna came next, followed by Hawg and Badicus. The
rebuilt battle lance was covering the rear, and Esmeralda
and Bell took the sides. The repair of the *Marauder II*
had turned out to be surprisingly easy. Most of the internal damage had been confined to the cockpit module,
which they'd completely replaced. Using the module from
the *Stalker* and adapting it with components from the
Zeus and the *Awesome*, Esmeralda and Antioch had managed to put together a dependable, if unorthodox, control
system.

Dodging the militia and staying out of sight turned the
trip into a three-week affair. Although the mercenaries
covered a lot of ground in that time, they were actually
only a long day's march from the outskirts of Houston.

Rianna had kept one ear and one eye on the civilian
news services, trying to stay up-to-date on events in the
capital. As Rose had predicted, the Clan invaders were
being treated as honored guests. The media was careful
to point out that the Clan force was small, but the arrival
of more troops was inevitable and there was no word
about Federated Commonwealth assistance.

Colonel Bahlyard had discovered that the invading Clan was the Jade Falcons. Rose wasn't surprised. Both the Falcons and the Steel Vipers had planets within two jumps of Borghese, although the Vipers were slightly more concentrated at the head of the Clan advance than the Falcons. Initial reports put the invaders at approximately company strength, about fifteen 'Mechs, with at least twenty-five Clan Elementals, the specially armored infantry that the media called Toads. Bahlyard had been unable to get a better count than that, as the Clans had performed a combat drop on the capital rather than debarking from the DropShip. Rose knew that was standard combat procedure, but even this small force descending on the city had a profound effect on the populace.

Since the initial drop, the Clans had kept their forces on the move, making accurate estimate impossible for the militia. Resistance up to this point had been nonexistent. The Council, which meant Crenshaw, had ordered the militia to surrender instead of fighting. Colonel Bahlyard had initially refused the order, but finally agreed to return to the city with his men. It was hard on the colonel, but it was a necessary part of the plan he and Rose had cooked up the night before the militia left the mercenary's camp.

Colonel Bahlyard and his men would start back to Houston, apparently obeying the orders of the Council. Such a large body of troops was bound to attract the Falcons' attention. The Falcons would have to send part of their force to watch over the incoming soldiers, leaving the rest to keep watch on the city. Rose planned to use the distraction of the militia to cover the arrival of his force. The militia would enter the city from the east, while Rose entered from the north.

It would require icy calm on the part of the militia. When the Falcons were in range, the militia was supposed to proceed toward the capital under the invaders' guns. Once the Clansmen learned that the city was under attack, they would be looking for a reason to fire on the militia. One false move and they'd have their chance.

The Black Thorns' part in the plan called for less courage during the initial stages. As the militia got closer to the city, so did the mercenaries. When Colonel Bahlyard finally made contact with the Clans, the Thorns would race the final distance toward Houston and the hyperpulse generator station. Timing was critical because the mercenaries didn't know just when the militia would make contact with the Falcons. If the Thorns moved too soon, they'd be discovered, and if they moved too late, the Falcons would have time to react to their approach. In addition, every step closer to the city increased the chances that they might be discovered by a Clan patrol or a passing recon flight.

Rose checked the chronometer under his display. They'd been marching for eleven hours, the last two at an infuriatingly slow pace. It was well past dark and Rose could see the lights of Houston to the south when the comm unit signaled an incoming call. Rose's hand shot out to open the channel before the light could flash a third time.

"This is Black One."

"Green One here. We have company. Three plus five."

"Three plus five, confirmed. Black One out." Rose opened the command channel.

"Move out, Thorns. Pursuit, you have the lead. Speed is six-five kph." As the mercenaries picked up their pace, Rose filled them in on Bahlyard's message.

"The militia has three 'Mechs and five Elementals providing an escort." Per their plans, Rose understood that the first number of Bahlyard's message indicated the number of 'Mechs and the second indicated the number of Elementals.

"They broke a Star?"

"Affirmative." Rose had not initially considered it, but the question made him think for a moment. The Clans operated in groups of five. Five Elementals made a Point. Five Points made a Star. The same principle held true for 'Mechs, but each 'Mech was a Point all by itself, which meant the escort group was missing two 'Mechs or five more Elementals.

"Pursuit Two, crank up the Beagle. We might have some stragglers."

Rose split his eyes and his concentration between the primary screen and the long-range scanner, the kilometers clicking away under the long strides of the 'Mechs. In fifteen minutes they were passing the houses on the outskirts of Houston. Five minutes after that and they were moving through the industrial section of the city's north side. Whenever possible the mercenaries marched along the side streets, forcing civilian traffic to move over or get crushed. Damage was light to the civilians, but Rose knew it was only a matter of time before they were discovered by the Clans monitoring the police frequencies. Even if no one was looking for them, seven 'Mechs marching through town caused too much commotion to be missed.

"Command One, this is Pursuit Two. Two inbound blips on an intersect course. Either they've got damn fast 'Mechs or a pair of hovercraft."

"Confirmed, Pursuit Two. Switch to Guardian." Rose watched the long-range scanner become suddenly cloudy as Ajax activated the Guardian electronic countermeasure suite. The ECM system was designed to provide a cloud of electromagnetic disturbance that would make targeting the mercenaries virtually impossible until the Clans got to close range. It was the perfect counter to the Clans' longer ranges. As long as the enemy didn't have a line of sight, they would have a difficult time tracking the Thorns inside the cloud. Of course, the cloud itself was very easy to spot.

Under the umbrella of the Guardian the Black Thorns picked up the pace. Rose switched to the short-range scanner because the long-range version was effectively blind while the Guardian was engaged.

"Report all contacts, people. If it's got two legs, shoot first." It was still early in the evening as Rose piloted the *Charger* past the factories and staring pedestrians, many of whom had come out to watch as the 'Mechs charged by. Rose knew that more than one observer would mistake them for the Clansmen.

"Target two sixty-nine degrees, approaching fast." Rose swung to the left as Rianna announced the target's approach. As he watched, two OmniMechs rounded the corner one street away, then began running toward the mercenaries. Rose and Rianna were in the middle of an intersection, with the pursuit lance in front and the battle lance behind. From their position in the street, only Rose and his sister could see the Jade Falcon OmniMechs under the glow of the streetlights.

From their chassis to their jade green paint jobs, the OmniMechs were identical: two headless humanoids, their gangly arms pointed directly toward the mercenaries. Long legs began pumping faster and the 'Mechs' considerable speed increased.

"*Dasher*s at nine o'clock!" The duo started their charge at a distance of three hundred meters. They'd covered half the distance to the mercenaries when Rianna triggered one large laser. The ruby shaft of light missed, flying past the Falcons to strike a slow-moving car four blocks away. The driver survived, but the car didn't.

In return the *Dasher* fired five lasers back at Rianna's *Phoenix Hawk*. Although none had the power of Rianna's Sunbeam laser, the combined effect was devastating to the medium 'Mech, especially since the *Dasher* hit its target, and Rianna did not. Armor boiled and fell away under the cutting beam of the Clan lasers. Gouges marked her 'Mech's chest, arms, and left leg. Rianna triggered the other Sunbeam at her attacker, but with the same results.

Rose moved slightly forward for a better shot around the *Phoenix Hawk*. He carefully aligned the cross hairs of the targeting computer, then fired. By the time the lasers reached the OmniMech's position, however, the *Dasher* was no longer there.

With a high-pitched whine, the 'Mech seemed to leap forward. The *Dasher* fired at Rose, sending four of the five shots into his center torso. The chest-mounted spotlight exploded and armor seared away. A small part of Rose's mind realized that the *Dasher* had activated the myomer acceleration signal circuitry, which poured additional power to the OmniMech's legs, but the thought hadn't made it to Rose's conscious mind when he reacted.

As the *Dasher* streaked past the *Charger,* Rose swung out with the Mech's huge right hand. The *Dasher* almost avoided the blow, but Rose struck the right shoulder a glancing blow. At the *Dasher*'s speed the effects were devastating. The OmniMech's right arm sheared away, taking most of the right torso with it. The pilot, suddenly off balance, slipped on the concrete and staggered off to the left. Completely out of control, he slammed the twenty-ton 'Mech into the brick wall of a corner factory, punching several holes into the structure, but failing to bring down the wall.

The second 'Mech waited to engage the MASC system until he was past Rose. Both Rose and Rianna tried to swing around for a shot, but neither could bracket the retreating 'Mech. Rose was about to give up when he saw a flight of long-range missiles crash down on the fleeing 'Mech. Rose counted eight initial explosions, then the components of the *Dasher* began to fail and explode. The MASC whined as it went out of control, but the 'Mech's legs had already stopped receiving signals from the pilot. The *Dasher* slid down the street, slamming into cars until it finally came to rest against the side of a bus.

Rose looked skyward and saw Angus and his *Valkyrie* descend on three columns of flame, then land in the middle of the street. "Nice shooting, Pursuit One. Tell me, how did you know where to shoot?"

"I just figured they'd keep running. If they went the other way, nobody could catch them. If they tried a strafing run, they had to come out on the other end of the street. I hit the jets when you shouted the warning."

Rose was impressed with the young man. The reflexes

he'd demonstrated could not be taught. A warrior was either born with them or he wasn't.

"Keep up the good work, Pursuit One. Now confirm the kill and let's get out of here. Pursuit Two, Guardian off."

Rose switched back to long-range scan as the mercenaries went deeper into the city. Gradually, offices replaced factories and the lighting improved. Rose knew that the Clans were fully aware of his approach. Panicked civilians were reacting to media reports of the first encounter, sending most away from the battle zone, but others toward it. Traffic became increasingly congested, forcing the mercenaries to divert from their original path three separate times.

"This is Pursuit Two," said Ajax. "I have three inbounds. I'm not sure what they are, but they're putting out sizable shock waves with each step. They've got to be assault class."

The approaching Omnis were beyond the range of Rose's conventional scanner so he was forced to take Ajax's word for their size. If the invaders had committed two Trinaries to the conquest of Borghese, these three accounted for all but one of the Stars.

"Pursuit One, we need a visual on the inbounds. Get to the top of that parking structure across the street: the height should give you the range to see them. Battle Lance, clear out the civilians. We might be fighting here."

While Rose considered the fire lanes for deploying his unit, Angus jumped to the roof of the parking garage. Meanwhile the three members of the battle lance began to broadcast warnings to the civilians over their external speakers.

"This is Pursuit One. I have a visual on three *Masakari* Class Omnis at approximately six hundred meters. They're just crossing over—" As Rose listened and watched the *Valkyrie* on top of the parking garage, two azure beams suddenly cut across the sky. One PPC beam passed by the *Valkyrie*'s right shoulder, but the other struck the 'Mech squarely in the face. The force of the blast cut neatly through the armor, the skeleton, the electronics, and the flesh underneath. With energy to spare, the beam blasted its way out the back of the *Valkyrie*'s head and into the night sky. The 'Mech paused for a moment as if stunned by its own sudden death, then it fell forward, draping itself over the edge of the roof.

Nobody moved for long moments, then Ajax broke the silence. "Three *Masakari* OmniMechs approaching at flank speed."

Rose was shocked to awareness as the three eighty-five-ton 'Mechs suddenly appeared. "This is Command One to all Thorns. Mobile advance, right flank. Stick together, people. We've got to get to the HPG station."

"This is Pursuit Two. I have one inbound. Weight is most heavy. Enemy left flank is secure."

Rose slammed his fist in frustration. "Most heavy" meant the 'Mech topped the weight scale. That translated into ninety-five or a hundred tons of Clan technology underneath a genetically engineered pilot. It was probably the invasion commander. Even though the Clans were outnumbered, Rose doubted he had the strength to fight them successfully. Rose scanned the terrain and made a quick decision.

"This is Command One. Fall back at best speed. I say again, best speed." The lead *Masakari* fired three PPCs at extreme range. Fortunately for Antioch Bell, the target, the Falcons had evidently used up all their luck with the shot that killed Angus.

"Where to, Command One?"

"I don't have a clue. Maybe we can outflank them. McCloud, I hope you're listening, 'cause we're about to require your services."

32

As Rose broke away from the OmniMechs, he outlined his plan to the rest of the unit. If they were going to make it to the ComStar compound, they'd have to use their firepower to better advantage. Rose knew the Black Thorns couldn't withstand another toe-to-toe battle like the one against Morgain. He'd hoped not to have to bring McCloud into the fight, but he was going to need her to turn the tide in his favor.

"McCloud, you'd better get airborne. We're going to need your help after all."

As the main column of the militia began making its way toward Houston, McCloud and a squad from the Green Team took off for the coastal town of Le Jeune. The town itself wasn't much, but it boasted an airport with the second-longest landing strip on Borghese. It was also the home of the Green's fighter flight, the 312th Planetary Defense Wing.

The wing was composed entirely of fixed-wing aircraft, which made them easy targets for both faster aerospace fighters and the more maneuverable VTOL craft. Under normal circumstances Rose would never have sent fixed-wing craft against the Clans, but one of the craft was a 'Mechbuster.

The 'Mechbuster was about as simple a design as aerospace engineers had ever created. Build an airplane around the biggest autocannon yet produced. Hollow out the fuselage and pack in enough shells to justify the cost of the fuel, then point it at the enemy. Although slow and unmaneuverable, the craft was capable of taking out a 'Mech in a single pass. Of course the pilot of such an aircraft was bound to draw a tremendous amount of attention.

"This is Pursuit Two. I have two incoming blips. I don't think these are the *Masakari*s. The footprint is too soft."

"This is Battle Four. All four Omnis from downtown pulled up when we ran. They seemed to be afraid of a trap. When I lost track of them, we had a five-minute lead on them, which was widening."

"Command Two, Pursuit Two, get a fix on the Omnis that shot Angus. Battle Three, follow them and provide back-up. Everybody else follow me.

"McCloud, what's your ETA?"

"Fifteen minutes to the center of the city. Where are you?"

"We're in the municipal park on the edge of the business district. Use my channel as a beacon. We're going to try to sweep past the heaviest resistance, but first we have to clear a path."

"I copy. I'll be there as soon as possible. McCloud out."

Although Rose had promised himself he would not split up the unit, there didn't seem to be any other way. The *Phoenix Hawk* and the *Raven* sprinted across the football field toward the buildings that surrounded the park, the *BattleMaster* in hot pursuit. Rose turned with the remaining force to prevent the Clan forces from boxing them into a trap.

The scanners immediately registered two approaching 'Mechs. Switching to thermal, he could see only eerie blots of heat coming toward him, but the computer positively identified those blots as a *Thor* and a *Mad Cat*.

"Open field engagement, Thorns. Nothing gets past

us.'' Rose watched the scanner and repositioned the *Charger*. Around him were several utility vehicles and the squat outlines of maintenance sheds, but little hard cover. To his left was a small arena and a crowd of civilian cars. He reminded himself to keep well away from the arena to protect the civilians.

At six hundred and fifty meters, the two OmniMechs opened fire with their extended-range PPCs. Both shots directed at Antioch missed, but the single bolt at Rose hit, laying the *Charger*'s right arm bare. Warning lights flashed amber as the limb was breached in three places.

The Black Thorns waited until the Omnis were within six hundred meters before opening fire. Clan missiles passed Inner Sphere missiles in flight to explode on and around the targeted 'Mechs. Rose thought he counted several hits against the *Mad Cat*, but without his spotlight, it was hard to tell at their current range.

Missiles left the launchers of both sides as the 'Mechs continued to close range. Esmeralda and Antioch moved forward and fired their PPCs. Esmeralda's bolts were both cut short, a sure sign that they'd hit, but Rose couldn't track Antioch's shots because the *Thor* was swinging his way. Rose triggered another flight of missiles and ran toward the *Thor*.

Missiles rained down on the *Charger* and a PPC blast tore off most of the armor on its right leg before Rose managed to close to within a hundred and fifty meters. Triggering all his pulse lasers, he saw the heat scale spike, then begin to decline as the heat sinks worked to dissipate the waste heat generated by the lasers.

To his left Rose was dimly aware that Antioch was engaging the *Mad Cat* at close range, trading Gauss rifle and PPC fire for PPCs and short-range missiles. Esmeralda seemed to be shifting targets in the center of the Thorn line. Both Clan 'Mechs were damaged, but neither seemed ready to fall, which looked bad for the mercenaries. Rose's armor had been destroyed in several locations and it had been worn paper-thin in others. Knowing he wouldn't be able to take much more punishment, he realized that the fight had to end soon, one way or another.

Taking his feet off the control pedals, Rose slammed his boots down on the large studs to either side. Deep in the heart of the *Charger,* something roared. The sound was amplified as three columns of flame appeared from the legs and back of the 'Mech. With a slight wobble, the three flaming jets carried the *Charger* toward the startled *Thor* pilot. Before angling the 'Mech down, Rose was briefly treated to a spectacular view of the area around the city park.

Although jump jets were common among lighter 'Mechs, few heavy 'Mechs bothered to mount them because of weight. The jets needed to lift sixty or more tons into space were just too heavy to be practical. The few 'Mechs that did mount the massive jets were normally limited to jumps of less than a hundred meters. Not the *Charger,* though. It had a jump range of 'Mechs half its size, and covered the hundred and forty meters to the *Thor* without effort.

Clenching his jaw and tightening his grip on the controls, Rose prepared for the jarring impact of landing. Landing on level ground during practice jumps had rattled him around in the chair, but landing on the *Thor* turned the world upside-down. The *Charger* actually hit the *Thor* in the pelvis with both feet on the way down. When the *Charger*'s knees hit the *Thor* in the chest, the momentum folded the flying 'Mech over the top of the OmniMech. Both machines crashed to the ground as the *Charger* drove the *Thor* down.

The *Thor* fell backward and the *Charger* fell over the top of the OmniMech. Rose threw both hands out to slow the fall and managed to partially brace the 'Mech for the final impact with the ground. Just when he thought he was about to hit, the world exploded in a flash of white light.

The next thing Rose knew, he was hanging from the restraining straps of the command chair. The *Charger* was still on its stomach and the *Thor* was still flat on its back, its chest belching thick gray smoke. As Rose disentangled himself, the *Thor* remained still. Looking down at the fallen 'Mech, Rose realized it would never rise again. If somebody had dropped a house on the *Thor,* it couldn't have been smashed more completely.

Rose looked around for the rest of his command and discovered them approaching from two sides. Of the Clan 'Mechs, however, there was no sign. As he began to try to move the *Charger,* he found that its legs were still intertangled with the *Thor.* After a few minutes of careful maneuvering, he was back up.

"This is Command One, how long have I been out?"

"Only ten minutes, Captain."

Rose's head was still foggy. He thought the speaker was Ajax, but it could have been Bell. "What's the situation?"

"The *Thor* at your feet is down. We chased the *Mad Cat* off, but the rest of the company got jumped on the way back from the recon. Battle Three chased off a pair of medium Omnis with support from the rest of the unit."

Rose finally decided it was Ajax. "Is McCloud still inbound?" Rose tried to keep the fear out of his voice, but ten minutes was a long time to be out of a fight this close.

"Still inbound and on time, sir."

"Hey, why isn't Battle One on the line?" As the gray cloud fogging his brain turned into a sharp pain in his left temple, Rose realized that Esmeralda should be giving the battle report.

"Either a freak hit from the *Mad Cat* sheared away an antenna or that patchwork cockpit is showing its heritage. Whatever the case, she can hear, but she can't transmit."

"All right, Battle Three, that makes you the temporary commander. Battle Four, stick with Three and get us to the ComStar compound. Pursuit Two and Command Two, stay in the center. Battle One and I will take the rear guard.

"Battle One, if you read, raise your right arm." Rose waited until Esmeralda raised the *Marauder*'s right arm.

"All right, Thorns, this will be our only chance to punch through to the compound, so we've got to make it count. Don't stop for anything. If somebody goes down, we'll have to trust that they'll be all right. Right now, securing the facility is more important than any one of us.

"Command Two, coordinate with McCloud on targeting and support fire. I know I don't have to tell her to watch for civilians, but I'll do it anyway. That goes for everybody. Make the shots count.

"Let's move out."

As Hawg and Bell started out of the park, Rose ran another check of the *Charger*'s systems. He still had plenty of missile reloads, but that would change soon. Although the armor had been breached in several places, there was no significant damage to the internal structure, except for the right leg. The red banks of indicator lights confirmed what Rose suspected as he tried to stand. The previous repair to the lower leg had failed. Despite the limp, he was still as fast as the *Marauder II,* but the *Charger*'s hallmark was speed and now he was deprived of that advantage.

Ajax and Rianna fell in behind the assault 'Mechs, with Rose and Esmeralda following. Rose's thoughts drifted up and toward the 'Mechbuster approaching the city. He didn't think McCloud would be in any danger, but that could change dramatically at any moment. Compared to the *Charger,* the 'Mechbuster was a difficult target, but Rose knew that a solid hit could take out the aircraft. He had destroyed similar aircraft before.

Marching toward the Clan 'Mechs, Rose realized that the chances were good that he wouldn't survive this encounter. There were so many things he'd wanted to tell Rianna and McCloud, but there'd never been the time. Something always came up and now it might be too late.

"This is Battle Three. We're approaching the Clan line. Multiple heavy targets are close."

"Command Two, vector the 'Mechbuster. We're going to need some supporting fire." Rose considered transferring coordination of the aircraft to his 'Mech, but despite the desire, he knew his attention was needed on the ground.

"Pursuit Two, how many Clanners ahead?"

Ajax's calm voice answered immediately. "Four heavy signatures to the front. Two medium swinging around from the left."

"Battle One, secure the left flank. Don't let those two mediums on our backs. Pursuit Two, provide support." Rose didn't like the idea of sending their eyes and ears to the side, but the *Raven* wouldn't last long in a firefight with heavy and assault OmniMechs. At least with the mediums, he'd have a chance of survival.

"Command Two, fall back. I'm taking your place." Rose picked up speed and passed Rianna as Esmeralda and Ajax went down the next cross street. "Two, see if you can find some high ground to direct traffic."

As Rose took his position next to Bell, he toggled through his scanners. The ComStar compound was only five kilometers away, but the Clan 'Mechs had intercepted their path and were at just under four.

"Command One, urgent, this is Command Two. McCloud is ahead of schedule; either she hits the Clans now or she has to wait for the next pass. She is requesting permission to engage."

Now that was a first. Rose had never known McCloud to ask permission for anything. "Affirmative, Command Two. Hit the Clans now." Rose knew that by the time the aircraft circled around for another pass, the Thorns would be too close for her to risk any shots.

"Pick up the pace, Thorns. Don't give them the chance to recover from the air attack." Rose fed the *Charger* more power and the distance between the two sides fell away. Over his head something loud rumbled across the sky and headed toward the Clans.

In the ambient light of the city Rose could see the underbelly of the aircraft in a shallow dive as it approached the Clan position. McCloud had slowed the 'Mechbuster as much as possible to line up her shot. He could see the flaps of the two wings fully extended to provide more lift at the slow speed. The weapon port was already open and ready. He urged more speed out of his 'Mech as the 'Mechbuster continued ahead.

The Falcons had always been good fighters and the arrival of a single aircraft did little to shake them. Confident that the Black Thorns were still too far away for concern, they cranked up their guns and waited for the 'Mechbuster to come into range. It was traveling at more than two hundred kilometers per hour, which normally would have made it a difficult target. But with all the guns pointed upward, something was bound to hit.

Rose could see the exhaust trails of long-range missiles as they leapt from their launchers and streaked toward McCloud. An instant later, the Clan pilots had triggered their lasers and PPCs. Although triggered second, the beam weapons struck the 'Mechbuster first. Many of the shots missed, flying past the aircraft as it approached. Several shots hit the craft, however, raining armor down on the city.

In the darkness Rose could see the beams cut short as they struck the armored belly of the aircraft. He couldn't see the damage, but he knew the composite armor was separating from the frame and falling to earth. The subsequent missiles tore through the damaged armor, ripping away larger pieces under the impact of powerful explosives.

As the Clan weapons recycled, the 'Mechbuster triggered the weapon that gave its name to the craft. The front of the aircraft was briefly illuminated as McCloud kept the trigger fully depressed. The aircraft's forward momentum was virtually halted as the recoil from the autocannon held the aircraft back. Rose tore his eyes from the primary screen to check the scanner. One of the Clan assault 'Mechs glowed brightly on the display for a moment, then disappeared. Rose wanted to cheer, but when he looked back at the primary, the shout stuck in his throat.

The 'Mechbuster's exhaust ports were clogged with

thick black smoke. Rose lost sight of the craft for a moment as it disappeared behind its exhaust, but re-sighted it as the ship turned slowly to the right. As he watched, the right side engine failed completely and more smoke began to trail from the ship.

"Rianna, patch me through to McCloud!" Rose forgot all about protocol as the 'Mechbuster continued the sharp turn. He watched the ship attempt to right itself several times during the arc, but each time he thought McCloud had it under control another explosion would rock the ship. On his display another comm light went green.

"Rachel, are things as bad as they look?"

Rose heard her reply as though it were light years away. She was using both hands to control the bucking ship and speaking into a wide-area microphone. "Is that you, Jeremiah?"

"It's me."

"This thing is headed down, Jeremiah. I can't give it any more power or the remaining engine will blow. Without more thrust, I can't get the nose up."

"Can you land it?" Rose had stopped his advance as the aircraft circled above his head. Following their leader the other 'Mechs had also temporarily halted the charge.

"If I had a flat spot, I could try, but I don't see anything that qualifies. None of the streets I can see are wide enough. If—" Her words were cut off by another explosion.

Rose wracked his brain for a place to land. The spaceport was the obvious answer, but the runways were too far away for the stricken ship. "Rachel, can you make it to Assembly Avenue?"

There was no answer. Just when Rose was sure their link had gone dead, he heard McCloud's ragged voice.

"No chance, Rose. I've got a fire in the electronics bay. I can barely see my hands, let alone the ground."

Rose wanted to scream, but he tried to think instead. There had to be something he could do.

"Rachel, I know you can do something, even though

I don't know what. You can't die now, Rachel. I need you here. I love you.''

Rose waited for a reply, but none came. He wasn't even sure she'd heard his last message. As he watched in horror and frustration, the aircraft disappeared behind the rise of the intervening buildings. Rose switched to his scanner, but the aircraft still did not register. He was tempted to run to the crash site, but he saw that the Clan 'Mechs had not been idle during his brief transmission with McCloud. Not content with the downing of a 'Mechbuster, they were advancing on the Black Thorns at full speed.

33

Rose turned to face the Clan pilots. The remaining three 'Mechs were approaching in a straight line, each traveling down a separate street. The Clan pilots either didn't know what they were facing or else they had a poor opinion of the mercenaries. Rose knew he could fight past one of the 'Mechs and make a run for the compound, but that would still leave the other two on their trail. Taking them on one by one was his only chance.

"Thorns, move toward the left-hand street. Maybe we can take one out before the others arrive." Rose heard the other two members of his unit confirm, but his mind was still very far way. The sky where the 'Mechbuster had gone down was glowing red.

"Any sign of Battle One?" Rose checked his scanners, but the *Marauder* was not on his screen.

"Negative, Battle Two. She's probably cloaked by the Guardian."

Rose hoped it was true. Between the Guardian and the intervening buildings, the main body of mercenaries were unlikely to reconnect with him and Ajax until they reached the compound, if they made it that far.

"This is Command Two. I have a target behind us." Rose turned his attention to the path they'd just traveled. Behind them was a single 'Mech, just out of sight. If

Rianna hadn't been sweeping the rear quarter, the 'Mech would have taken the lance by surprise. Without the Beagle active probe it was impossible to tell what type of 'Mech was following them. On the other hand, Rose knew what was up ahead.

"Command Two, follow Battle Lance up the side street. I'm turning to engage the rear 'Mech. Remember, keep moving toward the ComStar compound."

Rose swung the *Charger* around and headed back down the street. Hawg and Bell would be able to take a couple of shots each before the other Clan 'Mechs arrived to assist their besieged comrade. If Rose could stop the trailer, they stood a good chance of breaking free.

Walking back down the street Rose saw that the civilians were coming out to stare at the war machines now that they had passed. Rose's surprise turnaround had caught several out in the open. As the civilians fled for cover, an OmniMech appeared at the other end of the street. Seeing it bathed in the glow of the street lights, Rose could easily see that it was the *Mad Cat* his unit had engaged earlier at the city park.

The 'Mech was at least as damaged as the *Charger*, but Rose knew that the Omni had begun the engagement with more protection and better weaponry. Like ancient gunfighters, the two 'Mechs squared off briefly. The civilians thought the move was perfectly normal, but Rose knew it was a quirk of the meeting. Nobody stood in the middle of the street and traded shots with an OmniMech.

It took Rose only an instant to center his targeting cross hairs and trigger his missiles. The Clan pilot was a second slower as he triggered his 'Mech's right-arm PPC. Rose braced for the impact, which caught the *Charger* in the right torso, then ran toward the *Mad Cat* as the blast died away. The missile flight scattered explosions across the *Mad Cat*'s shoulders and chest. One boxy missile launcher exploded as a cluster of missiles tore through the housing and detonated the missiles still in the rack.

The missile launcher was still reloading when Rose triggered the medium lasers in the *Charger*'s chest and arms. All four beams found their mark, one striking the damaged *Mad Cat* squarely in the face, which housed the 'Mech's cockpit and life-support system.

Either the shot or the charging 'Mech scared the Clan pilot, because he triggered all his remaining weapons. Six short-range missiles flew from the rack to explode five seconds later against the hull of the *Charger*. The right-arm PPC also fired again, but the beam sliced past Rose. Rose felt the *Charger*'s right arm go limp, the red lights of the weapon-status board confirming the destruction of the arm-mounted laser.

Rose continued to close ground as the missile system completed its reload cycle. Despite the close range, he fired another flight of missiles. Twenty more warheads flew toward the *Mad Cat* as Rose approached. Although all twenty hit, only three did any harm. Three small explosions chipped away more armor, but the rest were simply crushed against the *Mad Cat*'s ferro-fibrous plates.

The impact of the missiles had distracted the Falcon pilot enough, however, to let Rose get close. Under the street lights Rose could see that the Omni was in bad shape. The left arm was still attached, but the PPC and actuators had been destroyed. The remaining armor was as pitted and gouged as the *Charger*'s. The Clan pilot tried to back away from the *Charger*, but Rose wouldn't let him get far enough away to fire the PPC. As the Clan pilot swung his right arm around like a metal club, Rose looked for, and found, a weak spot.

He shifted the *Charger* slightly, taking the damage on his reinforced shoulder plating. Shifting again he kicked the *Mad Cat* in the right leg. Metal popped free on the foot of the *Charger*, but the plates of the *Mad Cat*'s shin crumpled like foil under the blow. Rose fired his chest-mounted pulse lasers, then braced the *Charger* to receive another punch.

The shoulder plate buckled under the blow and smashed into the shoulder actuator. The arm still had some mobility, but Rose could no longer use it for balance as he aimed another kick at the *Mad Cat*'s shin.

Trusting his own balance and piloting ability, Rose kicked out again. The blow met with very little resistance as the metal bone of the OmniMech broke in two. The *Mad Cat* fell to the right and Rose staggered in the same direction. Pounding metal feet tore through the pavement as Rose struggled for control. While the *Mad Cat* was hitting the concrete, Rose regained control of the *Charger,* but smashed the front end of a car in the process.

The Omni pilot struggled to stand on one leg, but Rose didn't give him the chance. Careful to keep his 'Mech out of sight of the PPC barrel, Rose crossed over to the fallen 'Mech. He took careful aim at the cockpit and waited until the struggling ceased. The pilot crawled out of the cockpit hatch and Rose turned back toward the ComStar compound.

Three struggling steps was all he needed to realize that the *Charger*'s right leg was again badly damaged. At his current pace he'd never catch the rest of the Black Thorns. Thinking only of the people in his command, he triggered the jump jets. The *Charger* leaped over the street and landed in the middle of the road a hundred and fifty meters away, breaking through the concrete with both feet. The right leg groaned, but held, and Rose triggered the jets again. He jumped five times before the computer announced that he had only enough reaction mass for two more jumps. Rose hesitated, then decided to limp after his unit.

Five minutes later he reached the site of the first encounter. Looking quickly around the location, he saw only the carcass of the *Masakari* and several destroyed cars. Checking the scanner, Rose pushed on toward the ComStar compound, no longer checking each cross street or alley for hidden Clan 'Mechs. He knew he was taking risks, but he didn't care. If he was to have any part in the ongoing battle, he had to make up the time he'd lost.

Cresting a hill, Rose briefly saw the battlefield, where Hawg and Bell were fighting a retreating action against two damaged *Masakari*s. Though Rose couldn't see the full extent of the damage to the four engaged 'Mechs, it was easy to tell that Antioch was in serious trouble because Hawg had the remains of the *Banshee*'s right arm in his *BattleMaster*'s left hand. It would have made an excellent club, but the Clan pilots weren't coming close enough to let Hawg use his improvised weapon. There was no sign of the *Phoenix Hawk*.

Rose jumped again and tried to steer toward the fight. At the apogee of his flight he triggered a cluster of missiles at the back of the nearest OmniMech. He saw the missiles begin to explode across the back of the *Masakari*, then he was too low to see more. While the missiles reloaded, Rose ran a last check over his status board. He knew another jump was foolish, but he triggered the jets as the missile launcher came back on-line. Burning the last of his fuel, Rose angled toward the Omnis, vainly searching for Rianna as the *Charger* flew toward the enemy.

To his surprise, neither *Masakari* had turned to face him. He assumed that was because of Bell and Hawg, but he wasn't sure. Perhaps their backs were covered by another force? Knowing he didn't have time to worry about it, Rose triggered his missiles just before the *Charger* touched down. Now the two OmniMechs stood between him and the battle lance. He'd just fired the three lasers at the nearest Omni when something thumped against his back. Secondary explosions rocked the Omni, but the *Masakari* kept firing at Hawg and Bell.

Although Rose had never encountered a Clan Elemental, he knew one had just jumped onto his back. Almost immediately the armor over his right rear torso was breached. He took a step forward and found that his right leg was dragging worse than before. Thumbing the external camera he saw another Elemental burning away the remaining support of his right leg.

His 'Mech was about to fall, and Rose knew it. With his left arm useless and his right arm damaged, he couldn't swat away the Elementals, nor would his damaged right leg let him outrun them. He checked the jump jets, but as expected, they lacked the fuel to get the eighty-ton 'Mech off the ground. The missile launcher came back on-line as Rose resigned himself to his fate. The *Charger* was about to die.

He took a deep breath and fired the long-range missiles at the *Masakari*. The Artemis fire-control system functioned perfectly, sending all twenty shots into the OmniMech's back. Rose heard metal ripping and then an Elemental claw appeared above the view screen. The secondary screen shorted out in a shower of sparks as the claw ripped through the electronics. The nearest *Masakari* crashed into a row of parked cars just before the main viewer exploded. Rose looked up at the widening gap above his head as the Elemental struggled to shove his arm-mounted laser into the breach. He pushed the weapon into the gash as his Point mate finished his work on the right leg.

With a resounding snap, the *Charger*'s right leg gave way. Rose didn't even try to keep the 'Mech upright. Instead he concentrated on falling forward. The Elemental hesitated, torn between jumping to safety and finishing off the pilot inside. When he finally decided to jump clear, it was too late.

This time, Rose managed to remain conscious and felt every blow his body received on impact. The *Charger* bounced slightly and slid a few meters before coming to rest. Rose fumbled with the safety restraints and finally managed to free himself from the harness. Gravity immediately pulled him into the shattered remains of the main viewscreen. He pulled off the neurohelmet and looked around the shattered cockpit. Seeing the protruding laser of the crushed Elemental within easy reach, Rose sat the helmet over the end.

Standing proved more difficult than he imagined, mostly because of the awkward angle, but also because of the pain of the crash and the stiffness that always accompanied too many hours sitting in the command chair. Rose checked that the laser pistol was still on his hip and the boot knife was still strapped to his heavy combat boot. He climbed onto the back of his command chair and reached up for the rear entry hatch. The locking bolts swung back easily, the hatch popping open on the second push.

Rose climbed onto the rear of the *Charger*'s head and watched Hawg finish off the last *Masakari* with a barrage of laser fire. The *Banshee* was still standing, but the 'Mech was obviously out of the fight. Even from a distance, Rose could tell that its chest had been pierced in three different locations.

The Elementals had begun running to help the remaining OmniMech, but when it went down, they changed course and headed back into the night. Rose slid down the head of the *Charger* and landed on the street. As he trotted toward the *BattleMaster,* he heard the sound of other 'Mechs. Turning to face the new arrivals, he watched Esmeralda lead Rianna back to the rest of the Thorns.

That the *Marauder II* was even moving was a surprise. The autocannon hung from a broken mount across the right side of the hull. The right arm was still attached, but it hung almost to the ground, occasionally scraping against the concrete as Esmeralda moved. Both jump fins, which improved the flight profile of the jump-capable 'Mech, had been blasted away, leaving only blackened stumps of metal.

Rianna's *Phoenix Hawk* had been just as badly abused. The right arm had been severed at the elbow. Power couplings sparked blue and green as the arm moved, showering the area with the flash of electricity. The right jump jet had been destroyed, and from the way the 'Mech moved, the right leg seemed to be locked at the knee.

Rose turned and ran toward the *BattleMaster,* which seemed content to wait for the arrival of the other two 'Mechs. Rose arrived just after those two, and tried vainly to get their attention. He finally succeeded by firing a laser shot into the air in front of Hawg's cockpit. The mercenary looked down at him and finally bent over as he began waving his arms.

"Can you hear me?" Rose raised his voice, but did

not quite shout. Hawg lowered his left hand and Rose stepped into the upturned palm.

"Yes, sir. We can all hear you." As the *BattleMaster* stood up again, Rose had the sinking feeling he always got when riding an express elevator. He let his stomach catch up before he risked speaking. He looked over at the *Banshee,* and saw Bell emerge from the cockpit to stand on the 'Mech's battered shoulder.

"Pick up Bell and head for ComStar." The *Battle-Master* raised its hand toward the *Banshee* and Antioch jumped onto the palm. Esmeralda and Rianna were already moving as Hawg completed the transfer.

"Where's Ajax?" Rose shouted to the wind.

The reply came over the *BattleMaster*'s external speakers. "Rianna sent him ahead to scout the compound."

"Any word on the situation there?"

"Infantry defense. Looks like some of the more militant members of the Preservationists have taken up residence."

"What about Toads?"

"Looks like the defenders are all local."

Rose turned to Bell and lowered his voice slightly. "How are you doing?"

Antioch shrugged, offering the ghost of a smile. "I'm still alive." He paused and Rose nodded. "I think my left thumb is broken, though."

Rose tried to examine the digit in the passing street lights, but he couldn't see well enough to tell if it was broken or dislocated. He looked back at Bell, who only shrugged.

"Captain, Ajax reports increased activity at the compound. Still no sign of the Elementals or the additional 'Mechs."

"Hawg, get us into the compound. Tell Rianna to follow. Esmeralda should guard the approaching streets until we've got the compound secure. Tell Ajax to remain in position."

As Rose watched, Esmeralda kicked in the main gate to the compound and stepped back. Two short-range missiles flew out of the compound, but both warheads hit a factory on the next block. The *Phoenix Hawk* stepped into the gap with its left arm extended, firing a long burst of machine-gun fire, punctuated by a single shot from the medium pulse laser. The missile fire stopped and Rianna disappeared into the compound, followed closely by Hawg with his human cargo.

The two 'Mechs moved past the two small outbuildings and toward the main building at the far end of the court-yard. Rose kept his eyes on the outbuildings, but when the doors remained closed, he turned his attention back to Rianna.

"This is Rianna Rose, executive officer for the Black Thorns. The rebels occupying this compound are ordered to lay down their arms and surrender. You have thirty seconds."

"Hawg." Rose pointed to the main building. "Set us down. Bell and I will enter the station." Hawg set the two men down and returned to a standing position as Rose and Bell drew their pistols and sprinted for the cover of the near wall.

As Rose watched, a single man charged out a side door and muscled a missile launcher to his shoulder.

"Follow me, free men. We will return to the glory of the Star League." Both missiles flew up toward the *Phoenix Hawk*. Rose could hear the high-pitched whir of the anti-missile system, but the system was empty. One arced over the *Phoenix Hawk*'s shoulder, but the other glanced off the 'Mech's head. Both of the side-mounted antenna were blasted away as the warhead punched through the thick armor.

Rianna's response was immediate. She triggered the machine gun and swung her 'Mech's left arm in a long arc. The huge bullets tore through the wall of the ComStar facility and kicked up spikes of dirt as the slugs raced toward the missile-carrying man. The infantryman threw down the launcher and turned toward the door, but the machine gun caught him before he took another step. His body spasmed uncontrollably as the bullets punched through him. Rianna released the trigger of the machine gun, and the man fell into a boneless heap. Shifting targets, she fired a single burst from the pulse laser through the open door. Rose heard screams from inside.

"You have fifteen seconds."

The main doors opened and two missile launchers dropped into the courtyard. Men and women emerged from the two doors with their hands held high. More Preservationists stepped through the smoldering frame of the side door.

Rose rushed past the two groups and the motionless body. In the poor light he could barely make out the features of Hoffbrowse, contorted in pain and fear. Without a second thought, Rose continued toward the main doors. As expected, the Demi-Precentor in charge was at his desk, seemingly oblivious to the deaths around him.

"I wish to send an emergency message to Hauptmann General Stella Dmowski of the Kelenfold Command. I request the message be sent right now."

The seemingly unflappable Demi-Precentor looked at the two hard men before him and then at their sidearms. He wordlessly stood up and ushered them into the sending room. Five minutes later the message was on its way.

"Now what?" asked Bell.

"Now we wait for a reply." Rose looked toward the silent Demi-Precentor, who nodded. Evidently he was not a Preservationist.

It took more than six hours to receive a reply, time which the Black Thorns passed looking over their gun sights and preparing a defense against any counterattack by the Clans. Esmeralda moved inside the compound, but Ajax continued to prowl the streets searching for signs of the Jade Falcons. Dawn was just breaking when the Demi-Precentor handed Rose a message. He read it once, then sprinted into the courtyard.

"The cavalry is on the way," he shouted at the top of his lungs.

Bell looked at him as if annoyed. "Who needs them?"

"We do, unless you want another night like the last one. A regiment's on the way."

"I'm not sure that will be necessary," Antioch said. "The spaceport reports that the Clan DropShip blasted into orbit ten minutes ago. They seem to be heading back to their JumpShip." Antioch let Rose stand there for a few seconds with his mouth open before continuing.

"It's over. We won," Bell said, and relief washed over Rose like a warm wave. A grin spread over his face, which Bell returned in kind.

"Councilwoman de Vilbis is calling the Clan arrival an invasion and the Preservationists a terrorist organization. Rianna called for the police to pick up the prisoners.

"We did it, Jeremiah. We beat the Clans."

Then Rose's smile began to drain away as though someone had pulled the plug. "You're right, Antioch. We beat them, but at what cost? The price for this planet was just too high."

"Captain, this is Command Two. I have an emergency call from the Mother of Mercy hospital. Captain Mc-Cloud requests your immediate presence."

Rose felt his eyes fill with tears as he listened to Rianna over the *Phoenix Hawk*'s external speakers. Bell's smile was back in full force and Rose couldn't help but mirror it.

Perhaps, he thought, the price hadn't been so high after all.

Glossary

POLITICAL TERMS

After the fall of the Star League General Aleksandr Kerensky, commander of the Regular Star League army, led his forces out of the Inner Sphere in what is known as the first Exodus. After making their way beyond the Periphery, more than 1,300 light years away from Terra, Kerensky and his followers settled in a group of marginally habitable star systems near a large globular cluster that hid them from the Inner Sphere. Within fifteen years, Civil War erupted among these exiles, threatening to destroy everything they had worked so hard to build. In a second Exodus, Nicholas Kerensky, son of Aleksandr, led his followers to one of the worlds of the globular cluster to escape the new war. It was there on Strana Mechty that Kerensky first conceived and organized the system that would one day become known as the Clans.

Though Wolf's Dragoons originated among the Clans, they have repudiated their allegiance to the Wolf Clan. Nevertheless many Clan traditions, concepts, and customs still prevail among the Dragoons.

CLANS

Out of the ashes of the civilization that Kerensky's forces tried to create rose the Clans. The Clans are a warrior society that is rigidly divided into castes, with the warriors as the elite. To create this warrior caste the

Clans use genetic engineering, using the genes of prestigious living and dead warriors to produce potential new ones.

COMSTAR

ComStar, the interstellar communications network, was the brainchild of Jerome Blake, Minister of Communications during the latter years of the Star League. After the League's fall, Blake seized Terra and reorganized what was left of the League's communications network into a private organization that sold its services to the five Successor Houses for a profit. Since that time, ComStar has also developed into a powerful secret society steeped in mysticism and ritual. Initiates to the quasi-religious ComStar Order commit themselves to lifelong service. After the climactic battle between ComStar and the Clans on Tukayyid, ComStar splintered into two factions: the reformed ComStar and the archconservative Word of Blake.

INNER SPHERE

The Inner Sphere was the term originally applied to the star empires that joined together to form the Star League in the mid-2700s. The term currently applies to human-occupied space within the bounds of the Periphery.

PERIPHERY

Beyond the borders of the Inner Sphere lies the Periphery, the vast domain of known and unknown worlds stretching endlessly into interstellar night. Once populated by colonies from Terra, the worlds of the Periphery were devastated technologically, politically, and economically by the fall of the Star League. At present, the Periphery is the refuge of piratical Bandit Kings, privateers, and outcasts from the Inner Sphere.

STAR LEAGUE

The Star League was formed in 2571 in an attempt to peacefully ally the major star systems inhabited by the human race after it had taken to the stars. The League prospered for almost 200 years, until civil war broke out in 2751. The League was eventually destroyed when the ruling body, known as the High Council, disbanded in the midst of a struggle for power. Each of the royal House rulers then declared him or herself First Lord of the Star League, and within months, war had engulfed the Inner Sphere. This conflict continued for almost three centuries. This era of continuous war is now known simply as the Succession Wars.

SUCCESSOR LORDS

Each of the five Successor States is ruled by a family descended from one of the original Council Lords of the old Star League. All five royal House Lords claim the title of First Lord of the Star League, and they have been at each other's throats since the beginning of the Succession Wars in 2786. Their battleground is the vast Inner Sphere, which is composed of all the star systems once occupied by the Star League's member-states.

SUCCESSOR STATES

After the fall of the Star League, the remaining members of the High Council each asserted his or her right to become First Lord of the Star League. Their star empires became known as the Successor States and the rulers as the Successor Lords. Five ruling Houses make up the Successor States: House Kurita, House Liao, House Steiner, House Marik, and House Davion. The Clan invasion has temporarily interrupted the centuries of war—the Succession Wars—that first began in 2786. The battleground of these wars is the vast Inner Sphere, which is composed of all the star systems once occupied by the Star League's member-states. The Successor Lords have temporarily put aside their differences in order to meet the threat of a common foe, the Clans.

TRUCE OF TUKAYYID

The Truce of Tukayyid establishes a fifteen-year cease-fire between the Clans and the Inner Sphere. Khan Ulric Kerensky, ilKhan of the Clans, made a bargain with Com-Star's Precentor Martial, Anastasius Focht, to fight a battle on the planet Tukayyid. If the Clans won, ComStar would hand Terra over to them; if the Com Guards won, the Clans would agree to a fifteen-year truce. Signed by the Clans and ComStar after the Com Guards won an overwhelming victory against the Clans on Tukayyid, the truce establishes a boundary marking the front line of the Clan incursion into Inner Sphere space. The treaty forbids the Clans to advance beyond this boundary for a period of fifteen years.

MILITARY TERMS

The Inner Sphere and Clan militaries both use BattleMechs, DropShips, JumpShips and other similar weapons and equipment, but the Clans are superior from a technological standpoint. Clan warriors live by the Way of the Clans, a code of honor that affects even their style of combat. The Inner Sphere has never been able to defeat the Clans' superior technology. Their victories have *only* come through strategies that turned the tables on the code by which Clan warriors live and fight.

AUTOCANNON

An autocannon is a rapid-firing, auto-loading weapon that fires high-speed streams of high-explosive, armor-piercing shells. Light autocannon range from 30 to 90mm caliber, and heavy autocannon may be 80 to 120mm or more.

BATTLEMECH

BattleMechs are the most powerful war machines ever built. First developed by Terran scientists and engineers, these huge, man-shaped vehicles are faster, more mobile, better-armored, and more heavily armed than any twentieth-century tank. Ten to twelve meters tall and equipped with particle projection cannons, lasers, rapid-fire autocannon, and missiles, they pack enough fire-power to flatten anything but another BattleMech. A small fusion reactor provides virtually unlimited power, and BattleMechs can be adapted to fight in environments ranging from sun-baked deserts to sub-zero arctic ice-fields.

BATTALION

A battalion is an Inner Sphere military unit usually consisting of three companies.

CLAN MILITARY

Clan military organization, strategy, and tactics differ radically from those of the Inner Sphere. The basic element of the Clan military is called a Point, consisting of a 'Mech, or two aerospace fighters, or five infantrymen. Five Points constitute a Star. Groups of Stars are called Clusters.

Point	1 'Mech or 5 infantry Elementals
Star	5 'Mechs or 25 Elementals
Binary	2 Stars
Trinary	3 Stars
Cluster	4 Binaries
Galaxy	3–5 Clusters
Nova	1 'Mech Star and 1 infantry Star
Supernova	1 'Mech Binary and 2 infantry Stars

COMPANY

A company is an Inner Sphere military unit consisting of three BattleMech lances or, for infantry, three platoons with a total of 50 to 100 men. Companies are generally commanded by a captain.

ELEMENTALS

Elementals are the elite, battle-armored infantry of the Clans. These men and women are giants, bred specifically to handle Clan-developed battle armor.

JUMPSHIPS AND DROPSHIPS

JumpShip

Interstellar travel is accomplished via JumpShips, first developed in the twenty-second century. These somewhat ungainly vessels consist of a long, thin drive core and a sail resembling an enormous parasol, which can extend up to a kilometer in width. The ship is named for its ability to "jump" instantaneously across vast distances—up to thirty light years per jump. Before it can make another jump, however, the ship must recharge its interstellar drives by gathering up more solar energy. This process can take up to a week.

The JumpShip's enormous sail is constructed from a special metal that absorbs vast quantities of electromagnetic energy from the nearest star. When it has soaked up enough energy, the sail transfers it to the drive core, which converts it into a space-twisting field. An instant later, the ship arrives at the next jump point, a distance of up to thirty light years. This field, generated by the Kearny-Fuchida hyperdrive, is known as hyperspace, and its discovery opened to mankind the gateway to the stars.

JumpShips never land on planets, and only rarely travel to the inner areas of a star system. Interplanetary travel is carried out by DropShips, vessels that are attached to the JumpShip until arrival at the jump point. Jump points are the locations within a star system where the system's gravity is next to nothing, the prime prerequisite for the operation of the Kearny-Fuchida drive. Every star has two principal jump points, one at the zenith point at the star's north pole, and one at the nadir point at the star's south pole.

DropShip

Because interstellar JumpShips must avoid entering the heart of a solar system, they must "dock" in space at a considerable distance from a system's inhabited worlds. DropShips were developed for interplanetary travel. As the name implies, a DropShip is attached to hardpoints on the JumpShip's drive core, later to be dropped from the parent vessel after insystem entry. Though incapable of FTL travel, DropShips are highly maneuverable, well-armed, and sufficiently aerodynamic to take off from and land on a planetary surface. The journey from the jump point to the inhabited worlds of a system usually requires a normal-space journey of several days or weeks, depending on the type of star.

LANCE

A lance is an Inner Sphere BattleMech combat group, usually consisting of four BattleMechs.

LASER

Laser is an acronym for "Light Amplification through Stimulated Emission of Radiation." When used as a weapon, the laser damages the target by concentrating extreme heat on a small area. BattleMech lasers are designated as small, medium, and large. Lasers are also available as shoulder-fired weapons operating from a portable backpack power unit. Certain range finders and targeting equipment also employ low-level lasers.

LRM

This is an abbreviation for long-range missile, an indirect-fire missile with a high-explosive warhead.

OMNIMECH

The Clans' military success against the Inner Sphere is mainly due to the OmniMech. Based on advanced Star League technology that the Star League Defense Forces took with them when they left the Inner Sphere, Clan scientists developed the OmniMech, a BattleMech whose modular weapons systems could be easily reconfigured to suit any mission. This innovation gave the Clans tremendous flexibility on the battlefield. Coupled with their vastly more efficient cooling and sensor systems and destructive firepower, the OmniMech made the Clans virtually invincible. Since encountering the OmniMech, Inner Sphere scientists have tried to incorporate Clan technology into Inner Sphere 'Mech designs.

PLATOON

A platoon is an Inner Sphere military unit typically consisting of approximately twenty-eight men, commanded by a lieutenant or a platoon sergeant. A platoon may be divided into two sections.

PPC

This abbreviation stands for particle projection cannon, a magnetic accelerator firing high-energy proton or ion bolts, causing damage through both impact and high temperature. PPCs are among the most effective weapons available to BattleMechs.

REGIMENT

A regiment is an Inner Sphere military unit consisting of two to four battalions, each consisting of three or four companies. A regiment is commanded by a colonel.

SRM

This abbreviation stands for short-range missiles, direct-trajectory missiles with high-explosive or armor-piercing explosive warheads. They have a range of less than 1 kilometer, and are accurate only at ranges of less than 300 meters. They are more powerful, however, than LRMs.

CRUSADER

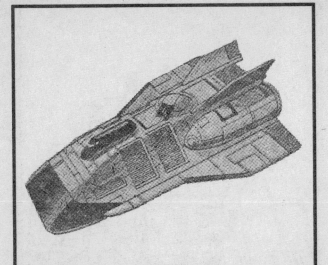

LEOPARD CLASS DROPSHIP

UNION CLASS DROPSHIP

LOCUST

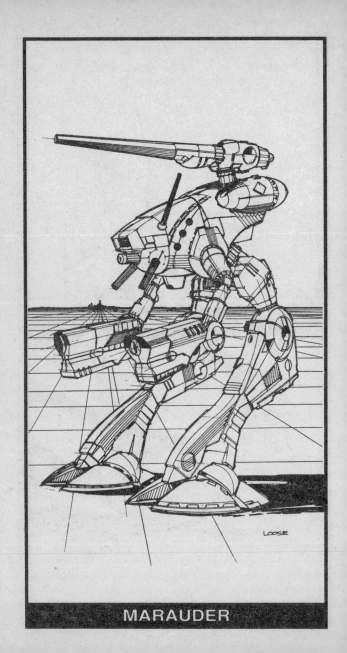

MARAUDER

PHOENIX HAWK

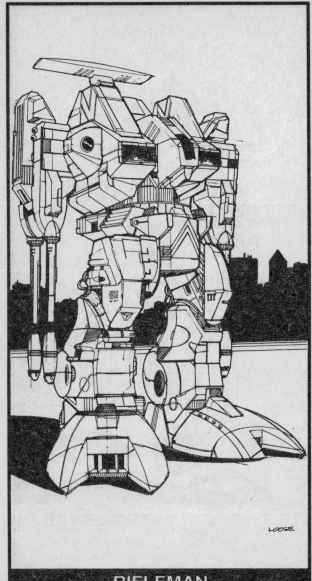

RIFLEMAN

SHADOW HAWK

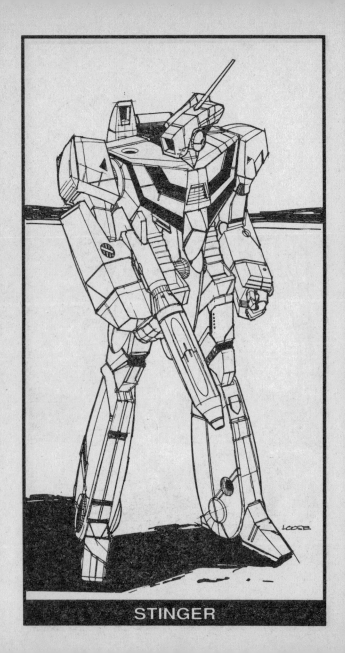

STINGER

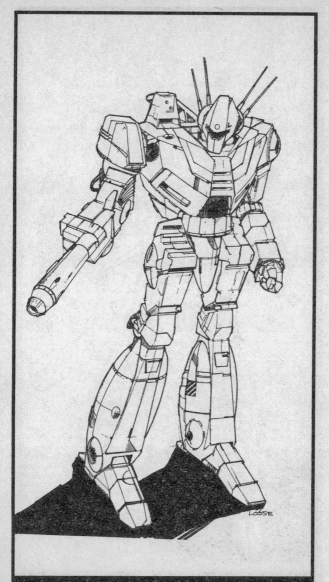

WASP

LOOSE

WOLVERINE